this is horse
manure

CRITICAL PRAISE FOR TERRY C. JOHNSTON'S
PLAINSMEN SERIES—AN EPIC SAGA TO RIVAL
DANCES WITH WOLVES

"EXCELLENT . . . keep[s] readers in suspense."
—Fred Werner, noted Western historian

"JOHNSTON'S BOOKS ARE ACTION-PACKED!"
—Colorado Springs *Gazette-Telegraph*

"Compelling, memorable characters, a great deal of history and lore about the Indians, whites and wild animals of the period . . . FASCINATING!"
—*Topeka Capital-Journal*

"GUTSY ADVENTURE-ENTERTAINMENT . . . larded with just the right amounts of frontier sentiment."

—*Kirkus Reviews*

Terry C. Johnston is a two-time Golden Spur Award nominee, and award-winning author of *Carry the Wind*, the *Plainsmen* series and *Long Winter Gone*.

*The Plainsmen Series by Terry C. Johnston
from St. Martin's Paperbacks*

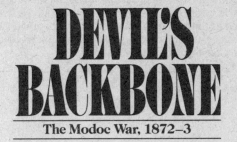

DEVIL'S BACKBONE

The Modoc War, 1872–3

TERRY C. JOHNSTON

ST. MARTIN'S PAPERBACKS

DEVIL'S BACKBONE

Copyright © 1991 by Terry C. Johnston.

Cover art by Frank McCarthy.

All rights reserved. No part of this book may be used or reproduced in any manner whatsoever without written permission except in the case of brief quotations embodied in critical articles or reviews. For information address St. Martin's Press, 175 Fifth Avenue, New York, N.Y. 10010.

ISBN: 0-312-92574-3

Printed in the United States of America

St. Martin's Paperbacks edition/August 1991

10 9 8 7 6 5 4 3 2 1

for what the years ahead
can mean to us both,
I lovingly dedicate this novel
to my son,
Noah

The Modocs are not yet extinct. But the spirit that drove them to resist the inevitable westering of the whites died in the lava beds. Occasionally, on frost-biting nights, the cries of coyotes haunt the ghostly, star-lit Stronghold, bringing back the memory of that time. A time to remember.

> –Erwin N. Thompson
> *Modoc War—Its Military History*
> *& Topography*

[General Jefferson C.] Davis should have killed every Modoc before taking him if possible, then there would have been no complications.

> –General William T. Sherman
> 6 June, 1873, correspondence to
> General Philip H. Sheridan

The Modoc War bathed none of its participants in glory, or even credit . . . The army made a mess of almost everything it attempted. Commanders quarreled or simply did not cooperate; underestimated, then over-estimated the enemy; hesitated when they should have acted, acted when they should have hesitated. Enlisted men proved too easily panicked, repulsed, and demoralized. In the end, Modoc defectors provided the key to military "victory."

> –Robert M. Utley
> *Frontier Regulars*

Few among them felt they were their brother's keeper; the Good Samaritan spirit scarcely existed. Some of the men had been officers during the Civil War; because they had been in some kind of trouble, they had re-enlisted under assumed names as a way to spend a few months or years until their failings had been forgotten. A few were said to have been Confederate veterans. Enlisted men were considered beneath the notice or concern of their officers, and the casualty reports scarcely took note of them. Officers were mentioned by name; sometimes non-commissioned officers were mentioned; privates were almost never listed. If they died, they were buried, frequently without a marker of any kind, and they wore no identification unless they pinned notes on their clothes saying who they were. If they were unfortunate enough to be killed, frequently these scraps of paper would be discarded, and they were interred simply as unknown dead. There they lay, unmourned, in uncared-for graves, many times lost to the knowledge of their loved ones.

—Keith A. Murray
The Modocs and Their War

Modoc War Chronology

October 1864 . . .	treaty signed with Klamath-Modocs
April 1870	Jack leaves the reservation
November 29, 1872	Battle of Lost River
December 21, 1872	Battle of Land's Ranch
January 17, 1873 .	First Battle for the Stronghold
January 22, 1873 .	First Battle of Scorpion Point
January 29, 1873 .	Peace Commission appointed
April 11, 1873 . . .	murder of Peace Commission and Lieutenant Sherwood
April 14–17, 1873 .	Second Battle for the Stronghold
April 26, 1873 . . .	"Thomas-Wright" Massacre at Black Ledge
May 2, 1873	Second Battle of Scorpion Point
May 10, 1873 . . .	Battle of Sorass/Dry Lake
May 22, 1873 . . .	Battle of Willow Creek Ridge
June 1, 1873	Captain Jack surrenders
July 1–9, 1873 . . .	trial of Modoc leaders
October 3, 1873 . .	execution of Modoc leaders; exile of Captain Jack's band to Oklahoma/Indian Territory

Characters

Seamus Donegan

Civilians

Ian O'Roarke—Donegan's uncle, rancher, Hot Creek, California

Elisha Steele—onetime superintendent of Northern California in Yreka, friend of Captain Jack

John Fairchild—rancher, Cottonwood Creek, California

Pressley Dorris—rancher, Butte Valley, California

O. C. Knapp—Indian Agent, District of the Lakes

Oliver C. Applegate—Yainax sub-agency commissary operator; interpreter, head of company of Oregon volunteers

Ivan Applegate—rancher, Clear Lake, California/one-time agent to the Klamaths

Jesse Applegate—rancher, Clear Lake, California

Bob Whittle—ferryboat operator on Link River; interpreter (wife: Matilda)

H. Wallace Atwell—known as "Bill Dadd the Scribe,"
reporter for Sacramento *Record*

T. B. Odeneal—Superintendent of Indian Affairs for Oregon

Patrick McManus—civilian packer for the army

Eugene Hovey—civilian teamster from Yreka, California

"General" John E. Ross—Commander, Oregon Volunteer Militia

Eadweard Muybridge—San Francisco photographer

Dennis Crawley—settler on Lost River

Louis Land—settler on east side of Tule Lake

Louis Webber—head packer for Thomas-Wright Patrol

H. C. Ticknor—local settler, surveyor of Ticknor Road, guide

Charley Larengel—civilian packer/Battle of Sorass Lake

George Fiocke—civilian in on capture of Hooker Jim's village

Jack Thurber—civilian in on capture of Hooker Jim's village (killed)

Army

General Edward R. S. Canby—Commanding Officer, Department of the Columbia and Acting Head, Military Division of the Pacific (SCOTT—orderly; MONAHAN—personal secretary)

Colonel Jefferson C. Davis—successor as Commanding Officer, Department of the Columbia

Lieutenant Colonel (Bvt. Major General) Frank Wheaton—Commander of the 21st Infantry, District of the Lakes, director of Modoc Campaign from 11/72 to 1/23/73 and after 5/22/73

Colonel (Bvt. Major General) Alvan C. Gillem—Commander, Modoc Campaign, January 23–May 22, 1873

Major (Bvt. Colonel) John Green—First Cavalry, commanding officer at Fort Klamath; field commander in Stronghold battle

Major (Bvt. Colonel) Edwin C. Mason—21st Infantry, commander east side of Stronghold

Captain (Bvt. Colonel) David Perry—First Cavalry, Troop F, wounded January 17

Captain (Bvt. Major) James Jackson—First Cavalry, Troop B, commander during Battle of Lost River

Captain (Bvt. Colonel) James Biddle—First Cavalry, Troop K, captured Modoc ponies in March during sweep of Lava Beds

Captain (Bvt. Colonel) R. F. Bernard—First Cavalry, Troop G, cavalry commander on east side of Stronghold; commanding officer during Battle of Land's Ranch

Captain (Bvt. Major) Evan Thomas—Fourth Artillery, Battery A, killed April 26

Captain H. C. Hasbrouck—Fourth Artillery, Battery B (mounted and serving as cavalry), commanding officer at Battle of Sorass Lake in May; escorted defeated Modocs to Kansas

Captain William Trimble—H Troop, 1st Cavalry, captures Captain Jack, June 1

Lieutenant Thomas F. Wright—Twelfth Infantry, Company E, killed April 26

Lieutenant John Kyle—Troop G, 1st Cavalry

Lieutenant John Quincy Adams—Signalman, 21st Infantry

Lieutenant Albion Howe

Lieutenant George M. Harris

Lieutenant Arthur Cranston

Lieutenant William Sherwood—killed on April 11, 1873

Lieutenant Boyle

Lieutenant Charles C. Cresson

Lieutenant George R. Bacon

Lieutenant E. R. Theller—Company I, 21st Infantry

Lt. Frazier A. Boutelle

Lieutenant J. B. Hazelton

Sergeant Robert Romer—4th Artillery

Sergeant Malachi Clinton—12th Infantry

Sergeant Michael McCarthy—H Troop, 1st Cavalry

Sergeant Maurice Fitzgerald—K Troop, 1st Cavalry

Private James Shay—F Troop, 1st Cavalry

Private Charles Hardin

Dr. Cabaniss—army surgeon

Dr. Bernard A. Semig—Assistant Surgeon

Henry McElderry—Assistant Surgeon

Scouts and Interpreters

Bob Whittle—ferryboat operator with wife Matilda; interpreter

Frank Riddle—trapper and hunter on Lost River; interpreter for Peace Commission and at trials

Toby (Winema) Riddle—Frank's wife; interpreter for Peace Commission

Donald McKay—half-breed guide and interpreter, leader of Tenino scouts/mercenaries from Warm Springs Reservation in Oregon

O. C. "One-Arm" Brown—Superintendent Odeneal's scout/interpreter from Fort Klamath

Dave Hill—Klamath Indian in on capture of Hooker Jim's camp, leader of some Klamath mercenaries

---

Settlers Murdered by Modocs, 29 November 1872

Wendolen Nus

William Boddy

Richard Cravigan

William Brotherton

Henry Miller

Christopher Erasmus

John Tober

Joe Penning (severely wounded and left for dead)

Frank Follins

William Schira

William Cravigan

W. K. Brotherton
Nicholas Schroeder

Robert Alexander
Adam Shillingbow

Peace Commission Representatives

Alfred B. Meacham—Head of Peace Commission (one-time Indian superintendent for Oregon)

Rev. Eleazar Thomas—peace commissioner (killed by

Boston Charley, April 11, 1873)

L. S. Dyar—peace commissioner (Klamath sub-agent/ succeeding Knapp)

Modocs

Captain Jack/Kientpoos

•

PEACE FACTION:

Scar-Faced Charley—leader after Jack's execution, lieutenant under Captain Jack

Humpy Joe

William Faithful (Wild Gal's Man)

Queen Mary—Jack's sister

•

WAR FACTION:

Curly Headed Doctor

Schonchin John—second in command

Bogus Charley—messenger between Modocs and army, "bloodhound"

•

Hot Creek Band

Shacknasty Jim—murderer, "bloodhound"

Steamboat Frank—"bloodhound", later a Quaker lay minister

Bogus Charley

Ellen's Man George—one of Canby's murderers, killed 10 May, 1873

Boston Charley—hanged for the murder of Thomas

Black Jim—hanged for murder

Barncho—died in Alcatraz prison for part in murder

Miller's Charley—killer of Sherwood, never brought to trial

Curly Headed Jack—killer of Sherwood, suicide in June, 1873

Sloluck—pardoned and exiled after term in Alcatraz prison

Hooker Jim—killer of settlers in November, "bloodhound"

Duffy—killer of settlers in November

Long Jim—killer of settlers in November

One-Eyed Mose—killer of settlers in November

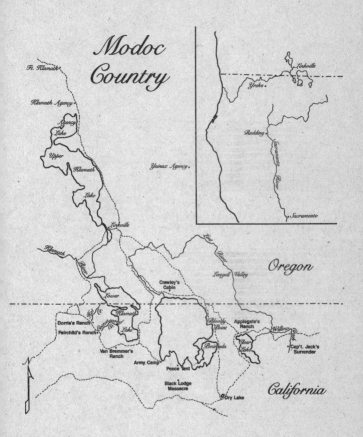

Modoc Country

Ft. Klamath

Klamath Agency

Agency Lake

Upper

Klamath Lake

Linkville

Klamath River

Lower Klamath Lake

Yainax Agency

Lost River

Langell Valley

Oregon

Crawley's Cabin

Dorris's Ranch
Fairchild's Ranch

Hot Cr.

Cottonwood Cr.

Van Bremmer's Ranch

Army Camp

Peace Tent

Black Lodge Massacre

Bloody Point

Peninsula

Clear Lake

Applegate's Ranch

Willow

Cap't Jack's Surrender

Dry Lake

California

N

Linkville

Yreka

Redding

Sacramento River

Sacramento

Maps drawn by author, with his appreciation,
compiled from maps drawn by
Doris Palmer Payne and Erwin N. Thompson

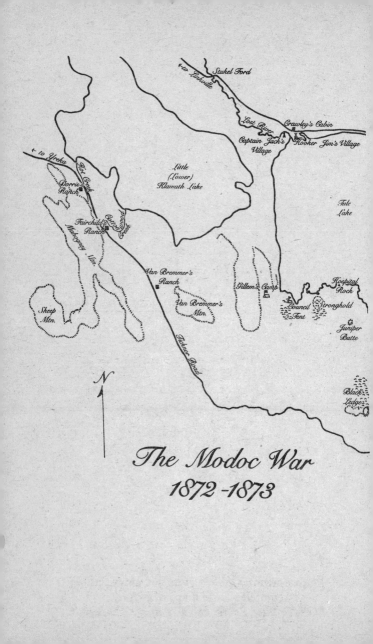

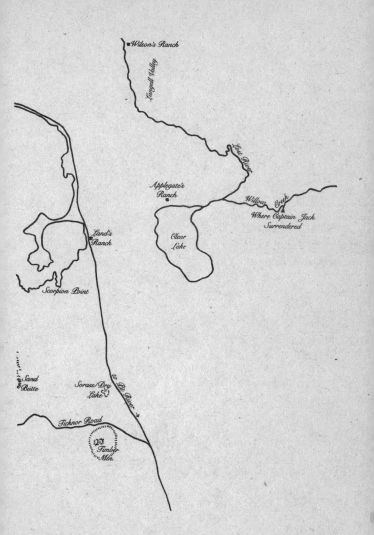

Wilson's Ranch

Langell Valley

Lost River

Applegate's Ranch

Willow Creek

Where Captain Jack Surrendered

Land's Ranch

Clear Lake

Scorpion Point

Sand Butte

Sorass/Dry Lake

to Tule River

Ticknor Road

Timber Mtn.

Maps drawn by author, with his appreciation,
compiled from maps drawn by
Doris Palmer Payne and Erwin N. Thompson

Prologue

Season of the Raven Calling

$\mathcal{F}$ear rose in his throat like bile.

He had been afraid before, but nothing like this.

For the first time in his life—afraid of dying.

Captain Jack swallowed the fear down and shuffled forward, dragging the heavy chains that encased his ankles across the wooden floor of the tiny guardhouse. Heading for the door and the patch of cold October sunlight the soldiers allowed to enter this close, stinking place.

Three others already shuffled ahead of him. Two more trailed behind Jack.

"Ho! Captain Jack!" hollered a soldier as the Modoc chief emerged into the sunlight.

That's what the white men called him. His adult name, bestowed upon him many years before by the white miners over at Yreka, California. So many seasons gone the way of the snow geese. Captain Jack remembered this was to have been his thirty-third winter as his eyes finally rose to the pine-plank scaffold and the ugly beam arching over the platform. And the six knotted ropes dangling still as death itself, their shadows smeared darkly over the first rows of wide-eyed, gape-mouthed spectators.

Jack and the rest were manhandled up into the back of

an army wagon where they were crowded together atop four crude coffins. The mules lurched forward at the insistence of an impatient teamster, carrying the condemned through the muttering crowd of white and copper-skinned faces, everyone straining to catch a glimpse of the great Captain Jack of the renegade Modocs.

The soldier wagon halted beside the pine-plank scaffold. Jack could smell the newness of the timber as four of the six prisoners were dragged down from the wagon bed by blue-clad soldiers. The other two, an interpreter explained without emotion, would not be hanged this day. This, Jack did not understand as he was shoved forward into a group of grasping arms.

He forced himself to believe it did not matter. He could face this, as he had faced everything else in its season.

Death too had its own time.

After two sweating soldiers had chiseled the iron shackles from his ankles, Jack was hurriedly hoisted up the ladder to the narrow platform. Reaching the platform, he noticed the cutaway trapdoor where he and the other three would stand, each beneath a dangling noose. Then he looked away to the sun overhead.

A tight-faced soldier came forward quickly, shuffling Jack into position before he dragged a black, airless bag over his head. Jack swallowed hard. Even though no one could see his eyes, he vowed he would not let them know he was afraid. It would be over quickly, he prayed.

He remembered hearing that a man did some dreaming when he died—while he was crossing over. It was all the shamans had taught him as a boy.

He hoped the dreaming would not take long today, beneath this cold autumn sun.

The old white shaman's words were muffled, coming through the black hood, but Jack could tell the man was fervently praying to his white god.

His legs were shoved together. A soldier, someone, was wrapping and tying, lashing his legs together securely.

I'm not supposed to kick when I start dreaming, he vowed to himself.

As the hands left his legs pinched beneath the tight rope, a stillness came suddenly over the platform. He heard some boots scuff across the new timber planks, then a nervous cough. Jack strained, and listened to the heavy breathing of the young soldier who had been standing to his left when he was shoved into position—the fresh-faced youth dressed in soldier blue who stood stiffly with his two freckled hands clamped on a long pole near the end of the platform.

He will be the one to kill us. No . . . Curly Headed Doctor and his foolish warriors are the ones who have killed me. Not this young soldier—

There came a rustle to his left, surprising him—the creaking of the huge lever the freckle-faced soldier stood against—and the floor fell away beneath Jack's bound feet.

For a moment he struggled as the rope cut into his neck, jerking his head to the side—he fought to control his legs, which convulsively drew up against the tight bindings. Jack did not want to fight it now.

Only air, fight only for air, he told himself. Like being down in one of the swimming ponds too long and clawing his way back up.

The hands tied at his back with cruel hemp did not feel like his, wrenching against one another now, fighting to get freed.

Then as he watched in utter amazement—the surface of the blue water above him grew placid, smooth and untroubled. Not churned as he remembered from the days of his youth.

With trouble, he opened his burning, tortured eyes, staring up at the shafts of sunlight diffused through the many feet of water left for him to crawl through . . .

. . . and then it did not matter any longer that he hurry to the top.

Kientpoos, chief of the Modocs, slipped into the dream

where there was no longer any struggle. No more did he fight against the ropes, gasping for air.

No longer did Captain Jack fight for the very life of his people . . .

Until the white man began crossing their land, the home of the Modocs was as limitless as the blue sky domed overhead. As long as he could remember, there had been word of settlers far enough away to the north, in what they called Oregon Territory. And even some much closer, to the south and west where lay the raucous mining camps of northern California.

To the west stood the massive Cascade Range, a land of once-active volcanos where ancient legend said the thunder and sun had gone to rest. And through the thick forests on the north, bounded antelope, deer, bear and mountain sheep. Overhead flew ducks and geese, even swans in a sweeping winter migration, while pelicans and loons and sea gulls all made this place their home year-round. Fish was to be found in every stream: sucker, perch, and trout as well. Modoc men hunted the hills for the small animals and large while the women dug camas roots from the soil or, from their canoes, dragged water lilies from the surface of many lakes, pounding the seeds into a meal they would use for food. Other seeds and berries could be found at every turn. As a boy, Kientpoos loved most the pine nuts.

Far away to the east of their land lay the desolate alkali flats. Beyond them, the Paiutes and Snakes and Pit River Indians against whom the Modocs had warred for decades beyond count.

And to the south of their green country along Lost River lay the undisturbed, pristine lava beds. A long narrow strip of volcanic upheaval that reminded a man of rugged surf breaking upon the shore, black and foamy, frozen for all time. Lying in this land like some monstrous, bony spine stripped of all flesh—black as evil itself.

This place had not always been Modoc land.

At one time, beyond the remembering of all but the oldest among them, the Modocs paid tribute to the Lalaca tribe, in later years, with the coming of the white man called the Klamaths. Eventually the Modocs grew weary of living as slaves to the more numerous Lalacas—so weary that chief Moadocus declared that his people would no longer owe allegiance to the Klamaths. In many battles Modoc warriors fell—but sweet freedom was won.

So the Modocs came to live in a state of wary peace along Lost River—given its name because it rises in Clear Lake and disappears in Tule Lake, without an outlet. Life was good when Kientpoos was but a boy.

Most of the rivers were too brackish for drinking, so the best water was found in clear, cold springs that dotted Modoc country. Sagebrush and bunch-grass dotted the hillsides, while down in the meadows along the rivers and creeks grew the richer, taller grass that fed the Modoc ponies, descendants of the finest horses long-ago brought to California by the Spanish. The cold, still waters of the lakes nurtured the swamp and tule grasses the Modocs used to weave their clothing before the coming of the white man.

Kientpoos, son of a chief, grew up in the Lost River land of fog-shrouded lava ridges dappled with juniper and scrub pine, where a man had to strain to hear the sound of geese sweeping overhead each autumn. The very vastness of the land itself swallowed sound as easily as it swallowed a man.

He could remember when there were no white men in Modoc country. Until 1850 there had been but few—and those only crossed in a hurry to go someplace else. But one or more of them left a disease that decimated half the tribe in 1847—smallpox.

For a few winters it was a struggle for the Modocs to grow healthy once more—while in their breasts they nursed a hatred of this deadly curse brought by the white man. As the white settlers began slowly pressing down from the north, squatting on some of the best of the meadows for their cattle and plows—it seemed they expected the Modocs to turn their cheek.

Instead, under the leadership of Kientpoos's father, the Modocs began to randomly attack small wagon caravans passing through their country, most times attacking at a place on the eastern shore of Tule Lake where the South Road strung itself between a rocky outcrop of lava and the water of the lake itself. In 1852 alone, thirty-six whites were slaughtered at Bloody Point.

In the midst of all the killing, young Kientpoos could not understand why his people and the whites could not live in some harmony.

"The white man must be driven out, my son," the chief told Kientpoos. "He is a treacherous devil who is here to take everything that God gave us. There is no peace living with the white man. He must go—then we will have peace."

Indeed, for every ambush, the white man came to retaliate. That fall the white miners at the nearby California town of Yreka, founded only the year before when gold was discovered along Greenhorn Creek, formed into a posse under an Oregon frontiersman named Ben Wright to revenge the killings.

The white men came to the Modoc camp, promising peace and preparing a feast for the Modoc men, women and children to prove their good intentions. Yet the Indians grew suspicious when the white men would not eat the food they had prepared for the Modocs. His elaborate plot to poison the tribe foiled, Ben Wright's men opened fire on the village. Less than a third escaped into the forests—never to forget the evil that lay behind the smiles of some.

That day would long remain in the heart of Kientpoos —a day when the white man's promise of peace was nothing more than a shabby cloak for his treachery.

With his father murdered, the embittered young man struggled to become chief against a weak leader, Old

Schonchin. Kientpoos was at last convinced there were indeed some white men who wanted to kill Indians as much as there were Modocs who wanted to kill the white-skinned. Still, he reasoned, there surely must be some white men who wanted peace as badly as he.

"I have always told white men when they came to my country, that if they wanted a home, to live there they could have it," Kientpoos said, "and I never asked them for any pay for living there as my people lived. I liked to have them come there and live. I liked to be with white people."

In years past he often visited the mining settlement at Yreka, California, some seventy miles west of Modoc land, where Kientpoos grew fond of the white man's things: clothes, wagons, houses, tools and weapons. In turn, the miners gave the friendly Modocs white names: Hooker Jim, Scar-Faced Charley, Curly Headed Doctor and Ellen's Man George, among others. Attorney Elisha Steele gave Kientpoos his white name—"Captain Jack"— after a miner he resembled. Steele and the Yreka miners did not recognize Old Schonchin as chief of the Modocs. To them, Captain Jack was the head man.

Too, the Modocs soon found that the lonely miners had grown fond of the Modoc women, and would pay a price for their services. As they became more familiar with the miners and shopowners, the Modocs more and more frequently bartered away the favors of their women for the precious articles of white civilization they could take back when they returned to Modoc country. They began to dress like white men, became drunk on the white man's whiskey and learned to crudely speak the white man's tongue.

The relations the Modocs shared with the miners was much better than the strained, uneasy peace the tribe maintained with the white settlers who kept moving into the Lost River country. All too soon the farmers and ranchers found themselves every bit as split as were the whites back in the east fighting their great war. While most settlers in Modoc land grumbled and complained to white officials and the army about the Indians, a few settlers who often hired the Modocs to work as hired hands on their claims said the tribe had every right to take a cow or horse here or there. Captain Jack's people were due that small "tax" for the white use of their tribal lands.

With each passing season, the Modocs learned better who to trust. And who they must be wary of.

Tensions grew and ebbed over the years, so much that Jack finally went to Yreka on St. Valentine's Day in 1864, to approach his friend Elisha Steele with the idea that a treaty with the white man would settle much that threatened to flare into full-scale war. Although Steele had no authority to negotiate a treaty, the attorney hoped that he could nonetheless forge a lasting peace.

By terms of Steele's agreement, the Modocs would no longer steal stock and would cease selling their women to the miners. They conceded the right of the army to punish them if they broke the terms of the agreement. What they received in return was permission to trade with the white man, to serve as guides to army and civilian alike, and to operate ferries for a profit.

Bound only by the strength of his word, Steele promised Jack he would try to win the Modocs a permanent home along the Lost River.

At the same time, the cries of the settlers grew so loud the army and the white man's government could no longer ignore them. Peace commissioners finally came among the Modocs and the Klamaths, a tribe more than twice as large as Jack's people, living just to the north of Modoc land. A new treaty was proposed that would move the Modocs from the Lost River to resettle on a part of what had long been traditional Klamath hunting ground. In their ignorance the white men believed the two tribes were alike and could live in harmony together. They promised the Indians that every man's family would be provided with stock and a wagon, tools to work the land, clothing and food.

Terms the Modoc did not like, nor want.

Yet Old Schonchin made a grand show of his acceptance of the treaty. After making his mark on the talking paper, the old chief turned to face the south, placing a hand over his heart, then moved the other from left to right, showing in sign that as steadfastly as the sun moved from east to west, he would keep his word.

Although something in his gut told Captain Jack not to affix his mark to the white man's talking paper, he reluctantly signed with the other chiefs that October in 1864 and moved his people to their new homes on Klamath land.

Trouble began immediately. The Klamaths considered the smaller bands of Modocs as intruders. They harassed Captain Jack's people: shamed them, took the fence rails they had split and lumber they cut to build their homes. It ate at the soul of the Modoc men to live as tenants and beggars on land controlled by their former enemies. During those same dark seasons, the white man's promises went the way of goose down before a wind. The promised clothing and food never arrived on the Modoc reservation, although the Klamaths were always well-fed and had plenty of clothes to fight the chill of winter.

That humiliation was ultimately more than Captain Jack could take. He found his tribe split in two factions. Those who believed in making the peace work allied themselves behind Old Schonchin, who had always been most agreeable to everything the white man offered. On the other hand, the more militant, freedom-loving Modocs arrayed themselves behind Jack. Even Old Schonchin's brother, John, vowed he would leave the reservation with Captain Jack.

Daring the white man to make good his promises, Chief Jack led his people back to Lost River, his very birthplace, by the end of 1865.

Along the streams and in the rich meadows that dotted the country of the Lower Klamath, Tule and Clear lakes, the Modocs discovered more cabins and fences and cattle than there had been when they left for Klamath country. For the next four years, Jack did his best to keep his people away from the whites as best he could, while the Modocs went back to hunting the hills for game, netting the streams for fish and gathering seeds and nuts for meal.

During the next four years, Jack continued to visit his white friends in Yreka, coming to respect Elisha Steele all the more. At the same time, Jack's Modocs watched Old Schonchin's band on the reservation with growing interest.

It was enough to convince them they should go on living free, as their ancestors had.

In that Lost River country, the white settlers were quick to complain that the army must do something about the nearly six hundred Modocs who had jumped their reservation behind Captain Jack—surly Indians returning to old tribal haunts to harass the God-fearing white folks who had come in peace to subdue and till this rich land so like a Garden of Eden.

With the inauguration of war hero Ulysses S. Grant in 1869, a new Indian superintendent for Oregon stepped to the fore—A. B. Meacham. In his lap landed the Modoc problem.

Meacham came south with a pair of interpreters, white man Frank Riddle and his full-blood Modoc wife, Winema. Also along were some civilian teamsters and a small escort of soldiers to guard Meacham in his talk with Captain Jack on the Modoc's Lost River stomping ground. Wisely, the Indian superintendent listened to the advice of Riddle and his wife, and left the soldiers in hiding some distance from the Modoc camp—not wishing to alarm Jack's people.

After the Modoc chief refused to hear of moving from Lost River, Meacham showed Jack the Modoc's own signature on the 1864 treaty. After a long, brooding silence, Jack reluctantly agreed he would go if he could live near a friend, Link River Jack.

Suddenly the fiery shaman, Curly Headed Doctor, leaped to his feet and shouted, "We will not go!"

At that moment Jack knew the fat had been thrown in the fire: if his band indeed did return to a reservation, any reservation, the tribal shaman would not enjoy his current prestige and authority among Jack's people while they lived in unfettered freedom.

Guns were drawn as more of the Modocs circled Meacham and his interpreters.

"Don't shoot—wait until we talk!" Winema Riddle shouted.

"Hear us!" Frank Riddle pleaded.

Jack himself strode into the center of the council arena, stepping between Meacham and the shaman to ask his question of the white man.

"If we do not go to this new reservation, what will become of us—you and me?"

Meacham considered his answer a moment. "My little group will have to fight you until we are all dead. Then more soldiers will come to kill your people—on and on, until there is not one left alive among you."

Jack adjourned the council and retired to his lodge to debate the matter with his head men. For two days they debated, and talked with Meacham. Then debated some more.

While Meacham ground through those two tense days of wrangling with the Modoc leaders, the escort company of soldiers grew restive and finally, charged up with enough of the whiskey they had brought along, they rushed the Modoc camp—scattering the warriors but capturing many women and children.

Infuriated, Meacham had little choice but to play the cards dealt him. As it turned out, the Modoc warriors had little choice as well: with their families held hostage, they eventually came in to surrender and hand over their old muzzle-loaders, agreeing to give the reservation a second try.

Although the Modocs were moved to a new area on the

eastern side of the Klamath reservation known as the Yainax Agency, matters proved even worse than ever. Now the Klamaths prevented Modoc children from gathering nuts and seeds in the hills, preventing Modoc women from hunting with snares to supplement what moldy flour the Indian Bureau gave out. As well, the women were kept from fishing, bullied and even beaten by the Klamaths. Not only did the Klamaths continue to steal the fruits of Modoc labor, but the white officers at Fort Klamath itself appropriated a few of the younger Modoc women for their own recreational use.

Three times Captain Jack went to the Indian agent for the District of the Lakes, Captain O. C. Knapp, to register his complaints. And each time Knapp waved the Modoc delegation away with his assurances he would talk to the Klamaths.

Nothing was done.

By the spring of 1870 the gall had finally risen in Jack's throat.

"The agent has no heart for us," Jack told his people. "He does not keep Meacham's promises. I no longer have a heart for Knapp—no heart for this place. The Modoc and Klamath cannot live together. We will go where we belong—to our homes on Lost River."

Chapter 1

Early Spring 1871

"*B*loody right we'll share a drink one day soon, old man," Seamus Donegan whispered quietly to himself as he folded Sam Marr's letter and stuffed it in one of the big pockets on his canvas mackinaw, his heart awash with memories of the man who had started north up the bloody Bozeman Road with him five years before.

With a sigh, he stepped down from the shadows into a stream of sunshine that poured through the breaks in the pewter clouds like liquid butterscotch.

The tall Irishman, who stood inches over six feet, had to admit there was something about this high country that could capture a man's heart. Both that country down around Cripple Creek in Colorado Territory, and this up here in the Montana diggings. He left the first behind a year before to follow the ghostly trail of his uncle, which led here to the gold boomtowns sprung up along Alder Gulch. Seamus had passed his thirtieth birthday getting this far up the backside of the snow-washed Rockies.

He smiled as the sunshine warmed a freshly shaved cheek. Seamus still favored the sweeping mustaches and the long, bantam tuft sported just beneath his lower lip first grown when he spent nearly a year fighting off Red Cloud's Sioux. The smile was as warm as the sunshine—

warmer in remembrance. Was a time he and Sam Marr had tried their luck getting up the Bozeman Road into this part of Montana—and both had been lucky to come through those days with their hair.*

Unconsciously Seamus's fingers sought to caress the old mountain man's medicine pouch he carried, tied around his neck on a buckskin thong there beneath his woolen shirt. He swung into the saddle atop the ugly roan he had traded from Teats at the Elephant Corral in Denver City back in the fall of '69. Coming there from Fort McPherson and his brush with death at the hand of a renegade mulatto.†

Seamus nodded to the owner of the shanty mercantile, a bookish sort of elf who also served as Nevada City's postmaster, before he reined up the street, headed out of town. Bound now for northern California.

He had been some time getting this far, learning this much. But at this moment beneath the Montana sun he sensed he was at long last heading down on the final leg of what seemed to have been a life's journey. Spring was breaking winter's hold on the high passes, and Seamus figured he could be in the California diggings by early fall.

What would happen when he arrived there was no way to tell. If only he could run across another wisp of a clue to the whereabouts of Ian O'Roarke out there in northern California.

Perhaps that fickle, fickle bitch called fate would smile on him as warmly as the sun caressed his neck right now. It had been a long winter going, here in Montana Territory. After a long winter before that, spent down in Colorado as well. Both winters filled with too damn many lonely hours put in remembering faces, tastes and smells—and the touch of a certain woman who alone still kicked around inside his empty heart.

---

* THE PLAINSMEN Series, vol. 1, *Sioux Dawn*
† THE PLAINSMEN Series, vol. 4, *Black Sun*

Back to the fall of '69 he had arrived in Denver City, his wounds from that brush with death still taut and pink and puckered. But the work he hired on to do at Teats's Elephant Corral slowly loosened up hide and sinew. Through that winter he had bedded down in the corner of a spare room at the back of a gambling hall beside the Chase Hotel on Fifteenth Street. Denver City was full of gambling halls and dance halls and whore cribs, and there was never any lack of something to do in that town for a man with healthy hands and strong back. Nor were there any lack of diversions and leaks for a man's purse.

The whiskey was strong—better than a thirsty man would find out among the string of posts and forts dotting the high plains where the sutlers invariably watered down their stock, padding their already substantial profit margin.

Besides the more potent whiskey, in Denver City a man could always find the girl of his liking: be she fleshy or thin, dark or pale, Mexican, Oriental or a smoke-skinned buffalo-haired chippie.

Many were the times it ate at him—this not knowing why the coffee-colored mulatto had hunted him down and nearly killed him in that stinking slip-trench latrine back of Bill McDonald's watering hole serving the frontier soldiers stationed at Fort McPherson, Nebraska Territory.

If it hadn't been for Bill Cody come back to the latrine looking for him that sundown . . .

Time and again he shook off the dread of the thought and learned to celebrate each new night he allowed himself to share with a new chippie in a different crib. One hurrah a week was about all Donegan could afford dipping into his purse, what with the way he went at the whiskey and the women.

As those months following the summer battle of Summit Springs had become years, he had noticed some subtle changes that warned him he was getting older. Besides the tiny cracks at the corners of his eyes that crinkled when he laughed or squinted across the great distances of this western land, no longer did he revel in all-night celebrations, wearing down the whiskey and the women both as he had once done. No, it was plain as paint he was slowing. It took longer to pull himself from the blankets the morning after when the sun came brutally calling.

As if that weren't the damndest thing about aging now —not only were the bad times getting him down all the more, but the good times took their toll on him as well.

Come the spring of eighteen and seventy there in Denver City, Seamus admitted he finally had his gullet fill of it all and promised himself he would follow down the only clue Liam O'Roarke left of his brother Ian. Remembering the two had their falling out in a place called Cripple Creek, Colorado Territory.

Not that there hadn't been times the Irishman wondered why he was even trying to follow the ghostly trail of his uncle when it seemed the only one who cared was his mother. But each time, Seamus finally admitted it mattered every bit as much to him.

It was family.

To his surprise, it hadn't taken all that long to run across some sign of Ian. A few questions asked at the marshal's office led him to track down a one-legged exprospector who lived in a shanty down below the creek. It was he who had known the O'Roarke brothers in better days.

"You do resemble 'em both, come to look at you," said the old man as he hobbled back to allow the Irishman room to pass into the low-roofed shanty built back into the hillside.

They both settled at the sheet-iron stove. Eventually, that night, Seamus eased around to telling the man how Liam had died—buried in an unmarked grave out on the prairie.*

"Heard something of that fight you had out there on

---

the Arickaree, son," the old man admitted with no lack of admiration in his watery eyes. "There was talk of it for weeks." He shook his head. "Must've been something—nine goddamned days. Shame though . . . Liam going under that way."

Seamus found the old man's eyes boring into him.

"He was the better of the two, boy. You know that, don't you?"

Donegan had to nod. "You're not the first to tell me."

The old man went back to gazing at the glow of the fire radiating through the slots in the stove door. "Not that the older one was really a bad sort—just that . . . seems he was weaned on sour milk. Always took offense at everything."

"You really knew them well—both me uncles?"

He finally nodded. "We panned—worked the same sluice. You work with a man like that, with your backs day after day—you get to know him."

"Threw in together?"

"For a time, we did," he replied. "Until the woman came to mess things up."

"The woman?"

With a gap-toothed smile he answered, "Woman always does make for the devil with a man, don't she?"

"I suppose she does at that," Donegan admitted. "What happened?"

"She belonged to another man. A cruel fella—he bought her in Denver afore crossing over the hills here to Cripple Creek."

"She was bought?"

"Paid for proper—and not with paper money. A young thing too. Her folks was poor-off, so they up and sold her to the fella with five gold pieces in his pocket."

"How was it Ian O'Roarke ended up with her?"

"She tired of the beatings from the man what owned her—so cast her eye out for someone who'd help her, I imagine," he replied. "Ian was there—and under her spell from the start. Not that I blame the girl none. She was needing help—and that's the Bible's truth of it."

"They ran off—Ian and this girl?"

"Not before things got ugly, son. One Sunday morning, it was. The fella—this husband of hers—he found out she had been talking to O'Roarke—lots. Others with loose jaws that liked to flap had seen 'em together a'times in secret. He come roaring in, saying she was his property, bought and paid for proper. If O'Roarke wanted her, he'd come up with the money or leave Cripple Creek for good."

Seamus wiped a hand across his dry mouth. "How much?"

"Five thousand in gold."

"That's a lot of money."

"Damn tootin' it is. Especially to buy a woman!"

"Ian have that much?"

He laughed. "Shit, son. All three of us together never seen that kind of dust in our lives!" Then he wagged his head. "Ian stood there, looking like he was figuring on it hard. Then finally told the woman to get out of the way. Up and told the gal's owner that he didn't have enough gold, but he figured there was lead enough in the pistol he carried in his belt to pay his debt."

"He killed the gal's owner?"

The old man nodded, a smile caressing his eyes. "Weren't clean, though. After they shot it out that morning, that fella's friends showed up that afternoon and set up a ruckus. Ian skeedaddled from town."

"How'd Liam figure in all of this?"

"All along he told his brother to stay clear of another man's woman—said there was always enough whiskey and enough women to go around. No sense worrying about one woman over another. But Ian seemed like he was bit something bad, that he just couldn't stay clear of her. Shame of it—Liam and he broke up our outfit over that woman."

"You sound like you figure Liam wanted the woman too."

"Liam? Shit, he wasn't the kind to get caught up yoke and traces in a woman. Not that one. He just . . . just didn't want to stir up no trouble."

"Where'd Ian go?"

"I heard later from Liam that his brother headed up to Silver Plume."

"Where's that?"

"North of here a ways."

"When?"

He thought on it, tapping a finger against his lower lip. "Eighteen and sixty."

"The woman went with him?"

The old man nodded. "Bad blood she caused between them brothers. Women just naturally have a way of stirring things up a'tween men."

"You've been a lot of help. I'll head out for Silver Plume in the morning."

"You might. Then, you might not," the old man said quietly, cryptically. "No sense heading there when I heard Ian didn't stay long in Silver Plume. Moved on north with the gal, fixing to make a clean break."

"Liam ever know of this?"

"I figure he did. But I suppose from the way he talked that he figured there was no sense in trying to mend things a'tween him and his brother. A woman can cause a deep wound that oft times won't heal just right—like a bad bone growed back crooked."

"Where'd Ian head off to?"

"By 'sixty-two he was pushing north to the Idaho fields. What was Idaho then—called Montana now."

"Alder Gulch? Virginia City, Nevada City, Bannack?"

His well-seamed face brightened. "Lordee! Does sound like you know of the place, son!"

"I'll be blessed!" Seamus exclaimed. "Of a time I was heading there meself. Glory . . . glory be."

* * *

Captain Jack told his people they were once more returning to their homeland, this time when he returned from visiting the agent O. C. Knapp. He promised them they would stay on Lost River for all the seasons to come.

No more would they listen to the paper-thin promises of food and clothing, of safety from enemies and a peaceful life. A small minority of the Modocs chose to stay on at Yainax under Old Schonchin, while the majority followed Jack's dream of freedom, sharing his undying thirst for the old life.

And return to their old ways they did. The men resumed their visits to Yreka, where they frequented the watering holes, getting drunk and selling their women to the white miners for gold and horses and weapons.

During this time the fire-eyed, wavy-haired shaman the miners had named Curly Headed Doctor rose to some prominence among the Modocs and split off from Jack's band, taking some nine or ten hot-blooded warriors who steadfastly believed war would one day come to Modoc land—when they would drive the white man out forever. To the Doctor's camp flocked the worst of renegades, who immediately renewed causing trouble for the settlers living in the Lost River country—frightening women and children while the men were away in the fields, demanding food here or an iron kettle there, occasionally killing a stray cow or stealing a horse.

Again the white man's cry of indignation was raised, louder than before. Most of the settlers demanded government action to force the Modocs back to their reservation. Yet a few white men counseled prudence—saying it was the Klamaths causing all the turmoil. If not those other tribes, surely it was nothing more than a few bad seeds among the Modocs.

Even if they had wanted to, by mid-1870 the army could not provide the help needed to quell the growing unrest along Lost River. Most of the western posts had been emptied of all but a skeleton force as the army shipped troops to General George Crook's drive to round up the renegade Apache in Arizona. With Crook himself dispatched to the southwest from the Division of the Pacific, General Edward R.S. Canby was placed in charge of the Department of the Columbia.

At nearby Fort Klamath, built in 1863 mainly to watch over the local reservation, there remained but two companies of infantry: only seventy-two soldiers. Over at the nearest relief station, Camp Warner in Paiute Territory, could be found another two units—one infantry and one cavalry.

Matters were growing steadily warm in the Lost River country by the week, not all of it local. In the summer of 1871 a new religion was spreading across the great basin. Over toward Nevada a Paiute named Tavibo was promising the destruction of the world as it was presently ruled by the white man. Earthquakes would swallow up the unfaithful whites while the red man would be allowed to repopulate the land in peace and prosperity.

A wild-eyed Curly Headed Doctor accepted the new religion with a vengeance. It was everything he had been praying for and preaching about among his zealots. As prescribed by the Messiah, Tavibo, the Modocs began dancing back the ghosts of their departed relatives in their camp beside Lost River.

Finally, in that summer of the year the white man called his 1872, Captain Jack was sternly warned by Indian agent Knapp that his people must return to the reservation or suffer the consequences.

Unhappy with the lack of progress in the Modoc affair under the old regime of Alfred B. Meacham, the agent informed the Modoc chief, the government had replaced the aging superintendent with T. B. Odeneal. That meant a new era of stricter control had dawned for the tribes.

Knapp went on to declare strongly, "The army has grown tired of you and your kind thumbing your noses at them and living off the reservation, Jack. Mark my words: the soldiers will soon come and remove your tribe by force if they have to."

"I am but one man. Yet I am the voice of my people. Whatever their hearts are—those are my words. I want no more war. I want only to be a man. You deny me the rights of a white man. My skin is red; my heart wants what a white man's heart wants; but I am a Modoc. I am not afraid to die. I will not fall on the rocks. Hear me! When I die, my enemies will be under me."

The agent slammed a palm down on his desk. "You sound like you're goading for war with the white man, Captain Jack."

"I have always told the white man to come and settle in my country; that it was his country and Captain Jack's country. That they could come and live there with me and that I was not mad with them. I have never received anything from anybody, only what I bought and paid for myself. I have always lived like a white man, and wanted to live so. I have always tried to live peaceably and never asked any man for anything. I have always lived on what I could kill and shoot with my gun, and catch in my trap."

"Shut your mouth and go back to the reservation with the others," Knapp replied brusquely, settling back in his chair. "There you will get the flour and pork we will give you. You don't need guns—don't need to hunt. Swallow your idiotic pride and make up with the Klamaths before it is too late for you and your people."

"We can never live with the Klamaths," Jack protested, his short, stout body tensed like a spring as he turned to leave the agent's office, fuming. "You white men may try to force us to live on a reservation—but we are Modocs. So we will make our home somewhere on Lost River . . . where my people have been born and cremated for centuries before your coming. If we are to die—don't force us to die on Klamath land. Let it be among the bones of our grandfathers!"

Chapter 2

Early Fall 1872

*F*rom Colorado, Seamus Donegan had pushed due north into Wyoming Territory. Company for that journey was no problem, what with all the freight outfits plying the roads north up the backside of the Rockies into Montana. From both Colorado and Utah the roads were bustling that summer of 1870.

When he had reached the diggings, the Irishman quickly eased himself in with the hard-drinking lot hanging on by their nails to their hardscrabble existence before winter snows shut down their scanty operations. In amongst the long string of gold camps and boomtowns he asked after Ian O'Roarke and the woman.

And kept his eye open for the gray-headed horse-breeder from Missouri—Sam Marr.

In Nevada City he came across a man who remembered Ian and the woman. Remembered too those two small children with them. A girl and her little brother. The boy was still a babe in arms, the shopowner said, when the O'Roarkes pulled out.

"Going where?"

"Said they would try the California gold fields again," with a thick Slavic accent.

"Ian had been there before," Seamus explained. He

sighed. "I was bloody well hoping my search would end here. Now it seems I'll be moving on west as well."

The shopowner laughed, wringing his hands on the dirty apron he had cinched around his chest, just below his armpits. "You'll be doing nothing of the kind—less'n you plan on leaving your bones for some winter-starved wolf to gnaw on before spring." He chuckled again, pulling the Irishman to the smudged and smoky window, pointing up the street.

Seamus nodded as it sank in. The mountain peaks hulking over them reminded him of the Big Horns standing guard over the Piney Creeks where Carrington built his beloved fort.

"The passes all closed up?"

"Oh, a man could go back down to Salt Lake, I suppose. Be hard going too. Then he'd have to make his crossing down along the south, moving over the desert this time of year."

Seamus sighed again. "I'll wait. And head out come spring. Been this long." He turned back to the shopkeeper at the window. "Any idea what a man can do with his time come winter here in Montana?"

With an easy laugh, the shopkeeper walked back to station himself behind his single, modest counter. "Lots a honest man can do if he takes a mind to. I've work at least one day a week for you. Others might surely find something to fill your time out too."

"I appreciate the offer." He felt a bit embarrassed, as if the man were offering a handout. "But I need to find me a place to keep the horses and lay my head."

"Thiebalt's—down the road. Tell him I sent you. Make you a good deal on boarding them horses. When you're done there—come on back here and have dinner with me and the missus. We'll fix you up something of a bed in the storeroom, if you like."

He held out his hand to the man. "I thank you, sir. And by the by, you ever hear of a fellow named Sam

Marr? Lot older'n me—gray of hair. Stocky. Little banty rooster of a man."

The shopkeeper cupped his chin in a hand thoughtfully. Then wagged his head. "So many . . . no, I suppose not. But, there is a gent who might know of this Sam Marr. Inquire for Billy behind the bar down at Henrietta's Roost, down the street."

"He'll know?"

"Billy's been here from the start, almost since water first come down this creek. He's seen 'em come and seen 'em go—good times and the bad. He been here, Billy will know him."

The bartender did know of Sam Marr, as it turned out.

That Missouri horse-breeder had pushed on north from Fort Phil Kearny in the late spring of 1868, not long before the army pulled all its troops and its tail out of the forts along the Bozeman Road. As Billy told it, Sam came to the area and staked a claim far enough away from the others that many laughed at his foolishness. But Marr ran across a little dust. Not a killing—but enough to keep a man at it.

Then late this past spring Sam Marr had packed up and rode off north with itchy boots once more, heading for the gold camps up by Jefferson City and Helena.

Seamus had to roar at that, bringing a look of consternation to the bartender's face.

"Ain't that just like my luck?" Donegan snorted. "I'm a day late and more'n a dollar short following any of these trails—be it following Ian O'Roarke or Sam Marr!"

But it didn't deter him from the difficult task of composing two letters to Sam Marr—both of them worded the same, but addressed to different towns. One to Helena and the other posted to Jefferson City. And throughout that miserable winter among new friends in Nevada City, Seamus wrote letters to various towns in southern Ohio— never allowing himself to believe they wouldn't reach her.

One . . . if only one.

Winter came in and descended on the land with a vengeance. But two or three days after each storm, the sun reappeared and the townspeople were back at it once more—digging out pathways between the shrinking cabins, making long, cavernous trails down the middle of the main street. Having caught up on the snowstorm gossip, each person went back to his or her chores, renewed by the enforced hibernation, no matter how short or long.

One day, in late winter it was, when the Slavic shopkeeper who also acted as postal agent hailed Seamus over. Donegan slogged across the muddy street, each of his gummy boots weighing as much as a small sack of horseshoes.

"You've a letter, Irishman."

"Ohio?"

The man shook his head, confused by the question, his brow knitting. "No. Helena."

Though disappointed, he raised himself to cheer, "By damned, it must be Sam Marr!"

He looked up from the envelope. "That's the name on it. Here. Been here for a couple days—and it slipped my mind that it come for you."

Seamus was gone, reading and rereading every one of the long, folded pages right out in the winter sun at the edge of the snowdrifts hugging that narrow street where cold melt ran gurgling with a voice all its own, singing of spring come to the high country. It was worth a third read as well, when Donegan plodded off toward a watering hole to have a solitary drink there, sitting with the memory of the faraway Sam Marr.

Less than a month later a second letter arrived from the old Missourian—coming the morning Seamus loaded the packhorse and rode south for California. Sam was doing well in Helena, operating a livery for a wealthy man, and was overjoyed to learn of the Irishman's miraculous return to the northern plains after so many planning the end of Mother Donegan's oldest boy.

"From what you write me of your battle on Beecher's Island (and what we here were told by word and print of that bloody siege)—you are blessed indeed, son. Like the rising of the mythic Phoenix from the ashes, you have risen from your grave more than once, Seamus Donegan."

He planned to write Sam all the way to California. That would mean a letter from the City of the Saints. Another from somewhere in Nevada, and still another he'd write in Sacramento, where the storekeeper said a man could begin his search for his oldest uncle. Perhaps even a letter from San Francisco, should he get that far west in his search for someone who would remember the name Ian O'Roarke.

In Utah he paid in dust for a Central Pacific rail ticket that would take him to Sacramento, a ride on those singing iron rails for one long-haired plainsman clear across the great central basin, along with passage for both animals. A marvel it was to travel so quickly, so steadily up and down the mountains and across the great expanse without slowing, halting only infrequently for those line stops where the train took on fuel and water and where the passengers tromped on or off, some travelers taking the opportunity to stand in line to eat at dusty station diners.

In the half a decade since he had fled the east, Seamus brooded, the east had done everything in its power to thrust itself west. And thrust itself fiercely it had.

Sacramento was a teeming, throbbing mass of comings and goings, filled with the smell of coal oil and wood smoke, fresh-cut lumber and the earthy dung of draft animals mixed a'tumble with the fragrant sweat of human labor that summer of 1871. He was but two days in town before learning enough of the location of the old gold camps to know he had to work himself east and north again. But ever closer still. First to Placerville, then due north to Nevada City and Downieville in the mountains, where a man might expect to find himself some gold.

But no answers did he dig out of those hills. Nor shred of a clue. Winter closed down on Donegan in Oroville hard beside the Feather River. He was six weeks stranded there. Already the new year of 1872 had the shine worn off it by the time he could bust his way out of winter's lock and continue to work his way north. Word had it there were some profitable diggings for a man closer to the Oregon country.

"If a fella was to ask around Yreka, Horse Creek or Hornbrook," explained a blacksmith making Seamus an extra fore and back shoes for the long trip, "he just might dredge up something on this man named Ian O'Roarke."

"I'm beginning to fear it's not likely," the Irishman brooded at the corner of the shop.

The blacksmith looked up from the hot work over his anvil. Salty sweat stung his blinking eyes. "You'll not find what it is you're looking for if you ever give up, mister. But then, I'll admit—not many a man would go off crossing half the goddamned country looking for one man neither. My hat's off to you. It takes a special breed of fella to spend so much of his life tailing after a ghost that may not even exist."

"He exists, all right," Seamus protested, feeling nonetheless the blacksmith's words were driven home with every stinging ring of that hammer colliding with fired steel glowing atop the anvil.

"Is he alive?" asked the man as he immersed the shoe with a resounding hiss from the oak bucket.

Donegan had only shaken his head and looked away into the late winter sunshine streaming into the central California valley that day he finally continued north. From gold camp to boomtown and on and on, he made the circuit, pointing his nose always north it seemed. Drawing closer and closer to the border that marked the end of California and the beginning of Oregon country.

Early that summer the Irishman sat in a tonsorial parlor, wincing each time the local "physician" tugged on the household thread he was using to sew up the ugly laceration on Donegan's brow where a miner had clubbed him with a broken chair leg in a saloon brawl.

"What you looking at so close?" he asked the doctor, who, it seemed to Seamus, drew back and stared more at his face after every second or third stitch, more than he was inspecting his handicraft.

The man shook his head. "I'd swear—but you look the spitting image of someone I knew years ago."

Seamus's big eyebrows lifted as much as his hopes were raised. "Irishman?"

He nodded and forced the needle through Donegan's flesh again.

It did not hurt near as bad now as that first puncture had. "You said years ago . . . when?"

The man bit a lip for a moment, concentrating on tugging the two raw edges of the wound together. " 'Sixty-five. Yes—going on eight years now. He had just come in from Montana."

"Anyone with him?"

"No, he was traveling alone."

There came a sinking feeling—Ian had family now.

"Can't be the man I'm looking for. He has a wife and two children."

The physician drew back. His brow knitted, then cleared like a prairie sky after a spring thunderstorm. "Yes. Why, yes! Two small children. Both of them caught their deaths of colds that winter of 'sixty-five . . . we just about lost the boy."

Seamus shoved the man's hand from his hairline. "What was his name?"

"Irish, of course. Seems it was O'something."

"O'Roarke?"

"Could be. Sounds—"

"Ian?"

"Yes—as a matter of fact." Now the man took a good, long, and appraising look. "You're related, ain't you?"

"If it's Ian O'Roarke, we are." He fidgeted, ready to get out of the chair. "You finished on me yet?"

"Two more . . . no, we'll make this the last one. Sorry, I know that one pulled."

When he had snipped the ends of the thread and handed the scissors to his wife, the physician held the lamp up close to inspect his work.

"Where can I find O'Roarke? He prospecting outside of town?"

Seamus watched the way the man glanced at his wife. She hurriedly took her sewing kit and left the room.

"Lord, he don't work a claim no more," the man answered quietly. "O'Roarke gave that up after them children got sick and nearly died. Him and the woman told us they were pulling out—going to make a change in things."

Donegan felt all the hope sink in him like the foam on a beer gone flat. "They've gone?"

"Yes, I'm afraid."

"Not around here?"

"Last I heard of O'Roarke—he was not far north. Up in Oregon. Not far over the line. Place called Linkville."

"What's a man like O'Roarke doing there?"

"He lives out from town some, south from Linkville."

"What's he do?"

"Raises a few cows, I understand. Grows some crops."

Seamus had to smile, remembering Eire. It was like the O'Roarkes, it was. They were farmers—connected to the soil as surely as a newborn is still connected to its mother by the umbilicus. The O'Roarkes, clinging to the rich, loamy land still.

He stuffed a hand down in his pocket and pulled out a small pouch of dust. "How much I owe you."

"Ten dollars worth sound all right?" the physician replied, dragging up a small scale he used to weigh the gold dust paid for his myriad services. "You could use a haircut."

"You'll leave this long hair alone today," he replied, digging open the top of the pouch. "But you've done more than ten dollars worth to this ruddy head of mine, you have. Here, make that fifteen for your help."

"He'll be glad to see you, Ian will?"

The question stopped Seamus at the door, his hand on the brass knob. "I don't know. The last time we laid eyes on each other, I was but a wee lad in Ireland. And he was setting sail for Amerikay."

The man pursed his lips, patting his vest pockets, in search of an old pipe. He cleared his throat nervously. "Then I wish you well . . . if you find this the end of your search for Ian O'Roarke."

She was a troublesome cow, this one—but the big, brooding Irish farmer felt he understood her. If he could live these past dozen years with sweet, unpredictable Dimity —then Ian O'Roarke felt he could get along with anyone.

Not that she was the first woman he had ever loved. Just that more than anything, he wanted Dimity to be the last.

"Sweet-sweet. Sweet-sweet."

The homely man with the rugged, angular face coaxed and prodded the cow back into the stall where he could examine her. She didn't like it any more than he did, this process of lifting her tail and easing nearly the length of his entire arm inside her. But there was no easy cure for the colic, and once a cow went down with it—likely she would never get back on her feet again. And he would have to put her down for good.

Life had been like that for him—pure colicky—until he found something to hold onto. And that was back there a dozen years in Cripple Creek when he fell madly, passionately, no-two-ways-of-Sunday in love with Dimity. She was hardly a month over eighteen when he killed a man for her and left his brother behind.

Just about the hardest thing Ian had ever done, besides saying farewell to the land of his birth and setting off for Amerikay with brother Liam. Seeing the look on the face of his sister and the other family all huddled at the landing as the big ship eased into the wind.

No turning back.

But there in that Cripple Creek street he had come to

the decision to leave everything that was behind—and grab onto everything that could be.

At least all that he hoped it would be with Dimity.

Patience had been born in Colorado Territory that first year after fleeing Cripple Creek and turning his back on Liam. Little Seamus came along almost two years later during their first winter in the Montana diggings. Whereas Dimity had named their daughter, Ian claimed right to name his firstborn son—especially a lad who so looked like O'Roarke's nephew.

. . . Perhaps it had been his nephew Seamus after all, the one who was asking up to town after Ian O'Roarke, he thought to himself, his mind torn from the work at hand.

Ian was all bone and sinew. Tall to be sure, but nowhere with the weight of his brother Liam. And the thought of his younger brother always weighed heavily on the dark-haired Ian O'Roarke.

His neighbors in this part of the country had been up to Linkville over the past two days. Friends John Fairchild and Pressley Dorris had gone into town for supplies and any news on the growing concern with the nearby Modocs living off their reservation, squatting along their old tribal grounds of Lost River . . . when the two were introduced to a tall, big-boned fella who had been making himself a nuisance asking the whereabouts of Ian O'Roarke.

"You catch his name?" Ian inquired of his neighbors when they came out to report the chance meeting in Linkville.

"Donegan."

"Seamus, it is," he replied, his eyes lighting up.

"You know him then?" John Fairchild asked.

"He's my nephew. The lad was the namesake for my firstborn son."

Pressley Dorris nodded. "I figure he'll be along in a few days. Not everyone going to keep as quiet about you as we did, Ian."

Ian had nodded. "Seamus got this far on my trail—he won't be long coming these last few miles, I suspect."

"We weren't so sure you'd want him—"

"That's all right, John. It's time . . . time we talked, this nephew and me."

After Fairchild and Dorris pulled away without ever dropping from their saddles, continuing on down the road to their own ranches of tilled ground and cattle pasture, O'Roarke put on his oldest pair of patched britches, pulling on his worn boots before he tromped across the rich-smelling mud to the log barn where the cow was enduring her pain noisily. With a strong but gentle touch, he had set to work on the animal, thinking back to the tall, raw-boned youth with smooth cheeks he had last seen standing at the edge of the crowded pier—the boy's arm clutched fiercely about Ian's sister.

It made him think once more of his brother Liam and the years they spent roaming this terrible and exciting new land of Amerikay. Together as more than brothers—wandering souls each day more like true friends . . . wandering happy until Cripple Creek and those terrible words spoken like spilled whiskey between them that neither one would swallow and take back.

Brother Liam—would that he ever see him again, Ian prayed.

Little Liam was born on the road to Oregon from Yreka after the awful, gray winter when they nearly lost Patience and Seamus. Then better than two years later in 1867 another daughter was born, named Charity. Finally, two years after her, the baby was born—Thomas, named after Dimity's father.

That never failed to raise some sort of dark chuckle in Ian, recalling how set-footed Dimity was about naming the boy Thomas, after the man who had sold his own flesh and blood to a miner who had enough twenty-dollar gold pieces to buy her.

But set-footed Dimity was about it. And Thomas their youngest was named. So long had it been since she had been sold by her father that perhaps she had forgotten the venal brutality of the man.

"Just perhaps, Ian O'Roarke," he said to himself as he stroked the cow's flanks, her tail whipping hard against his ribs, "time is indeed the healer the priests and holy-ones say it is."

Five children across their first eight-odd years together. Traveling in search of the pot of gold the brothers O'Roarke had come west to find.

In the end realizing his wealth did not come of shiny metal or hoarded riches.

So it was each evening Ian O'Roarke spoke his own private prayer as his family gathered around its table for supper.

It was in their eyes and smiles and the love that he felt from this new family that each day convinced the aging Irishman that he had truly found his fortune.

So rich were his blessings that he realized this life was all he had ever wanted, and surely more than he figured he would ever deserve.

Chapter 3

November 28, 1872

"*More* coffee?"

Seamus looked up at the rose-cheeked woman, reminded of his mother's ruddy face as she would kneel over some steaming pot hung from the trivet at the fireplace. He figured his mother must now be about the age of the woman who stood at his elbow.

"One more cup of your coffee would do nicely, thank you."

She poured, then left him to himself at the tiny table where he sat in the gloomy, autumn afternoon light straining through the glass window that looked out on the muddy street of Linkville, Oregon.

This unpretentious settlement of square storefronts surrounded by an ungainly assortment of rough-hewn cabins had arisen years ago on the east bank of the Link River, close by the southern tip of Lower Klamath Lake, to serve the commercial needs of a growing number of white settlers moving into what had once been Modoc tribal lands.

Most of those who came to trade in town of late were now of one mind: raising enough ruckus with the government so that officials would forcibly remove the Modocs from their Lost River camps where they had been squatting for some years now. The time had come for action.

Outside the smoky café window where Donegan sat watching that late afternoon, officials an entire continent away in Washington had already set in motion the gears of a small, yet immensely tragic piece of history that was about to be played out along the Oregon-California boundary. Gears that no man at this point would be able to stop until they had run themselves dry of blood.

In a letter recently telegraphed to Superintendent T. B. Odeneal, the Indian Department passed on explicit instructions regarding the immediate removal of the Modocs to their Yainax Reservation: ". . . peaceably if you can, forcibly if you must."

From Linkville, Odeneal had promptly informed the military commander of the department, General Edward R.S. Canby, who in turn had informed Major John "Uncle Johnny" Green, commanding officer of the First Cavalry at the nearby Fort Klamath, that soldiers were in all likelihood going to be required for that peaceful removal.

As only a footnote at the time, Canby had cautioned his subordinates that if troops were to be used in the removal, then "the force employed should be so large as to secure the result at once and beyond peradventure."

In the meantime, from the safety of Linkville, Odeneal had sent Klamath agent Ivan Applegate to visit Captain Jack in his camp on Lost River. Applegate returned the next day muttering about his trip being an abominable waste of time. Jack, Applegate announced, was not about to meet with any white man who talked about moving his people, nor were his people going peacefully back to Yainax to live under Old Schonchin.

Yet what Applegate had most heatedly reported upon his return was that while he had been a guest in the Modoc camp, many of Jack's young warriors had clamored for killing him and his interpreter—if only to precipitate a war with the white man.

The Modocs' shaman, Curly Headed Doctor, had the

hotbloods all fired up with war-talk . . . convincing the warriors that their powerful spirits would protect them and defeat all white men who marched against them.

Captain Jack and a few others had stood against the talk of murder—and in the end the chief's words had kept Applegate alive while he slipped away from the Modoc camp.

When Applegate relayed the critical situation to Odeneal, the nervous superintendent immediately dispatched his agent to see Major Green up at Fort Klamath, requesting the army to immediately "furnish a sufficient force to compel said Indians to go to Camp Yainax, on said reservation, where I have made provision for their subsistence."

At five o'clock that morning Applegate had stood before Green, delivering the superintendent's urgent message. For some reason not waiting to communicate with either his superior, Lieutenant Colonel Frank Wheaton of the Twenty-first Infantry, or Wheaton's superior, General Canby, the major had by eight that morning dispatched a seasoned officer, Captain James Jackson of Company B, First Cavalry, to lead Lieutenant Frazier A. Boutelle and thirty-eight troopers to assist Applegate's removal of the Modocs. Assistant Surgeon Henry McElderry would ride behind the troops with a small pack-train carrying three days rations for the soldiers.

"With all due respect, sir," Lieutenant Boutelle said haltingly to Major Green in private after Applegate had stepped from the major's office, "as I understood General Canby's orders, no direct action is to be taken against the Modocs until a force large enough can be sent against them."

Green was clearly perturbed with his Officer of the Day. "What do you think will be a sufficient number, Mr. Boutelle? A hundred? *Two* hundred?"

"All due, sir—Captain Jackson's company is not enough, Major. I figure we'll be only enough to provoke a fight with them."

Green whirled on the lieutenant, cheeks flaring. "God-dammit! If I don't send you troops down there—the whining, carping civilians in this region will think we're all afraid of those bloody Modocs!" He looked down at his desk and sighed. Then swept up the sheet of paper and handed it to Boutelle.

"Lieutenant, here are my orders."

Boutelle scanned them quickly.

Orders No. 93:

   In compliance with the request of the Superintendent of Indian Affairs for Oregon . . . Captain James Jackson 1 Cav. with all the available men of his troop, will proceed at once . . . to Capt. Jack's camp . . . endeavoring to get there before tomorrow morning, and if any opposition is offered . . . he will arrest if possible Capt. Jack, Black Jim, and Scarfaced Charley.

Beyond the peaks to the west, the sun was setting as Seamus emptied the burnt dollop from his stub of a pipe and refilled the bowl. Smoke wreathed his face as he peered from the window, watching the last of Captain Jackson's soldiers disappear down the street, toward the livery corral where he imagined the troopers would be quartering their horses for the night.

"Your name was Donegan, right?"

Seamus turned, peering over his shoulder at the settler he had met two days before, upon his arrival in Linkville.

"Yes," he replied, coming 'round in his chair and start-ing to rise, his hand extended. "You're John Fairchild—"

But he stopped dead in the middle of climbing to his feet, slowing, that big hand still hung out before him like a clumsy prop now. Over Fairchild's shoulder he caught the eye of the other settler, a man named Dorris. Yet beside him—the ghost of an uncle, stepping now out of the late afternoon gloom of the tiny, smoky café.

"Seamus Donegan, is it?" the tall rail of a ghost asked

sternly, dark eyes glowering, having taken two menacing steps closer. "Of County Kilkenny?"

"Ian . . . Uncle Ian O'Roarke." The words spilled like iron filings from a blacksmith's rasp. He stood there a moment longer, not knowing what to do first—after all these miles and so many years.

Then Ian moved first. Initially it was his face that softened, the sharply-cut eyes widening and the chiseled corner of the mouth coming up like the soft curve of a butt stock. O'Roarke's arms came up, widening in warmth and welcome as he moved forward at a rush.

They met in the middle of the floor, knocking aside two armless chairs with a clatter as they embraced.

"You . . . you were so small when we left, Seamus," Ian said quietly, his words all but lost against his nephew's bulky shoulder.

"I haven't missed many meals, Uncle," Donegan replied, squeezing the shorter, thin man all the tighter, still unable to believe it was Ian O'Roarke. He had remembered his uncle being so much taller, of a much more massive frame as he carried a young nephew around from place to place on his own shoulder.

Instead, as Seamus drew back to arm's length to look into the older man's eyes, he was astonished to realize Ian was actually smaller than Liam had been. Every bit as tall perhaps, but nowhere as big. The cruel tricks that time and solitude of thought play with the mind.

"Where—" he started to ask his uncle.

"We can save that for later, Seamus," Ian replied, slapping his callused, farm-worn hand on the back of the young man's neck and pulling him close once more. He kissed his nephew on both cheeks, only then realizing Seamus was crying too.

His uncle smelled as he always had: of animals and sweat, of hard work and the land, so rich and dark and alive. "I've been looking—"

"I know you have, nephew. I—I only wanted to disappear. Didn't know anyone'd come looking for me, or that it'd be you who did. Most of all, never knew when I would have to come back up for air. Now's as good a time as any. By the Virgin Mary—how you've grown!" He snorted back some dribble at the end of his nose. "How old are you now, let's see . . ." He bit his lower lip in contemplation.

Seamus could see that his uncle was only keeping the lip from quivering. "Thirty-two winters come and gone now, Uncle."

The dark eyes gazed up into his, moistening anew. "You make an old man feel older still, lad."

He flung a fist at his uncle's midsection very much as he had done as a youngster. Seamus marveled at the taut washboard of a belly on Ian O'Roarke. "That's not the belly of an old man."

"Fifty-eight I am—but the plow and animals keep a man younger than I'd ever be, wading ice-water sluice boxes, hungering for yellow dust."

Of a sudden, Seamus wanted nothing more than a drink of something hard, strong and potent to settle what had unnerved him. His heart awash with so much.

"A drink we should have, Uncle," Seamus proposed, his eyes going to the other two men as well. "To celebrate—"

"There's not time, nephew," Ian explained, smiling gently behind that dark, full beard that encased his sharp jawline.

"If it's home you must return to—I'll come along . . . you let me invite meself—"

"It's not home we're going to," Ian interrupted, wagging his head and tossing a thumb over his shoulder at Fairchild and Dorris. "There's bloody business afoot and we've got to be sure the hand of it is played square, Seamus."

This time Donegan wagged his head. "I—I don't understand."

Ian gently nudged his nephew back to the smoky window. The sun had disappeared, but enough light still spilled across the icy puddles gathered in every rut and bootprint to give the street a metallic, orange luster.

"You saw the soldiers come this afternoon?"

He nodded. "Aye."

Ian turned to his nephew. "We—the three of us—have long had good relations with these Modocs. And those soldiers out there don't know it—but they are about to bring some evil matters to a head, Seamus."

"Modocs?"

"Indians in these parts. John and Press here are among the few who got along with Captain Jack's people the last few years his band's been out on Lost River."

Fairchild came up. "The soldiers are leaving tonight— to be at the Modoc camp by dawn."

"Trouble?" Donegan asked, sensing the inevitable of it already.

"These soldiers don't know what they're starting," Ian replied. "When Press and John come by the other day to tell me a stranger'd come to town, asking about me . . . it sounded like my own nephew had dogged the trail long enough."

"You came to see for yourself?"

He nodded, laying a hand on Donegan's forearm. "Nephew—before things get bloody, I wanted to see you face to face. To send you out to my place."

"Your family—they'll be safe?"

Ian nodded quickly, but seriousness clung to his eyes. "You can wait for me there."

Seamus clutched his uncle's arm. "By the saints—I'm not letting you go now, Ian. After looking for you all this time, I'll be damned if you walk out of here and into some trouble without me."

"This is none of yours—"

"Bleeming well it is. Time and again you picked me up off the ground and wiped the blood off me. Where you're bound this night—I'm bound there as well."

Ian O'Roarke glanced at the other two. They nodded quickly. He himself measured his young nephew. "You know how to handle that hog-leg you've got weighing you down?"

"If I need to."

"The war in the south we heard so much about years ago?"

"All four years, Uncle. Cavalry."

O'Roarke looked at his friends, a sad smile cutting his beard. "Looks like the blood's held true, boys." He pulled Seamus aside to whisper out of the hearing of the rest of the patrons in the café. "There's much to talk of, Seamus. So be it. You want to ride with me, you can come."

"Where is it we're going in the dark, with a chance of snow smelling strong in the air?"

Ian O'Roarke snorted softly as Press Dorris and John Fairchild seemed anxious to be on their way, inching toward the door. "Come along then, nephew. We're going to try to keep the army from stirring up more than they can handle with the Modocs."

Outside, a freezing rain had settled hard over the land.

Never before had Ian O'Roarke seen the little settlement of Linkville so alive with commotion and hubbub.

For months now the antagonized citizens of the surrounding countryside had goaded the army and government to make a move against the Modocs or, the settlers threatened, they would themselves raise a volunteer militia to do what the army was incapable of doing.

When Ian and Seamus, along with Pressley Dorris and John Fairchild, marched through the icy sleet to the edge of town, they found Captain James Jackson's forty cold soldiers hugging the trees at the edge of the nearby corral. Puffs of gauzy vapor betrayed every man in that gloomy darkness as the civilians approached a small, animated circle of men arguing in hushed tones. Jackson and his Lieutenant Boutelle stood quietly aside as Superintendent Odeneal reimpressed his agent, Oliver Applegate, with the seriousness of what was about to take place. Applegate was unsure of moving too hastily.

"I think it better to wait for more soldiers to come—"

"Dammit," Odeneal growled, freezing rain crackling along the arm he used for gesture, "we don't have the time—and we don't have the need. The Modocs will move peacefully . . . or the captain here will herd them up to Yainax."

"I don't figure Captain Jack and his bunch will do anything peacefully, once you send the soldiers in there after him."

Odeneal rocked back on his heels, smiling. "Chances are good you'll be proved right, Mr. Applegate. But, after all, we'd better give those Indians the chance to come in peacefully before we start shooting, don't you see?"

Applegate bit his lip, clearly worried. "There's a couple Yainax men in Jack's bunch."

Odeneal ground his jaws angrily. "What the hell are they doing in that camp?"

"Gambling. Let me go in there and get them out before these soldiers of yours start shooting."

"I can't allow you to ruin our advantage of surprise now, Mr. Applegate."

At this moment a pair of civilians heavily bundled in coats and mufflers crossed behind the Indian agent, leading their horses out of the corral. They climbed into the saddle and started away at a lope when Applegate noticed their departure.

"Who are they, Odeneal?" he asked, agitated, signaling Jackson closer. "Captain, perhaps we should send some soldiers to stop them?"

Odeneal shook his head. "No, Jackson. There's no reason to stop those men."

"Why, the devil there isn't!" Applegate said. "They might be going off to warn the Modocs of our coming. Then your plans will be ruined."

"Balderdash," Odeneal sighed. "That's merely two men who rode down here with me: a scout from Klamath named One-Arm Brown and a fella named Crawley— owns a ranch on Lost River, near the Modocs' camp.

They've gone ahead of us to warn the other settlers near his place of what's afoot. We're giving them a chance to move out before trouble starts."

"So you are expecting trouble, Odeneal?"

"Aren't you, Applegate?"

The agent eyed the soldiers a moment before he answered. "Yes. I suppose I am expecting trouble now."

Chapter 4

November 29, 1872

The jolly mood that had lightened the whole affair back at Linkville had gone the way of a man's breath smoke on the freezing wind by the time Captain Jackson's outfit had plodded through the darkness and walls of freezing sleet for more than six hours. Agent Oliver Applegate's brother, Ivan, a local rancher, had joined the five settlers and Ian O'Roarke's nephew in following Jackson's Company B south into the icy wilderness.

Tiring of the plug tucked in his cheek, Ian reached up to yank it from his mouth. His heavy canvas mackinaw crackled like splintering plaster. Just up the road, Jackson signaled a halt at the Lone Pine Ford on Lost River. None of them dismounted as the captain reined around and came back to Applegate and the civilians.

"We're close, aren't we?" the agent asked of Fairchild in a hushed whisper as the soldier brought his horse to a halt nearby.

Fairchild nodded. "Six, maybe seven miles now. I figure it'll be dawn soon, when you want to move in."

"Good," Jackson replied to the rancher's declaration, shuddering with the freezing rain that drove at them in gusts of icy torture. "It's a little after four. I've determined to split up here. But we're going to do something a bit different than what we planned with Superintendent Odeneal—" He winced, an arm clamped at his belly.

"You don't look so good, Captain," Applegate said.

"My belly's giving me fits again," Jackson replied, gritting. "Applegate, your civilians here tell me there's another, smaller band of Modocs camped over there on the east bank of the river."

"That's right," Pressley Dorris answered. "The shaman, Curly Headed Doctor, and his bunch."

"How many?"

"The Doctor's son-in-law, Hooker Jim, and a dozen or so warriors—their women and kids."

Jackson swiped a glove under his nose. "At first I was planning to send Lieutenant Boutelle across to keep a lid on that bunch. But with my belly giving me trouble the way it is, Applegate—I'm going to send you and your civilians across the river instead—while I'll take the soldiers with me into the main camp. So, just in case trouble starts . . ." His voice died off as he leaned forward, clutching his belly again, suffering a cramp.

"You don't want that small bunch breaking loose across the countryside, do you, Cap'n?" Seamus inquired.

Jackson raised his eyes to peer through the gray sleet at the tall civilian. "You know something of fighting Indians, do you, mister?"

"Some. But in different country. Different Injins."

The soldier nudged his horse up and came to a halt to have a closer look at the man in the soggy hat. "How different?"

"As different as Sioux and Cheyenne can be from these Modocs, I suppose."

"What's your name, mister?"

"Seamus Donegan."

"He's my nephew, Captain," Ian explained, more for Applegate's benefit than Jackson's.

The captain straightened, took a deep breath of the cold air that seemed to momentarily settle his discomfort. "You'll ride with me into the main camp, Mr. Donegan."

"I'd like him to stay with me," Ian protested, "if you're sending me off with Applegate from here."

Seamus grinned at O'Roarke. "It's all right, Uncle. Riding with soldiers into an Injin camp is nothing new to this Irishman."

O'Roarke felt a swell of pride for his nephew—something akin to how he felt for the accomplishments of his own children in years gone the way of winter snow. "This ain't your fight, Seamus. It might be safer you come with us."

Donegan patted his uncle's arm with a crackle of breaking ice. "It's all right." He turned to Jackson. "I'm yours, Cap'n."

The soldier flashed a grin before his face drained serious once more. "All right, Applegate. Take your men across to the cabin Fairchild told me isn't far from Hooker Jim's camp."

"That'll be the Crawley cabin," Fairchild added. "Sitting up on the hillside the way it is, we can watch both camps from the windows."

"If trouble breaks out," Jackson said somberly, "hold on to the cabin at all costs. And, Applegate—do not allow any of your civilians to initiate any action against the Modocs. We're not here to start any war, mind you."

"Captain, this is entirely Odeneal's show," Applegate replied sourly. "I was all for waiting for Colonel Wheaton to send you some reinforcements."

Jackson chewed the inside of his cheek as another wave of nausea swept over him. "I suppose the fat's in the fire now. You have your orders, Mr. Applegate."

"Keep your head down, Seamus," Ian said as he rode past his nephew on the way down the bank to the ford.

For the better part of two hours, Jackson led his soldiers, surgeon, and Donegan through the lush countryside rather than using the trail. The Irishman had been quick to advise the move—to lessen the odds of running across Modoc sentries. A tough trip that took them straight on to first light, and still they found themselves a mile from the village.

Here the captain formed his men into two platoons: one to follow himself, the other under the command of Lieutenant Boutelle. The troopers were told to dismount quietly and were given five minutes for tightening cinches and readying for the final ride into the village.

"You men take off your coats," Boutelle ordered.

There was a bit of grumbling from some of the darkened faces.

"I know it'll be cold," the lieutenant replied. "But I'm giving the order for your own good. The coats restrict your movement."

"Lieutenant's right," Donegan said quietly to a couple young soldiers who glanced over their shoulder at him as he started to pull the icy horn buttons from the frozen holes in his canvas mackinaw.

Here, with the graying of light along the tops of the hills climbing up from the banks of Lost River, Seamus got the first good look at Jackson's entire outfit. Clearly exhausted without a night of sleep riding down from Fort Klamath, and numbed to the bone by the bitter, icy cold, both men and animals plodded off once more through the icy mud, caked with ice. Horses and soldiers alike hung their heads wearily against each renewed blast of sleet hurling against them like tiny lances of pain.

Jackson and Boutelle led them the last mile until the officers finally made out the first dim outlines of the brush arbors and earthen wickiups of the Lost River Modocs. The captain halted his troops and ordered Boutelle's seventeen men forward on foot.

The lieutenant and his troops dismounted and began inching into the village as a dull sun rose like a pewter button illuminated behind the thick, icy clouds.

A gunshot cracked the still air as the soldiers reached the center of the quiet village.

Boutelle's squad dropped to their knees. The Modoc tongue hurled at them from all directions. Up from the bank came a Modoc man, carrying a rifle. He suddenly stopped, totally surprised—raising his arms, his face filled with shock to find the soldiers in the middle of the village.

"Who is that, Applegate?" Captain Jackson asked Ivan Applegate, who was expected to interpret.

"Scar-Faced Charley. At one time he was Captain Jack's best friend."

"Tell him to drop his gun," Jackson ordered as the village came alive.

Many heads poked out from the earth shelters, then disappeared as quickly into the darkness as the Modoc warrior began gesturing, talking excitedly.

"Get those men out here now!" Jackson hollered.

"Charley doesn't know what you want with him," Applegate explained excitedly, turning to the officer. "Says he's just visiting from Yainax—here to gamble with Jack's people."

"I'm letting none of these men go," Jackson hissed, eyeing the Modocs who inched away from their shelters now, stripped to the waist and armed, slowly moving toward Scar-Faced Charley and the riverbank. "Is Captain Jack here among these warriors?"

Applegate searched. Then shook his head. "No. I don't see him."

"Tell all of these men to lay down their weapons, Applegate. Carefully and quietly."

The twenty-two-year-old Scar-Faced Charley took this opportunity to wheel and lope to the nearest lodge. In a moment he reemerged carrying several rifles. With one at ready in his arms, he dropped two at his feet, handing the others to Black Jim. In the gray light his horrible scar stood out like satin against his dark face, running nearly from forehead to jaw, the result of a childhood fall from a white man's wagon. He waved his rifle menacingly.

"Get these Modocs to settle down, Applegate!" Jackson snarled, clutching a hand over his gut. "Explain that we're here to escort them to Yainax. Convince them, goddammit—we don't want to fight. But they've got to turn over their weapons—tell them!"

In his stuttering Chinook jargon, Ivan Applegate began a painful, time-consuming dialogue with the armed warriors who jockeyed with one another for cover behind the earthen houses. Behind the interpreter, the young soldiers likewise made themselves as small as possible throughout the negotiations.

After more than forty-five minutes of hollering between the two groups, immense pain crossed Jackson's face. He straightened somewhat, still grimacing, signaling Boutelle closer.

"What the devil's going to come of this?"

The lieutenant shook his head anxiously. "There's going to be a fight, Captain—I have no doubt of it now."

"Our surprise was ruined."

"The sooner we start the fight, the better, Captain. Longer you wait —the better armed these boys get. That scarred one there seems to be one of the leaders of this bunch—despite what the agent says about him just visiting from Yainax."

"You're right, Mr. Boutelle," Jackson agreed, gritting his words in pain. "Applegate! Help the lieutenant here disarm that Scar-Faced Charley there."

As Boutelle passed the agent, pulling his service revolver up and heading for the armed warriors, Applegate started to protest to Jackson. It was too late for words already.

Boutelle was trying on his own to spook the warriors, talking loudly, profanely, in hopes of cowering the enemy, distracting them—anything so that he could get close enough to grab Scar-Faced Charley's weapons. "You sonsabitches better drop those guns now—or your carcasses will bleed in hell before the sun's half-high!"

Charley muttered his own oath, "You no call me dog names!"

Applegate had no time to translate as the Modoc suddenly brought his rifle to his hip and Boutelle lunged aside. The pistol and rifle exploded together, a bullet raking along the lieutenant's left arm. Another cut through the bright red bandanna tied at the young Modoc's neck.

Donegan pitched forward into a crouch while the whole village sprang to life.

Warriors poured from every lodge, firing guns or bows at the skirmish line of startled soldiers. Horses reared and bucked, yanking free of their holders as bullets whistled and whined among them. Troopers dove for cover, returning the Modocs' fire. Every few moments another soldier grunted, falling dead or wounded, crying out to his companions to pull him to safety.

All too quickly the soldiers were retreating, giving way, being driven from the village.

As he reached the wounded lieutenant, Seamus realized that in moments Jackson's outfit would likely be overrun.

Donegan crouched over Boutelle, his eyes wary on the approaching warriors. "You hit bad, Lieutenant?"

He shook his head. "Just a scratch."

"C'mon, we'll get you out of the line of fire." Donegan grabbed the back of the lieutenant's tunic, pulling Boutelle behind an earthen lodge.

"Thanks, Irishman." He twisted painfully, getting to his knees and glancing around the side of the lodge. "We've got to move against them, and now. Or we'll be swallowed up."

Donegan peered over the village quickly, appraising what he could through the gun smoke and sleety haze. "I'm in for this hand. If you're in shape to lead—let's go."

"Second platoon!" Boutelle hollered. "Spread out, on the skirmish! Forward."

It was a shaky charge at best, but the soldiers began to eat up some ground, forcing their way back into the heart of the village as the Modocs now gave ground.

In a spare handful of minutes more, the shooting tapered off as the Modocs backed into the sagebrush and trees, fleeing into the low, scrub-lined hills south of the village. They were fleeing along the west shore of Tule

Lake, quickly disappearing into a forbidding, fog-shrouded wilderness.

Boutelle doggedly kept after them for another ten minutes, then turned back to the village.

By the time Donegan and the soldiers reached the Modoc camp, Jackson had ordered his squad to clear the lodges. Old men and women were herded out of the village, dragging two bodies with them to the icy riverbank. There, the Modocs pulled aside brush and tule reeds where they had hidden their canoes. The old and the very young, bringing along one dead warrior and another seriously wounded, quickly pushed off and paddled off downstream toward the nearby lake.

"What are our casualties, Mr. Boutelle?" asked a weary, ill Jackson.

"One dead, sir. Seven wounded."

"Seriously?"

"One won't make that trip back to Linkville, Captain."

"Are you in any condition to fire the village, Mr. Boutelle?"

The lieutenant glanced at his left arm. "You want to destroy the village? Yes, sir."

"Better search the lodges for any old ones left behind in the escape, Cap'n Jackson," Seamus Donegan suggested.

"The old ones have left—you saw them yourself, dammit," Jackson growled. He wheeled on Boutelle. "What are you waiting for, Lieutenant? Put this camp to the torch!"

To a gully some seventy-five yards from the Crawley cabin, Ian O'Roarke led Oliver Applegate and the rest of the civilians. Here they squatted and watched, less than a mile from Hooker Jim's village.

In the spreading of a murky, gray light, One-Arm Brown and Dennis Crawley bolted from the cabin door and joined the seven.

"You spread the word to the rest?" asked Pressley Dorris.

Crawley nodded, huffing air. "Warned everybody from the edge of town, clear down to my place here."

O'Roarke squinted at him, grabbing Crawley's shirt angrily. "You didn't warn nobody on down the lakeshore?"

"Superintendent doesn't think there's gonna be a fight," Crawley said.

"Anyone else in your place?" asked O'Roarke.

"Bybee and his family come down here for safety. Four other fellas and Dan Colwell, my partner."

A few tense moments passed as a murky sun rose behind the sleety clouds. Across the misty river they could begin to make out the movement of soldiers approaching the outskirts of the village. A single gunshot rang from the far shore.

Breathless, the civilians waited for more gunfire. Minutes passed and the only thing heard from across the river were the loud voices from Captain Jack's camp.

"What you suppose is going on?" Crawley asked the bunch.

"I don't know," One-Arm Brown answered, "but I'm fixing to find out."

"Where you going?" O'Roarke demanded.

"Ride down to the bank—see if I can find out what's going on over there."

A moment later Brown slipped from the trees and pointed his horse down the soft bank to the edge of the water. He moved upstream several yards, stopped for some time, then reined back to the gully.

He rode up shouting, "It's all right! Captain Jack's boys are throwing down their weapons."

The civilians set up a whoop. But somehow, something just didn't sit right in O'Roarke's gut.

"Jackson's got 'em!" Crawley led the cheer.

Brown was back among them then. "Let's go on down to Hooker Jim's camp and drive those fellows in."

Chapter 5

November 29, 1872

*F*rom the sound of those first loud voices carried across the waters of Lost River, the Modocs in the camp of Curly Headed Doctor had awakened and gathered along the shoreline to watch the drama unfold in Captain Jack's village.

They turned suddenly as better than a dozen white men clattered into camp on horseback.

Oliver Applegate was off his animal even before it had come to a stop, trotting the last few yards, his hand out-stretched to the startled Modoc shaman. Confused, Curly Headed Doctor eventually shook the offered hand.

"The soldiers have come," exploded Applegate enthusiastically in Chinook jargon.

The shaman's eyes shot a glance across the river. The eyes grew lidded with sinister suspicion.

The agent continued, buoyed by Jackson's success. "I have come to save you from the trouble happening to Captain Jack's band. I come to befriend you all. You know I am the chief at Yainax—and I treat your relatives well who are there with me."

O'Roarke slid from his saddle, wary and watchful as more of Hooker Jim's warriors formed a rough crescent around Applegate.

"That's right," the agent was saying effusively. "Come here to me and lay down your weapons. Now. It's good you lay them down and I will see that the soldiers do not trouble you anymore."

It grew so quiet that Ian could hear the cold river lapping icily at the nearby bank. That, and the pounding of his own apprehensive heart. He thought quickly of home and Dimity—the children . . . as a handful of the Modocs stepped forward and laid down their collection of old rifles and pistols. A few bows found their way atop the scattered pile.

Like a jackrabbit scurrying through the maze of sagebrush, Hooker Jim suddenly bolted for the riverbank, a rifle in his hand.

Spurred by his action, some of the rest of the warriors started to retrieve their weapons. They stopped when the white men's rifles were quickly lowered at their chests. Out of the tense confusion sprang the interpreter, O. C. "One-Arm" Brown, skidding down the slick, icy bank after Hooker Jim.

He caught Hooker Jim as the Modoc was pushing a canoe into the icy river still being pelted by the diminishing sleet, with a sound like dried beans plopping on a taut drumhead.

"Give it up, Hooker," Brown snarled, holding a derringer on the Modoc.

"Do what he says," O'Roarke said, coming up behind Brown, his own rifle pointed and ready.

The Modoc took a step up the slick bank and slipped, falling to his knees in the icy mud. Hooker Jim tried again, clawing up the bank.

"Your gun—drop it," Brown demanded as the Modoc reached the top.

"Who's that coming across the river?" Crawley called out, drawing everyone's attention.

A canoe with two Modocs paddling furiously neared the bank. This momentary diversion was all the warriors needed.

A warrior called Miller's Charley lunged at Brown, snagging Hooker Jim's gun from the white man.

In the next breath Dave Hill was on the Modoc, struggling to free the rifle.

"Better keep talking to them, Oliver," O'Roarke said from the side of his mouth. "The fat's gonna drop in the fire, you don't."

Applegate started chattering in Chinook once more, trying to calm the Modocs who milled and muttered among themselves, looking over their shoulders at the frightened women and children huddled close to the earth lodges.

"What's taking things so long?" Brown grumbled, nodding his head across the river.

O'Roarke shrugged his shoulders. No matter what happened now—this hadn't turned out to be the clean, tidy removal everyone had said it would be. Dimity and the children were on his mind—

—when the two shots echoed across Lost River, the roar heavy on the cold, dawn air.

As the white men whirled, confused and frightened, the warriors acted. Sweeping up their weapons, Hooker Jim's men knelt and fired into the civilians.

George Fiocke fired his double-barrel shotgun into the milling, terrified Modocs.

A young mother cried out as an infant sagged in her arms, bloodied. An old woman pulled the wailing, wounded mother behind a drying rack, screaming that the young squaw should run—that the child was already dead.

As puffs of ugly, gray gun smoke billowed between the two groups, the white men fell back toward their horses while the warriors disappeared among their lodges. Women, children and old ones tore into the trees, shrieking hideously in pain and fear, anger and rage.

In his confusion and fright, one of the civilians bolted from the clouds of gun smoke in the wrong direction. At the very moment he found himself among the deserted lodges, a bullet smashed into the side of his face. Jack Thurber's heart pumped the last of its shiny blood onto the ice-slicked ground, steaming into the air of that gray dawn.

"C'mon, dammit!" screamed O'Roarke. "Pull back! Pull back—everyone back to Crawley's place!"

They really didn't need that much prodding to retreat from the hail of fire coming out of Hooker Jim's village. Wild Modoc yells of vengeance and rage followed the civilians as they struggled to catch up their horses. Most of the white men hurried up the slope, straggling toward the top of the hill on foot.

The women inside the Crawley cabin drew back the heavy bolt and flung open the door as the first of the men reached the muddy porch.

Modoc bullets randomly slapped the side of the house and smashed windows. The Indians shot from long range, concealed down in the hillside sagebrush. A few daring warriors had mounted and rode back and forth provocatively at the end of the slope, daring the white men to come out and fight. Beyond them, on the far side of the village, the women and children continued their flight.

Dorris and O'Roarke quickly took a head count. Every man had made it out of the village. But Thurber was dead before he was dragged up the hill. Another settler's arm hung shattered and useless from its bloody socket. It would have to come off, and soon. Three more were wounded and oozing blood from the wild melee when the shooting broke out.

Ian wiped the back of his hand across his dry lips as the Modocs drew off. The women in the cabin sobbed while some of the men cursed their pain and anger. Some of them talked in hushed tones—for the first time wondering why they had not seen or heard from any of the settlers living on south of Crawley's.

Brown bit his lip and looked at Crawley.

Dennis Crawley quietly admitted again that they had not warned anyone below his place. "Brown and me . . .

we both figured it would be wrapped up quick—with no bother," he moaned.

All Ian was thinking about was Dimity and the children, far to the southwest for the time being—praying they would remain safe.

"Damn you, bastards," he hurled his oath. "There's Injuns busted loose, and them poor folks don't know they're coming."

In Hooker Jim's heart boiled the blood of vengeance.

Less than a mile below the Crawley cabin, he halted the fourteen warriors who were covering the retreat of the women and children along the shore of the lake. They collapsed into the sagebrush and grass, heaving with their exertion.

Three of his warriors were wounded: Miller's Charley, Black Jim and Duffy. But there was more rage electrifying that tiny clearing than there was fear of the white man and his soldiers.

"They have all turned on us!" Hooker Jim growled.

"I say we let the spirits take care of the white man!" Curly Headed Doctor said, leaping to his feet, stomping the beaten, soggy grass in a sudden chant for power.

"It is a time for fighting—not for dancing," Hooker Jim replied.

Curly Headed Doctor stomped in his direction, shaking a small fan of withered feathers. "Yes—it is a time for fighting. The spirits are with us."

"We must get our women and children to the Stronghold where Jack will take his people," Miller's Charley said as he inspected the bullet wound in his thigh.

"Good!" Hooker Jim replied, rising in a leap. "We will leave a trail of blood and white scalps on our way to the Lava Beds!"

"We should kill them all?" Black Jim asked, fear again etching his face.

"Every one!" Curly Headed Doctor shrieked. "The white man came into our camp this morning . . . not his soldiers. The pale-skinned men who always claimed to be our friends—then they turned their guns on us, our women and children." He threw his head back, cackling, raising his chin to the sky. "The spirits cry out for their blood!"

"Let us go," Hooker Jim said, leading them out of the clearing. "This morning we'll give the spirits so much blood they'll choke on it!"

Two hundred yards down the trail skirting the north shore of Tule Lake, the warriors ran into two white settlers who had heard the shooting and were coming to find out what was going on. Greasy smoke burst from the trees lining the road. The two horses reared, pitching their riders.

Wendolen Nus spilled from his saddle, dead from a head wound. In a heap, Joe Penning landed in an ice-slicked puddle, unconscious and barely breathing from the gaping hole in his chest, which slicked the warming ground beneath him with shiny pink.

"This one's not dead," Long Jim snarled, bringing the muzzle of his rifle down to Penning's head.

"Leave him," One-Eyed Mose said. "Don't waste your bullet. He is as good as dead now."

They moved on, herding the women and children toward the scattered settlers' cabins hugging the lakeshore meadows.

Three and a half miles from Crawley's place, they fell on a group of Australian immigrants just arriving in their fields for the morning's labors. The shooting was over in a matter of seconds. The team of horses pulling the settlers' wagon bolted, taking their clattering load back down the road. William Boddy, his son-in-law, William Schira, and Boddy's two stepsons, Richard and William Cravigan, lay dead in the muddy hayfield. The Modocs pounced upon the bodies, mutilating them, tearing off each scalp with a sucking pop.

Back at the cabins, Mrs. Schira heard the frightened team clattering her way down the hard, frozen road. The animals skidded into the yard with the empty wagon. She called out for her mother. Together they bolted from the cabin and went running up the road, long skirts flying. Knowing something terrible had befallen the menfolk.

Halfway to the fields they slid to a halt in the icy ruts of that road, clutching one another in fright as the grim-faced, blood-splattered Modocs appeared like apparitions from the woods.

"We no hurt you," Hooker Jim explained in his poor English. Like most Modocs, over the years of contact he had learned a passing amount of the white man's tongue from those friendly miners in Yreka.

The women shrieked, trying to escape. Four of the warriors leaped behind them. Their dark faces drawn, eyes like ten-hour coals of hate.

"We want men. More men in your place?"

"N-No," Mrs. Boddy stammered. Her daughter was sobbing. "No more . . . don't hurt us—please . . . please—"

"We want men," Curly Headed Doctor explained, stepping up with a wild, crazed expression twisting his face. He held up his hands to the women, palms out. "This is Boddy's blood. Look, I drink it!" He licked his fingers clean, relishing it as the women shrieked, sobbing, clutching one another in terror.

"We are Modocs," Hooker Jim explained. "White man and soldiers—they kill women. We Modocs. We no kill women. Go find Boddy, in the woods." He pointed behind his warriors. "Go now. You are safe."

Not much farther to the east around the shore of Tule Lake, Jim's fleeing Modocs came upon the land claimed by brothers William and W. K. Brotherton, a spread squatting directly upon the border between Oregon and California. Both were near their cabin, chopping firewood among a stand of junipers when the warriors were upon them without warning. They fell without a sound.

Hooker Jim remounted his men and moved a few hundred yards on south into California. On the road nearing Bloody Point, they ran across settler Henry Miller.

"Where you go?" Jim asked the white man as the Modocs surrounded him in the middle of the icy road.

His eyes grew wide with suspicion and fear. He licked his lips gone dry. "To Linkville, Hooker Jim. I have some . . . need some supplies there."

Jim inched his pony closer. "Why you no tell us the soldiers come?"

He coughed, trying to chuckle. "S-Soldiers? What soldiers? Honest, Hooker Jim—I don't know nothing of any soldiers."

"He didn't tell us the soldiers were coming," Curly Headed Doctor growled in Modoc to the rest. "Henry Miller said he would warn us—he didn't."

Miller tried to duck as Hooker Jim's rifle came up, but the bullet met him full in the face, blowing out the back of his head. His body spilled from the back of the pony, sprawled in the icy ruts, and voided its bowels, steamy on the frosty air.

From there Hooker Jim led his warriors down the east side of Tule Lake, where they ran across two herders tending some sheep belonging to the Brothertons. At the first sight of the armed Modocs, the twelve-year-old son of William Brotherton turned to flee. Bullets whined overhead as young Joseph leaped over the scattering sheep, fleeing on foot and heading for the main house. In that next moment, German-born Nicholas Schroeder clambered aboard his horse. The warriors pursued, firing until they hit the sheepherder. His body still quivered in death throes when they set upon it with their knives.

Mrs. Brotherton had come running at the first sound of gunfire, carrying a Winchester repeater and finding her son sprinting toward her. She handed young Joseph a pistol then fired a series of shots at the advancing Modocs while she slowly retreated back to the cabin. There the two joined another son and Mrs. Swan, a Klamath woman who lived with the German sheepherder. From the pantry the four quickly dragged out fifty-weight sacks of flour to bulwark the walls. Mrs. Swan and the boy plopped down behind the sacks while the cool-headed Mrs. Brotherton bored auger holes through the house walls.

In the meantime the Modocs had crept up behind Henry Miller's cabin, standing only some fifty yards from the Brotherton's place. For the better part of an hour the warriors kept up a hot fire, while bullets still came from the main cabin.

It was not worth the trouble, or the wait, the Modocs decided. They mounted up and plodded off to find easier quarry. There would be a total of fourteen to mark the passing of Curly Headed Doctor and his zealots that bloody day.

Christopher Erasmus, Robert Alexander, John Tober, Adam Shillingbow and Frank Follins—one by one fell that late icy morning along the eastern shore of Tule Lake as the Modocs fled south for the Lava Beds.

To the safety of the Stronghold among that great volcanic eruption where the Lost River Modocs would prepare for the coming siege.

Seamus had heard the gunfire from across the river—a few shots clustered together, then a flurry, and finally a dying away. Minutes later more random shots had cracked the air on the far side of Lost River. Eventually those too tapered off by the time Captain Jack's village was burning on the west side.

Jackson mounted up the wounded who could ride and his platoon, moving north upriver to the Stukel Ford.

Left behind to complete the destruction of the camp were Lieutenant Boutelle and his platoon, along with the Irishman.

No sooner was Jackson gone upstream than gunfire suddenly rattled the trees surrounding the village clearing. Boutelle's soldiers dove for cover, hollering warnings and shrieking in surprise as the Modocs whooped, making themselves brave for their counterattack.

Lead whistled overhead, thunking into the earthen lodges, splintering drying racks for boned fish. A good half of Boutelle's men huddled suicidally behind a lodge, refusing to budge. Seamus was among them after a wild dash across open ground.

Donegan's chest heaved as he hoarsely rasped his words. "I suggest you boys start using them rifles of yours —if you plan on any of us making it out of here with our scalps!"

"There's been enough killing for the day," one of the braver spouted off.

Donegan snorted. "Not for the Modocs, there ain't. They plan on doing some more—and now. Use those bleeming rifles or the Modocs will have your hair inside of a handful of minutes!"

One by one they turned from him, loading cartridges in their Springfields and finding a place to return the Indian fire.

Across the open ground at the center of the village, Donegan found Boutelle watching him taking command of the reluctant soldiers. The lieutenant saluted quickly before he went back to firing his sidearm.

Within minutes the gunfire coming from the surrounding woods began to die off. Then the rustling of leaves and brush faded on the freezing air.

Boutelle's men were alone once more in the eerie quiet of the smoldering village.

Chapter 6

December 1, 1872

The day following the Battle of Lost River, Captain James Jackson rested his weary company at a temporary camp he had established near Crawley's cabin. Surgeon McElderry kept himself and a hospital steward busy tending to the wounded and keeping the casualties as warm as possible in the freezing, wet weather.

Beneath the dripping canvas of his tent, the captain wrote dispatches to Major John Green at Fort Klamath: "I need enforcements and orders as to my future course."

At this point in time Jackson and Boutelle were convinced they had killed not only Captain Jack, but Scar-Faced Charley and Black Jim—the three they had been ordered to bring in.

Late the next afternoon, 1 December, two long-faced civilians rode their muddied horses into the soldier camp, carrying news of the settlers murdered for the startled Jackson.

At sunrise on 2 December, Lieutenant Boutelle led a small patrol out to locate the total number of dead, and to look for the women at both the Boddy and the Brotherton settlements, who were said to be fleeing cross-country toward Linkville to avoid any roving Modoc war-parties. Returning to Crawley's from Clear Lake, Boutelle met the women who had minutes before met up with Ivan Applegate and some other enraged civilians from Linkville. The women returned to the soldier camp to personally tell Jackson of the horror in the attacks.

With the presence of the Linkville citizens at the scene, Jackson realized he no longer needed to warn the civilians north of Lost River that the Modocs had broken out. Word of the army's failure was already spreading like brushfire.

Back at Fort Klamath, Major Green was doing some fancy explaining of his own to his superiors, Lieutenant Colonel Wheaton and General Canby: "It was believed that the Modocs would submit."

Canby was clearly angered: "Troops at Bidwell and the District of the Lakes . . . ought to have been in the Modoc country before the attempt to remove the Indians by force was commenced." He ordered Major E. C. Mason with three companies of the Twenty-first Infantry to march immediately from Fort Vancouver for Fort Klamath.

In those first few hours of alarm, Governor Grover of Oregon Territory had issued a call to raise volunteers who would remain in the Tule Lake area only until "the regular troops take the field in force sufficient to protect the settlements."

Meanwhile, Colonel Wheaton ordered veteran Captain Reuben F. Bernard, along with his G Troop of the First Cavalry, to join up with Jackson's soldiers at the scene. Most of the civilians who had accompanied the army to remove the Modocs immediately returned to their homesteads to see to family and make fortifications, what with Modocs running loose.

"So this is your nephew, Ian," Dimity O'Roarke appraised as she ground her roughened hands into her dirty apron, then presented Seamus with one of them.

"He favors his mother—God bless her," Ian replied.

"Saints prithee," Dimity replied quietly, stepping back

to measure the young man, pushing a loose sprig of hair behind her ear.

She had a gentle smile that softened the hard lines of her angular yet simple face. A hard life for most of her thirty years could be read by any man taking but half a notice of that beauty beneath the sturdiness there. While she was clearly near the same age as Seamus, Dimity nonetheless showed the signs of child-bearing, homemaking and the frontier in every story-telling line that creased her well-tanned face.

Like a midgets' lynch mob, Ian's children immediately descended upon the tall newcomer who was but two years older than their mother, clamoring for his attention, asking all manner of questions as they tightened their noose.

"Scoot—all of you," Ian scolded them. "Let the man breathe." He slung an arm easily over Donegan's shoulder. "You'll have all the time in the world to get your answers."

"I'm named Seamus too," declared the nine-year-old to the tall stranger. "Are you staying with us?"

Donegan looked at Ian. He nodded.

"Yes. I'll stay with you for a few days."

"Be more than that . . . now," Ian replied from the mantel of the moss-rock fireplace where he was stuffing tobacco into the bowl of his old briar. "What with all that's happened," he said, turning around to stare now at his nephew. "All along that ride home, I've been hoping you'd see clear to stay on until all this is put to rest. We'll start by going into Linkville after breakfast in the morning—pick up some more supplies and ammunition, in case there's a long siege of it here."

Ian could tell Seamus wanted to stay on, if only for a while, just by the way he was looking at what Dimity had cooking on the stove, smelling its mingling of fragrant aromas that filled every corner of the main room.

"Aye. I'll stay for a few days," Seamus replied. "What could take long about digging a handful of Indians out of these hills?"

Ian wagged his head. "John and Press agree with me," he said sadly. "That bunch isn't loose in the hills. They're already safely bedded down in the Lava Beds."

"Lava Beds?"

"The devil's own playground—barren and fit for no man or beast, that."

"The army'll go in and dig 'em out soon enough, Uncle."

He brought the pipe to smoke, then tossed the sulfur-headed lucifer into the fireplace. "Sounds to me like my own nephew is bound to find any reason he can to leave—when he just got here!"

Seamus finally grinned, settling in a big rocker little seven-year-old Charity dragged up for him. "Yes, Ian. We have much to catch up on."

From the corner at her dry sink, Dimity cleared her throat. That had always been signal to Ian that she had something of import to say.

"Have you ever thought of putting your roots down, Seamus?" she asked, not turning from the work of her hands over the vegetables she was slicing directly into the cast-iron kettle. "Thought of doing the honest work of a farmer like your uncle here?"

Ian was still angry with her for those pointed words the next morning when he and Seamus stepped from the low-ridged door into the main yard, their breath frosty on the warming air. Everything was still slick with icy sleet; fence rails and barn siding. But the sun was emerging over the low hills, giving a pink glow to the thick glaze.

"She didn't mean to cause you hurt, Seamus," Ian said as they slipped bridles warmed under their arms on the horses brought out of the barn.

"No hurt to me, Uncle."

"She was talking out of turn."

"Sounds to me like you took more offense than I."

"Perhaps I did at that."

As Donegan smoothed the blanket then laid the saddle atop it, he asked, "You happy settling down, are you?"

Ian stopped and sighed. "Sometimes, Seamus. It's hard sometimes. But the pain of staying planted in one spot like these big trees comes less and less to hurt me with the work of every spring. I've done it for so long—for Dimity and the children." He climbed into the saddle and adjusted the reins, waiting for his nephew. "A man grows older—and so he learns to swallow down a lot of the pain."

On the way down the road past Pressley Dorris's ranch, Ian pointed out Hot Creek to their right. "A small band of Modocs lives downstream under a fella called Shacknasty Jim."

"Shacknasty?"

"Miners named him that 'cause his mother didn't keep a too tidy place, Seamus."

They chuckled, and Ian went on to explain that the band had no connection to Jack's or Hooker Jim's troublemakers. Instead, they lived by themselves, causing no man harm.

Donegan and O'Roarke were rounding a curve in the rutted road when the clatter of many horses and the creaking of wagons greeted them.

"Ho, Ian! Morning to you, Mr. Donegan!" called out John Fairchild.

"Morning!" shouted Pressley Dorris, waving.

"Shacknasty," Ian said, acknowledging the Modoc warrior on horseback between the two settlers. Then he looked at his white friends. "What's going?" Ian asked, the jut of his chin indicating the small cavalcade of horsemen and wagons filled with women and children.

"Shacknasty brought in his bunch to my place late yesterday afternoon," Fairchild replied. "They don't want to go join up with Captain Jack—'cause they realize it will mean their deaths. But with all the soldiers roaming the countryside, they came to me for help."

"Well, we're gonna help, ain't we?" Ian asked.

Fairchild and Dorris smiled.

Press Dorris said, "Of course we are. I've convinced

Jim to take his bunch on up to the Klamath reservation—as long as I can get them there without trouble from the army or Oregon militia."

"I hear things are nasty in town," Fairchild muttered under his breath so that Shacknasty would not catch his pessimism.

"They're all here?" Ian asked, his eyes counting off Jim's brother, Shacknasty Jake, along with Bogus Charley, Steamboat Frank, even Ellen's Man George.

Fairchild said, "Last night I sent my hand, Sam Culver, into town to wire agent Dyar up at Klamath that I was gonna bring this bunch in to the reservation. How 'bout you coming along, Ian? You ride with us into town?"

Ian glanced at Seamus.

- "We were headed to Linkville anyway, Uncle."

"We'll ride along," Ian replied, "to make sure no one ruffles any feathers there."

Yet the town had a bad feel to it as the escort slowly plodded down to the first buildings scattered crudely on the outskirts of Linkville.

"I got a feeling we better cut short of town and ride down the back street to Whittle's Ferry," suggested Dorris.

"Good idea, Press," Ian said quietly.

As they were starting to turn the procession away from the main street, an agitated Sam Culver pushed himself off the boardwalk and signaled Fairchild to heel over.

"I don't know how it happened, John," he began, huffing, his eyes big as penny saucers.

"What happened, Sam?"

"Somehow they found out."

"Who found out what?"

"Lot of drinking going on already today—knowing you and Press was bringing them Injuns into town."

Ian eased back in the saddle as some heads popped out of doors farther down the street. There was some muffled shouting as the excitement grew along the main street.

"Whiskey and blood don't mix well, John," Ian said.

He leaned over to Seamus. "This is turning into something bigger than we thought. You can ease yourself on out of here and get back to the ranch now before—"

"I told you, Uncle—I was riding into town with you. And now's not the time to leave you by yourself."

Ian smiled with his eyes only as he turned to watch the crowd congealing in the middle of the street. The smile completely disappeared as the mob turned, rumbling up the street toward them.

"Ho, Fairchild!" hollered the man leading the bunch. He wore a surly look on his face, chicken-tracked with burst blood vessels.

"Fritz Dinkins," the settler replied, pulling the flap of his coat aside to expose the handle on his Colt revolver.

Dorris and the rest did likewise. Donegan brought up the Henry into plain sight.

Dinkins wiped a hand across his mouth, that grin still there. "We hear the army's sending two hundred soldiers down here. Won't be a Modoc worth a greasy spot on a barn floor by the time they get through with these murdering bastards."

"You been working yourself up some, ain't you?" Ian said, easing his horse up beside Fairchild's. Now he could clearly see the hard red lines checkering the German's eyes, the rosy glow tattle-telling his cheeks and nose.

Dinkins stared back hard. He threw a thumb over his shoulder even before his voice rose a pitch. "You seen the bodies of your friends they've got laying in the back of the hotel?"

"Boddy and the rest? Well, I know what you're thinking," Dorris spoke for the first time. "But this bunch didn't have a thing to do with those murders."

"They're goddamned thieving Modocs, ain't they?" shouted someone from the crowd.

The rest surged forward a moment, jostling roughly, muttering their oaths.

"One of the bodies had the heart ripped out, Dorris!"

" 'Nother had his balls cut off!"

"They didn't find all the pieces of the German!"

"Hold on, dammit!" Fairchild hollered above the commotion.

"This bunch is giving itself up to avoid trouble," added Dorris. "Going to the reservation peaceable. So you boys just go on back to town and let us get down to the ferry where we can make the crossing."

"I figure we owe it to those dead friends of ours laying back there in the hotel to even the score a bit. Fourteen of these red bastards—for fourteen of our white friends!"

"Simmer down, Fritz—I don't wanna have no trouble here!"

"Shit, Fairchild! You're leading trouble right there!" shouted Sam Blair. "Just ease on out of the way now and let us string 'em up. We'll damn well save you the trip to Klamath!" He patted his pocket. "I got a order right here from Governor Grover says I can hang the nine Injuns murdered our citizens!"

"This ain't that bunch!" Ian hollered. "I was there when Hooker Jim's band broke out and ran off to do their bloody work."

"I say hang these bastards anyway!" Blair shouted.

Donegan cocked the Henry as the crowd surged against itself again.

"Listen—we're trying to get this bunch to the reservation so they aren't loose . . . so they can't join up with Captain Jack's renegades," Fairchild tried reasoning again.

"It's a shame, Fairchild," Fritz snarled with some morbid humor. "The ferry ain't working."

"It ain't?" Dorris asked, looking down the long slope toward Whittle's buildings.

"Whittle says it won't be till morning he gets it going again," Fritz said, and many in the group laughed.

"We got no choice but to keep the bunch under guard till then," O'Roarke said for the four of them. "Any the rest of you feeling as spry as Fritz here—come on and start your trouble now."

"Better than waiting until later," Fairchild said.

For a few tense moments the crowd muttered, then first one and a handful inched away, moving back up the street to the hotel beckoning with warm, yellow light on what was turning into another gloomy afternoon of leaden skies.

"Let's get Jim's bunch camped—and quick. Down there by Whittle's place," Ian suggested.

Late that afternoon before all light drained from the sky, the five civilians sat in Whittle's warming shed, planning their rotation of guard duty. As best they could, they had explained their situation to Shacknasty Jim and his men. His Modocs were armed to a degree—but the faces of that lynch mob had clearly frightened the women and children of the band.

Ian stood first watch, then Seamus. Behind him came Fairchild, then Dorris. Last watch of the night was Sam Culver.

And when the rest came to relieve Culver at dawn, there wasn't a Modoc left anywhere near Linkville, Oregon.

Scared of the white citizens, the entire band of forty-five Indians had slipped away in the darkness while Culver snored.

"Goddamn the luck!" Fairchild cursed.

Ian only wagged his head. "Shame. It's a shame. Fourteen more warriors on their way right now."

"Way where?" Donegan asked.

He looked up at his nephew. "On their way to join Captain Jack's holdouts and Hooker Jim's cutthroats."

Chapter 7

Freezing Rain Moon

*I*t could only be the sort of place a man might come to die.

Captain Jack brooded as he peered out on the drizzling sleet that pounded the section of the Lava Beds where his people had fled after the soldiers attacked their Lost River village. Smoky fires sputtered and hissed whenever the cruel wind sent a gust of wind into the caves, accompanied by a spray of the icy sleet.

The children cried for water or from empty bellies or because they could not go out to play—escaping the captivity of the dank, smelly caves where the Modocs hid from the rain and ice and cold. Always the children were crying.

And now there were even more mouths to worry over. Late yesterday the Modocs from the Hot Creek area had come in with stories to frighten the women and children —stories of the white men in Linkville preparing to murder them all, even though they were desiring only to hurry to the reservation.

If the white man would kill women and children who were willing to surrender themselves to the reservation life—then there was no hope to make talk that would see his people out of this tragedy.

He hated the way the cold of that realization had settled in his belly and wouldn't leave—like an unwelcome relative come to live off his family. One who would not admit his welcome was worn-out. He first noticed the cold in his belly when Hooker Jim, Curly Headed Doctor and the others had come roaring into the caves in this central part of the Lava Beds located at the south shore of Tule Lake.

It was to this place the various bands had agreed they would flee if ever attacked.

But when Curly Headed Doctor's fourteen warriors showed up with their women and children, they were also carrying the scalps of fourteen white men. Fresh scalps, dripping not only with freezing rain, but dripping still with gore. So there was great celebration among Jack's people when the others arrived—singing and rejoicing over the scalps. The killings were justified because other white settlers had attacked their camp across Lost River from Jack's village. They had simply avenged a blood debt.

Still, the cold knot of doubt troubled Jack. He did not like all white men. But those he had come to know, like Elisha Steele in Yreka, had taught him enough about white men for Jack to realize the white men and their own avenging armies were going to consider the killing of the settlers by Hooker Jim's warriors as simple murder. Not as war.

Racing some thirteen miles across the choppy surface of Tule Lake in their dugout canoes, the Modoc women and children had joined their men who hurried overland, all fleeing to the middle of the Lava Beds—this narrow, forbidding landscape covering something on the order of fifty long miles of uninhabitable terrain.

Except for some dried bunch-grass and an abundance of sagebrush, the maze of caverns was notable only for its austere lack of vegetation and absence of animal life. If it weren't for the freezing rain captured in tiny pockets on the shredded rock, his people would be without a source of water. The place was nothing more than blackened, volcanic rock scattered in a long and narrow bed, angling south from Tule Lake into the sage-dotted foothills like a slightly deformed spine of some monstrous demon long ago fallen to the earth in a fiery time gone—leaving nothing but its blackened bones to tell of its evil passing.

So rough was this three-mile-wide strip that it appeared the ground had suffered eruption after violent eruption of volcanic activity. And during the lull between each successive eruption, more of the lava flow cooled, until in the end there were no more massive, cinder boulders to hurl into the air. The landform solidified into a cruel, sadistic smear of hulking black jutting across the countryside, from afar looking much like a stream of old blood gone cold on the sand.

In between each violently uplifted ridge of cruel rock the size of a San Francisco city block were a maze of chasms and crevices forming winding pathways where smaller, even the tiniest of pebbles, waited to quickly slash through a thick, cowhide boot. Over some of the Modocs' caves the walls of the canyons towered as much as twenty, forty, sixty feet above a man—man thereby made to feel especially small and unimportant in the midst of the bleak ugliness assaulting this dead place.

Just less than a mile from the south shore of the lake, the winding, tortuous trail through the ugly chasms led to a large crater in the lava flow. Here in this small, natural amphitheater, Jack stationed his people. Here would be his Stronghold where they could hold out against the white man. To reach this hollowed pit, the soldiers would have to run the gauntlet of that rugged trail, on either side of which stood walls of jagged lava-cooled spires jutting up like the fangs of some prehistoric creature. Here the Modoc warriors could rain their riflefire down on all who trespassed on this, their last bastion of hope for their people.

Surely, Jack kept brooding as the first cold, gray days ran into freezing black nights, the white man and his soldiers will leave us alone now that we have come here. They cannot want these abandoned beds of frozen fire where no crops can grow and no cattle can graze. Only the Modoc can survive here—if the spirits allow. Only the Modoc can survive here.

But as fervently as he hoped his people would be left alone to eke out a living here among these lonely chasms, Jack was certain the white man would follow. Curly Headed Doctor and his bunch had seen to that by murdering many of the white settlers Captain Jack had called friends. This was a cloak he could not take from his shoulders—he was leader of the Modocs. Jack realized that in the end he would suffer for the crimes of his people.

His heart had grown heavy earlier that morning when he and a few others had gone scouting to the edge of the fractured terrain, scaling some of the higher lava rocks to see what they could of any attempt to follow or dislodge them. To his surprise, Jack discovered some of his white friends approaching from the west side of the lake, come for a parley. They left their horses to graze where they could on the soggy bunch-grass.

Though the wind was cruel and the sleet slashed at the openings of a man's clothing, Fairchild, Dorris and O'Roarke talked long with the chief. Jack told the settlers they were free to use the Ticknor Road south of the Lava Beds without danger.

"But the Emigrant Road going around the north end of the lake is closed," Jack told them sullenly. "Any man found on that road will be killed."

Standing with the chief were Shacknasty Jim, Steamboat Frank and Ellen's Man George. No longer was there any doubt of it—the lynch mob at Linkville had driven the Hot Creek Modocs into the arms of Curly Headed Doctor's stirred-up warriors.

By the end of their council, the settlers found that their horses had wandered off. Jack called to his warriors to bring up three more of their own to exchange for the lost animals.

"I bring your saddles here—this place—if my men find your horses," said the Modoc leader as the white men clambered bareback aboard the ponies.

"We do not want to fight you, Jack," Ian O'Roarke sighed.

He nodded. "I know you—know all my friends. We want not to fight friends. Send soldiers away. We live happy on Lost River again."

Fairchild and the others shook their heads sadly. "The army is coming, Jack. Come out and surrender now before any of your people are killed."

This time Jack backed up several steps, straightening his stocky frame in the midst of the driving, icy rain, his hair dripping in rivulets down his dark face. "I cannot come out and give my body to the soldiers. Jack is a dead man already."

Already the might of the U.S. Army was converging on the Lava Beds.

Lieutenant Colonel Frank Wheaton, commander of the Twenty-first Infantry, would become the first director of the campaign. He ordered Captain Reuben F. Bernard of the First Cavalry to immediately take all available mounted troops west from Camp Bidwell and march for Tule Lake, there establishing one of two army camps at the ranch owned by Louis Land. On that site directly across from the Peninsula jutting out from the east shore of the lake, Bernard went into camp some five miles from the Modoc hideout.

At the same time, Wheaton ordered Captain David Perry to take his F Company, First Cavalry, from Camp Warner and join up with Bernard. Wheaton himself would establish his own, and the second, camp at the Van Bremmer ranch fifteen miles west of the Lava Beds.

Fort Klamath was now all but stripped of its manpower and armaments for the coming campaign.

Until the heliographs were set up on the surrounding hillsides, and until the weather cooperated by providing enough sunlight to operate the signal mirrors, the two camps were forced to communicate by using either the rough Ticknor Road to the south or taking the easier, longer route looping completely around the north end of Tule Lake.

While Major Green and Captain Jackson were left to man their camp at Crawley's cabin as a supply link north of the lake, Wheaton ordered Major Edwin C. Mason to lead B and C companies of the Twenty-first Infantry, who had only recently returned from chasing after the Apaches with Crook in Arizona, out of Fort Vancouver. Their confidence in their abilities to rout a motley band of coastal Indians was high.

A correspondent who would travel south with the command wrote, "Today the garrison is alive with preparation for war. Major Mason makes an interesting and conspicuous appearance mounted upon a snow-white war steed and wearing a fur cap. The greatest excitement prevails, but the troops are in good condition, and joyous over the expectations of coming events."

Mason's eager soldiers crossed the rain-swollen Columbia on a paddle-wheel steamer, and at Portland boarded a train that would carry them south by rail to Roseburg. From there the soldiers trudged on foot along muddy, rutted roads up the Umpqua Valley and over the snow of the Cascades. For three long weeks the freezing rain held dominion of the skies, slowing the troops and bogging down their wagons in a mire of mud and ice. The troops arrived at Van Bremmer's ranch, cold and soaked to the skin after a journey sure to take much of the ardor out of any young man's war-fever. The day they slogged into Bernard's camp, the sleet turned to an icy snow.

With their arrival on 22 December, there were now 250 regulars readying to attack the Stronghold of the Modocs.

Meanwhile, the local citizenry of both California and Oregon were consolidating their desire to avenge the deaths of the white settlers. Besides a band of twenty-five California volunteers loosely confederated under the leadership of John Fairchild, a larger group of 120 volunteers had formed themselves into the Oregon militia under the leadership of General John E. Ross. Upon their arrival at the scene, these men placed themselves under Wheaton's command. Most of the sixty-eight Oregon volunteers under the command of Oliver Applegate were Klamath trackers who jumped at this chance to assist the white man wipe out their old enemies. So they would not be mistaken for Modocs, the Klamath trackers were provided regulation army kepi hats with white badges emblazoned on them.

The rest of the men under Applegate were Linkville citizens, itching all on their own for a shot at the Modocs gathered with Captain Jack.

Since Fairchild's volunteers were in a large part hired hands working neighboring ranches, over the next several months they would continue to tend cattle and sheep and account for their chores between sporadic scouting and fighting. For that service to the Modoc campaign, these California volunteers would receive their regular wages, in addition to fifty-five cents per day and a clothing allowance from the army.

Eventually, four hundred men were assembled in camps on the south shore of Tule Lake to dig seventy Modoc warriors from the Lava Beds.

While the troops arrived with their meager supplies and the Oregon militia rode into camp intending to eat from the largesse of the quartermasters, the army's supply line soon bogged down. After requisitioning every horse and mule in the Klamath region to serve as a pack-train to haul supplies, Wheaton's officers had no other place to turn but to the merchants of nearby Linkville, who promptly marked everything up a hundred percent. Sorely in need of saddles, the army found itself paying forty dollars for a saddle priced the day before at twenty. Determining that it could not live with such exorbitant prices, the army strung out its supply line all the way west across the Cascades to Jacksonville. Since wagons could not force their way over the muddy, snowy passes, the horse and mule pack-trains were put into service. Adding insult to injury, little of the army's whiskey ration arrived at the scene. Civilian packers claimed most of it had leaked out on the hazardous trip over the icy mountains.

At the same time, rumors circulated hinting that the Modocs had somehow rustled themselves a herd of more than one hundred head of cattle now grazing on the limited grass in the Lava Beds. Yet Jack and his head men were not satisfied, and determined to somehow get their hands on more supplies in the event of a protracted stalemate as the white man slowly drew his noose tighter and tighter on their Stronghold.

Despite the gloomy situation in the field, District Commander General Edward R.S. Canby remained cheerful:

> "I do not think the operations will be protracted. The snow will drive the Indians out of the Mountains and they cannot move without leaving trails that can be followed. It will involve some hardships upon the troops; but they are better provided and can endure it better than the Indians. In that respect, the season is in our favor."

Canby and the rest were about to find out how wrong they could be.

For several hours beneath the pewter sky of 21 December, the Modocs had shadowed an incoming quartermaster's wagon from Camp Bidwell.

Following the disastrous events of 29 November, Captain Bernard had so hurried to the scene that his troops found themselves running low on supplies. In addition, the captain realized the forthcoming attack on the Stronghold would require more ammunition. As important as that shipment was to his encampment, an overconfident army sent only five soldiers to ride as escort for the single wagon carrying those much-needed commissary staples and Bernard's additional ammunition.

"That was gunfire, Lieutenant!" shouted the captain as he rose from his camp stool, stepping from beneath the canvas awning. It was drawing close to three o'clock that dreary winter afternoon.

John Kyle huffed to a stop before Bernard. "From the south, sir."

"What detail do you have out?"

"None, Captain."

Bernard slammed a fist into his palm. "It can only be the supply train we've been expecting from Bidwell!"

Kyle was already turning when the captain barked his orders.

"Take the men you have ready and ride to their relief, Mr. Kyle! I'll send another platoon right on your tail to support you."

In the time it takes a man to fly to his saddle, the young lieutenant was riding at the head of a column of ten cavalry troopers and a single gray-eyed civilian. As Kyle was disappearing up the road toward Clear Lake, Bernard was scribbling the dispatch he would send with a rider to the headquarters camp, requesting reinforcements.

The veteran lieutenant turned once to look over his platoon, finding the civilian easing up on the outside of the galloping column. Kyle waved him on, then waited for the stranger to come alongside him as they raced up the icy road. "You familiar with this terrain, mister?"

"Not from this country, Lieutenant," Seamus apologized.

The older Kyle regarded the civilian as the cold wind whipped tears from his eyes. "I thought you were one of the settlers from around this country."

"Me uncle is," he answered, easing the Henry out of its saddle scabbard. "I don't know the country—but I know fighting Injins."

Kyle grinned as he appraised the brass-mounted repeater, but it was as quickly gone. "Glad to have your gun along."

As the road brought itself around a large stand of timber, pointing east, they finally saw the wagon far ahead, stopped in the middle of the dark, rutted smear across the countryside, still at least an eighth of a mile away.

With a shift in the wind at that next moment, the Modocs heard the soldiers clattering and slogging down the icy road. The warriors were just then crawling atop the wagon, ripping through the oiled canvas stretched over the high-walls.

Try as he could, Seamus could not find sight of a single one of the military escort for the shipment. There were a few army mounts wary and nervous, some prancing and rearing, held by a handful of the Modocs. But no soldiers as Kyle's unit came within rifle range.

Over the Irishman's head buzzed some angry wasps. A soldier behind him grunted. Seamus turned to find one of the young troopers gripping his upper arm, blood beginning to seep between the fingers of his woolen gloves. Donegan was just twisting back in the saddle when he found Kyle looking at him.

"They're going to make a fight of it, Lieutenant!" he shouted into the cruel wind.

Kyle threw up his arm, signaling a halt. "Dismount and form a skirmish line—there!"

"Three horse-holders to the rear," shouted a young sergeant, directing a trio of soldiers to handle the mounts for the entire platoon. With hunched shoulders the three hurried back down the road and into the trees as Kyle and Donegan led the other seven into the brush.

"Spread 'em out, Lieutenant." Seamus waved an arm to the left, then to the right. "Keep your heads down, boys—don't shoot less'n you have a good target."

"We don't want to waste ammunition now," Kyle repeated. He looked up the road as some of the Modocs continued work in the back of the wagon, the rest fanning into the timber. "How many you figure to be up there?"

"Two dozen. Maybe more that we never saw," was Donegan's answer.

From the left flank of their pitifully small force came a volley of riflefire. Lead slapped the leaves of the trees, stung the brush about the soldiers. And with it arose many shrill, eerie Modoc war cries. Enough to send a jolt of cold down the Irishman's spine. He knew the inexperienced soldiers were likely worrying about soiling their blue britches.

"There!" he shouted, catching some movement through the brush and shadow of the thick timber lining the road.

More gunfire erupted, this time from a few of Kyle's men. In answer, more formless war-cries greeted the right end of the flank. The young soldiers returned a frantic fire.

"We're pinned down now, Lieutenant," Seamus growled.

"They've flanked us, haven't they?"

"Appears so—I'd better get back to those holders before the Modocs eat them for supper," he whispered out of hearing of the other soldiers as he rose to a crouch. Donegan burst into the timber, at a dead run, hunched over and making himself as small as he could.

A bullet whined past his nose, cutting through the branches. A second snarled close at his heels. Seamus kept going, dodging and weaving until he drew close to the horse-holders. Two of the mounts were already down. The rest just then clattering out of the timber, no longer held by the three soldiers who huddled behind the two heaving, thrashing brown carcasses.

One of the soldiers, frightened and wide-eyed, pulled up his rifle on the Irishman as Donegan came sprinting up. Modoc bullets slapped the dying horse as Seamus made himself small behind the carcass.

"Just about killed you, mister," whispered the soldier.

"I know, sojur," he replied, the remnant of a grin disappearing now. "Let's you and me turn our guns on them Injins."

"We ain't got a chance!" shrieked another of the three.

Seamus grabbed the youngster's tunic with his left hand. "We don't have a chance you give up like this. Now use that goddamned rifle!"

As they laid their rifles over the ribby side of the still-warm carcasses and began firing back into the trees, the gunfire from the Modocs intensified. Along with the hair-raising war-whoops. Then, as suddenly as it had thickened, the gunfire died off.

"They pulling back?"

Seamus nodded at the young soldier. Then he understood why. Down the road to their right plodded the double-timing infantry, huffing out of the gray of the soggy afternoon along the icy scar of the Fort Bidwell Road that poked itself from the timber. Above their heads hung a seeping cloud of breath smoke, like sheer muslin, cold and gray.

"We've just been rescued, Private," Seamus announced quietly. Then he fell silent as he heard the mumbled prayer of a youngster lying on his side, eyes clenched tightly, blood seeping from a shiny hole in his side.

". . . and deliver us from evil . . ."

Chapter 8

January 17, 1873

*W*hen they had driven off the Modocs back on that cold December day, the soldiers found all five of the troopers serving as wagon escort. Three were wounded, along with another so seriously shot up he did not last the night. Kyle himself found the body of the fifth escort twisted beneath the rear tailgate of the freight wagon.

Completely stripped of his uniform and underclothing, his entire scalp gone, including the tops of both ears, Private Sidney Smith lay in a ice-slicked puddle turned red from the many bullet wounds in his head, belly and legs.

Near dark the infantry had marched back to the scene after a running fight with the fleeing Modocs, who eventually disappeared around the south end of Clear Lake, evidently retreating to the Lava Beds.

After a harrowing chase by some mounted Modoc warriors who nipped dangerously at his heels, Bernard's courier had reached Jackson's station at Crawley's cabin. Without delay the captain had led his reinforcements down to Land's ranch, where they went into camp with Bernard's troops.

In the past few days, Seamus had grumbled to Lieutenant Kyle and a few other officers what poor marksmen the young soldiers had turned out to be. The lieutenant had wagged his head sadly.

"Even with the ammunition we saved on that wagon—we still have less than ten rounds for each man now. We can't even begin to consider letting them practice with their weapons. You use the rounds to practice—or you use it to fight the Modocs. Word has it we'll be going in after them soon enough."

"You know how soon?"

"Captain Bernard figures by the middle of the month."

The army and civilians had marked time, waiting for any action after the first flurry of activity moving men and matériel to the scene. Yet as the days ground on, more of the soldiers grumbled about the food, about the weather, about the icy wet, about most anything, simply because there was nothing else to do but complain.

Over on the west side of the Lava Beds where Ian O'Roarke and the other Californians were stationed, there was some brief excitement when a train of mules arrived from Oregon for use as pack animals by Mason's forces. When it came time for the civilian packers to put the animals into service, they and the soldiers were surprised to discover the mules were green to sawbucks and diamond hitches. For a few days the breaking of those mules kept the packers busy, keeping their minds off the cold and the wet and the poor food.

Christmas itself had been a dismal day. Most of the countryside found itself under a foot of new, wet snow when Lieutenant Colonel Wheaton himself arrived at Crawley's cabin to discover Mason's sixty-four men shivering around smoky fires. He pressed on to Van Bremmer's ranch, where he established his headquarters for the planned assault on the Modocs' hideout.

While out on a scout on 5 January, fourteen of the Oregon volunteer militia had themselves a hot skirmish with some Modocs. Despite the amount of lead flung back and forth, no one was hurt on either side.

A few days later, when Governor Grover mustered out

his Oregon volunteers, stating that they had completed their thirty-day enlistment period, Wheaton grew anxious. If the militia marched home, it would deprive the lieutenant colonel of a full fourth of his fighting force. He requested General Ross to keep his men on, which made the federal government responsible for all future expenses incurred by the volunteers.

Despite the aborted attack on the supply wagon and the long wait in the cold, wet weather, much of the talk in camp remained jovial.

Another supply wagon was attacked several days later when the first shot from the Modocs grazed one of the lead mules. The driver immediately put the team into a gallop, losing most of his load by the time he made it in to Bernard's camp—his wagon box lighter by a few canteens, a keg of whiskey, and more of the sorely-needed ammunition. That night the men in camp watched the glow of a bright fire and listened to the distant war-cries as the Modocs celebrated not only the soldiers' supplies, but the white man's liquid fortification as well.

When final battle orders were issued on Sunday, 12 January, every man grew more expectant with the coming assault on the Lava Beds scheduled five days away. Wasn't a soldier or civilian who didn't believe they wouldn't have a short time of it when it came to digging the Modocs out. A simple matter throwing several hundred soldiers against seventy warriors.

Captain Perry and his cavalry were sent ahead to a ridge at the southwest side of Tule Lake. His troopers were to clear the area of any hostiles and establish a staging area for the bulk of Wheaton's forces, including the artillery detachment with their two twelve-pound mountain howitzers, who would move over from Van Bremmer's ranch on Thursday, 16 January. Major Green would assume command of this arm of the attack.

Perry and Oliver Applegate took a combined force of soldiers and Klamath volunteers to the ridge on Monday to establish their advance base. But when Modoc sentries on the bluffs overlooking the west side of Tule Lake heard the clattering approach of the ghostly forms swimming out of the thick fog, the warriors opened fire.

Quickly dismounting, Perry's troops and the Klamaths prepared to attack. But when they pressed forward they found the Modocs had retreated into the labyrinth of the Lava Beds. Again, apparently no damage was done to either side, although the volunteers captured one old Modoc rifle. Moreover, what caused Applegate the greatest worry during the brief fight was that between flinging shots at the white men, the warriors had hurled their threats at the agent's Klamath trackers—telling them to come over and fight on their side.

When his Indians hollered back that they would help Captain Jack, Applegate became gravely concerned and sent his trackers far from the front lines.

All hope of surprise had melted away like summer snow in the Cascades. Unless they were blind and deaf, every Modoc in the Lava Beds realized the soldiers were moving against them at last.

Through the next few days both staging camps were filled with the normal bragging of men assured of quick success as the moment of attack drew nigh. Ian O'Roarke often wagged his head ruefully as he listened to the boastful chatter of Wheaton's soldiers and Ross's Oregon volunteers alike—every man seemingly afraid of nothing more than that the battle would not last long enough for him to collect a scalp for a souvenir: something valuable in return for his weeks of eating bad food, wearing damp clothing and sleeping in wet blankets, huddled around smoky fires as the sky argued whether it would rain or snow each new day.

"These boys here will show the army how fighting Injuns is done!" spouted one of the Oregon militia as he pointed to a knot of nearby soldiers. "I'll ride Jack's horse back here to camp myself."

"Don't matter now how bad the food's been for us,"

chimed in another. "We'll be eating Modoc steaks soon enough!"

"As for me," said a third, joining in the fun, "I'll let you boys raise scalps. Me—I'm grabbing me one of them squaws to take back home and be my dishwasher!"

On Wednesday the fifteenth Wheaton reported to General Canby that "a more enthusiastic jolly set of Regulars and Volunteers I never had the pleasure to command." While repeating his assertions that Captain Jack would not make a fight of it, he nonetheless wrote that "if the Modocs will only try to make good their boast to whip a thousand soldiers, all will be satisfied."

The sixteenth had been consumed with the movement of men. A series of rocky upheavals in the terrain, all running north and south in direction and having created a series of nearly insurmountable bluffs, existed between Van Bremmer's ranch and the lake itself. Each successive bluff was followed by a gradually sloping plateau, until the country rose toward its next ridge.

Rather than fighting this terrain, Mason had his wagons ramble north some distance until they could come down along the lakeshore itself. At the same time, his cavalry and pack-train marched directly east, going overland to a point three miles from the Modoc stronghold.

On the east side of the Lava Beds, Wheaton's plan dictated that Captain Bernard was to draw close to his own staging arena as well. Wheaton desired his combined forces to spring into action at dawn on the seventeenth, battling their way by skirmishes through the Lava Beds until the two wings could converge on the central fortification held by Captain Jack, thereby preventing the hostiles from escaping south. While the lion's role would fall on Green's troops coming in from the west, Bernard's forces were stationed on the east by and large to keep the Modocs from fleeing when the attack came.

Fleeing is just what they expected the Indians to do. So it was no important matter that time and again the officers had tried to downplay the significance of the shortage in ammunition the troops were suffering. The soldiers expected only to have to round up the ragtag band of renegades and herd their prisoners north to the reservation.

Late on the sixteenth Seamus rode with Captain Jackson's troops as Bernard moved his men toward their staging area through a thick, inky fog that soaked a man if it didn't downright freeze him. The rocky trail they followed for more than sixteen miles through the soupy veil wiped out most of the landmarks Bernard was using to guide him into position for Friday morning's attack. From that point he was to send out patrols to capture any Modoc canoes they could find along the lakeshore. The Indians would thereby be prevented from making their escape when the mad rout the army was expecting would take place.

The Modocs were waiting not only on the west side of the Lava Beds, but on the east as well.

When the winds shifted and the fog rolled out momentarily, Bernard was startled to find out he had led his men to a position far too close to the Modoc Stronghold. He immediately ordered a judicious retreat, only to discover that a band of warriors had been tailing his men.

They fired into both Jackson's left flank and pack-train, causing more confusion and stark terror than casualties among the soldiers and twenty of the Klamath scouts under Dave Hill. Four men were slightly wounded in the terrifying skirmish before Bernard got his men pulled back, formed up, and the Modocs drifted away into the maze of black monoliths like dissipating fog. They made camp at the base of a large outcropping known as Hospital Rock.

Now Captain Jack's warriors could not help but realize the attack would be coming at them from two directions with the coming of day. And they alone realized what effect the terrain would have on the pending battle.

As officers from both flanks peered across the Lava Beds that late afternoon, 16 January, 1873, the fog contin-

ued to hug the ground, obliterating all the upheavals of
that black, bone-shard terrain in the Lava Beds. From
where the soldiers stood, it plainly looked as if they would
easily gain access to the Modocs' Stronghold—thereby
quickly whipping Captain Jack's small band of poorly-
equipped warriors.

Modoc sentries reported the many sagebrush fires they
had seen being lit at twilight, both to the east and west.
Now it was the Ice Moon.

The soldiers had been a long time in coming.

Tomorrow would be the test of Captain Jack's people,
and their Stronghold.

The area he had chosen to make his stand was roughly
rectangular in shape, a thousand feet wide by a half-mile
long, stretching south from the shore of Tule Lake. The
rocks standing like sentinels around the center of this
Stronghold were like a thrashing ocean surf of frozen
lava. Wave following tumultuous wave of sharp, back-
boned pumice made for an impregnable fortress, complete
with banquettes and watchtowers, loopholes and fortified
breastworks. As nightmarish as the terrain might appear
to the white man, the Modocs knew every foot of it: each
crevice, cavern and chasm.

Down in the heart of the Stronghold, they had discovered patches of grass for their ponies and cattle. For fuel
they had used the greasewood which abounded. The fires
now warmed the Modoc hands and feet while Jack
watched Curly Headed Doctor warm the war-spirits of
the warriors.

As the shaman harangued the people, readying them
for the coming fight, Jack could only look on, sullen and
bewildered. Carrying two thoughts in his heart. He
wanted the white man gone from his land on Lost River
—gone for good. But the bitter truth he had to swallow
was that the white man was not going to go away without
a fight. The dilemma for Jack was how to protect his
people. A war with the soldiers would mean many women

and children would be killed. Why should he sacrifice the innocent ones for the lives of those who had murdered the white settlers back in the Moon of Freezing Rain?

But most of his people were now enthusiastically behind Curly Headed Doctor.

This was to be the supreme test of the shaman's power. For many moons now as the trouble brewed and finally erupted, the Doctor had been promising that those faithful who followed his teachings could not be harmed by the white man. Throughout that great circle of black rock, the women and older children were busy with one preparation or another for the morning's fight—polishing weapons, loading powder horns, making lead balls. Everyone had a task.

Curly Headed Doctor clapped his hands and called some young warriors forward into the firelight. They each carried a huge coil of handwoven rope made from tule fibers found along the lakeshore. Totaling hundreds of feet together, each rope had been dyed red—the magical color of war.

"These ropes I will now string end to end entirely around our stronghold," the shaman declared loudly before his hushed audience. "They will form a magic circle the white man cannot cross when he comes to drive us out tomorrow!"

Clearing his throat in nervousness, Jack slid from his rock and stepped up to the shaman. He felt cornered—like a desperate animal—caught here between the soldiers who were coming and the bloodthirsty medicine man who now held so much sway over his tribe.

"We are a brave people. Let no man, white or Klamath, mistake that. But look at us," Jack said, an arm sweeping the gathering. The light from the huge fire caressed the faces of only fifty-one warriors, along with 175 women and children.

"We are few—against the many," he continued, hoping to silence the shaman. "We have seen what happens when the soldiers die. More come. Let us talk of peace with the white man before our people are gone forever."

"Ha!" snorted Curly Headed Doctor. "Your bowels run cold with water, eh?"

"All these will die before this war ends," Jack protested.

The shaman shook his finger at the chief. "Suppose we do die? I will take many soldiers with me before I fall."

Hoots of agreement from many of the young warriors echoed in the Stronghold.

"At last we will be able to pay the white man back for the treachery he brought us. You remember Ben Wright, don't you, Kientpoos? Ben Wright and his white brothers murdered your father and mother!"

"I remember," Jack answered. "I too nursed revenge in my heart. And in the end, it was my spirit being consumed by hate. Let us send word to the soldiers that we will talk of peace with them."

Again he was hooted down by the young warriors, their blood heated by the shaman.

Curly Headed Doctor dropped his rope at his feet, holding up his hands, palms out. "See? My hands are blackened with the blood of many white men! But still the spirits of Ka-moo-cum-chux cry out for more blood. A hundred should die for every Modoc woman and child killed—and that means war. Kientpoos talks like a scared animal." He slapped his chest. "I will make medicine to turn the white man's bullets to harmless puffs of smoke. Your shaman calls for war!"

"You would not surrender, I know that," Jack said as the fleshy medicine man stooped to retrieve his sacred rope. "I would not expect any of you to surrender—those who murdered the white settlers who were our friends."

"Friends?" shouted Hooker Jim. "Friends would take our land from us and not repay us!"

"Fairchild, Dorris and O'Roarke are our friends—each year they pay us for the land they use."

"If they get in our way—we will crush them too!" shouted the Doctor.

"War! War!" was the word echoed off the black rocks dancing with eerie smears of firelight.

When Jack held up his hand for silence, he called for a vote. Of the fifty-one warriors not on guard duty and present in the Stronghold, only fourteen sided with Captain Jack and Scar-Faced Charley.

Thirty-seven voted to follow the seductive war medicine espoused by Curly Headed Doctor.

Chapter 9

January 17, 1873

*A*t four o'clock that Friday morning, buglers blew reveille.

"Damn," Ian muttered to himself, "if that don't tell them Modocs we're coming, I don't know what will."

O'Roarke pulled himself reluctantly from his frozen blankets. The air made a frosty halo before his face as he stomped into his boots, wiggling toes to stimulate warmth.

Last night had been hardest, that night before this coming unknown. As the temperature dropped and the heavy, humid air began to freeze a coating on everything, he had tossed in his blankets. Thinking hard on Dimity. Yearning to roll over and feel her warmth. Wanting more than anything right now after all these years to gently lift the bottom of that worn flannel gown and feel the softness of her hips as he ground himself into the heat of her—there in the blackness of their cabin beneath Mahogany Mountain.

But here he was among the hundreds of soldiers and volunteers. His hands shook with cold as he knelt to pull wood from beneath the oiled shelter-half where he had kept the firewood dry. Starting the fire as Fairchild and Dorris and others grumbled and kicked around, Ian lis-

tened to the high-spirited soldiers boasting of their coming march right into Captain Jack's fortifications, when
they would kick some Modocs all the way back to their
reservation.

"We'll be back by lunch!" came a cheer from a nearby
soldier bivouac.

One of those Twenty-first fellas, Ian brooded as the
split kindling clawed at his match flame and held it
dearly. Ruddy foot-sloggers don't have no idea the living
hell they're about to face they go in that devil's cauldron
to pull Jack out.

In a matter of minutes the assembly was blown, then
orders grumbled through the massive encampment and
the men began moving out.

For more than two hours the cold and apprehensive
white men stumbled through the dark of winter's predawn to reach the bottom of the bluff. From there the left
flank led the way, marching carefully to the lakeshore,
where the entire outfit filled their canteens for the coming
fight. Once they were again formed up, Wheaton gave the
order to establish a skirmish formation. The infantry deployed first: Company C on the far left, followed by Company B on the right. Next to them stood the Oregon
volunteers, while Fairchild and his California volunteers
were deployed on the left as flankers for the infantry itself.
Perry's cavalry, armed with repeating Spencer rifles, were
on the far right as the command was given.

"Move out!"

The order was repeated up and down the line as men
shuffled forward into the gray-black of that cold morning
with a clatter and rattle of arms, both Springfields and
Sharps rifles, along with the squeak and groan of each
man's own equipment. From this point on no one man
would be able to see the rest of the formation. Ian could
look both left and right, recognizing beneath the dim starshine no more than a half-dozen men in either direction.
The broken, unforgiving terrain made it impossible for
him to see any more of the command.

About six-thirty Wheaton ordered the howitzers to fire three shots—a signal to begin the battle. Yet instead of answering gunfire, there was an eerie lull from the Lava Beds.

One of the Klamaths who could speak Modoc was sent far forward to announce to Captain Jack's people that they had ten minutes to surrender or be prepared to suffer the coming attack.

The sun came up late and lazy beneath the sodden clouds, to shine with a chilly light devoid of any warmth on this left arm of the attack. Ian could now make out the full extent of the thick fog souping the battleground below them. From this far right came the sound of sporadic riflefire.

"Sounds like the soldiers over yonder run onto some Modoc pickets," said one of the soldiers as they continued to cautiously feel their way across the forbidding terrain.

Ian heard John Fairchild snort. "I doubt it," the settler said.

"That's right," Ian replied. "It'll be those soldiers over there shooting at shadows in the fog—thinking they're Modoc warriors."

Ghosts, Ian thought as some of the sharp rocks slashed through the thick hide of his boots. He felt the first nagging trickle of warm blood seeping into his torn, cold stocking.

Ghosts is what we're sent in here after.

Jack hadn't slept all night.

He was sure the dancing and singing had been heard miles away in the soldier camps. The white men were coming with the rising of the sun—so Curly Headed Doctor led the warriors in a wild, frenzied celebration of their war-spirits.

At the center of their Stronghold the Doctor had some young men raise a medicine pole—nothing more than a large limb cut from a nearby juniper. Once again, he declared, they would dance back the ghosts as the prophets in Nevada had taught them. From the limb's grotesque shape the women hung several white-haired dog skins, hawks' feathers, a white weasel skin and a glistening, dark brown otter hide. Then the music began. And the dancing.

With the women chanting the prescribed words to the ghost-song, Curly Headed Doctor started to dance the one-foot-step-then-drag that characterized the dance brought to them from Nevada. As he circled the pathetic little medicine pole, the women and warriors threw tiny bits of food and roots and other sacrifices into the bonfire casting throbbing shadows on the black walls surrounding their fortress.

With a wild flourish, time and again the shaman bent over the smoke rising at the edge of the fire. He would inhale deeply, drawing its potent power into his lungs.

Suddenly there had been a shriek—then many shrieks. Jack had turned to find the Doctor had fallen, convulsing on the ground, his eyes rolled back, arms and legs akimbo, thrashing in a frenzy.

"He is visiting the land of the ghosts!" shouted Hooker Jim, pushing the many back out of the way.

"Let him talk to our ancestors!" shouted Steamboat Frank.

"Their spirits help us drive the white man away!" Ellen's Man George joined in.

First a few, then more of the women started dancing in the way shown them months before by the shaman. Shuffling, bent-kneed, hop-stepping, then dragging the trailing foot, they circled the medicine pole, chanting and keening all the while as the drummers pounded out the steady, hypnotic rhythm.

As the night wore on and the dancing ended, Jack dispatched his men to various stations on either side of their Stronghold. Forced to spread his warriors across a wide front, he brooded angrily that he had less than sixty men to throw against the might of the white man come the new day's sun.

"It is not our numbers," Scar-Faced Charley had said in the cold darkness of that morning-coming. "In each of us now is the strength of our departed spirits. Ka-moo-cum-chux has shown the Doctor that we will be protected from the soldier bullets. We will fight like demons—destroying ten times our number! They cannot touch us with their bullets."

"Yes," Jack replied, forcing himself to feel better for the coming fight. "And we have captured many of the white man's guns and bullets for our own warriors to use."

"Do not worry, Kientpoos," Charley said. "We may be spread thin—but when the soldiers attack a portion of our defensive ring, we can rush more warriors to that position. When they attack another part of our defense, we will rush warriors over there. The soldiers will never reach our Stronghold."

Jack regarded his old childhood friend carefully. "Because of the shaman's red rope he has strung far around us?"

Charley shook his head. "No. Because we will be fighting to protect our families."

After a bit, some of the frantic, scattered far-off shooting from Green's and Mason's soldiers tapered off.

Ian marched at a snail's pace with the other Californians, listening for any sign of the enemy looming out of the roiling fog.

As the minutes passed into hours, more shots and shouting were still heard to echo from the right end of the formation. So retarded were they by the thick fog making their advance agonizingly slow, that by eleven A.M. they had only put some two miles behind them since leaving the staging area.

The only good thing about the pace was that few men had been hit during that morning of bullets coming out of the fog from unseen snipers and shadowy ghosts with sprigs of sagebrush camouflage tied atop their heads.

"Where's more of that howitzer fire Wheaton ordered to soften the Modocs up?" grumbled Pressley Dorris.

"I figure Green canceled Wheaton's order," Fairchild replied. "In this damnable fog, I wouldn't want those gunners not knowing where any of us are."

"Listen!" yelled someone off to Ian's right.

"Yeah," replied another as every man strained to listen to the distant gunfire. "Sounds like Bernard's outfit has gone and opened up on them at last."

"Hurraw!" several cheered.

"We'll send them Injuns straight to hell!"

"Here we go! Straight up their backsides while Bernard's got 'em penned down!"

There was a wholesale rush by the Oregon volunteers and some of the young soldiers as the morning's optimism reached its climax.

"Straight to hell!"

Ahead and to the right, rifles of a sudden cracked out of the soggy haze.

A nearby soldier called out as he fell. "Come get me! Pull me outta here! Oh, God—"

Two of those closest to him rushed forward into the whitish mist. More gunfire rattled. One of the rescuers spun around, his jaw gone, the bottom of his face gushing blood as he fell senseless, thrashing to the ground.

The second rescuer grabbed his leg, hollering as loudly as the first soldier hit. "My goddamned leg—don't make me crawl outta here!"

"Fire!" ordered officers up and down the line.

Yellow and orange spat into the rainy mist of the clouds enveloping the whole battlefield in a surreal glow as the sun continued to rise far behind the fog. More men hollered out in pain and panic. Nearby Modocs answered with their own shrill battle-cries. The air stank of sulfur and blood and burnt powder.

"Charge that position!" yelled some officer, standing and pointing at the dim muzzle-flashes seen through the fog. "Charge!"

By now the white man's bullets were ricocheting off black boulders and ridges looming out of the thick, icy mist. And soon the Modoc fire diminished as the warriors drew back, disappearing, only to reappear and attack farther down the skirmish line.

"We're getting eaten alive!" growled Pressley Dorris.

Ian looked on all sides of him as the wounded were dragged back to cover, the dead allowed to lie where they had fallen in silence. "Not even given a chance to get our own licks in, are we, boys?"

The entire advance ground to a halt, men yelling at one another, suggesting orders, giving orders, refusing all orders to continue.

Major Green was among them suddenly, whipping them with his courage. "Up there!" He pointed with his pistol. "We've got to take that ridge—that's where the buggers are! Drive them off—now, charge!"

The first handful obeyed, rising to plunge toward the nearby ridgetop. Two of them fell backward as orange bursts brightly split the fog.

"More—don't give up now!" Green was hollering. "Charge!"

"You heard the major!" another officer took up the call. "Let's take the ridge!"

But for every two men who rose to fling themselves against the Modocs atop that foggy ridge, there was a casualty who stumbled and fell. The soldiers left unhurt watched petrified as the wounded and dead piled up, until there was no courage left within them that could make the soldiers continue their suicidal charge.

For the next hour and a half the Modocs continued at will to snipe their way up and down the long skirmish formation, picking off soldiers from place to place while Oregon volunteers bolted and got themselves separated from Mason's infantry. They had quickly recognized their peril, out on the far flank like ducks in a barrel for the shooting. Now they scurried backward in a rapid withdrawal. Most of them hunkered down behind larger boulders, heaving the cold air into their straining lungs after their narrow escape, listening to Modoc bullets smack the rocks or whine harmlessly overhead.

"You boys aren't near as brave about eating Modoc steak now as you was the last few days," Fairchild said to a knot of the Oregon militia.

"Give us a crack at something we can see," one of them complained.

Ian shook his head. "Funny how them Modocs find targets to shoot at—but you boys can't see a thing to make war on."

Far in the distance the cold of the early afternoon air carried on it the sound of sustained volley firing coming from across an inlet of the lake.

"Sounds like Bernard's got his men into the thick of it now," O'Roarke commented, dragging a match over the heel of his scarred boot. He lit his pipe and set back with a sigh, trying not to dwell on Dimity and the children.

"Mayhaps Wheaton's going to let them have a go at Captain Jack for a while now—and give us a break," Dorris replied.

"Don't mind this little rest, I don't," Ian said, blowing a thick column of blue smoke into the whitish, foggy air. "Shame of it is, this time gives a sane man time to think on just what the devil he's doing here anyway."

Bad as things were for Green's troops on the west, things couldn't be any worse for Bernard's hundred men moving in on the Stronghold from the east.

Although the terrain they had to cross was not near as formidable as was the terrain on the west, Bernard's men still suffered from the thick fog and the eerie black monoliths that loomed out of the cloudbank before them.

Perhaps halfway through their march, the soldiers and Klamath scouts reached a collapsed lava tube that formed a chasm some twenty feet deep. As their skirmish line came to a confused halt, the Modocs nearby opened a random fire.

No man was hit in those first few, frantic seconds—but the lead whistled overhead or zinged against the black lava formations, splattering with a lot of noise that caused every man to find the biggest place where he could make himself small. As much as the officers yelled at the soldiers, as much as they threatened with orders—the line did not rise from its bulwarks and advance.

"We can't cross that chasm!" a soldier shouted above the din when the order to charge the Modocs was first relayed.

"That's no goddamned chasm," Seamus Donegan muttered, near under his breath.

Beside the Irishman, Captain James Jackson wagged his head. "Right now, that hole may as well be a chasm. We'll not get these men across it."

"Your sojurs still afraid of the Modocs after all this time?"

Jackson nodded. "Almost two months since that fight we had with Captain Jack in his village—and yes, they're still spooky."

Donegan poked his head up then down the skirmish line. "I don't know how many warriors are out there in the fog, but they sure have a hundred of us pinned down here."

"Jackson?"

Both Donegan and the captain turned at the sound of Bernard's voice. He was crawling on his hands and knees across the rough ground topped by lava pebbles. They nodded to the senior captain as he came to a stop at their boulder.

"I'm deviled on what to do, Jackson," Bernard hissed.

"We'd better pull back a little. There's a spot we crossed—about a hundred fifty yards back. It's there we can set up a defensive perimeter."

Bernard wagged his head ruefully. "All right. We'll pull back without joining up with Green's flank as Wheaton ordered."

"You're not going to move this bunch of sojurs in this fog," Donegan said.

Bernard eyed him severely. "I'll be damned if we aren't having to fight the whole of Jack's army out there."

Jackson shook his head. "No way of telling—but I figure I'm of the same mind as the Irishman here. There's a handful of snipers out there—picking away at us, holding one hundred soldiers down and turning their nerves to water."

Bernard chewed at the inside of his cheek a moment. He looked overhead at the dim sun scorching a cold hole in the thick, whitish fog. "Perhaps if we hang on long enough, the sun will burn off this cloud. Pass the order along to pull back to a defensible position."

In small groups and pairs the soldiers obeyed that order to retreat.

Scrambling back the way they had come, the men hurried more than a hundred yards and found what they were seeking: a place they could defend against an unseen enemy. Bernard and Jackson moved up and down the new picket line, stretching their defense from the lakeshore for more than a mile and a half by placing a soldier to cover every eighty yards of rocky terrain. Here the men piled up what rocks they could to form more protection against Modoc lead that continued to whine overhead. From time to time throughout that long afternoon, the soldiers would occasionally fire random shots in the general direction of their red-skinned tormentors.

Most of those bullets sailed harmlessly over Captain Jack's Stronghold, chipping away at the rocky fortifications on the far side of the Stronghold, where Green's and Mason's troops huddled, pinned down by the rest of the Modoc leader's ragtag band of ill-equipped warriors.

Chapter 10

January 17, 1873

*H*ere in the middle of the Ice Moon, Captain Jack was doing his best to lead his men in battle. He had never fought the white man before. None of his band ever had on anything close to this scale.

With less than sixty armed warriors, Kientpoos spread his fighting force across three miles of terrain, forced to cover two fronts, both east and west. Most of Jack's men kept moving, using the fogbank to their advantage: firing randomly at a portion of the soldier line, then disappearing, to reappear somewhere else where they would wreak havoc for a few minutes before disappearing there as well.

While the fog tied the white men down, it could only help the Modocs, who knew every foot of these terrifying Lava Beds.

Jack was sure this hit and run approach to fighting the soldiers had to give the army the unmistakable illusion they were fighting a much larger Modoc force.

Within their bastion the Modocs had been using a few large pits one could not really call caves for shelters. Over them they had suspended their blankets or a few old animal hides against the freezing rain. Splitting their Stronghold was a series of three or four long, lateral cracks in the lava rock, making a space wide enough for a man to squeeze through—and now used to move small groups of warriors back and forth across the Stronghold itself, from front to front.

The increasing noise coming from the lakeshore alerted Jack that the soldiers were moving once more, this time from the west to the north—toward the lake itself. Inching closer to the edge of his Stronghold.

He quickly ordered Scar-Faced Charley and Steamboat Frank to take a handful of others to that section of the rocks that would overlook the shoreline. There his warriors would be hidden among the rocks some twenty feet above the approaching soldiers—able to fire down on the unsuspecting attackers.

If they were going to instill cold fear in the bowels of the white men, his Modocs had until sundown to do it. He gazed overhead, watching the sun fall off mid-sky and slip into the western side of the world, as the Modocs knew it.

By sundown that relentless winter sun could in all likelihood burn off the fog.

His fifty warriors would then be up against four hundred soldiers and Klamath scouts.

Jack willed the sun to stand still in the sky.

The whole area Green had been trying to force his way across since dawn was a rumpled landscape scored by ridges and gullies of lava flow frozen long ago in time. Each deep gully, some a hundred feet wide, had to be crossed by the soldiers while exposing themselves to Modoc fire. When they would reach the far side, the white men still had to climb a steep twenty- to thirty-foot wall of black rock, cross the top of that ridge, then drop down into the next deep gully. It was hard going, and the young soldiers resisted every step of the way.

No one could blame them. They were called on to bare themselves to Modoc riflefire for every foot of ground they gained.

Because of the hard going and the effective use of the

terrain by the warriors, by one o'clock in the afternoon the entire advance had slowed to a halt, pinned down by the random, yet uncannily accurate fire of the ghostly Modocs hidden somewhere in the white fog.

During the painstaking crawl forward, Mason's infantry had somehow lost track of the slower Oregon volunteers. Major Green soon realized that there was more than three hundred yards of open field between those two outfits. He dispatched his scout Donald McKay with an order for the volunteers to close up the ranks. Instead, the civilians turned around and sent that order on to Captain Perry's cavalry unit, then the Oregon volunteers retreated, carrying along the body of one of their own casualties.

Not long after this mysterious move, Green had to send word back to Wheaton that his right flank had become mired down, unable to move and taking heavy fire from the unseen Modocs. Even more distressing, the major reported, his positions were not only hearing fire from Bernard's troops dug in on the far side of the Stronghold, but some of Bernard's bullets were falling among his skirmish lines—although it seemed Bernard's forces were not moving forward at all.

"Wheaton wants us to get your cavalry and Mason's infantry shuttled down to the lakeshore, where he wants us to make a junction with Bernard's men," said Major Green as he raised his eyes from Wheaton's orders, just brought in by half-breed scout McKay.

"What good will that do us?" Captain Perry asked, rows of thick flesh furrowed between his eyebrows.

"Yes, I agree," said Mason. "Our plan was to join on the south, not on the lakeshore. If we join on the lake, we'll be driving them toward open ground where they can flee."

Green shook the orders angrily, frustrated. "I don't understand, gentlemen." Suddenly he turned to the Californians standing nearby, observing the officers' conference. "Fairchild—you and O'Roarke—come on over here. Can you tell me what happens if we form a solid line of troops at the lakeshore then attack inland toward the Modocs' Stronghold?"

Fairchild looked at O'Roarke, some confusion in his eyes. He stared back at Green, unblinking. "You're opening the corral gate, Major."

O'Roarke snorted, wagging his head in exasperation. "Don't you soldiers see it's like flushing your breeding pens? You'll never catch the Modocs then."

Green turned to Perry after some moments of deep thought while staring at his boots. "Perhaps it would be better for the soldiers among us not to second-guess Colonel Wheaton."

"With all due respect, Major—"

Green held a hand up and silenced Perry. "Captain, we will proceed with our orders as received."

"Sir—I'll take heavy casualties if I send my men across that terrain. They'll be exposed every time they climb—"

"Captain, take your men and commit to making a junction with Bernard's stalled offensive."

Perry straightened and sighed. He saluted. "Yes, sir."

"We're going too, aren't we, John?" Ian O'Roarke asked Fairchild, still tasting in his mouth the stale coffee and greasy salt-pork the army had fed the civilians that morning in the predawn darkness.

The settler looked at the handful of others who stood watching Perry march off, flinging his arms at his men, ordering them from behind their boulders, demanding they form up for the advance. He turned back to O'Roarke.

"We're going, Ian. But, by God, some poor soul is gonna pay for this fool's errand."

O'Roarke spoke a silent prayer he would soon be walking back up that muddy, rutted path from the Ticknor Road, seeing Dimity in the distance, waving her bonnet at him, raising herself up on her toes the way she always did when she first spotted him coming up the path, gone long to Linkville or beyond, watching for him out the front window and rushing into their tree-shaded yard in her still-youthful excitement. Ian prayed.

Foot by foot Perry led his troops and the Californians along the dangerous shoreline. When they were less than 150 yards from the rocks ringing the Stronghold, the Modocs opened a sudden, devastating fire. Two of the volunteers dropped, dead where they lay on the black sand. Then, as suddenly as the gunfire had erupted, it slowed, trickled off and stopped.

"Hello, white mens!" sang out a Modoc voice.

Ian turned to Fairchild. "That sound like Steamboat Frank?"

The rancher nodded as the disembodied voice continued.

"Charley—don't you see some Yreka boys with those white mens?"

"Yes—I see them good down there," came a second voice.

Pressley Dorris crabbed up on hands and knees to collapse between Fairchild and O'Roarke. "Scar-Faced Charley—know his voice anywhere."

"Look—that was old Dorris talking! What you Yreka boys want with us, say? Dorris, what you want doing here?" The Modoc brazenly raised his rifle and fired a shot at the soldier lines.

"Fairchild with you?" Charley asked, and fired a shot.

"How about O'Roarke?"

Another shot fired.

"How long you boys going to fight us?"

Again and again Scar-Faced Charley emphasized each question by firing a round from his captured rifle. Keeping soldier and civilian heads down as he had his fun.

"What's matter with you, Dorris?" Steamboat Frank asked this time, and fired his own rifle.

"Can't you hear us, boys?" Charley chimed in again.

Frank laughed loud enough for the soldiers to hear. "Ain't you got no ears, white men?" He fired another shot. "Can't you talk?"

Scar-Faced Charley laughed with Frank. "These white boys ain't got mouths!"

As the afternoon dragged on, the Modocs slowed their funning with the white men and began to have real sport with the attackers. By that time most of the canteens had been drained while the lake lapped invitingly close. Trouble was, each time a soldier attempted to belly-crawl to the shore, he had to cover the last ten yards without the protection of any boulders, exposing himself to fire from the warriors stationed high in the rocks above the soldier position.

Lieutenant John Kyle was himself hit, yet not seriously, as he emerged from the boulders, four canteens slung over his shoulder. Down he went with a clatter. Grunting with the pain of dragging his bleeding leg back across the sharp lava-laced sand, Kyle made it to the shelter of the rocks.

"Well done, Mr. Kyle," Perry said quietly as he helped drag the lieutenant back to safety.

"Well done, hell," Kyle growled. "I didn't get any water—"

"Leave that to me," Perry said as he began pulling the canteen straps from Kyle's shoulders.

"They'll get you too."

"Maybe not," Perry replied.

"Chances are good they will," Ian O'Roarke said quietly as he knelt beside Kyle, pulling off the last of the canteens from the lieutenant's body. "I'll try to cover you best I can."

Perry tore his eyes from O'Roarke to stare out from the boulders across that last ten yards of bare shore, measuring something unseen. His eyes came to rest on the civilian once more. "Might work, mister."

Ian patted two more canteens he already carried for the other Californians. "If it doesn't, Captain—I don't want you blaming me for trying."

Perry smiled wryly. "Never hold a fool accountable for his acts, mister." He held out his hand.

"O'Roarke."

"Let's crawl, Mr. O'Roarke."

Together they went to their bellies, pushing with their legs and pulling with their hands dug into the surface of black pebbles. The empty tin canteens clattered softly beneath each arm as they inched from the rocks. Slowly at first—then more quickly, perhaps frantically, as they moved each successive yard, nearing the beckoning water that lapped lazily against a slick of opaque ice that coated the black shoreline.

The first shot noisily struck a canteen O'Roarke dragged beside him.

A second shot caused a short spout of earth to erupt between the two men already scrambling apart and turning about. O'Roarke rolled onto his back, pulling up his Spencer repeater and snapping off two shots of his own. From the corner of his eye Ian watched the captain cover the last few yards on his hands and knees, fall to his belly at the water, where he plunged two of the canteens beneath the cold surface at once.

Ian fired a third round at the tall, black monoliths where the Modoc marksmen hid. Just above those rocks the white fog hung suspended, blotting out the falling sun overhead. More Indian fire rattled from the loopholes above the white men.

"Arrrghgh!"

Ian fired once more, then twisted his head to find Perry grasping his upper arm. Dark, bright blood filled the spaces between his pale fingers, oozing over them, staining his tunic and blotting on the black sand below.

"Goddamn, that hurts!" Perry hollered again.

Derisive laughter rang from the rocks above them. Then, "I'm shot!" shouted in a high, mocking voice.

"Oh, I'm shot!" another voice jeered.

"Lemme get us out of here," O'Roarke whispered, firing his rifle toward the rocks. "Can you do it yourself?"

Perry nodded.

"You come here to fight Indians," a squaw's voice

hurled itself down at the two at the shore, "and you make a noise like that when a bullet hits you?"

Modoc warriors laughed with her.

"You are no man, soldier," the woman's voice continued mocking him. "You a squaw instead!"

With every bullet that kicked up a spout of dirt around them, O'Roarke and Perry crawled that much faster back to the boulders.

Perry collapsed, breathing hard behind the rocks as a soldier wrapped the wounded arm with a strip of dull bandage. By now the captain had three dead and several wounded.

"How long you figure we can sit here?" Perry asked those gathered around him.

"I don't figure we can afford to stay here much longer," Kyle replied, bobbing his head back up the trail at the sound of footsteps.

Perry and the rest turned to find Major Green and some of his staff shuffling their way in a hurry.

"What's the hold-up, Captain?" asked the commander as he brought his eyes from Perry's wound to the captain's face.

"We can't get down to the lakeshore without suffering heavily, Major."

Green yanked one of his woolen gloves from his right hand. "By damned, we have to. We have to."

"We've taken heavy casualties, Major—"

"I damn well never thought it would be easy once we started this morning, Captain!"

Green got to his feet, standing above the rest of the soldiers who hunkered down among the rocks.

"Major! Get down!" Kyle shouted.

"Get down!" other voices rose here and there.

A shot rang out, kicking up some black dust from a boulder behind Green.

"Damn you, heathens!" the major hollered, turning toward the Modoc position, flailing an arm in indignation.

"And damn you—all of you soldier mans!" Charley

hurled his oath at the white men refusing to budge from their rocks. "You all die in hell you don't stand and fight like mens!"

"Major—we can't expect—"

"I damn well do expect . . . and order every last one of you on your feet. You sonsabitches better get moving, on my command—and join up with Bernard. We have our orders. Are any of you men prepared to suffer courts-martial for cowardice?"

There arose a smattering of angry muttering from the group scattered among the rocks. Three more shots came whining past Green as he stood there, alone and unmoving, making himself a dandy target.

"Get down!" more men shouted.

"Get up and fight like soldiers, you yellow-bellied dogs! Get up, dammit!"

Ian reached over and tapped Fairchild on the arm. "You and Dorris ready to show 'em how?"

"What you got in mind, Irishman?"

"I say enough of us give these soldiers some covering fire—they can make that crossing of the open ground without too many getting hit."

The pair nodded and led the rest of the Californians to their feet.

"C'mon, boys," O'Roarke announced to the knots of soldiers hiding in the boulders. "We've got business to attend to on the other side of them rocks off yonder."

"You figure to find your nephew with Bernard's men?"

He nodded at Pressley Dorris. "I pray I do find him, friends. Pray I do."

Spurred by the courage of the Californians who took possession of some rocks and began delivering a hot fire back at the Modocs, Green got Perry's and Mason's men moving as bullets angrily slapped the rocks around them. Every man capable made that trip past the exposed lake-shore, not tarrying in the least where so many had been wounded. Cavalry and infantry both followed the settlers' example: while a few of the soldiers hurried east past the boulders into the naked no-man's land, the rest laid down a hot riflefire to cover those crossing to the far side.

This maneuver dragged on and on for the longest time under a deadly hail of Indian bullets. Many of the Californians and soldiers prayed for darkness to come. Only then would they be able to drag their dead and wounded from the rocks and join Bernard's troops.

As a shimmering, hazy sun shrank behind Mount Shasta near five o'clock, the last of Green's men collapsed among the rocks on the far side of the Stronghold, near the shore where they effected their reunion with Bernard's troops safely ensconced behind big boulders. In the growing twilight the Californians were the last to scurry to safety, having covered every soldier who dared make the crossing.

Darkness was sinking over the land as the wind shifted once more out of the north, bringing with it a cold, icy spray off the lake.

Among the rocks, only a hundred yards away, the wounded who had been abandoned began to howl in distress as the black of night swallowed the land.

"Don't leave me here for them Modocs!"

"For God's sake—come drag me outta here!"

They moaned pitiably and cried out for help.

His gut twisted in remorse, Ian tried to shut his ears to those cries of pain and anguish as night came down around them all. When he could no longer take it, he turned to Fairchild.

"I need your help," he whispered. "Can't go in there all by myself."

"I'm in with you," Dorris agreed.

Crawling back into the lengthening shadows cast across the lakeshore by the lava boulders, the trio moved out followed by more volunteers.

Five yards, ten then twenty—and the deepening gloom of twilight opened up with spurts of yellow fire. Modoc bullets sought out first one, then a second of the volunteers. Ian turned to find all but Dorris and Fairchild had abandoned the search for the wounded.

"We don't have a chance, Ian," Fairchild whispered.

A bullet ricocheted from a rock nearby.

"They're aiming at sound now," Dorris hissed, inching backward toward safety, disappearing into the gloom.

"Give it up, O'Roarke," Fairchild said, tugging at his friend's leg.

Reluctantly, the Irish settler swallowed down the bile at the back of his tongue.

And like the rest, abandoned the wounded.

Chapter 11

January 17–18, 1873

*A*t sundown on 17 January the short but electrifying Wheaton finally moved up close enough to the Stronghold to see for himself the lack of progress made after more than twelve hours of march and skirmish.

The thick, whitish ocean of mist lifted for the first time since sunrise. On every high point from the Lava Beds to the rough-cut rumpled bluffs themselves, the Modocs lit signal fires of greasewood. Beneath a blackening, moonless sky, no soldier seeing all those flickering fires could help but catch the "yellow flu" already running its course through the command.

By the time Wheaton arrived on the scene, he found only a handful of Oregon volunteers and fifteen regulars left from Green's entire command who had started out that morning assured of an easy victory.

He waved his adjutant to his side. "Signal Captain Bernard's command. The attack is suspended."

"Suspended?"

Wheaton snapped at the lieutenant, "This battle's over, goddammit!"

"Yes, sir."

The lieutenant colonel scanned the knots of men huddled behind the boulders from the cruel wind and Modoc bullets, then found the leader of the Oregon militia.

"General Ross?"

"Colonel."

"I now believe it will be impossible to carry the enemy's position by another direct attack, unless more artillery is used."

"We had two howitzers at your disposal today, Colonel."

"And we could have damn well killed a lot of our own men in that fog too. As it is, I have seven dead regulars and nineteen seriously wounded. Have you assessed your own casualties?"

Ross looked a little sheepish with his answer. "Only two dead, Colonel. And nine wounded. I'm afraid two of those won't last the trip back to Van Bremmer's ranch." He cleared his throat, then spoke his mind. "Wheaton, my men feel that we could have wiped out that Stronghold—had you turned us loose earlier in the day—"

"My good General!" snapped Wheaton like a broken mainspring in a pocket watch. "The problem is not with me—nor is the solution resting with your volunteers."

"Colonel—"

"I'll break one of my own hard and fast rules, Ross—speaking my mind to a civilian. Something I rarely do," he hissed, shutting Ross up. "Today proved one thing to me if nothing else. Your volunteers learned the hard way that the Modocs will fight—that they won't run when you or my soldiers draw near. I think these men of yours are far less eager to fight now than they were this morning."

Ross glanced at some of his men, including battalion commanders Applegate and Kelly. Every one of the volunteers wore a chastised look, unable to meet Wheaton's gaze.

"What would you suggest we do now?" Wheaton asked of Ross.

The general wagged his head as it sank between his shoulders. "We'd better get out of here, by God!"

Wheaton's hands clenched into fists as he finally choked on the failure of his own soldiers and the volunteers. In the end his anger subsided just as quickly. He sighed. "General Ross, I leave this matter in your hands."

Both the remaining soldiers and what was left of the Oregon volunteers watched as Wheaton disappeared with a few members of his staff into the deepening twilight.

Ross stood, stretching. "I figure it's dark enough now to get this outfit out of here without taking any more casualties. Let's move back up the bluff."

To follow Ross in pulling back were less than seventy-five men remaining on that west side of the Stronghold. The rest of the volunteers had been wounded and were already evacuated, or they had simply abandoned their positions when the shooting really heated up, many leaving behind their weapons and their rations in a frantic wholesale retreat.

In their hurry what with full darkness descending, the hungry and the cold took only a few of their wounded with them in that retreat. They hauled the battered and bleeding over the rugged rocks in improvised stretchers made of gray army blankets. The dead and those wounded they could not safely reach were left behind among the cold, black lava flow.

"For God's sake—don't leave me here for those butchers!"

Listening to the whimpering cries from the nearby battlefield raised the hair on the back of Donegan's neck as the night came down.

"In the name of all that's civilized . . ." another voice called pitiably, "someone shoot me, please shoot me!"

He looked at his uncle in what moonless light the starry sky had to shed on them as they sat protected by the boulders, the humid air crackling with frost about them all.

For better than ten hours four hundred men had hopelessly thrown themselves against a mere fifty—that fifty and the formidable fortress of the Lava Beds.

·Ian O'Roarke shook his head in resignation. "I doubt that's the first time you heard men begging for someone to kill 'em, nephew. You fought that war."

Seamus sighed, his head slung between his shoulders like a worn-out singletree. "That was a long time ago, Uncle. And a lot farther away. We fought white men."

"And you're saying white men don't butcher their wounded prisoners? If you are—you're a ruddy fool. Ben Wright and his bunch come to the Modocs at Bloody Point twenty years ago, with murder in their heart, dead set on wiping every last one out: man, woman and child. Wright and his butchers are as much to blame as Captain Jack or Curly Headed Doctor for what's happened this day."

For the longest time Donegan stared off to the east where Green's troops had abandoned the wounded in their passage. "I don't suppose I'll ever get used to fighting Indians, let's say. More than six years since I killed my first on a hot day near a trickle of a stream called the Crazy Woman Crossing—and I bloody well know this won't be my last fight with the h'athens, Ian." *

"Heathens, you say. Ah, now—be wary you're in the right, nephew. Whenever you're fighting—no matter who or when—make ruddy sure you're in the right before you go raising your fist or pointing your gun."

"Who's right here?" Donegan asked quietly.

Ian wagged his head, watching the eerie reflection on the lake's cold and tortured surface of the huge bonfire the Modocs were building nearby to celebrate their victory. "I doubt there'll ever be a right in this bloody little war."

As the white men sat brooding over their failure in the day, the Klamaths began calling out to their long-time enemies. One of the Californians translated what he could —learning that at the beginning of the battle the Klamaths had guaranteed they would not shoot at the

Modocs. And now when the fighting was all over, it was plain to see written on each Klamath face the undisguised contempt they had for the white soldiers and volunteers who instead of bravely attacking the Modoc Stronghold had held back under the protection of the ever-present rocks.

Wary of any treachery, Bernard suggested the Klamaths be ordered back to their reservation.

Agreeing, the slightly built Lieutenant Colonel Wheaton wrote in his report, "Our enlisted Klamath scouts have proved to be utter failures. We want Warm Springs Indians. Donald McKay, my district guide, will take charge of them."

Later in his dispatch to General Canby, Wheaton admitted the lack of solid accomplishment by his troops after a whole day of fighting.

. . . all they did was to take about eighty [ponies] from the Indians . . . [my men are so near to the breaking point that] they could hear the whizzing of the balls, and the War-whoop of the Indian . . . besides, two-thirds of the command was so badly bruised and used up that they are limping about yet . . .

Then, stretching the truth, he claimed,

We fought the Indians through the Lava Beds to their stronghold which is the center of miles of rocky fissures, caves, crevices, gorges and ravines, some of them one hundred (100) feet deep.

In the opinion of any experienced officer of regulars or volunteers, one thousand men would be required to dislodge [the Modocs] from their almost impregnable position, and it must be done deliberately, with a free use of mortar batteries. The Modocs were scarcely exposed at all to our persistent attacks. They left one ledge to gain another equally secure. One of our men was wounded twice during the day, but he did not see an Indian at all, tho' we

were under fire from eight A.M. until dark. No troops
could have fought better than all did, in the attack advancing promptly and cheerfully against an unseen enemy
over the roughest rock country imaginably. It was utterly
impossible to accomplish more than to make a forced
reconnaissance, developing the Modoc strength and position. It is estimated that (150) one hundred and fifty Indians opposed us.

. . . Please send me three hundred foot-troops at the
earliest date . . . Can the Governor of California send
volunteers to protect this threatened portion of his state,
which is open to Modoc raids?

Having no better option with Wheaton himself retreating for the night, Green decided to take Bernard with him
and withdraw to Land's ranch. That slow, sad withdrawal of walking wounded began just past ten-thirty
P.M. Forced to move carefully in the moonlit darkness
through the blackened Lava Beds, stopping often to rest
for the wounded and those carrying them alike, the last
soldiers did not arrive until after one A.M. the next morning.

Those who were hungry enough waited for coffee to
boil at greasewood fires. Those who had had enough
hardtack for the day collapsed to the ground and were
quickly asleep where they fell.

While the cold stars whirled overhead, Donegan and
O'Roarke snored as loud as any.

As darkness sank over their Stronghold, the Modocs had
no desire to sleep. In every breast tingled the energy
brought of resounding victory. They gloried in not only
holding the soldiers at bay—but in driving the white man
back from the Lava Beds.

Not a single Modoc had been seriously injured, much
less killed, in the day-long fight, although they had been
outnumbered by more than six to one. For all of that, the
band was giving thanks . . . to Curly Headed Doctor.

But Captain Jack knew the white men would be back. Despite the victory dancing of the mystical shaman and the keening squaws—the soldiers would not give up.

Of that he was certain.

Jack realized it now might be up to him alone to keep his fighting men ready when the next assault came. To convince them not to let down their guard because of one day's victory. But to continue to steadfastly hold out against so many, his people needed food, weapons and bullets.

When the moon came up splaying silver light over the blackened, bone-sharp landscape, the warriors moved out. Crawling over the positions once held by the enemy, they found haversacks filled with pig meat and hard crackers, a Springfield rifle here and there, along with some much-needed ammunition picked up at every turn. Ironic that they were now better armed than they had been more than twelve hours before, when the battle had started.

Among the jumble of boulders a few warriors found some of the bodies still warm and unconscious, others attempting to crawl away in a clatter of sharp lava rock as the Modocs came close. They plunged knives into hearts or slashed the throats of those soldiers still living—rather than waste a precious bullet or ruin the scalp by bashing in the white heads with war-clubs. And there were always the dark blue, wool uniforms the warriors stripped from the white bodies—clothing that would protect Modoc man and woman alike until the coming of a fateful spring.

Besides the pair of army field glasses they picked up on the battlefield, the hotbloods carried back many fresh scalps to the Doctor's victory celebration held in the freezing darkness of that early morning.

"My red war rope protected our people with its great power!" exclaimed the shaman. "The powerful magic given me by Ka-moo-cum-chux turned the white man's bullets to water!"

"We will drive them all back over the mountains!" vowed a warrior.

"Those soldiers we don't kill will run home to his mother's skirts!" cried another.

Jack listened as the warriors joined the noisy squaws now in a wild orgy of dancing and feasting at their bonfire reflecting from the choppy surface of the nearby lake. They would go on like this until sunrise caused many to finally crawl off to sleep in their caves and blanket-shelters.

His heart was heavy, yet—his heart was Modoc. Their chief, Kientpoos, would not make peace until his people wanted peace.

The cold grew inside him like a cold wave off the lake crashing against the side of his canoe. Worst of all, Jack could not shake the feeling that he would not live to see his beloved Lost River country again.

With a gnawing of deep, personal pain at that loss, the chief of the Modocs prayed his people would remain strong, resolute and united the next time the white man came. And the next time. And the next . . .

Chapter 12

$\mathcal{F}$ollowing a day to recuperate, Major Green assigned Bernard's Company G to remain on the east side of the Lava Beds while he led the rest of the troops and Fairchild's California volunteers back to Colonel Wheaton's headquarters established at Van Bremmer's ranch on the far side of Tule Lake. From there, Captain Jackson would lead the military escort for the freight wagons loaded with those wounded pulled from the battlefield before the Modocs murdered the rest who had been abandoned. Their painful ordeal on that long and jarring seventy-mile ride north to Fort Klamath would last three full days.

On that road heading out of Modoc country, the wagon train of wounded was unofficially escorted by most of the Rogue River Oregon volunteers who were quickly scattering now after their resounding defeat, and were most eager to put the Cascade Mountains between them and the Lava Beds.

There was little enthusiasm for continuing the fight among Wheaton's regulars as well. With their own eyes, many of those soldiers had personally witnessed what the Modocs had done to the bodies of fallen comrades carried out of the Lava Beds and buried at the base of the bluff the day after the disastrous fight.

Realizing his immediate need was to relocate to a new base camp, the colonel left Van Bremmer's ranch and the outrageous prices the civilian was charging the army for its stay. He moved the entire command north to the Stukel Ford of Lost River once more.

There among an abundance of tall, sheltering trees a spare handful of miles above Crawley's cabin where the butchery had begun the end of last November, Wheaton's men established their camp on 21 January alongside the river, just below a steep bluff that would protect the site from most but the harshest of winter gales.

The great cogs inherent in the army command were already grinding into motion: reinforcements were on their way. General Canby alerted Troop K at Camp Halleck in Nevada to march to the scene. Artillery Batteries A and M were dispatched from the Presidio in San Francisco. In addition, Battery E of the Fourth Artillery from the Department of the Columbia, Companies C and E of the Twelfth Infantry, along with Company I of the Twenty-first Infantry, both from the Department of California, were given their marching orders.

That same day, Wheaton had Captain Bernard abandon his camp at Land's ranch and instead establish his G Company farther east at Applegate's ranch, on the north shore of Clear Lake. Upon receiving those orders, the troops moved out that very afternoon, taking all their supplies except for three tons of grain for the horses.

The following morning, the twenty-second, Bernard dispatched Lieutenant John Kyle and twenty men to escort two wagons back to Land's ranch for the grain. A lone, gray-eyed civilian rode along with the troopers, helped load the forage, then remounted for the return trip to Applegate's.

"Stretching your legs again, are you, Mr. Donegan?" Kyle asked the tall Irishman on the big-headed, ugly horse beside him.

Seamus smiled. They had put some two miles on the return trip behind them and were nearing Scorpion Point on the road hugging the east side of Tule Lake. "Aye, Lieutenant. Horse sojur like me can't take all that sitting around in camp like those foot-sloggers of Green's or Mason's."

Kyle laughed. "Horse soldiers we are—"

A flurry of shots whined through the escort, knocking two men into the road. The rest struggled to control their frightened animals, bucking and rearing, twenty different voices raised, every one screaming in fright, surprise or outright shock.

With a shrill yelp of pain, a civilian teamster pitched backward off his seat like a sack of oats into the frozen shards of grass at the side of the trail. He thrashed, crying out as bright blood spurted from his belly between his gloved fingers.

"Take cover!" Kyle ordered.

Seamus could see there was no need in giving the order —the soldiers were already doing just that.

Barely four days had come and gone since the brutal lessons learned in the Lava Beds. Like quicksilver, the soldiers reacted to the frightening Modoc war-whoops. A few dropped from their horses, coolly aiming at the puffs of smoke dotting both sides of the road, which betrayed a Modoc rifle. Most, however, either abandoned their mounts or savagely kicked their horses in a wild retreat that left the two heavily-loaded wagons standing in the middle of the road.

Glancing over his shoulder, Donegan realized in a matter of seconds there would in all likelihood be only four of them left to hold off the Modocs.

"Best you get someone riding to tell Bernard!"

Kyle nodded. "And then we're pulling back ourselves!"

Seamus nodded. "Best idea I've heard all day."

As the lieutenant slapped his sergeant on the arm and gestured toward their rear, Donegan slammed home more cartridges into the Henry. He wasn't sure he was doing any damage through the thick growth lining the road that hid the enemy. But he had them at bay for the moment.

And the moment only.

First one, then a second shot whistled by. This time from his right.

"They're flanking us, Irishman!"

"Ruddy well I know that!" he shouted above the clamor. "Let's retreat while we still bloody can!"

After getting less than a hundred yards down the road, the Modoc fire lessened. Kyle and Donegan found the rest of the escort and the wounded teamster spread out along both sides of the muddy, ice-slicked path.

"You thinking what I think you're thinking, Donegan?"

He nodded to the lieutenant. "Two or three of 'em followed us to make sure we'd stay pinned down here—while they finished plundering the wagons."

A big grin creased the older man's face. "What do you say to it being our turn at making a charge?"

"That's the medicine, Lieutenant!"

Kyle turned, hurling his voice all about him. "Two of you, stay with the teamster—make him comfortable as you can. The rest of you—form in two squads: one on each side of the road. Mr. Donegan will take the left flank. I'll lead the right. Reload now while you can, boys. We'll let those Modocs know we're not going to take this licking laying down."

"We might be too late," Donegan grumbled, pointing up the road.

Above the frost-shrouded trees emerged the first oily smudges of black smoke.

"They're torching the wagons, men. Let's march!" Kyle ordered.

Donegan splashed through the jelling mud and over the ice-slicked ruts, eight soldiers tromping behind him. They double-timed it across the frost-rimed grass, ducking beneath the icy, dripping branches of the trees lining the wagon trail.

As soon as the Modocs heard the soldiers huffing up the trail, they whirled and fired a ragged volley. Then backed behind the roiling smoke all but obscuring the two wagons they had set ablaze.

With a wave of his arm, Seamus brought his squad up in a solid front. On the far side of the road Kyle did the same.

"That smoke's no better for us than the fog was," growled an old soldier.

"We're going through the smoke after 'em," Donegan replied. "Get around and flank 'em."

Into the trees he led his squad, eyes scanning the thick timber for an ambush—feeling himself sucked in just as Major William Judd Fetterman must have felt, lured on and on by Crazy Horse himself . . . until it was too late.*

"They're gone!" the old soldier whispered, pushing the kepi back on his receding brow.

"What you make of that?" another asked.

They all came to a halt at the edge of the road on the far side of the burning wagons. The fire was licking along the high-walled boxes—with little hope of slapping the flames out now.

"Damn!" Kyle cursed as he came upwind of the smoke with his ten men.

"At least they didn't get the wagons to use, Lieutenant!" yelled a soldier.

Some others muttered their grudging agreement before Kyle silenced them. "What the hell would the Modocs want with our wagons in that goddamned devil's den of a place anyway?"

"Lieutenant's right, fellas," Donegan said. "The Injins didn't want the wagons or the grain."

"What they ambush us for?"

Donegan turned on the soldier who asked the question. "Because they didn't want us to have it either."

* THE PLAINSMEN Series, vol. 1, *Sioux Dawn*

* * *

In the midst of planning to snatch victory from the jaws of his defeat in the Lava Beds, Colonel Wheaton received notice that he was being replaced by Colonel Alvan C. Gillem from the Benicia Barracks, north of San Francisco.

"So much for Wheaton's grand scheme to float four flatboats laden with artillery across the lake and bombard that goddamned Stronghold," Lieutenant Thomas F. Wright commented that night of the twenty-third to some of the Californians at the fire where most men huddled as soon as the sun began to sink in the west. Wright had taken a liking to the volunteers and spent as much time among them as he could spare.

"Just might work at that," Donegan replied.

O'Roarke eyed his nephew a moment. "You know about artillery do you, nephew?"

Seamus snorted, then dragged his sleeve under a raw, runny nose that for days had refused to stop dripping. "Aye, Uncle. I've had so much grapeshot and mother-rounds both flung me way—I ought to qualify as expert!"

"Your nephew's right, Mr. O'Roarke," Wright said, then turned to Donegan. "Wheaton will do his damndest to make every last regular an expert in drilling by the time Gillem comes in."

Seamus nodded. "No sojur can be happy with the account they gave of themselves that day in the Lava Beds," he grumped, staring at the flames licking at the inky darkness.

"I just don't understand it, Donegan," Wright brooded. "As long as the army's been fighting the Indians, a detail of soldiers—no matter if they are numerically inferior to the hostiles in numbers—has always taken the day in an open fight of it. Yet on this ground, when we had them by a superiority of numbers and arms—we got whipped."

"It was their ground, lad," O'Roarke commented. "They knew every foot of it."

"That, and the fog working on their side," John

Fairchild put in. He turned to see his friend Dorris walking up. "Halloo, Press! What's news from our Hot Creek country?"

Dorris nodded to the friends gathered at the fire, then accepted a cup of coffee from Donegan and squatted, blowing steam from the tin's hot surface. "Modocs paid our side of things a visit few days back."

Fairchild didn't appear ruffled on the surface. "Oh?"

"Just a scouting party, I figure from the sounds of it."

"Who told you?" Wright asked.

Dorris glanced at the lieutenant. "Some of the Hot Creeks who didn't go to join up with Captain Jack . . . or head north to the reservation. I didn't tell nobody, but they've been holing up at my barn. Hooker Jim and his cutthroats found them there and shot the hell out of my barn to scare the Hot Creek bunch."

"Damn," O'Roarke muttered. It was as if a big hole had opened up inside him and much of his belief in the fight had gushed out. "Everyone safe up and down the road—you talk with Dimity?"

"She and the young'uns just fine, Ian. Nothing to worry about."

"Nothing to worry about, is it? We've done this to these innocent Indians, Press. You and me and John. How long can we go on blaming the Modocs for what's happened?"

"It ain't just them—it's those goddamned Klamaths that started it long before a white man ever stomped his boot track into this part of the country," Dorris replied, blowing at his steaming coffee, making his face disappear behind the wispy gauze film.

"Shit, Press," O'Roarke said. "It's our moving in on their land—"

"We damn well pay for the use of it, Ian," Fairchild broke in.

"That's right—but we're only three. All the rest have just gone in and taken what they wanted of that Lost River country."

"What's that got to do with Klamaths?" Donegan asked his uncle.

Ian glanced at Fairchild, then at Dorris, before he poked a stick in the fire. "We took the land away from the Modocs, nephew. Not from the Klamath tribe. And somewhere along the line then the government ordered Captain Jack's people to go live with old chief Schonchin on Klamath land. You can't do that to a man who has any pride."

"Goddammit, I hate it when you're right, Ian," Fairchild grumbled. "You can't take a man's home away from him—then expect him to live as a boarder in the house owned by his old enemy."

"That what this is all about?" asked Seamus.

Ian nodded. "I suppose."

"Perhaps we are all a little to blame for the way things turned out," Dorris said.

"And now the Modocs are split down the middle," O'Roarke said. "Hot Creeks and Schonchin's band on one side—Captain Jack and Curly Headed Doctor on the other."

"It ain't so simple as that," Fairchild said with a shake of his head as he tossed the last of his coffee into the fire. "I still can't understand that match, Ian. Jack joining up with Hooker Jim and the Doctor. Something smells awful wrong there—Jack being in cahoots with those butchers. I just can't believe it's so."

They turned at the sudden disturbance at a nearby fire —a struggle between two of the volunteers and a blanket-wrapped woman.

"Bring her over here, Schearer," Fairchild ordered, standing. When the squaw was stopped before the rancher, he turned to Dorris. "Press, ask her what she's doing here."

Dorris spoke his slow and plodding Modoc, then she replied in her pidgin English learned from the miners at Yreka.

"She's come with a message from Captain Jack himself."

"You don't say?" remarked another of the volunteers as more of the civilians pressed forward.

"Someone—go find Wheaton. Tell him to get on over here and fast," Fairchild commanded.

Minutes later the colonel stomped up through the light snow that was beginning to fall. He parted the civilians to find the Modoc woman sitting at O'Roarke's fire.

"What's going on here? Just what is it she's doing here?"

"This squaw comes with a message for you from Captain Jack himself," Dorris announced.

Wheaton made a perfunctory grunting noise as he stepped closer, inspecting the squaw who sat dipping a hard cracker in some coffee laced with a lot of sugar. "So —let's hear what she has to tell me."

"Jack wants a meeting."

"With me?"

"With someone who will talk—to discuss a settlement."

Wheaton looked over his shoulder. "A settlement, huh? Perhaps we can get this wrapped up before Gillem comes in to take over command."

"Yes, sir," Wheaton's adjutant agreed at the colonel's ear. "If you can get the Modocs to surrender before Gillem shows up—it would be a feather in your cap."

Wheaton slapped both thighs as he settled atop a sack of white beans. "A meeting, is it?"

"How about us going along?" O'Roarke asked of Fairchild and Dorris. "You two and me?"

"Why you three? This is an army matter," Wheaton protested.

O'Roarke smiled, handing the woman another hard cracker. "Jack and his bunch don't know you soldiers. Don't trust you. But they do know us."

Wheaton brooded on it but a moment. "If that's the

way it must be to get Jack to come in to surrender," and he rose to his feet with a clap of his hands, "so be it. You men go to the bluff as soon as you can make ready in this storm—and see what Jack has on his mind about surrendering."

Chapter 13

February 1873

When the three civilians had been escorted by Lieutenant John Adams to the bluff on the western outskirts of the Lava Beds to meet with Captain Jack, what the ranchers learned was of a growing rift among the Modocs in the Stronghold. While Jack and Scar-Faced Charley led a faction that wanted to negotiate peace with the army, there was a strong and growing number of noisy warriors led by Curly Headed Doctor, Hooker Jim and Shacknasty Jim. If not intimidated into silence, Jack's supporters were threatened with death if they did not go along in continuing this big fight with the white man.

Nor was it the best of times for the regulars awaiting the arrival of their new commander. Already the Oregon volunteers had gone the way of the four winds. And the less than two hundred regulars who remained were stretched between two camps situated some thirty miles apart.

From the attack suffered by Bernard's supply wagons on the twenty-third, it was plain to see that the Modocs were free to roam from the Lava Beds at will. Rumors ran thick and fast that other tribes in the surrounding countryside were debating the wisdom of joining Captain Jack in the Stronghold. Officers argued among themselves over petty matters, and the enlisted brawled daily over one slight or another.

It was not a camp where high morale reigned.

When the weather cleared enough for Colonel Alvan C. Gillem to break through the snowbound countryside from Yreka, the first order of business for the new commander of the Modoc campaign upon arrival at his new headquarters on 7 February was to send Wheaton packing from the Lost River camp, back to duty at Camp Warner in Oregon. It was not the first, nor would it be the last, unpopular order ever issued by Gillem, commander of the First Cavalry.

Born of no-nonsense Tennessee mountain stock, he had long been a personal friend of former President Andrew Johnson. When Johnson was no longer in office, the future did not bode so brightly for the West Point graduate who constantly feared himself passed over for advancement. Yet Gillem was not the sort to wear the tunic of a desk commander: he fought his first Indians in Florida during the Seminole War. As one of the few southern officers to remain loyal to the Union at the outbreak of the Civil War, Gillem was held in high favor although he was not a brilliant tactician in the field.

Following Appomattox, Gillem was awarded his full colonelcy in the regular army and sent to Mississippi to command the occupation troops before he was transferred to California when Grant moved into the White House in 1869.

Although he had resentments of his own, the man himself was even more resented by those who had served under him. Gillem's lack of popularity among his officers apparently stemmed from the fact that his colonelcy had been acquired too easily, and much too quickly for those line officers who had to struggle for seniority in the postwar army. Gossip among the Pacific Coast army had it the man with the rapidly receding hairline was susceptible to flattery from some of his subordinates, while he dealt harshly, even capriciously, with others.

The men who had served under Wheaton were in no way pleased to welcome Gillem to their war-effort. And the line troops were in no way eager to have another go at the Modocs in the Lava Beds.

"Give the man credit," Donegan said to Lieutenant Wright the next evening at their mess fire.

"For stirring things up?"

"Bloody time someone should stir things up! How long you figure to sit on your arse, waiting for the Modocs to come to their senses?"

Wright snorted, then finally laughed. "Damn, but you're right. Perhaps I should give Gillem credit—he's the first commander of this campaign who finally believes that we've been snookered by no more than fifty-five to sixty warriors."

"How many troops does Gillem have here and on their way to reinforce you?"

"A little over five hundred."

"I rest my case, Lieutenant!"

"Damn you, Irishman," Wright said, then chuckled. "Maybe that old war-horse will get something done now that we've got those bloodthirsty bastards outnumbered ten to one."

"I doubt it."

They both turned to find Major Edwin C. Mason striding up.

"Good evening, Major," Wright said, saluting.

"You have any coffee brewed?" Mason asked, holding out his cup. "I'm damned tired of what my mess sergeant thinks passes for coffee."

Seamus picked up the bail of the blackened pot and poured. "You're welcome to all your bladder can walk off with, Major."

Wright waited for Mason to settle himself near the fire. "Why do you doubt we'll get anything accomplished soon, Major?"

"Because no sooner did Gillem arrive than did word come in that Washington's formed a peace commission to negotiate a settlement with the Modocs."

"A peace commission?"

He nodded, blew on his coffee and sipped before answering. "Former superintendent A. B. Meacham heads it. Along with Jesse Applegate and his nephew Oliver Applegate, who's the agent up at Yainax. And a fella named Samuel Chase, an agent from somewhere off in Oregon."

"The Modocs trust any of these fellas?" Donegan asked.

Mason eyed him a moment in the firelight. "Far as I've learned from your uncle and the other Californians who ought to know—the Modocs trust only Meacham."

"The commissioners on their way?" Wright asked.

Mason nodded. "From what I'm told, they'll be here in a couple days."

"You know what they're planning to do?"

"Get the Modocs to talk peace." Mason wagged his head. "Word is—Jack wants to talk peace to Fairchild and a squawman by the name of Riddle . . . but the rest of that medicine man's bunch won't let him talk peace. They're all hammering for more war."

In the third week of the Moon of Stars Falling, Captain Jack received emissaries from the soldier camp: Bob Whittle, who operated a ferry on Link River, and his Indian wife, Matilda. Also along was a Modoc woman, Artina Choakus, commonly called One-Eyed Dixie because of a childhood infirmity that had left her blind in one eye.

At that first brief conference, Jack's head men agreed to these initiatives by saying they would talk the terms of settlement with rancher John Fairchild and Frank Riddle, a trapper and hunter and sometime-resident of Yreka who had earned the Modocs' confidence more than a decade before by marrying into their tribe. His wife Winema was called Toby among her husband's people.

In the shadow of that long backbone of ridge overlooking the Lava Bed stronghold, the Riddles interpreted for Fairchild when he rose to speak to the Modoc leaders.

"I come with words of making peace from the white leaders," Fairchild began.

"Tell us these words you have written on your talking paper," Jack instructed. He was praying the white men would say something to magically lure his warriors from the seductive grasp of the shaman. It was a thin hope all the same.

> "To Captain Jack, Schonchin John and others:
>
> Captain Fairchild will talk for us a few things. We have come a long way to see you in behalf of the President and have brought you no bad words. Our instructions say we must look into the trouble that caused the war. We want to hear both sides and then we can say to the President what we think is best. He wants us to write down all about it. What Mr. Fairchild says we will agree to, about when and where the talk will be held. It is a disgrace for either side to take advantage while we are fixing for a council. Ben Wright did wrong—"

At the mention of the murderer's name by interpreter Riddle, anger flared among the Modocs like kerosene thrown on a fire. Jack whirled, his arms out and waving to calm them.

"Quiet—the white peace talkers say that Ben Wright did wrong."

"I say we kill these white men who come to us—reminding us of the treachery of Ben Wright's white-skinned butchers!" shouted Hooker Jim as his father-in-law, Curly Headed Doctor, chanted to the sky for blood and scalps.

"No!" shrieked Scar-Faced Charley. "These come in peace—they must go in peace. The first to lay a hand on them must come through me!" He leaped past Captain Jack and stood, defying Hooker Jim's cutthroats.

"There is too much talk of blood," Captain Jack said evenly, quietly, "when we should be talking of peace."

"Yes," Scar-Faced Charley agreed. He looked at Riddle. "Finish the talking paper from the white men."

Riddle swallowed hard, his hands shaking slightly as he continued with Meacham's letter.

> "Ben Wright did wrong. The white men do not approve of such things. What our men agree to do they will stand by.
>
> A. B. Meacham,
> Chairman of the Peace
> Commission."

"Does he say to us that what the peace-talkers decide with the Modocs—that all white men will abide by?" Jack asked, feeling a surge of hope for his people, yet wary not to allow his feelings too dizzy a ride.

Fairchild nodded and spoke. Riddle interpreted.

"We must stop fighting now while we are talking about peace. No more should your men go out from the Lava Beds and fight the Hot Creek band. No more should your men go out to steal cattle from other ranches. This should be a time when you show the white man that your word is straight and true."

"We should show the white man that we think his talk of peace is squaw's talk!" Curly Headed Doctor roared.

Several of his supporters hooted and cheered.

Jack waited for the explosion to subside, then turned back to Fairchild.

"It is good to talk of no more killing and stealing while we talk of peace between us," he began, then waved first his right arm toward the rocks behind him. Twenty Modoc warriors stood.

Watching the expression on the white faces, Jack waved his left arm. More than twenty more warriors stood, showing themselves for the first time.

Now he spoke in his bad English while he walked straight up to his old friend. "My men shoot not first bullet, Fairchild. Jack keep Modocs here all time we talk peace to you."

What followed between the Modocs and the Californians in early March was one inconclusive and unsatisfactory meeting after another. The two sides could not even agree on a place for the peace commission to meet with Jack and his head men.

"Meacham will not come with his peace talkers unless some soldiers come along as his escort," Ian O'Roarke said, then waited while Frank Riddle interpreted. He glanced at Fairchild quickly to see what his friend's face told.

Jack waited for the words to be spoken in Modoc, then shook his head and sighed. He appeared exasperated.

"No, I say again. We cannot agree to have the soldiers come with the peace talkers. If our concern is to talk of peace—why are there soldiers coming?"

This time O'Roarke sighed. Another fruitless meeting. "The soldiers come to escort the peace talkers—just as your warriors come to escort you here to talk with us, Jack."

"No. I have said it for the last time. Enough talk on these soldiers coming. No more talk now. I am tired of so much talk. If white man wants peace with the Modoc—let us see your peace talkers come in peace."

Ian glanced over at the gathering of warriors who attended every one of these frustrating meetings. In reading those smug smiles painted across the faces of Bogus Charley and Boston Charley, he thought he saw some hint of sinister victory. Near the pair sat Hooker Jim, Schonchin John, and the shaman himself. His instincts made him instantly suspicious.

"John," Ian whispered to Fairchild as Riddle went ahead interpreting. The two ranchers put their heads close. "All these weeks gone by—and those two jokers show up over in Gillem's camp every day."

"Bogus and Boston?"

Ian nodded. "That pair is up to no good."

"What you mean, Ian?"

"Smooth talkers, aren't they?"

"Always have been," Fairchild replied. "But we've been on to 'em for sometime."

"Soldiers aren't." He watched the light come on behind Fairchild's eyes. "That's right, John. Every day they come in, friendly as can be. Get fed and drink whiskey with the soldiers—sometimes the officers. But they reap much more for all the time they spend in camp than a full belly and a hangover."

"Those bastards have been carrying vital information back to the Stronghold, haven't they?"

"Those two aren't the simple-minded fools the soldiers take them for."

"Goddamn," Fairchild hissed.

O'Roarke straightened, putting his hand on Riddle's shoulder to silence the interpreter a moment. "Jack—I want to ask you something very important. Your men there—those two," and he pointed. "Bogus Charley and Boston Charley—they come to the soldier camp every day, don't they?"

Jack nodded as Riddle's Modoc words caught up.

Ian smiled slightly. "Tell us what those two have been telling you about the soldier talk in our camp."

"They have not been telling us anything of soldier talk."

Shaking his head, Ian's smile disappeared. "Tell me, Kientpoos," O'Roarke said, using the chief's formal Modoc name, "they have been telling you bad things about the hearts of the white men for the Modocs—haven't they?"

Jack appeared stunned by the sudden sting to O'Roarke's words. Behind the chief some of the others began shifting nervously as Riddle translated. Both Bogus and Boston licked their lips and ran their palms down the front of their soldier pants. Ian and Fairchild kept their eyes more on the gathering behind Captain Jack than on the chief himself.

He finally relented. "Yes—the two tell us that the white men have a bad heart for me and my people."

"We do not have a bad heart—"

"You may not—for we have been long friends, O'Roarke. You and Fairchild are fair men. My friends in Yreka too—men like Elisha Steele. I want Steele to come to talk with me too."

Ian glanced at Fairchild, who nodded. "I think we can get Steele to come with us next time."

"It is good," Jack replied, his lips pursed in a line of stern determination. "Good to have my white friends here with me when I talk of serious things. A few of your kind are fair men. But these soldiers talk with two voices. One we hear through you—and it is filled with kind words of hope that we can settle this trouble." He sighed, taking his hat off and scratching his head. "The other voice we hear is what the soldiers say behind our backs. They want to kill us—man, woman and child—for the time they came to attack us in the Lava Beds and we killed the soldiers to protect our families."

"Vengeance is not what this is all about, Jack," Fairchild said.

"We hear talk in the soldier camps that they want to capture us—to hang us from a tree. This hanging is very bad, Fairchild."

"I know, I know," the settler answered. "I will not lie to you and tell you that every soldier heart is truthful and that every soldier will not wish you harm. My heart speaks the truth to you when I say that there are a few—a very few soldiers—who would like to paint themselves in Modoc blood."

Jack smiled as Riddle translated, wearing that smug, self-assured look that could drive an adversary into a frenzy. "I know there are many who want to kill us."

O'Roarke shook his head, taking a step closer to Jack, watching the chief back up that same single step. "Kientpoos—look at your own men—now. See how many of them who stand behind you at this moment— how many want to kill us. Fairchild and me. Without good reason—just because we are white men. Look for yourself and then judge us fairly."

Eventually Jack turned and studied the faces of his men. When he looked back at O'Roarke, the chief's dark eyes were lit with a dark fire.

"Yes, my old friends. Neither of us must ever forget that there are Modocs who would kill you both just because you are white men."

Chapter 14

March 1873

*E*lisha Steele was promptly summoned to the army's camp from Yreka by commissioner Alfred B. Meacham.

After a day of conferring with the peace commission, attorney Steele selected his delegation to accompany him to the Modocs' stronghold. Not only would he need Frank and Toby Riddle as interpreters, but Steele requested two of his fellow Californians along because they too were held in high esteem by Captain Jack: John Fairchild and Ian O'Roarke. Ian then convinced the Yreka lawyer that his nephew, Seamus Donegan, would be a good man to ride along: a level head, and good in any sort of scrape, whatever came of the council.

Rounding out the delegation was H. Wallace Atwell, a California newspaperman who wrote under the name "Bill Dadd" and had invited himself along to cover the momentous meeting with Captain Jack's "renegades."

The horses were loaded with provisions, a rubber poncho and several blankets needed by each delegate, who, because of the distance to be covered, would be required to stay the night in the Modoc Stronghold.

Donegan was perhaps alone in feeling a thick and pervasive wall of suspicion in the Modoc camp, sensing the dark, smoldering eyes on him as well as the other visitors the moment they emerged from the maze of catacombs and fissures, guided by Scar-Faced Charley and two others into the center of the Lava Beds where Captain Jack's people had held out for better than three months.

The rest of the white men appeared hopeful, if not ready to believe in the friendly gestures and words coming from the Indians.

"My good friends gathered here know I speak with straight words," Jack said, nearing the end of his opening remarks. "You white men know my heart. It is not white. My heart is Modoc. But—a war can only mean disaster for my people. While I cannot stand by and see my people slaughtered by the Ben Wrights among the white men moving into our Lost River country—so too I cannot stand by and see my people kill themselves in a foolish war."

For a few moments the chief stopped near H. Wallace Atwell, watching in silence as the reporter scribbled across his notebook while Frank and Toby Riddle interpreted Jack's words for the white ears.

"We are for peace—but we will not be treated like dogs. We can live in peace on Lost River. You must tell the army they cannot push us onto Klamath ground again."

When Jack had taken his seat, Steele rose to address the assembly.

"There are many among the white men who are for peace, my friends. I would hope that among the Modoc— there will be more who stand for peace than clamor for war against the soldiers."

The Yreka lawyer made his meaning plain as his eyes landed on Curly Headed Doctor, and stayed riveted there for the longest time before he continued. "I come to you today with the assurance of the chief of the peace commission—a man you remember named Meacham, who once served as chief for the Indian Bureau in all of Oregon country."

"Meacham?" Jack asked.

Several of the other warriors echoed the name as Riddle pronounced it.

"Yes, Meacham," Steele replied. "He has given me authority to tell you that he can grant amnesty for all who have committed any crimes, committed any killing since the twenty-ninth of November—under a state of war with the soldiers."

"What is this amnesty?" asked the chief.

Steele considered a moment, tapping his lower lip with a fingertip, walking slowing in front of the Modoc head men. "It means that your warriors will not be held guilty for the killing they did in fighting the soldiers."

Jack turned to his people, the smile broad across his flat face. "You see—we can win with the white man! He will not force us into turning over the guilty warriors to be hanged!"

There were hoots and hollers of agreement, which fell silent when Steele held his hands up.

"Jack, your people must understand that this amnesty is given your warriors only if you agree to removing your people to a reservation—but a reservation of your choice."

Jack came back to Steele quickly. "On our land beside Lost River."

Steele finally shook his head. "No, Jack. Almost anywhere but there."

"It is our ancient land."

"I know. Believe me, I know it is." Steele wrung his hands in desperation, sensing the momentous turn of things—if only it were still in his grasp. "You must do this, Jack. For your people. Take the reservation offered. Choose a beautiful place for your people to live out all their days. And—it will be all your people, as I said. No man will be hanged if you go to the reservation now. You have my word on it."

"You speak this truly?"

"I have never lied to you, Jack."

"No, my friend Steele has never lied to me," the chief

replied, then turned to his people. "We will sleep on these words tonight—and talk more tomorrow before the white men return to the camp of the soldiers."

Later that evening after some Modoc women had served supper to the delegation gathered at a small fire of their own, Steele and Atwell fairly bubbled over with the prospects of peace.

"Why the devil is it you don't agree with me, fellas?" the lawyer asked the others.

O'Roarke looked at Fairchild. Then Fairchild looked at Riddle before answering. "Elisha, I'm sorry—but I don't think we've made a damn bit of headway."

Atwell wiped the back of his hand across his greasy lips and shook his iron fork at the settler. "But I saw Jack's face myself—and if I know anything, Mr. Fairchild, I know people. I heard the chief's words myself—and sensed no double-dealing there."

"You're right, Mr. Atwell," Ian O'Roarke burst in. "Jack plays every card as it lands—fair as the day is long. But Fairchild here isn't talking about Jack."

"What the devil are you two talking of then?" Steele inquired.

"Jack doesn't control the whole band anymore."

"He's their chief."

"And fellas like you make that same mistake all the time," Seamus Donegan broke in.

"I'd expect a comment like that from someone who had a little experience with Indians on the high plains— but these Oregon tribes are as different from those as night and day."

"Are they, Elisha?" Fairchild asked. "There's more at work here to keep things stirred up than meets the eye."

"I believe you fellas will be proved wrong come tomorrow."

"Pray that we are," O'Roarke said, then blew steam off his coffee. "Pray that we are wrong."

The following morning more speeches were made— grand orations about how the Modocs would be cared for with annuities of clothing and food, education for their children and medical care for the infirm and aged. If Steele felt buoyed the night before, he was ecstatic about the mood he felt among the Modocs by the time his delegation pulled away from the Lava Bed Stronghold.

So eager was he to spread his happy news that in nearing the army camp, Elisha Steele spurred on ahead of the other delegates, urging a handful of Modoc escorts to accompany him at a gallop.

Into the clusters of tents and smoky mess-fires he tore, standing in the stirrups, hat at the end of his arm, waving from side to side. "The Modocs are for peace! They're ready to make peace!"

Meacham and the Applegates immediately burst from their tents in the late afternoon light. From a breathless Steele they heard all the happy details as the Yreka lawyer time and again pointed at the Modoc warriors who had come along to the soldier camp to reinforce the hopes for peace.

Soldier and civilian alike were all astir, ready for a great celebration by the time O'Roarke, Fairchild, Atwell, Donegan and the two interpreters arrived minutes later.

"I don't figure there's any new good news to tell, Mr. Meacham," Fairchild said as he and O'Roarke strode up to the commissioner's tent where Steele was reveling in telling messengers the news he wanted conveyed to Linkville and Yreka, from there on to Washington itself.

Meacham twitched, his eyes narrowing. The celebration subsided, then fell silent. "What are you saying, Mr. Fairchild?"

"The Modocs listened to Steele all right," O'Roarke said. "But they didn't agree to peace on our terms."

Meacham shook his head violently. "You mean they won't accept amnesty for their murderers in return for a reservation of their choice?"

"If that reservation is on Lost River."

"We both know that's out of the question."

"Then we're back to the word go again, Mr. Meacham."

Steele shouldered his way up, his old and lined face etched now with worry where moments before it had been smoothed with joy. "Atwell was there. He heard the speeches from all of us. Tell them, Wallace. Read the speeches."

When the reporter finished reading his notes to the growing throng, there was not a person there who could admit to finding among the Modoc words anything that would give them hope of making peace with Jack's people.

"What about the Modocs who came with us?" Steele asked, his voice edged with desperation. "Riddle—you ask them if they didn't come to show us the Modocs were ready to accept peace."

After talking in low tones for a moment with the visitors, Riddle straightened, his own mouth puckered at the corners like shrunken rawhide. "They said they come to listen to the white man talk of making peace. Listen only —no talk of peace for the Modocs."

Steele sensed the eyes of many turn his way. His jaw twitching, the lawyer finally said, "I'll return there tomorrow. You'll go with me, won't you, Atwell?"

"Suppose it will make for a good story—yes, I'll go."

"Good." Steele turned to the Riddles. Stepping before Winema, he asked, "Toby, will you go—to interpret for me?"

After glancing at her husband. "Only me?"

"Yes. Just you, Toby."

"I will go with you, Steele. Tomorrow. To talk to Captain Jack's Modocs."

By the time Jack's friend Elisha Steele returned to the Stronghold, the mood of the Modocs had changed as quickly as the wind itself changed in the Ice Moon.

In less time than it took the winter sun to travel from horizon to horizon, Curly Headed Doctor had once again wrested emotional control of the band from Chief Kientpoos. Jack wished the two white men and his niece Winema had stayed at the soldier camp. The mood in the Stronghōld had turned black and ugly, like the hard, cold and icy rocks that formed this bastion where his people hid like animals.

Unlike their last visit, this time Jack feared for their lives.

He kept his seat, watching the gray-headed Steele drop from his horse and look about him apprehensively. Knowing the white man could feel the hate in every pair of eyes on him, Jack knew his sole task would be to protect the lives of these three people—any way he could.

Slowly Steele came forward, then held out his hand, forcing a watery smile on his face.

"I come here as your friend, Jack. Are we . . . we still are friends?"

Jack nodded, his eyes half-lidded. "Yes, Steele. We friends long time to come."

It made him feel a little better to watch some of the apprehension drain from the white man's face.

"Jack, I come to see if I heard the Modoc words right when we talked of peace and a new reservation for your people."

"We are for peace, Steele," he said. "But when you come here to tell us we cannot have our reservation on Lost River—you do not know what pain and anger you make in the heart of Modocs."

Steele wrung his hands before him, something that made Jack pity his white friend as Curly Headed Doctor lunged forward, sticking his face inches from the lawyer's.

"No more talk now!" snarled the shaman. "We are all done giving in to the white man. Only lies you give us. But no more! Now we are free!"

"And we will drive the white man out of our country!" shouted Hooker Jim.

"You must remember that there are many white men like me who want to find peace—"

"Peace?" screamed the shaman. "You are here begging like a dog for peace because the Modoc is more powerful than the white man!"

Steele shook his head, eyes growing big as Winema translated the words. He glanced quickly at the reporter. Atwell was no longer hunched over, notebook pressed atop his knee—instead, he was watching the scene with growing alarm.

Steele swallowed hard before speaking. "Better that we talk tomorrow before I return to the soldier camp."

"There is no more talk!" Curly Headed Doctor said. "When your blood has cooled—we can talk tomorrow."

"Yes," Captain Jack agreed, rising. "The council is over for tonight."

While his people slowly dispersed, the chief watched, feeling no little fear for the lives of the guests. Here and there angry knots of warriors and squaws gathered, whispering, all the time staring at the white men and Winema. Scar-Faced Charley came up beside Jack.

"We cannot let these people be killed, Kientpoos," Charley whispered at Jack's ear.

"We'll take them to my own cave. Bring my sister to watch over Winema. I will guard Steele and you must guard the other white man with your life."

Charley nodded as Jack turned back to their guests. "Come with us now," he explained to Winema Riddle. "It is safe where I sleep."

Jack led the three to the cave his family had been using since arriving there at the end of the previous November. There he showed the guests where they could unfurl their blankets and make their beds. Then he joined Charley and his sister, called Queen Mary because of her size, at the narrow entrance to the lava cave.

The sun sank rapidly that night, bringing the cold and frost much quicker than normal. Jack hungered, his belly rumbling with a dull reminder that he had not eaten since breakfast on some dried strips of cow meat. With nothing else now, Jack sipped at the cool water from the canteen he had captured on the battlefield weeks before.

Sometime long after the moon had risen, then fallen far enough to shed its western luminance into the cave, Jack turned to look over the three guests he was guarding. He found his old friend Elisha Steele up on an elbow, staring at him in the silver light. When the white man spoke, Charley and Queen Mary turned quietly.

"Jack," Steele whispered.

"Ssshhh," Charley warned.

"No," Jack replied quietly. "It is all right. Speak softly, Steele."

"I . . . I feel in my heart that you and your . . . the three of you are all that stands between me and my death right now."

Jack squinted, hard. Sometimes that helped him better understand the white man's words when they came too quickly to grasp in one huge bite. The squinting helped him concentrate and sort out the words. When he had enough, he stopped squinting and nodded to Steele.

"Yes, my friend. You too all stand between me and rope hanging now. I save you now. You save me soon."

Jack watched Steele slowly sink back to his blankets, his face disappearing from the patch of silver light. Yet the white man's eyes continued to show bright and big for the longest time in that dark, cold cave.

Watching, always watching the three who stood between the white men and the rage of Curly Headed Doctor.

Chapter 15

Late March 1873

Ian O'Roarke watched Steele, Atwell and Toby Riddle ride back into the outskirts of Gillem's army camp. From the haggard, wind-blustered look of his friend, Ian immediately knew something had gone awry.

"Tell me, Elisha—you found out how wrong you were, didn't you?" Ian asked, walking along at Steele's stirrup until the Yreka attorney reined up his horse.

"Tell them, Steele," Atwell prodded angrily.

The attorney nodded and sighed. "I had to . . . had to promise them that the commissioners would come to a conference . . ."

"Yes, so?" Ian said, watching others coming up to the three on horseback.

"I promised the commissioners would come to a meeting with the Modocs in their Stronghold . . . unarmed."

"Unarmed?" O'Roarke asked, his voice rising two octaves.

"You actually promised the Doctor's butchers that the commissioners would lay their lives down on the Modocs' front step—unarmed?" John Fairchild asked.

"It was the only way he could get us out of that camp alive," Atwell said, still visibly shaken.

Ian looked at Winema, her head bowed. At that moment Frank Riddle shouldered his way through the crowd. The couple spoke quietly for a moment, then he lifted her down from the horse.

"I don't think Jack would let her be killed," Frank said as he turned to go, Winema beneath an arm. "She's his niece, for God's sake."

"Still, she might be caught in some fury provoked by the Doctor," Fairchild said.

Riddle nodded, obviously concerned for his distraught wife, and led her away from the growing crowd.

"They're planning nothing more than bald-face treachery," Ian said, "demanding Steele guarantee the commissioners come to that evil den of death, unarmed."

"You had no business making any promises on our behalf," said Alfred B. Meacham as he came to a stop.

Steele whirled, his hands before him, imploring. "I said what I had to—just to get us out of there before—"

"You might well have hamstrung us, Steele," Meacham growled.

"More than that, Alfred," O'Roarke said quietly, "you go and choose to meet with those warriors now—your life hangs by a most slender thread."

By the first week of April an impressive array of newspapermen had gathered at Colonel Gillem's camp, each one eager to feed his hungry readers back east with the latest morsels from what was now being headlined as the MODOC WAR IN THE LAVA BEDS. This would prove to be the first, and in many ways the only, campaign comprehensively reported on during the entire quarter-century era of the Indian Wars. And with the way things were going, it was sure to make headlines for months to come.

"A ragtag band of poorly-armed Injins holding the mighty U.S. Army at bay!" Seamus cried. "That damn sure will make news back east."

"One of the New York papers even has a veteran of the British army reporting here for them," Ian O'Roarke said as he stirred the coals of their evening mess-fire.

John Fairchild squatted down beside them. "Heard he was working for the New York *Herald.*"

"The stuff he's writing about—and how he's writing it —won't do Gillem no good," Seamus said. "Those articles get back east—all those politicians back there with their starched collars will cry even louder for the army to make peace with Captain Jack at any price."

"Just to avoid a war. A bloody shame," Ian growled, dragging the bubbling coffeepot from the coals.

"They haven't been kind to the commissioners already here to make their peace with the Modocs. Not that I really care for the rest of 'em." John Fairchild accepted a steaming cup. "But when they go sniping at Meacham— that's when I get my hackles up."

"What they been saying about the old man?" Seamus asked.

"Saw a soldier's paper yesterday. One of the reporters was writing that Meacham could 'talk the legs off a cast-iron pot in just ten minutes,' " Fairchild replied.

Seamus shrugged. "Sounds like Meacham's the man for the job. Them Modocs been hard as cast-iron so far."

They chuckled a bit, blowing steam from their coffee as night came down hard on the Lava Beds.

"I just don't like the way some of them others been reporting on Meacham," Fairchild continued. "Another one said that 'words roll from his silvery tongue like green peas from a hot platter.' "

"Don't let them worry you none, John," Ian said. "Those reporters are only angry because Meacham won't let them attend any of his conferences—or his meetings of the commission. They bloody well print anything these days."

"But Uncle," Seamus said, "the truth is that if Meacham is every bit as good as the reporters are saying he is at charming the pants off those Modocs—then he's the perfect man for what task lies ahead of them."

Ian and Fairchild both nodded. Donegan's uncle stared into the flames. "Then I suggest we all pray Meacham's

up to the task of making peace out of this dirty war,
nephew."

If the administration of Ulysses S. Grant back in Washington had anything to say about it, they were bound and determined to make peace with the Modocs. Twice in those past four months, the U.S. Army had tried, and failed miserably, to muscle Captain Jack's people onto the reservation.

A majority of politicians and power brokers alike back east were dismayed that Grant's Secretary of War, William Belknap, and his Secretary of the Interior, Columbus Delano, would not join forces to annihilate the Modocs. Instead, the administration had closed ranks to negotiate with that ragtag band of renegades holding out against the might of the frontier army.

Yet as the headlines bannered across the front pages of eastern newspapers, daily reporting the bumbling attempts of the army and the staggering, wavering efforts of the peace commission, more and more of the east came to debate the fact that it appeared the Modocs were doing only what could be expected of them—given a reservation on the homeland of their ancient enemies when their own Lost River land was stripped from them by white settlers.

Even more impressive, it was becoming more and more abundantly clear to a growing number of politicians who had their own agendas that this little war with the Modocs was turning into an affair lasting much too long, and by every means of accounting, much too expensive.

But try as A. B. Meacham and General Canby could, the Modocs were not cooperating in making peace.

Twice the Modocs sent word that they were ready to surrender provided they would not be hanged and the band would be given a reservation far from the Klamaths. Twice Canby sent wagons to the agreed-upon meeting place. Both times the wagons rumbled back to Gillem's headquarters empty.

Forces against surrender were at work in the Stronghold. Each time it appeared Captain Jack was making headway convincing his people that surrender was the best path to take—Curly Headed Doctor and his zealots intimidated and threatened. As murderers of the white settlers four moons before, these warriors knew that surrender for them meant the end of a white man's rope. Besides, everytime the mood of the Modocs huddled in the Stronghold seemed to inch toward giving up—the shaman would leap to the top of a boulder and harangue his believers.

Pointing each time across the lake to Bloody Point.

Where twenty winters before, a white peacemaker named Ben Wright had come among the Modocs—and savagely slaughtered most of their village.

As the frustrations had simmered week after week with complete lack of progress in the negotiations, the face of the commission changed. General Canby found himself dealing more with Meacham and the hope for peace talks every day. In addition, fifty-eight-year-old Methodist minister Eleazar Thomas was appointed to replace a departing commissioner. Also, the subagent on the Klamath reservation, L. S. Dyar, was appointed to take the place of the departing Jesse Applegate.

If it were to be a staying action meant to contain the Modocs in their Stronghold while the commissioners talked, then Canby would guarantee his superiors that the local settlers were protected and that he would know what the hostiles were up to. Accomplishing this had meant the construction of signal towers the soldiers would use in transmitting heliograph and semaphore signals between Gillem's headquarters and Bernard's camp, located at Applegate's ranch on Clear Lake.

It was there that Captain James Biddle received orders to lead his K Troop, brought in from Camp Halleck in Nevada, on a reconnaissance of the Ticknor Road that strung its way through the roughest of country skirting the south side of the Lava Beds.

Seamus led his horse up beside Sergeant Maurice Fitzgerald and mounted when the older cavalry veteran gave the order to his horse soldiers. Around last night's fire the two had shared memories and tales of battles, fighting units of J.E.B. Stuart's Confederate horse at Gettysburg and in the Shenandoah for Phil Sheridan.

"By God, Irishman," Fitzgerald bawled now within his black beard, already flecked with white, "what you and me could do to clean this little matter up and quick, eh?"

Seamus eased down onto the saddle as the sun warmed a cheek. "This ain't the kind of horse war I grew used to fighting, Sergeant."

Fitzgerald appraised him, then finally nodded. "If only those bastards back in Washington would turn the cavalry loose—we'd show 'em which way the Modocs run!" He urged his mount near Donegan's, flinging his fist at the big Irishman's arm. "If only we could get you back in uniform, you bloody renegade!"

"Things working out fine just the way they are, Sergeant," he said as Fitzgerald signaled his patrol to move out. "I get me fill of fighting when I want it. But I don't do no kitchen patrol and don't dig no latrines."

"Ah—you do have the best in life, don't you, Donegan!"

"If you love bad food and wet blankets and a drippy nose."

"What? You'd give up white beans and corn dodgers for the cooking of some soft-fleshed person of the female persuasion?" prodded Fitzgerald with a great smile creasing his dark beard.

"Before you could say *deserter!*"

They laughed together, joined by a few of the troopers within hearing distance, as they moved into the freezing fog of mid-morning, a milk-pale sun climbing overhead behind the thick clouds blanketing the land.

By early afternoon Troop K had plodded past Dry Lake and were heading west, nearing a low, yet prominent, outcropping known among the locals as Sand Butte. Like nighthawks flitting across the horizon at twilight,

Seamus caught the barest hint of movement—ahead and to the right.

When he glanced over at Fitzgerald, he found the sergeant squinting into the haze of foggy sunlight and smudgy clouds.

"I saw it, Irishman."

"Two of 'em?"

"Two, most like."

"You see any weapons?"

Fitzgerald wagged his head. "But you can be damned sure if there's a Modoc raiding party out here—they've got weapons." He turned in his saddle and threw up a hand, halting the column.

Captain Biddle pushed his horse ahead and reined up beside Fitzgerald. "You spot something ahead?"

"Both of us."

Seamus watched Biddle's eyes flick his way, then go back to rest on his sergeant.

"You're figuring an ambush."

"They like working that way, Captain," Donegan replied.

"Let's prepare this troop for action," Biddle said after a moment of thought. "I don't like the lay of this country." He flung an arm ahead, indicating the winding trail through the rocky landscape strewn with bluffs and ridges, boulders and a few stunted junipers and a profusion of sagebrush.

"They'll draw us in, Captain—and jump when they figure the place is right."

"Unless we make 'em jump first," Seamus said, a small grin beginning to carve his face.

Biddle regarded him sternly. "What's on your mind, civilian?"

"Me and Fitzgerald—best riders you've got, Captain. What say the sergeant and this civilian ride ahead to flush out what's up there?"

Biddle looked at Fitzgerald, asking with his eyes. The sergeant nodded. Then smiled.

"Sounds like something I can do. With your permission, Captain."

Once more Biddle regarded the torn, horrid country that lay just ahead as they approached the foot of Sand Butte. He sighed. "All right. But don't take any chances."

Fitzgerald chuckled. "Me, Captain? Not with this rummy to cover my backside I won't! C'mon, Irishman."

As they moved out, Seamus pulled free the mule-ear on the army holster and dragged out the .44 caliber pistol. He stuffed the long barrel beneath the belt he had tightened around his thick, blanket mackinaw. As they eased toward the foot of the butte, there were places where the horsemen had to ride single file through the boulders. They kept their eyes moving above them, on either side, expecting at any moment to see figures blot out some of the sky, firing down upon them.

Instead, as they rode free of a tangle of boulders, the two horsemen caught sight of the same two Modocs seen minutes before, but now hurrying away to the north around the base of the bluff, riding bareback on ponies.

"Wasn't no war-party, Sergeant."

"Just what I was thinking," Fitzgerald answered. "But what would two of them be doing out here alone—"

Seamus tapped the sergeant's arm. "There."

"I'll be go to hell right here, Irishman," he exclaimed, pushing his slouch hat back on his head, then turning in the saddle, looking downtrail.

"We've hit the jackpot. Let's go back and tell the captain he's captured some Modoc ponies."

"We don't have to, Donegan." He pointed behind them.

"Biddle got a little curious, eh, Sergeant?"

"His ass gets itchy if he don't know what's going on up ahead."

They waited for the captain and his troopers to come up, then showed off the thirty-five ponies grazing on dry, brittle grasses in a long, narrow meadow totally hidden from the Ticknor Road.

"If we hadn't come this far up the butte chasing those two herders, we'd never found those ponies," Donegan commented.

Biddle smiled, which was signal to many of the young, green troopers to shout their approval. "Good work, boys. I suppose it is about time we took something from the Modocs. Lord knows we've too damned little to be proud of in this campaign."

"Just take each day as it comes, Captain. You'll keep your hair that way," Seamus replied. "Might even win a scrap or two with these ruddy Modocs too."

Chapter 16

Early April 1873

Captain Biddle drove the captured ponies on west to Gillem's headquarters at Van Bremmer's ranch.

It was there, two days later, that a half-dozen Modoc women showed up to protest the capture of the herd.

Alfred Meacham advised General Canby against returning the animals. Agreeing, Canby allowed the women only to briefly visit their ponies before the squaws were escorted from the army camp, empty-handed.

As a staunch Republican and a God-fearing Methodist, Meacham was a former hotel and toll-road operator from the Grande Ronde Valley of the Blue Mountains in northeastern Oregon when President Grant appointed him to serve as the state's Indian Superintendent in 1869. Meacham had long been a supporter of the Grand Old Party and "Unconditional Surrender" Grant.

But his appointment had not come as his first experience dealing with Indians. Back in 1863 when he had arrived in Oregon, Meacham already possessed twenty-six years of fair-handed business dealings with Indians in his native Iowa. He himself had been instrumental in the government's 1844 removal of the Iowa bands to lands farther west on the plains.

This quiet, stocky and balding superintendent got the

shock of his life when he made his first visits to the agencies newly in his charge. Not only did he find most of the agents corrupt and venal under an effectively-oiled spoils system, but he discovered most of the Indian Bureau itself to be morally bankrupt. Meacham himself was enraged to run across several attempts of local agents to "wash out the color"—an expression of the time referring to the interbreeding between white and red to solve "the Indian problem."

Instantly indignant at the abuses, Meacham was quick to rid his department of those agents doing everything they could to personally hurry along the "mixing of the races." At the same time, he declared it mandatory that any man living on the reservations with an Indian woman had either to marry the woman in legal ceremony or abandon her immediately.

Yet his greatest despair, it seemed, was that he was unable to elicit the army's help in his reform. In fact, Meacham was unable to enact any substantial change in the moral climate at Fort Klamath itself, where the officers openly "borrowed" squaws from their husbands. Try as he might, Meacham was powerless as well to end the practice of the fort commissary officers and contract sutlers using the local squaws, who were unable to pay for their purchases, as prostitutes for the enlisted men.

So by this spring of 1873, Alfred Meacham found himself feeling older every day now. For more than two months he had been traveling this road of negotiation and hope, attempting to find some accord between the government and the Modocs. He took little joy in knowing the process was making an old man of him.

Immediately following the 17 January debacle in the Lava Beds, Secretary of the Interior Columbus Delano had asked Secretary of War William Belknap to suspend hostilities against the Modocs while Washington selected a commission to determine how best to bring about a lasting peace with Captain Jack's renegades. On 30 January military action was duly suspended, except for any action required by the army for the protection of settlers in the area.

At that same time, Secretary Delano did not have to cast far to find the head of what would be his peace delegation. Former Oregon superintendent Meacham was visiting in Washington. In a matter of hours his presidential appointment was made official and Meacham was on a westbound train, headed for Oregon country once more.

As mile after mile, and day after day, were put behind him, Meacham wrestled with the dilemma of where to begin and what to do once he arrived at the Lava Beds. Truth was, he had accepted the position with misgiving.

And ever since he had arrived on the scene, nothing had changed his most private of feelings. Down in his heart of hearts, A. B. Meacham sensed that he had accepted a task that may very well cost him his life.

By the last days of March, Meacham found himself dealing with a new group of commissioners. Joining him now in the peace efforts were the fifty-eight-year-old Methodist minister Eleazar Thomas from California, and the subagent from the Klamath reservation, L. S. Dyar. In addition, General Canby had in recent weeks become so active in the affairs of the commissioners that he was regarded as one of their delegation.

But back on the twenty-third of March, Meacham actually feared Canby had put his foot in it.

Colonel Gillem had suggested that the colonel and Canby journey over for their own firsthand look at the Lava Beds. Escorted by a full company of heavily armed troops, the officers marched east from Van Bremmer's to the bluff from which the disastrous 17 January attack had begun.

"At that point, I ordered the troops to dismount and rest," Canby had explained upon his return to Meacham. "I could look out over the placid expanse of Tule Lake stretching away many miles northward and eastward, while to the east and south lay the seemingly level expanse of the Lava Beds."

"That's when you saw the Modocs?"

Canby had bristled, nettled at Meacham's attempt to hurry along his own well-paced rendering of the story.

The general cleared his throat. "While leisurely gazing over the imposing landscape, we suddenly heard a shout from the rocks near the foot of the bluff where we were standing. I then observed an Indian waving his cap at us."

"Is that when Dr. Cabaniss approached the warrior?" Meacham asked, referring to one of the several contract surgeons assigned the regiments for the campaign.

Canby nodded. "He knows some of Jack's men and a few of the women."

"Yes. He's a good man," Meacham observed.

"That's when he and that English journalist, uh . . ."

"Fox?"

The general agreed, "Yes. When they went down and found out from the warrior that Captain Jack wanted to talk to me—personally."

"Cut through the brush, General," Meacham chided. "Did you make any ground in your talk with Jack?"

This time the pleasure drained from Canby's face. "No. Jack kept Cabaniss and Fox as hostage until we had finished talking."

"Wasn't it more of an argument?"

The general eventually agreed. "I suppose it was. Jack hasn't relented at all. Still wanting the army to disperse and his people allowed a reservation on Lost River. It was clearly not a pleasant encounter."

Meacham grinned darkly, his eyes moving over to a nearby fire where New York *Herald* correspondent Fox was having an army barber trim his long hair. "I suppose that unpleasant encounter is reason enough for Fox to want his hair sheared?"

"Yes," Canby agreed, attempting to smother a chuckle. "Immediately after the Modocs left us and we were heading back, Fox vowed he would crop his mane so short that should he have another encounter with Jack's renegades, no Modoc would want his scalp!"

And through it all, day in and day out, Captain Jack's band played the army and civilians alike for time. Almost any day expecting another terse, impatient telegram from Secretary Delano, Meacham feared the calendar would end up falling on Captain Jack's side of this war of nerves.

On the first day of April, Canby agreed with Meacham that they should stoke the fire beneath the Modocs. The general moved his headquarters from Van Bremmer's ranch to a site at the base of the bluff—three miles from and almost within hailing distance of the Stronghold.

After Gillem's camp had been impressively spread below the bluff, the following day saw the entire peace commission meet with a delegation of Modocs for the first time. The wary on both sides met in that no-man's land between the army's tents and the bastion of the Stronghold. Meacham was alone among the commissioners in realizing the Modocs had come with some women as a universal sign of peaceful intentions.

Yet, as things turned out, the two sides argued more on the form of future sessions than on matters of substance.

"Why are you moving your soldiers so close to my women and children?" Captain Jack asked angrily of General Canby through the interpreters.

Meacham watched the old soldier squirm some under the hard scrutiny igniting the Modoc eyes.

Canby cleared his throat, trying out an uncomfortable smile. "I—I moved my soldiers . . . my own headquarters—so I could be closer to talk with you, Jack. You have men in the trees behind you—there." Canby pointed.

"They are here to be sure I am not killed by your soldiers," Jack replied.

"My soldiers camp close by so that I am not harmed by your warriors, Jack."

The Modoc chief shook his head. "You do not have women and children in your camps. I am not a threat to any of your women and children. Take your soldiers away from here before we can talk about peace."

"Your warriors could most certainly be a threat to women and children."

Jack's face flared. "When the soldiers attacked our camp and the white settlers were killed—not a woman, not one child was harmed by my warriors!"

Canby shifted uneasily. "We want the murderers brought to justice."

"White man's justice?" Jack asked. "Did the white man hang the murderers of my people when Ben Wright came among us and slaughtered the Modocs who trusted in the word of a white man?"

"That has nothing to do with our situation today."

Jack stood abruptly, surprising everyone. "There will be no more talk between us until you guarantee me that Hooker Jim's warriors will be treated the same as the rest of my people if we surrender."

Canby shook his head, concern growing across his face. "I cannot negotiate their amnesty, Jack. They are guilty of murdering innocent civilians."

"Then we really do not have much to talk about."

At that moment a brutal spring storm that had been taking shape over Tule Lake, full of froth and foam, burst over the council area. A cold rain began falling, urged by maddening gusts of brutal wind hurled off the white-capped water. Canby rose, sheltering his face beneath his wide-brimmed hat.

"We will talk another time, Jack. When it is not raining."

Some on both sides apparently agreed with Canby that the changeable weather dictated that their council be suspended. A few Modocs were withdrawing for the Stronghold while Dyar and Thomas were turning away toward their horses.

"Where are you going?" Jack demanded, a smile creasing his dark face, black hair stringy and sopping in his eyes. "You white men are wearing better clothes than I am—and I won't melt like snow!"

Plainly Canby grew impatient as Toby Riddle translated. "We'll talk more another day, Jack. When I return to my camp, I will have some soldiers come to this place —to this meadow—where they can erect a tent for our future meetings. We can be safe from the weather in the days to come, Jack."

Canby waved the other delegates away from the area, leaving the Modoc men behind with their mocking laughter ringing across the open basin.

That same day, 2 April, Artillery Battery E arrived at Gillem's new camp. And on the fourth, while the soldiers erected the high-walled canvas tent in a flat meadow all but entirely free of the large lava boulders normally dotting the area, the Modocs most assuredly witnessed the arrival of Artillery Battery K.

"If that growing show of military might is not enough to awe Captain Jack and his people," sighed Alfred B. Meacham that gloomy twilight, "they'll think twice about doing anything the slightest bit underhanded now that our chosen meeting place actually lies closer to this soldier camp than it does to their distant Stronghold."

"Praise God! Perhaps now they'll not be so quick to dig in their heels," agreed the kindly Reverend Eleazar Thomas, the portly minister, at their evening mess-fire, "and Jack's cutthroats will begin to negotiate in good faith at last. I get the feeling you made some headway in your talk with the Modocs at the tent today, did you?"

Meacham considered his answer. "Jack wanted to see only me and Fairchild. Along with the Riddles. He does not trust Canby."

"Why doesn't he like the general?"

Meacham sighed. "Perhaps it is his uniform—the fact that he is a soldier. Jack says Canby talks too much of his friendship for the Indians."

"Jack doesn't believe Canby."

He nodded. "That's at the basis of it. A soldier who brings his army closer and closer to the Lava Beds cannot be trusted by Captain Jack."

"So tell me why our renegade chief did not want me there with you."

Meacham felt ill at ease saying it. "To the Modocs, you are what is called a 'Sunday Doctor.' They know you don't like them because your Christian religious views are so different from theirs."

Thomas snorted. "You're a Methodist yourself, Alfred. Aren't your beliefs different from that curly-headed witch doctor's?"

Meacham shook his head. "That's not the point, Reverend. Because you are a minister, they feel you can't give them the slightest consideration because you consider them outright savages."

"In the name of heaven! That's just what they are—ignorant and not in a state of grace, for they know not of the Lord Jesus Christ, our Savior."

Meacham waved his hand for quiet. "Because of those views you hold, they'll continue to distrust your intentions, Reverend."

Thomas drew his lips up into a line of determination. "They do that with no more fervency than I in continuing to trust to my God in guiding my footsteps as I trod this dangerous path to bring the Modocs to peace."

Meacham opened the cover on his pocket watch. "I must be going soon."

Thomas clucked in that righteous way of his. "So how many delegates do you think that renegade will bring to the talk?"

"It matters very little—"

"What really matters is that the renegade chief will continue to try every little ploy to drag this affair out, Meacham—if you allow him."

He shook his head, weary of the constant sniping he suffered from the other commissioners. "Canby's already sent word to Jack that he'll be moving his camp even closer to their Stronghold since the Modocs aren't attempting to negotiate with us."

"Who's carrying word between our camps now?"

"Three of Jack's warriors: Boston Charley, Hooker Jim and another called Bogus Charley," Meacham replied, watching the sun settle far beyond the high peaks of the Cascade range. "They want to spend the night with us in camp."

"Damn those godless Philistines, I say."

He wanted to smile at the preacher, as one might pat the head of an errant child, yet did not allow himself that pleasure. "For myself, Reverend—I believe it better that we have those two Philistines in our camp, if only for the night. Right where we can keep our eyes on them. They're trouble—I'll admit that."

"And the Lord knows they're stirring all they can of the cauldron of discontent among us, Meacham."

"The soldiers up in their signal post tonight must be cold," the commissioner finally said after a few moments, watching the distant flare of light illuminating a soldier's face as he would light his pipe.

From the elevation of the rock outcropping more than seventy-five feet above the camp, the soldiers could signal Hospital Rock on the far side of the Lava Beds, besides having a commanding view of the meeting tent itself. "When the sun goes down tonight—those boys up there going to be so cold they'll shiver keeping themselves awake."

Thomas appeared to have the least care for the enlisted soldiers on night watch as he cleared his throat. "When are we next meeting with the Modocs?"

"I'll determine that when I talk with Jack at the tent tomorrow," he answered anxiously. "I must be going for now."

"I'll pray for your guidance in the morning, Meacham. Pray that God Himself finds the words for you."

"Better pray that God Himself were attending these councils, Reverend. Then we might all sleep a little more soundly."

*   *   *

Meacham was wrong about the full commission meeting with the Modocs.

It was the very next day, the fifth of April as white man reckons his time, when Captain Jack sent Boston Charley back to the soldier camp, requesting a meeting with the old white man named Mee-Cham, along with his long-time friend John Fairchild and the Riddles.

Only they.

With the dying of each day, Jack had sensed a growing urgency pressing in upon him as the Doctor gloated that the chief's faith in negotiating a favorable reservation from the white man was itself dying a little more with each sunset glowing behind Mount Shasta.

More than anything right now, the young chief of the Modocs somehow had to get the white peace talkers to understand that matters would soon be wrenched out of his hands. The white men must make peace with his people, and now—or Jack could not guarantee the safety of those who came to that tent in the meadow to talk of peace, to talk of a reservation for his old people and the little ones who cried from empty bellies or the cold each night. The rest of his band were strong enough to suffer through this siege.

Captain Jack watched the three white men and his niece approach the high-walled peace tent, knowing he had come here to talk peace not for those who could survive at all costs holed up like cornered animals among these brutal rocks. No—he had come here to talk peace for those too old or sick or small—those who did not hunger for Curly Headed Doctor's war—those who hoped most of all for peace so they could return to their life of old among the Lost River camps.

But the army was moving again. Almost every day Jack received reports from his wide-ranging scouts that the soldiers were tightening the noose around the Stronghold in the Lava Beds. Not only had the largest group of white men on the west moved closer to the Modocs, but now the soldiers on the east were moving their camp from

Scorpion Point to Hospital Rock as well—as little as two miles from where he now stood.

"I know your hearts—I can trust you four," Jack replied when the old white man Mee-Cham asked again why he could not bring the rest of the peace commission with him to the council.

"What is it your heart wants to tell me?" asked the old white man.

"I came to this place of rocks when the soldiers drove us here," Jack said. "We had no place to be safe. Now we want to return to our homes on Lost River. I was born there—like my father before me. Give us back our homeland, and we do not need anything from the white man— not like the Klamaths up north. We will not need your food or your clothing. Leave us be to hunt and fish as we have always done. And we will leave you white men alone."

"I cannot do that, Jack. Things are too far gone now."

"The soldiers took our horses and would not give them back. Just like the land the white man has taken from us. One day—a man must stand up and fight for what another man takes from him."

"The horses were captured in war—"

"Your soldiers bring many guns to talk peace to so few Indians!" Jack did not allow Meacham to continue. He rose suddenly, pointing across an arm of Tule Lake. "See that place over there, Mee-Cham. I was just a boy then— when Ben Wright murdered my people . . . my father." He whirled on the commissioner. "But I remember. I will *always* remember the men who say they come in peace— then bring guns to do their talking for them."

"We are not like Ben Wright," Meacham started to protest, but Jack was there, his five fingers extended, wagging, forcing the white man back into his seat.

"You know how many escaped that butchery of Ben Wright's men? Five—one for each of my fingers."

"Yes! I agree! Ben Wright committed an unspeakable evil—but we are not here today to talk of him—"

"No! We are here to talk of peace while your soldiers prepare for war, Mee-Cham. Listen to me carefully: I will not fall on the ground when the shooting starts. I will fall on the bodies of my enemies."

Meacham shook his head sadly. He swiped the back of a hand across his mouth, appearing to form the words in his mind. He gazed steadily at the Modoc chief. "If you do not come out of these rocks in peace, Jack—then many will die. Not just soldiers. Not just your warriors. But sadly, many of your women and children will die. Are they as ready as you to die, Jack?"

The Modoc chief felt the same old desperation growing inside him, with the realization that the white man's words were right, striking the heart of his worst fears. When he finally spoke, Jack's words came out strong, yet were uttered so low that Frank Riddle leaned in closer to hear them.

"Give us the chance other men have to provide for their families."

Meacham shook his head. "I cannot talk about Lost River. That is in Oregon where some of your warriors murdered innocent settlers. That means there will always be bad blood between you and the white man in that country."

There. That was it, Jack decided. Yes—what the old white man said was true. There would always be much bad blood now that Curly Headed Doctor and Hooker Jim had murdered the white men. He sighed, capping his knees with his small hands.

"All right. Give my people this place. These black rocks for our new home."

"The Lava Beds?"

"I can live here and raise my families. Take the soldiers far from here. I will make this my home, Mee-Cham." He watched the white man's face drain of what he thought had been hope.

"We cannot allow you to stay in these rocks unless you

give up the murderers, Jack. They will have their say in our court of law."

Jack wanted to laugh, the pain was so big inside him. "Have their say? You white men have no right to judge a Modoc."

"It is our system of justice."

Riddle had a hard time finding words to explain that, while Jack hung on every word.

Then the chief spoke again after some thought. "So give us the civilians and soldiers who killed the women and children on Lost River many moons ago."

Meacham wagged his head. "I cannot do that. Your law is dead. White law is the only law that can live in this land now. There cannot be two laws living side by side in peace. Only one, Jack."

Perhaps another way would win a concession from this peace man, Jack thought. "Then you try those white men for murdering my people—under your white man's law, Mee-Cham."

"I cannot do that."

Jack was wringing the thick wool of his army britches in his hands. "Then the white man's law is a fool's law. If it is only for the white man—and cannot bring justice for the Modocs. If so, it is for fools to believe in."

"You are being unfair—"

Jack stood. "My people did not start this war. The soldiers and the other white men came and started it. The white man shot first. No, I shout! I will not give my young warriors over to your white man's law. Take the soldiers away and we will have peace."

Meacham rose too. Fairchild and the Riddles with him, all sensing the conference coming to a dark conclusion. "I cannot tell the soldiers to leave. They have their orders to stay until your people have left the Lava Beds."

As Meacham turned slightly to go, Jack lunged and grabbed the commissioner's arm, his voice cracking as he implored the old man.

"Tell me what to do, Mee-Cham! What path am I to walk now? I do not want this fight."

Meacham put his hand over the Modoc's hand locked on his arm so tightly. "The only way we will not have a fight is for your people to come out of the rocks."

Jack yanked his hand away, straightening. "I cannot come out and turn myself over to you. I am afraid—" But then he realized he did not want to say that. "No! I am not afraid—my people are afraid of what your soldiers will do to them . . . and I speak the heart of my people. I am their tongue—the voice of my people. Go tell that soldier chief I am not afraid to die. Tell this soldier chief in his fancy blue coat that I will show him how a brave Modoc dies."

"Come, Jack—back to the soldier camp with me so you can tell General Canby your words for yourself. We can talk more there."

"We are done talking now," Jack said quietly, sensing with his failure that the power of the shaman was growing all the more stronger than his own. "I must talk to my head men. We will decide if we will come here to this tent to speak to you anymore."

He watched the white men and his niece Winema Riddle mount. Then he strode to Meacham's stirrup.

"Tell the soldier chief that if he does not take his soldiers far from my women and children—I will show him how bravely a Modoc chief dies."

Chapter 17

Shining Leaf Moon

*W*hat the white peace talkers did not realize—what the soldier-chief failed to understand—was that by pressing his soldiers in on both sides of the Modoc Stronghold, the white men were making things tougher on Captain Jack.

If they only knew how dangerous things were growing between Jack and Curly Headed Doctor. As the soldiers moved closer and closer, flashing their mirror signals and waving their flags over the Stronghold every day—the shaman and his hotblooded warriors grew more angry, their tempers flaring and their actions unpredictable.

And now Boston Charley had just returned from the white man's camp with news that the soldiers were expecting some mercenaries in a matter of days—Tenino Indians being brought down from the Warm Springs Reservation in Oregon to fight the Modocs on their own terms.

No longer did things look bright, beckoning up that road toward peace. Now Jack prayed he would not be forced to walk the other path.

Earlier that day at the tent as he had watched the four riders disappear toward the soldier camp on the west, Jack had fully realized he was drained of much of his hope. His words spoken to the old white man in parting had said as much. His people had no chance of surviving this standoff with the white man. Sooner or later they would run out of food, or water, or ammunition for their captured weapons.

Why was it, Jack had been wondering as the sun sank that day, that the white men could not read in his words, see in his eyes, that he desperately wanted to make peace if the terms of peace were fair to his people?

But there was a great racket from the other forces in this camp among the cold, black rocks. No man boasted of his own power more than did the Curly Headed Doctor. His red medicine rope had kept the soldiers out of their rocky Stronghold. But more than that, the shaman now claimed he alone had kept his people free from the white man for years.

"Is there a man among us tonight who refuses to see that we have not been a slave to the ways of the white man for many winters?"

Hooker Jim and Bogus Charley hollered their agreement with the shaman, leading a chorus of the Doctor's supporters that echoed from the rain-slicked rocks encircling the central cavern.

"Ho! And is there one among you," the Doctor went on, glaring now at Captain Jack, "who will say that it was not my power to keep these talks with the white man from making any progress?"

"We do not want peace at the white man's terms!" Hooker Jim shouted.

"Let it be war! Let your medicine lead us!" others yelled.

Jack listened to the words, watched the faces screwed in anger—knowing more and more of his band were desiring war. They did not want to give in now that their strength had shown itself time after time.

But there was a quiet voice that rose among the tumult. "You do wrong to talk about our chief not wanting war when what he wants to do is protect the lives of our women, lives of our old ones and babies," spoke William Faithful, a young warrior. "We must not dwell on war— let us wait for the white man to give us back Lost River."

"Yes!" hissed the Doctor, quickly turning to regain control of the crowd. "But at the same time the white man waits for us to shrivel up and die in here. He sits out there with his army on both sides of us. This will not do! How can we drive the white man out of our land forever if we do not have a war? And how can we get the soldiers to fight us when he will not come in among these rocks to fight our powerful warriors? There is one choice only— we must start the war ourselves!"

"Tell us when we can attack, holy one!"

The Doctor shook his hands high. "No—we will not attack. They are too many."

"What—we cannot cower in here like frightened geese!" Hooker Jim protested, grabbing his father-in-law's coat.

"Yes, yes!" the shaman replied. "They must come in here to get at us!"

"But the soldiers cower in their camps."

The shaman turned on Boston Charley. "You are right —so we must get the soldiers to come in after us."

"How? Tell us how."

He whirled again, his face contorted in primal pleasure. They were in the palms of his hands. "We will kill the peace talkers!"

Jack stood, suddenly frightened. *"No!"*

Curly Headed Doctor leaped for him, stopping when his toes touched the chief's. *"Yes!* Kill them—butcher them—as the soldier guards watch from their camps! It will show the white man my medicine is strongest."

"The soldiers will come attack us!" Boston Charley shouted.

"We will wipe them out like before—send the rest running home far from here!" agreed Hooker Jim.

"Those men come to talk with us in peace!" Jack shrieked, growing more frightened as the firelight reflected from the angry faces in a noose tightening about him. "Your blood is hot as fire now—let us speak of this matter another—"

"The peace talkers want us to give ourselves up!" Hooker Jim screamed. "We will not be hanged by the white man."

As well as any man could, Jack knew how terrible a death it was—this hanging. A man's spirit could not fly from his mouth when he died. Both body and soul suffered death.

He wagged his head, reluctantly. "No—I cannot give you over to be hanged by the white man."

The Doctor waved his arms dramatically. "And when our people surrender, walking from these rocks—won't the soldiers shoot down our women and children?"

"I cannot say—I can only trust Fairchild and O'Roarke . . . perhaps too the old white man, Mee-Cham—"

"Stop!" yelled the shaman. "The time for talk is over." He waved an arm, signaling his son-in-law forward.

Hooker Jim confronted the older Captain Jack as if what the twenty-two-year-old warrior had to say had already been planned. "I can see you no longer have the heart to be chief of the Modocs. You are a squaw!"

Jack felt the hot breath flung in his face by his antagonist. "I am no squaw."

There was cackling laughter, led by the shaman, echoed from the black rocks surrounding their firelit council.

"Old squaw!" Hooker Jim continued. "You have done no fighting yet—and a chief is supposed to lead his men in fighting. I think you are no longer fit to be our chief!"

"I am your chief—and I have others to worry over in my heart. The little ones, the sick—"

"A chief leads his men into battle."

Jack patted the butt of an old pistol he carried in his belt. "If the soldiers come, I will fight."

Ellen's Man George pushed forward. "What do you need a gun for, Jack?" he sneered, showing the gaps in his teeth. "You don't fight. You don't shoot white men with it. Here—give it to me. I will do the job of a chief with your gun. I will kill the chief of the white peace talkers— with your gun I will kill their tyee—since you don't have the stomach for it!"

The wild, mocking laughter rang in Jack's ears, making them hot with the pounding of his blood.

"Kientpoos must quit sitting here on these rocks, waiting for our people to run out of food," the shaman urged, moving back up. "Fight with us, Jack—or get out of our way and stay with the women."

"Wait!" yelled Scar-Faced Charley.

For a moment Jack clung to hope that this talk of killing the white men would end. Charley was his oldest and most reliable supporter. A strong fighter with a quick mind. He would settle things now . . .

Charley stepped up to Jack, placing a hand on the chief's shoulder. He spoke quietly. "There is the time for talking, my friend. And the time for fighting. No more talking. This is the time for making war."

"What of the others—the children, our old ones?"

"Perhaps your heart has grown weak, Jack," Charley went on. "Perhaps you do have the heart of an old squaw."

No man's words could have stung more than did Charley's at that moment. "You are . . . are going with Hooker Jim?"

Charley nodded, smiling, his eyes firelit. "Yes. I will go in your place—and help kill the peace talkers since you do not have the stomach for it."

"You are my old friend. How can you ask me to kill the soldier tyee? To shoot him when we are talking of peace would be the act of a coward!"

"No," shouted Scar-Faced Charley. "We are asking you to do a brave thing."

"I cannot kill the soldier tyee!" Jack shrieked.

"Here!" announced Bogus Charley, pushing through the crowd.

Jack saw the warrior carried a woman's woven dress.

"Give that to me!" cried Hooker Jim. "I will put it on the old squaw with no warrior's heart."

Hooker Jim knelt to lap the woven reed dress around Captain Jack's waist. As he was done tying it, Jack's shoulders sank at the humiliation.

"Jack has a heart like a little bird!" a female voice cried out, flinging a woman's shawl over the heads of the crowd. "He must wear a squaw's clothing."

"You must wear this too—if you are going to have the heart of a squaw," said Scar-Faced Charley as he turned back from one of the women with a squaw's tule-reed hat in his hand. This he jammed atop the chief's bowed head.

The laughter grew louder, accompanied by shrieks of derision from the women, who no longer hid their sneers behind their hands. He was mocked, standing before his people totally shamed as they backed off—pointing, doubling over in laughter, dancing around him and gyrating their hips like men who wanted badly to rut with a woman.

In anger that boiled over like a cauldron too long left untended, Jack flung a flat hand out, smacking one of the young warriors across the jaw. His other hand flew upward like a mighty bird taking wing—another warrior stumbled backward into the noisy crowd, crying out in pain.

For the space of two heartbeats, the warriors surged forward, hands before them like the claws of angry beasts. But with a look into the eyes of their long-silent chief, they held. Stopped. And reconsidered.

This was unlike any look they had ever seen on Captain Jack's face.

He flung the squaw's cap back into Hooker Jim's sneering smile. Jim wiped the sting away yet did not move to provoke his chief.

Jack tore the tule-reed dress from his waist, held it before him as he ripped it asunder. Eyes wild with the terror of his own long-pent emotions, Captain Jack flung shards of the garment over the crowd.

"If there is a man among you strong enough to step before their chief and call him squaw—let him show his face now!"

Slowly he turned, watching their eyes fall, watching many of the younger warriors shuffle backward a step. The immense quiet that fell over that cavern in those brutal black rocks was now matched by only the black, pin-pricked sky overhead as the chief hissed his vow.

"Kientpoos—chief of the Modocs—will prove to you I am no squaw. In my heart I know we will kill some white men—but they will kill *all* of us."

He stepped up to the shaman and Hooker Jim, throwing down the woman's shawl at their feet. "You tell me you want war. We will have war!" He pounded his chest once with a fist, then held the same hand high, brandishing his pistol.

"Remember my words for all time—Captain Jack will no longer be the one who asks for peace!"

For two nights Jack kept to his cold, damp cave. Refusing food. Taking only water. Unable to sleep.

Worrying how this bloody task could be taken from him.

Now that Scar-Faced Charley had crossed over to join the shaman in calling for the murder of the peace talkers, Jack was left with few allies. One of the most stalwart was William Faithful—young, but never lacking in courage.

"You asked me to come?" William said, squatting beside his chief.

"Go to every cave, every fire. Tell them I wish to speak."

Without a word William rose and left to spread the news. In a matter of moments the Modocs of the Lava Beds had gathered, silently awaiting the speech of their chief.

He strode into their midst, then stopped before Hooker

Jim's most hardened murderers. With his arms crossed haughtily, Jack glared at them each in turn. Not a one met and held his gaze.

"My heart tells me I am among strangers now. I thought I was chief of a brave people. But it is a coward's errand you send me on, to murder the soldier tyee."

Jack watched the Doctor shift as if ready to rise, intending on interrupting. He waved the shaman down with a stiff arm.

"Do not make me commit this treacherous act—take it from me, I beg you!"

His fervent plea surprised the assembly. Especially those who stood closest and could see the mist gathering in the chief's eyes.

"A chief does not beg!" shouted the Doctor.

Jack turned on him. "Yes—I beg you. Do not hold me to that promise to kill the soldier tyee."

"Yes—you will kill him!" Hooker Jim shouted.

He whirled on the young warrior. "You make me do this—our people stand at the edge of our graves!"

"You gave us your word!" said Scar-Faced Charley.

"I spoke when my blood was hot," Jack replied, his hands imploring the warriors. He straightened slightly. "I will ask you all again—those who would have me kill the soldier tyee, stand with Curly Headed Doctor. And those who believe to do such a thing would be the act of a coward—stand behind me."

There was a loud shuffling of bodies. But the movement did not take long. In a matter of seconds the warriors who stood behind Captain Jack numbered only what he could count on two hands.

The rest stood glaring with wicked smiles behind the hate-crazed shaman.

Jack shuddered with the revulsion it gave him to see those faces. "You force me to kill the soldier chief?"

"Or you are not our chief."

His mind awhirl, swimming against the black, ugly tide

of cruel things awash against his soul, Jack fought for his breath, his heart thundering in his ears.

He licked his lips, then gazed back into some of the faces leering in the firelight around him.

"It is decided. I will kill Canby."

Celebration erupted: shouting, pounding backs, women trilling their tongues in joy.

Holding up his hands, Jack eventually gained their silence one last time. "I have said it—I will keep my vow. But first I will ask the soldier chief to give us our homes back on Lost River."

"If he says yes—that we can live again on our old homeland?" asked the Doctor.

"Then his life will be spared."

Hooker Jim inched forward. "And if the soldier tyee says no?"

Jack pulled the pistol from his belt—and stuffed the muzzle into Jim's belly. "Then—I will kill him."

The warrior glanced down at the pistol. And smiled. "That means that the rest of the white peace talkers must die as well."

"I do not care," Jack replied. "I have vowed to kill the one called Canby."

In a furious burst of crazed bravado, many of the warriors argued over who would have the honor of killing the others when the time came.

"We can kill the white men when they come to talk peace," said Curly Headed Doctor. "All of them!"

Chapter 18

April 8–10, 1873

"*I* am convinced that Jack truly desires peace," said Alfred B. Meacham as he sank on the canvas camp stool inside General Canby's Sibley tent, which served as commission headquarters at Colonel Gillem's camp.

Seamus watched the rotund Reverend Thomas lean back and lock his fingers together across his ample belly.

"They're beginning to see the light, I take it. Praise God!"

"Not so fast," John Fairchild added hastily. "Jack's fighting the tide."

"Like salmon swimming upstream to spawn," Ian O'Roarke muttered.

"Only natural," Seamus finally said. "The ones holding out for war are the ones with nothing to lose."

"Murderers," hissed agent L. S. Dyar. "Cold-blooded murderers."

"But I saw some hope when Jack finally showed he wasn't dead-set on having his Lost River reservation," O'Roarke added.

Meacham nodded. "Perhaps some hope there, yes."

"His people will never let you move them out of this part of the country," O'Roarke reminded them.

"Jack's in a dilemma," the reverend said, drumming

his fingers across his vest buttons. "The devil's at work among that shaman's warriors. I trust God Himself will be at work on Jack's side."

O'Roarke snorted. "God, Reverend Thomas? Aren't you preachers all alike now? God, you say? Why, God hasn't been in those Lava Beds all winter—and I don't see any sign He's about to go walking in there now."

"I beg your pardon—"

O'Roarke started to rise as Thomas pushed himself up from his stool. Donegan was there with his uncle, already restraining him.

"Excuse me, gentlemen," O'Roarke apologized, sitting back down. "I did not realize the reverend here was under the influence of his own foolish gruel."

"I'll have you know—"

"Reverend, please take your seat," Meacham instructed. "Yours too, Mr. Donegan."

"What about this plan of yours you mentioned a few minutes ago?" Dyar asked.

"Yes—tell me what you think of it," Meacham replied. "Offering the Modocs a chance to send out every woman, child and man who do not want to fight, before Canby moves his forces in for the kill."

"Yes, a grand idea to save the innocent," Thomas added.

O'Roarke shook his head, looking at Fairchild. "I think John agrees with me that it's a good idea that won't work. The warriors won't let the women and children out where they can't protect them from the soldiers."

"And the women simply won't leave their men behind," Fairchild said.

"A depressing alternative, I assure you, gentlemen."

They all turned to find General Canby pushing through the tent flaps, accompanied only by his orderly, Private Scott. The officer settled atop a case of hardtack and removed his dripping hat.

"I've just come from an informal round-table with my officers."

"Any new ideas?" Meacham asked, drawing a black cheroot from a vest pocket.

Canby was a few moments in replying. "In fact, there was a new idea."

Thomas inched forward on his stool. "Tell us, General."

"The officers asked me to come to you—the peace commission—with a proposal of sorts."

"What sort of proposal?" Dyar inquired.

"To have you gentlemen suspend your talks while my soldiers have a good crack at the Modocs."

Meacham straightened like a shot. Thomas gasped. And Dyar dropped his head into his hands.

"No—not when we're just making some movement with Jack on this matter of Lost River."

"Besides, General," Seamus said, snagging Canby's attention and pointing at Meacham, "at what cost to your men would you want to destroy the negotiations of this man?"

"Some of my line officers are ready to put money on it that they can whip those fifty or sixty warriors inside of minutes."

Donegan shook his head. "I'd wager meself that those officers who wish to be soon parted from their money were not here last January seventeenth."

Canby nodded, grudgingly. "Don't let word of this spread, gentlemen—but the past few mornings we've noticed an increase in desertions on morning report."

"Desertions?" O'Roarke asked.

"Yes," replied Seamus. "I'll wager you'll find the greatest number of desertions among those who fought the Modocs last January . . . and don't want to again."

"You're right, Mr. Donegan," Canby replied.

"With all this talk of going back to war with the Modocs—they're the ones remember best what kind of hell this war with the Modocs really is," Seamus added.

"Appears Jack's warriors are ready to make a fight of it again," Meacham said. "When sentries spotted some two-dozen Modocs hiding in the trees near the council tent this afternoon—I called off the conference."

"Didn't like the smell of that one," Fairchild said.

"Something's going on up there," Dyar added.

Meacham rose, stretching. "As head of the delegation, I want your approval on something. One last time—I want to offer Jack's people a chance to walk out of the Lava Beds without harm—before the general's troops are turned loose. Do I have your agreement to make that offer?"

"Here, here," Thomas seconded loudly.

"Any dissent?" Meacham waited. "Good. I'll send Toby Riddle to Jack's stronghold tomorrow with our final offer of safety for those who want out before the killing starts."

"Take him from here, Frank," begged Winema Riddle, her head bowed as she sat atop a soldier horse the following day, 9 April.

"His heart aches as much as mine," Frank replied as he stood beside her stirrup. He had one hand touching his Modoc wife, the other arm clutched around their sobbing twelve-year-old son.

"I will return to you both," Winema said, barely getting the words out as she reined away.

Behind her she heard the renewed wails of grief and anxiety as her only child howled. She knew Frank was having to restrain him, from the sound of the scuffle. Soldiers silently parted for her, others rose from their smoky mess-fires as she plodded by. Most of them took their hats from their heads in a sign of respect for her and the mission she had undertaken.

Winema straightened. Not only was she different from other Modoc women and therefore deserving of respect—but Toby Riddle was doing this brave thing. Called on by Meacham to carry an important message to her uncle, Kientpoos. Captain Jack of the Modocs in the Lava Beds.

It did not take that many minutes for her to pass

through the council meadow and cover the last two miles to the edge of the Stronghold where the first warriors appeared from the rocks.

"I come with a message from the white men for the ears of Captain Jack."

Without ceremony she was once more escorted to the heart of the Stronghold, where many warriors sat about cleaning and oiling their rifles. She did not find Jack among them. Dismounting, she handed the reins to William Faithful and climbed through the rocks to her uncle's cave.

"If you have important news," Jack announced, "we must tell it to all our people. Come—we will call everyone together."

When everyone had taken their seats in blankets and quieted the children, Winema explained, "The white men are offering safety to all those who will come out of the rocks now—before the fighting starts. They will be given a reservation of their own, far from the Klamath land."

For a moment there was some silence. Then Curly Headed Doctor started to hoot rudely. If the message bearer had been a man, he would be soundly shamed. But this was a woman, niece of the chief. Still, she suffered through a growing clamor of derision.

Jack quieted the noisy throng. "Let us vote. Those warriors who would accept the white man's offer of safety for our women and children—let them line up with me here."

A slow, deliberate shifting as first a few, then a handful, then eleven men jostled their way out of the crowd.

Winema watched Jack's shoulders sag when it grew painfully clear no more were rising to stand with him.

This time Hooker Jim began the crazed hooting, followed by more jeering laughter from the thirty-eight other warriors who wanted nothing of the white man's offer.

Jack turned to Winema. "My people have decided. They will not leave this place for their own safety."

Schonchin John suddenly surged forward, stopping before Winema, his eyes angry and glazed with hate. "Take the white man our message now," he spat like an angry cat. "Tell him that we are going to kill any Modoc who attempts to leave our Stronghold. No Modoc will give himself up and live."

She read the moistness in her uncle's eyes as he blinked the tears back. "I have heard your warriors speak," she said, turning to go.

Jack caught her arm. "Tell them . . . tell Mee-Cham that we are ready for war—ready to fight. But tell them Jack will not fire the first bullet."

"I go, Uncle. But my prayers stay here with you."

A teenage boy appeared from the crowd with her soldier horse.

Winema grew worried. "Where is William Faithful?" she asked.

"He asked me to bring you the horse. That is all I know." The youth cupped his hands and helped her aboard the animal where she spread her skirt.

Winema reined away, heading into the maze of pathways—fissures and crevices—that would take her back to the soldier camp.

She had not come much more than a half-mile from the center of the Stronghold when a voice whispered to her from a thick tangle of brush.

"Do not look my way when you stop your horse."

She appeared confused, frightened, gazing into the bushes.

"We will both be killed if you let them know I am here —talking to you."

She thought she recognized William Faithful's voice, but could not be sure, as it was spoken so softly.

"Get off the horse and adjust the stirrups while I talk to you," the voice instructed. "Those who are watching you must not be made suspicious."

Winema dropped to the ground and slowly, deliberately circled to the off side, where she began adjusting stirrups lazily.

"I come to warn you, Winema," the voice hissed in a harsh, frightened whisper. "They mean to kill the peace talkers when next they come to the tent. Everyone."

She froze, frightened, her heart caught in her throat. Then started to turn.

"Don't look at me hiding here! I am your friend. You warn your friends not to come to the tent anymore. Perhaps even your own life is doomed if you come with them. All will be killed!"

There was a sudden rustle in the brush and then all was silent. The voice was gone.

With her heart still in her mouth and her blood pumping hot in her ears, she slowly mounted, her eyes searching for any warriors who might kill her now if they knew she had learned of their deadly plot.

Talking to herself, lips slowly moving, Winema Riddle convinced her shaking hands to grip the reins tightly, nudging her heels against the mare's flanks. Slowly, ever so slowly plodding back to the white man's camp.

Where she would embrace her husband and son as she had never embraced them before.

It was plain to Meacham that Winema Riddle was spooked when she came tearing into the soldier camp, galloping the last half-mile or so as if the devil himself were right behind her.

Strange too that she refused to talk to Meacham, but dismounted only when she had arrived in front of her tent, where Frank Riddle appeared with their son. Frank helped his wife down, then clutched her to him. On her toes, Toby Riddle whispered something in Frank's ear. He drew back, his face gone white and drawn. She nodded.

And Frank motioned for her to go into their tent with the boy.

Meacham strode over as Winema disappeared behind the tent flaps. "Something's wrong, Frank. I need to know. Was Toby hurt?"

Frank turned on him with a look on his face Meacham had never seen worn by Riddle.

"I'll tell you in private."

Meacham yanked Riddle into a nearby tent they found empty. "Tell me."

"She won't dare tell anyone but me, Meacham."

"What is it?"

"You'll all be killed!"

Meacham choked on it, believing the warning instantly. "How? When and where?"

"At the tent—the next time they come there to talk with you."

The old man shook his head in disbelief. "Surely . . . they wouldn't try something so bold—"

"You don't believe Toby?"

He nodded. "I believe her, I do. Let's call the others together. She can tell them herself."

"If anyone finds out she talked to you—my wife is dead."

"We'll swear every man—"

"No, you can't. We know you. Toby trusts you. These others are strangers to us."

He grasped Frank's shoulders firmly. "Quiet—it will be safe with us. We'll swear each man to secrecy."

Which is what Meacham did when he had the other three men in the Riddles' tent.

"While I do not consider this woman a liar," General Canby began, "I can't put much stock in this plot to kill us. They simply wouldn't dare!"

"I quite agree with the general here," Reverend Thomas said. "What wicked evil is at work among those savages! Praise be, the power of God will be like a mantle for us all. The Modocs will have no chance to kill us while we carry forward the sword of God's power like Christian soldiers."

Staring at Dyar's fear-taut face, Meacham replied, "God will not watch over us if we don't watch over ourselves."

"Damn right," Frank Riddle replied, embracing his shaken wife. "I may not be as smart as any of you. But I do know the Modocs. And if they say they'll kill us—they will do it."

The general cleared his throat self-consciously in the silence that followed Riddle's warning. "We'll see what the morrow brings," Canby suggested. "For now, I cannot worry about some rumor the Modocs wanted brought back here to stir us up. Good evening, gentlemen."

While Meacham and the others were beginning their breakfast the next morning, a delegation of three Modoc warriors approached, escorted by armed soldiers.

"These Indians say they want to talk to Meacham," a young sergeant announced.

Bogus Charley nodded, smiling with that winning grin of his. "Mee-Cham. Yes, Mee-Cham. Good!"

After Riddle arrived to interpret, the rest of the civilian commissioners sat across from Bogus and Boston Charley, as well as Shacknasty Jim, all three of whom eyed the bacon sizzling in the cast-iron skillet over greasewood flames.

"You'll get some to eat, all right," Meacham said. "When it's cooked and when I'm ready to feed you. So, tell me what you come here for."

"Captain Jack wants to meet with you," Boston Charley announced in his halting English. His eyes bounced over the group, scanning the nearby soldier camp. "Where is the old man, soldier tyee?"

Something crawled up Meacham's spine, like January ice water. "He stays with the soldiers."

"He will come to meet with Jack too?" Shacknasty Jim asked.

"Yes, if we have something important to talk about, he will come."

The three heads bobbed eagerly. "Good things to talk about. Jack says come talk with him. Much important talk now."

"You can tell the soldier chief yourself," Meacham replied. "He's coming over now."

Canby strode up purposefully, his eyes darting over the three gape-mouthed prisoners. "What are these Modocs doing here now?"

"They bring us word from Jack," Meacham answered. "Wants to parley at the tent."

Canby nodded. "Odd, isn't it? I just got a message from our lookout tower. They've spotted a half-dozen armed warriors already at the tent. Armed, mind you. And two dozen more with rifles lurking in the brush and rocks a few yards off."

Meacham stood slowly, the look on Winema's face yesterday now plain once more by this morning fire. He stood before Boston Charley, held out his hand and dragged the Modoc up while shaking. "We are not ready to talk yet. Perhaps soon. But not yet."

The Modocs listened to Riddle's translation, then dove into a confused discourse that offered every reward should the white men come now to make peace talk at the council tent. It only served to make Meacham all the more anxious.

For the entire time, Reverend Thomas had been silent —watching only as the noise of the discussion grew around him. He finally stood, tugging at the points of his woolen vest, then stopped self-assuredly right before Bogus Charley.

"My son," Thomas began in that stentorian tone of his usually saved for the pulpit, "why would you and the others want to kill us? We are here to help you and your people. We come as your friends and benefactors—to make peace in this country for all time."

Meacham watched the impish light in Bogus Charley's eyes change to a flinty glare as Riddle translated.

"How you say we going to kill you?" he spoke in his own rough English. "Who tell you we kill white peace talkers?"

Meacham shook his head when Thomas glanced at him for support.

"I cannot lie to a man—not even an Indian," Thomas said, proud of himself despite stepping on his own tongue. He turned back to Bogus Charley. "It was Toby Riddle."

Charley glared at them. "She lies to you!"

"There," Thomas replied smugly as he turned back to the other white men. "I knew there was no real cause for alarm. She must have misunderstood something Jack said."

Frank Riddle was already moving away from the fire, anger etching his face, pounding one fist into the palm of his other hand as he cursed preachers and peace talkers.

Meacham turned back to find the three Modocs suddenly starting off in the opposite direction. At the edge of the soldier camp the trio began to walk faster, until they were loping across the broken country, headed for the council meadow.

Chapter 19

April 10–11, 1873

She did not know why she was going back to this den of death.

But here she was, inching her soldier horse back through the maze of slippery, black rock. Heading for Captain Jack's Stronghold behind a stone-faced Hooker Jim.

This morning, less than two hours after Bogus Charley and the other two had learned that Winema Riddle knew of the plot to kill the peace commissioners, Hooker Jim had arrived in the soldier camp. Unannounced, and surprising everyone, he had poked his face next to Winema's while she sat among the peace talkers and a handful of other white men.

"Jack wants to talk to you," Hooker Jim declared in Modoc.

Beside her, Frank Riddle began to rise. She placed a hand on his thigh, urging him to sit.

"What . . ." she said, swallowing hard, "what does Jack want to talk to me about?"

Hooker Jim shook his head, showing his brown teeth through his strained smile. "He wants to see you at his cave."

She glanced at her husband, now noticing the other white men studying her and Hooker Jim.

"Now—Winema." The Modoc's words were terse.

"What is this about?" Meacham asked, coming over quickly.

Hooker Jim straightened, his hands flexing. His eyes met Frank Riddle's for a moment. "Tell the old man this has nothing to do with him."

"It has everything to do with me," Meacham stated. "Tell this one I can have him thrown in irons here and now for harassing this woman. I'll have him held as my prisoner."

Hooker Jim licked his lips, smiling, drawing his lips back over his teeth, which reminded Toby of the color of pinewood chips flying from the blade of the axe when she had helped Frank build their cabin years before.

Finally the Modoc sputtered his answer, somewhat cowed by the white men who had risen to impress the warrior.

"Jack wants to know why his niece tells lies about him."

"How do I know you are not lying?" Meacham replied.

Hooker Jim pointed at the woman. "She tells lies! We do not plan to kill you!"

Toby wanted to cry, looking at the face of Meacham as he stood there. She could tell he did not believe a single one of Hooker Jim's protests.

"If Captain Jack wants peace—if he truly wants us to believe you and he are not lying," Meacham said, grabbing Hooker Jim's sleeve for emphasis, "then you go now and tell Captain Jack to come *here* to talk."

With a sneer, the Modoc yanked his arm from the white man's grip. "Modoc won't do what white man says no more. Modoc is not your dog. Woman lie about our chief. She come and face her people."

"She ain't going anywhere with you, Hooker," Frank Riddle said quietly.

"Winema is Modoc. She does not belong to you white men. She Modoc."

"She's not going anywhere," Riddle said in Modoc.

"I won't leave without her," the warrior hissed between his thin lips.

They stood glaring at one another, hands flexing, perhaps ready to pull a knife or pistol. She saw the same look darken Frank's eyes as she read in Hooker Jim's. At last Toby laid a hand against her husband's arm.

"This is important, my husband. I will go—to help make peace between our peoples." Toby spoke in English. She gripped his wrist tightly.

He gazed down at her. "They will kill you."

She bit her lip. "Perhaps. But I took that chance when I rode in there alone yesterday."

"That was different—they are angry with you now," he pleaded. "They might even kill you for betraying their secret."

She shook her head, sensing at last her own resolve beginning to glow like a valiant candle flame fighting a windswept gale. The look in Frank's eyes made it hard to pull away.

Toby turned to Hooker Jim. "I go. Because I am Modoc, I am brave as any warrior. I go with you now."

From time to time throughout the three-mile trip, Hooker Jim had glanced back at Winema and smiled that crooked, wicked smile of his between those two thin lips. And each time he gazed back at her, Toby vowed not to let him see her crying. She jut out her chin, blinked her eyes clear and held herself erect atop Frank's saddle. She was Modoc.

Yet she had never felt so alone, so much a stranger, as she did when she reined up within the heart of the Stronghold itself.

They inched forward, like coiling snakes, each of those warriors. Behind them the women and old people. Their faces each bore the same unmasked hatred for what they saw as her betrayal of her people.

Reluctantly she slid from the saddle, refusing to release the rein, as if it were her last remaining link with her husband's people, with their life together, her only link with life itself at this terrible moment—as first one, then a handful, and finally all of the Modocs closed in about her and began to fling their venomous words at her.

As suddenly as they had started to defile her, calling Winema the most vile of names, the Modoc men and women fell silent. Then slowly parted.

Before her stood her uncle by birth. Captain Jack. Chief Kientpoos of the renegade Modocs.

He strode up to her dramatically, then took his time circling her, appraising her up and down—as if stripping her of all self-respect here before her own people. Then he stopped and spoke.

"Why did you tell the peace talkers we are going to kill them?"

She started to choke, sensing the bile at her throat. "It —It is true, Kientpoos? You have murder even in your heart?"

"What right do you have to judge?" he shouted into her face. "You are no longer Modoc! You have a white heart. No Modoc blood flows in your veins!"

The words stung, but no more than the horror she felt as the crowd jostled and surged around her, yelling their profane oaths at her.

"I am Modoc," she replied quietly, raising her head high. "I tell the peace talkers because I do not want to see the little ones, the old ones, the ones so ill they cannot fight—I do not want to see them killed when the soldiers charge in here. And they will come, Kientpoos."

Jack was shaking, his hand trembling terribly with undisguised rage as he raised it to strike her. But as she stood there, not shrinking from the blow, not flinching in the slightest, he stayed his hand.

"Who told you we plan to kill them? Who!"

"I know it is true in my heart, Kientpoos. I have eyes— I can see when I come here that your heart has become bad toward the peace talkers. I have ears—I can hear for myself—"

"No!" shrieked Curly Headed Doctor. "Who told you? One of these warriors—who?"

Winema looked back and forth between the two men: Jack and the shaman. Here at last she was totally certain. The two of them allied in this terrible act. "My dream spirits tell me you kill them—"

Jack grabbed the front of her coat angrily, his other arm shoving the shaman back. "No dream spirits come to you—tell you of this! A man—one of these men here—tell you. *Who!*"

"I know in my heart—"

He yanked her about by her coat again. "You tell me, *now,* or these men kill you, Winema!"

She watched the rifle and pistol muzzles come up to stare at her with cold eyes. Then she swallowed, certain of her own death coming. And with one swipe of her forearm, bravely knocked Jack's grip from her coat.

In a fury that she knew would be her dying moment, Winema flung the rein aside and hurled herself into the crowd, pushing the shocked men and women aside. She reached the low outcrop of black rock that overlooked the main gathering area of the Stronghold, where the war councils were held.

There on high she stood, turning herself toward them, tearing open her coat. "Here beats the heart of a Modoc. Brave and strong. If you must kill me—then do it now, you yellow-spined *cowards!*"

There was a loud rattling of hammers as guns were leveled and men jostled below her. Jack and the shaman surged through the crowd toward the outcropping.

"Shoot me—Kientpoos—you frightened dog! You are right. No dream spirits told me. Yes—one of your warriors told me of your treachery. He looks upon me with his eyes now."

She watched the warriors glance at one another suspiciously.

"But I will not speak his name. I will never betray him
—because my heart is Modoc."

"You have a white squaw's heart!" yelled the Doctor.

Winema wheeled on him. "I am brave enough to die
here—now. You are so brave to kill an unarmed woman!
Is your medicine so weak that you cannot face an armed
warrior, shaman?"

"I curse you—"

"Kill a brave woman if you dare, cowards! But do not
kill the four white men who come among you to make
peace."

One by one the muzzles of those pistols and rifles fell
away. Hatred on those faces now replaced by something
close to grudging admiration. She turned to her uncle.

"You, Kientpoos? Will you kill a brave woman?"

Finally he shook his head. "No—no man will kill you.
Not today. Not any day. Your heart is as brave as any
warrior's." He turned back to the crowd. "Help this
woman who is possessed with a strong spirit down from
the rock."

A half-dozen warriors shoved forward as the crowd
surged back, among them her informer. For an instant
their eyes met in that noisy throng. Winema read gratitude written in his, there among the mist that moistened
his admiration of her courage.

"Accompany this woman back to her husband in the
white soldiers' camp," Jack ordered. "Let no one do her
harm!"

"She told them of our plan!" shrieked the shaman.

Jack whirled, grabbing the front of the Doctor's shirt in
both hands, shaking the older man in rage. "Today this
woman did a brave thing. With my own bare hands, I will
kill the man who harms Winema. You and your kind are
cowards. She is right, shaman. You have made me a coward with you. So understand my words I spit into your
face now: like her, I too am not afraid to die. But I will
take you with me, Doctor."

Jack hurled the shaman back against some of his supporters. "If any of your men lay one hand on my niece—with my dying breath, I will rip your heart out."

While Frank Riddle's Modoc wife was gone to the Stronghold, Seamus Donegan watched with growing alarm as two warriors expertly played on Reverend Thomas's most fervent hopes.

At the civilians' evening fire the Irishman listened while the preacher swallowed the Modocs' professions of a change of heart.

"We no longer have bad hearts for the white man," Bogus Charley said, waiting while John Fairchild interpreted.

"We want to live as God's children beside our friends—the white man," added Boston Charley.

"My sons," the reverend said, glowing in pride. He clamped hands on the warriors' shoulders. "God has truly performed a miracle among the Modocs. I must tell General Canby and Mr. Meacham of this immediately. We cannot betray this work of the Lord by carrying weapons into that meeting."

Seamus sloshed his coffee across the ground as he set his cup on a fallen log, heading to cut off the Methodist minister.

He put out a big hand and slowed Thomas to a crawl. "You surely aren't buying all that cock and bull, are you, Reverend?"

Thomas stopped, his face twisting. "How dare you speak to me of the Lord's business in that blasphemous tone, Irishman!"

Seamus felt the sting of the last word, spoken as if it were some profane oath of the devil himself. "They're lying to you."

"Unhand me, heathen."

Donegan took his hand off the man. "I'm no h'athen. Me mither always taught me to respect men of God. But you're something else, Thomas. You're a ruddy fool."

Thomas shoved an arm before him, pushing past Donegan. "Get thee behind me, Satan!"

He watched the minister go, and was standing there shaking his head when Fairchild came up on one side of him, Uncle Ian on the other.

"I always wonder why they called the Indians savages," Fairchild said. "Seems some of them Modocs are a bunch smarter than a lot of us, don't it?"

O'Roarke agreed. "He's the sort of small-minded Christian makes me think of the Inquisition. That preacher's got God and miracles on the brain—and nothing will keep him from convincing the others to go to their deaths . . . unarmed."

"We can't allow that," Seamus vowed in a whisper. "If Thomas's God wants him to go to that council with the Modocs unarmed—by the saints, *my* God has bound me to see the others are not so foolish."

Canby remained unswayed, believing with the fervent Thomas that the Modocs had undergone a change of heart.

"Despite what Toby has told you?" Meacham demanded of the soldier.

"Yes—she is Modoc. But perhaps she misunderstood something. My own instincts tell me to trust these Modocs. After all, Mr. Meacham—I've been dealing with Indians for over thirty years."

"You're going ahead with this meeting you've scheduled for tomorrow at noon?"

Canby nodded. "Yes. Good Friday, Mr. Meacham. Don't you agree it will be an auspicious day upon which to make peace with Captain Jack's people?"

Meacham wagged his head. "No peace meeting, General."

"But I quite agree with Reverend Thomas that God has wrought a miracle in that Stronghold. While I have slowly pressed in my army making for an ever-tightening noose about them, their own hunger and desperation has brought about their change of heart. God is to be praised—"

"Dammit!" Meacham cursed, flinging down his tin plate and standing. "God had nothing do with this—can't you see? God has been nowhere near the Lava Beds . . . and God most certainly will not be with us at that meeting tomorrow!"

That night, Bogus Charley slept in army blankets with the reverend's blessing, just outside Thomas's tent at the center of the soldier camp.

Not long after sunrise that Good Friday morning, 11 April, Boston Charley showed up as well, again professing that the Modocs were to surrender if a favorable home could be found for Jack's band of holdouts.

"That runt of a pie-faced one stayed with Thomas all night," Donegan whispered to his uncle as he soaked hardtack in his bitter coffee that clear morning. Out of the clear blue of a cloudless sky, a chill breeze rattled the restless canvas of nearby tents.

Ian nodded. "Aye. Bogus Charley doesn't want to see anything happen to their murderous scheme now."

"And the other one showed up to press the case," Seamus replied. "Look how he plays the part of the dutiful lap dog to the preacher."

Ian set his plate aside. "I've lost my appetite, nephew. Just look at that—Boston Charley: eating his breakfast off the preacher's plate now, drinking his morning coffee from the preacher's cup."

"Thomas really believes he has wrought his miracle with those two cutthroats—believing peace will be made on this holy day."

"Good Friday—the day long ago when Christ was crucified for our sins," Ian muttered, staring down into his coffee cup. "A day when Thomas will see the others butchered for his sin of pride."

Seamus drew the chill air of a spring morning deeply into his lungs. "Odd, isn't it, Ian—for it's the sort of

morning a man offers his thanksgiving for being alive."
He turned at the bustle of talk across the fire.

From bundles of brown waxed paper tied with manila
twine, Thomas pulled new clothes he had purchased from
the camp sutler, McManus, for his Modoc wards. Color-
ful cotton hickory shirts and woolen button-fly britches
were given both Bogus Charley and Boston Charley.

"He makes gifts to those bastards," Ian muttered as he
rose from his seat. "I can't take any more—watching this
. . . hearing those two butchers telling Thomas that the
fighting is over and that peace will be made with the white
man today."

"You're leaving, Mr. O'Roarke?" asked Canby as he
strode up with his orderly Scott.

"You have business with me, General?"

"Why, no. I'm here to dispatch these two Modocs to
their Stronghold with word to their chief."

Canby stepped away, around the fire, as O'Roarke
glanced at Donegan, deciding to stay.

"Mr. Fairchild—tell these two men to carry my message to Captain Jack," Canby began, accepting a cup of
coffee from Commissioner Dyar. "I will meet with his
men at the council tent—and no farther. At noon, as
agreed."

Fairchild translated as the two Modocs finished don-
ning their new clothing, proudly smoothing it with their
palms. They nodded without reply and loped on foot
from the camp, headed east to the Lava Beds.

Seamus looked into the blue of that clear sky overhead,
finding the sun bright, warming the chill from the air.

"Noon," was all he said as he went back to soaking his
hard cracker in the bitter coffee gone cold in his cup.

Chapter 20

April 11, 1873

"*I*'d put them both in chains, were it up to me," Seamus said to Meacham as the leader of the peace commission stood and smoothed the points of his vest.

Meacham wagged his head. "The gall of Boston Charley—begging me while I'm dressing . . . then bullying me to wear my new boots to the conference." He gazed down at the old shoes he had put on just to spite the Modoc.

"If that doesn't convince you they're up to no good, I don't know what will."

"Seamus," he sighed, "I'm about to walk into the unknown. But one thing I'm certain of—Boston Charley wanted my new boots."

"He plans on taking them off your feet."

Meacham glowered as he took his coat off the army cot and slipped it over his arms. "Off my cold, dead feet."

They pushed from the tent flaps to find Frank Riddle ready to burst in on them.

"Meacham—Toby wants me to beg you not to go today!" Riddle pleaded, wringing his hands.

"Easy, Frank," Meacham said. "You look a mess of it."

He shook his head. "Didn't get much sleep last night.

Neither of us. Thinking on what those butchers are going to do to you and the others."

Meacham tried a weak smile as he glanced at Donegan. "I'm praying Toby misunderstood something, Frank. Things are very tense right now. The Modocs are acting unpredictably because Canby has them ringed so tightly."

"No telling what a trapped animal will do, Meacham," Seamus said.

Meacham glanced at the Irishman then started away. "C'mon, Frank. Let's go find the others and let you tell them what you've told me."

Through the trees, they came to the tent where Thomas and Dyar slept. The Klamath subagent rose from his stool, coffee cup in hand, when the others approached.

"Where's Thomas?" Meacham asked.

Dyar pointed with his tin cup. "He headed over to Gillem's tent. Wanted to find out just what we were going to say when he goes to sit down with Jack today."

"It's close to time we were going, Dyar."

The subagent glanced at the sky. "Damn if it ain't." He sloshed his coffee into the little fire he had built beneath the blackened pot.

"Let's join Thomas and see what Gillem has on his mind."

The entire group went to the colonel's tent, where Meacham rapped on the pole.

"Come in."

The four pushed through the tent flaps to find Thomas seated on a canvas camp stool and Gillem still huddled beneath his blankets, his uniform draped over his footlocker and his boots askew by the sheet-iron stove standing nearby.

"It's time we were getting ready to set off for the council, Colonel."

His lidded eyes found Meacham, held for a moment, then shrank away. "I'm in no condition to attend any meeting today."

Meacham inched forward. "You're that ill, Colonel?"

"Would that I could die," he growled.

The four new arrivals looked at one another quickly. Scratching his chin whiskers, Meacham stepped closer to Gillem's cot. "That's . . . that's just what we've come to discuss with you. This threat the Modocs have made to kill us."

"Thomas has told me all about that," Gillem replied offhandedly. "Sounds like a nervous rumor to me. We've got the Modocs where we want them—bottled up. So they're bound to rattle their sabers a lot because they see no way out of this mess they've backed themselves into."

"This isn't saber rattling, Colonel."

Gillem's eyes found the tall Irishman who had spoken. "You a settler around here, mister?"

"No. But I figure I've better reason to trust Frank Riddle and his wife than I do two Modocs who talk from both sides of their mouths when they've got the preacher's ear here."

"I told you, Colonel—I've had a hard time convincing these men that the whole situation has changed among the Modocs," Thomas said.

"Nothing's changed." Riddle stepped forward, dragging his hat from his head. "Colonel, my wife heard 'em admit it. Two men going to kill each one of the commissioners going to that council at noon."

"Balderdash!"

"For once in your life—hush, Thomas!" Meacham ordered.

"By the Lord in heaven, I hope you're proved wrong," replied the reverend.

"By the Lord in heaven, I *pray* I am too." He turned to Gillem. "Colonel, with you being sick—I believe we should call off the council for today. We really need you as military representative to accompany us if progress is indeed going to be made."

"I can't possibly make it out of this cot—much less make it down to that tent."

"I'll be going—to represent the military, Colonel Gillem."

Every head turned as General Canby entered the tent with Scott, his orderly, and Monahan, his personal secretary.

"It does not change the fact that the Modocs have made plans to kill us all," Meacham said.

Canby smiled genuinely. "I'm not about to show my backside to a bunch of starving, ill-equipped Indians, Mr. Meacham. My soldiers will be close enough in the event of any trouble."

"You're taking an escort?" Donegan asked.

Canby shook his head, not even looking at the Irishman. "Our pickets will be watching from the bluff, and from the lookout post atop the signal tower. I've had field glasses trained on that meadow since sunrise. We won't be surprised by Jack's bunch."

"They'll have you shot and scalped before any help can arrive, General." Seamus watched Canby breathe deeply with the sudden sharpness of the image.

"The pickets tell me they've spotted the Indians on the scene—and none are seen among the rocks or timber nearby. I see no reason not to trust in the Modocs' word."

"They've kept us off-balance all spring, General," Meacham said, grinding his coattail in one hand. "Why the devil should they suddenly start telling us the truth now?"

"So why must we be dishonest ourselves at this point?"

"Perhaps only to save our lives. Nothing more dramatic than that."

"Are you suggesting we lie to the Modocs, Mr. Meacham?" Thomas asked.

He nodded. "Yes. If it becomes clear there is treachery afoot . . . if something doesn't fit right—by damned, let's agree to anything the Modocs want then get the hell out of there."

"God, no!" Thomas shrieked, a hand rubbing across his ample belly. "I can't be party to falsehood in the name of making peace. I'll trust to God and leave everything in His hands."

"Nor can I be a party to betraying the Indians when my whole career I have been steadfast in maintaining my honor with them, Mr. Meacham," Canby replied. "We have promised to go to this council unarmed. I will honor that pledge."

"I will go armed," Meacham said. "Having your soldiers back here will not protect us. I'll carry a weapon."

"And I will as well," Dyar added.

"No, no!" Thomas said, growing excited. "We made an agreement not to carry arms. If they suspect we have been unfaithful—it will ruin all the inroads we've made with them to get this far."

"Reverend Thomas is absolutely right," Canby agreed. "The importance of making peace at this point fully justifies us taking a moderate personal risk."

Behind them Frank Riddle threw up his hands, shrugging his way toward the flaps. He stopped and turned. "If you men want to go to your deaths—that's your business. I told you what the Modocs were planning. It's no more of my responsibility now."

"Are you still going along to interpret, Frank?" Meacham asked, his voice showing a hint of desperation.

Riddle nodded reluctantly. "I'm going. And so is Toby. I've been with that woman for twelve years—and never once has she deceived me. I know in my gut that those butchers out there are going to murder you today."

"Thank you for your concern, Mr. Riddle. But you do the translating—only what you're paid for," replied Canby. "And the rest of us will make this peace with the Modocs."

Riddle left the tent. Seamus pushed past the flaps and joined him, standing in silence as the voices rumbled low and indistinct within the tent for a few more minutes until Meacham and Dyar appeared.

"We have a few minutes left before we depart,"

Meacham stated, stuffing his pocket watch back into his vest.

Thomas came out of Gillem's tent with Canby. The general strode off, followed by his staff.

"I'm off to pay off my tab with the sutler," the preacher explained. "Those clothes and other things I bought Boston and Bogus yesterday." For the first time in days his face clouded over. "I'm not certain I'll return. But I mean to perform my duty faithfully and continue my trust in God to bring it out all right. I place myself in the hands of God. If He requires my life, I am ready for the sacrifice."

Every bit as stunned at the preacher's sudden admission as the others, Donegan watched the minister disappear through the gathering of trees and tents. Riddle left for his tent without another word. Dyar promised to be over in a matter of minutes. Then Seamus followed Meacham back to the commissioner's tent. Fairchild, Dorris and O'Roarke sat at the fire, watching Meacham come up.

"If you gentlemen will allow me a few moments of privacy, I have a letter to write to my wife."

Seamus watched Meacham disappear. Then he finally spoke low to the three civilians gathered around the coals of their morning fire.

"I think Meacham knows."

"That the Modocs plan treachery?" Dorris asked.

He shook his head. "No—that he's going to die."

A handful of minutes passed. The four watched from afar as Thomas and a very military General Canby, dressed in shiny brass buttons and glittering braid, strode from the outskirts of camp on foot. The pair moved off alone. Heading down the footpath toward the meadow where the Modocs awaited them.

Only ten minutes later Meacham reappeared from his tent, his suit coat draped over one arm. Standing still, drinking deep of the cool air, he seemed to search for something to say. "Have the others shown up yet?"

"The preacher and the general already set off for the tent," Fairchild replied.

Meacham sighed, then nodded slightly. He walked straight up to Fairchild and handed him a slip of paper folded once.

"Read this, John. Aloud."

As Fairchild began reading, Meacham shivered then pulled on his coat.

"Lava Beds, April 11, 1873
My dear wife:

You may be a widow tonight; you shall not be a coward's wife. I go to save my honor. John A. Fairchild will forward my valise and valuables. The chances are all against us."

Fairchild's eyes climbed from the page that trembled between his fingers. Those eyes were filled with a mist he attempted to blink away.

"Read the rest of it, John. So you are sure of what is expected of you . . . in the event of my death."

Fairchild cleared his throat, wincing.

"The chances are all against us. I have done my best to prevent this meeting. I am in nowise to blame. Yours . . . yours to the end.

Alfred.

P.S. I gave Fairchild six hundred and fifty dollars, currency for you.

A.B.M."

"Here it is, John," Meacham said quietly, stuffing an envelope into the civilian's hand. "You'll see that both the letter and the money reach my wife."

Fairchild held out his empty right hand, dragging Meacham's into his. "I'll go with you—"

"No. This is something I have promised I would do on

my own. Promised myself. Now you must make a vow to me."

"Anything," Fairchild said.

"Swear to me on all that is holy that if . . . if my body is found butchered in any way . . . that you will bury me yourself—right here—on this spot . . . so that my family will not have to see me. To be haunted by the memory of—"

"I promise, Alfred. On the grave of my mother, I swear that to you."

"No man would think you a coward," Seamus said, beginning to pull his pistol from its holster.

Meacham tried a smile as he reached out to shake hands with the Irishman, with his other hand pushing the pistol back into the holster. "Thank you, Mr. Donegan. I do not need to be remembered as a hero. But . . . I don't want to be remembered as a coward who ran—or a man who provoked violence when I was called on to work for peace."

"We'll come with you partway then," Pressley Dorris offered, patting his own pistol.

Meacham shook his head as they finished shaking hands. "No. I see Mr. Dyar and the Riddles coming now. We will go together as planned—with our interpreters."

Dyar came up first, his eyes moving across the civilians. "Mr. Fairchild—please deliver this money and letter to my wife at the Klamath Agency. Tell her . . . just tell her I love her. And always will."

Fairchild took the flat parcel from Dyar and turned away without a word, stomping off angrily into the trees.

Seamus felt the sour taste of tears spoil at the back of his throat, knowing that Fairchild had retreated before he himself broke down.

Dyar licked his dry lips, handing the reins of a horse to Meacham.

"Why are you going," Meacham inquired, not yet rising to the saddle, "if you too are convinced we are riding to our deaths?"

Dyar thought a moment, as if searching for words to explain. "If you go—I will go with you. I'm not going to stay if all the rest go. It would be nothing short of cowardice. We are in this together."

Meacham nodded as he watched Oliver Applegate hurrying up to the scene. "I understand. You are a good man, L.S."

"You have always been a friend to me, Alfred."

They touched hands then turned to their horses. Applegate brushed by Dyar clumsily, not succeeding in hiding the fact that he slipped a derringer pistol into the subagent's coat pocket.

"It is not a cowardly thing to protect yourself," Applegate whispered at Dyar's ear.

Dyar rose to the saddle, his eyes meeting Meacham's. O'Roarke once more presented his hand to the head commissioner, as if to shake. They clasped hands. Seamus watched a look of surprise come over Meacham's face as his hand came away from O'Roarke's.

"Protect yourself, my friend," Ian said in low tones.

Meacham cupped the tiny derringer in his palm and buried it in a coat pocket. "I will not die in dishonor—the Lord willing."

Bogus Charley sat on a nearby stump, watching the proceedings as if he were heedless of them. "You go now," he said in his poor English, dragging the blade of his belt knife along a twig, peeling back the bark. "Jack tired waiting for you. Go now."

At that admonition, Toby could no longer hold back her sobbing. On her knees to clutch her small son to her breast, the woman's cries of distress grew louder now as Meacham mounted his horse. "Do not go—you be killed!" she screeched.

"We must," Meacham replied, watching as she rubbed her face against her son's in parting. Toby finally rose to her saddle beside Frank.

Meacham urged his horse out of the gathering of spectators, followed by Dyar. The Riddles brought up the rear as they moved onto the footpath that would take them along the shore of Tule Lake to the council meadow.

"Godspeed," Seamus whispered.

The Irishman finally turned away, a sour ball in his belly, to find his uncle staring at Bogus Charley. The Modoc still sat on that stump nearby, whittling and humming a happy tune. Joining Fairchild and his uncle, Donegan strode over to the warrior.

"You're staying here to be sure no soldiers follow them —aren't you?" Fairchild demanded in Modoc.

Charley looked up, wide-eyed. Then he smiled. "Nothing will happen to them." He went back to whittling shavings off a green twig.

"Your friends going to kill them, Charley?"

"Nothing is wrong, Fairchild."

"You kill them—we kill you, Charley," O'Roarke vowed with a hiss.

Charley dropped the twig and slowly slipped the knife back in his belt. Rising, he dusted shavings from his new pants.

"Best you remember the man who bought those new britches for you," Fairchild reminded.

Charley tried a smile, but it turned into something painful. Without excuse, he turned and began walking east. Then he started to trot. At the edge of camp he was already running. Not staying on the footpath, but heading directly through the rocks.

"He's making a beeline to Jack before the commissioners get there."

"You think he'll try to stop things now?" Donegan asked.

Fairchild glanced at O'Roarke, then shook his head. "No. That bastard's hurrying to tell the rest of 'em that there's no soldiers coming to spoil their plans."

Chapter 21

Shining Leaf Moon

*C*aptain Jack waited impatiently with four others at the white man's tent in the meadow. Boston Charley trotted up.

"They're coming!" he said breathlessly, pointing back up the trail.

Jack turned casually and bent over to retie his cracked boots. That was the signal he had given to the two warriors hiding in the brush less than a hundred feet away, telling them all was going according to plan and the white men were approaching.

Sloluck grinned at Barncho. They had come here in the cold darkness before dawn to get into position, each with an armload of rifles, before the soldiers in the lookout tower could see movement come first light. Here the pair had shivered through the entire morning, waiting. Barncho grinned his slow-witted grin. Soon enough the shooting would start.

Jack straightened. He glanced over the rest. There was one killer assigned to each of the peace talkers. And each killer would have a backup to help finish off the victim.

"I will kill the soldier chief," Ellen's Man George said at Jack's ear. "You do not want him—but I do want his scalp."

"No," Jack said, raspy. "I am chief. I will kill the soldier tyee."

"I remember you wanted us to take this vow from you—"

Jack whirled on him, snagging his shirt. Ellen's Man almost fell backward, so surprised was he with the chief's assault.

"I told you—the soldier chief is mine."

Ellen's Man George would help Jack kill the soldier tyee.

Boston Charley and Bogus Charley had the honor of killing the "Sunday Doctor" who carried his good book wherever he went.

Schonchin John and Shacknasty Jim would see that old man Mee-Cham would not leave this meadow alive.

Dyar was to be killed by Hooker Jim, backed up by Black Jim.

Yet even Jack did not know that Scar-Faced Charley had crept through the sagebrush and lava rock to find his own hiding place. He was not here to assist in the killings. Instead, Charley had come here to keep his vow to kill any Modoc who raised a hand against Winema Riddle.

At that moment, Jack's attention was snagged by the pounding footsteps and rustling brush. Bogus Charley burst into the meadow, a wide grin wolf-slashed across his face. "They're here!" He ground to a chest-heaving halt before the others.

"Did they bring guns?" Hooker Jim asked impatiently.

He shook his head. "No guns. No soldiers!" He laughed. "We kill them all like squashing ticks!"

"Yes—we kill them, and the rest of the soldiers will run away. Just like the Doctor told us," Hooker Jim reminded them.

"There!" Ellen's Man shouted, pointing up the trail across the meadow.

Thomas and Canby appeared out of the trees, coming forward on foot at a brisk clip. The "Sunday Doctor" carried his Bible under one arm, dressed in a freshly pressed light-gray tweed suit. Canby was resplendent in his glittering buttons and braid and medals that caught the sunshine still draping the meadow in light despite the gathering clouds.

Jack wanted that coat. Perhaps more than anything he had wanted in a long, long time—he wanted the soldier chief's coat.

The Modocs surged forward, meeting the two white men far beyond the council tent. They talked loudly, excitedly, to the two commissioners, shaking hands, bounding up and down like schoolboys at play, pointing the way toward the tent in the front of which they had built a fire and dragged up some deadfall for seats.

Canby sighed when he reached the tent, glanced at Thomas then let his eyes slowly pan over the surrounding brush and rocks for any signs of movement. Jack watched the soldier chief's eyes every minute, hoping his two warriors would not become so anxious that they betrayed their positions.

For a tense moment the soldier chief eyed both Bogus and Boston Charley. They carried rifles they had with them while in the soldier camp earlier that morning. Jack saw the soldier chief about to say something to the pair.

He pushed forward, tapping the box beneath the soldier chief's arm. "What this?" he asked in his roughened English.

Canby stopped, diverted from confronting the warriors carrying rifles. "Ah, yes. Here," he said, dragging a box of cigars from under his arm. "I did not have a pipe to smoke with you, Jack." He pronounced each word slowly, deliberately, conscious of being without an interpreter for the moment. "These are good to smoke—good smoke. I got them from the camp sutler."

Jack was the first to step up and take one, then a second that he put in his pocket. He stood there a moment, gazing at the tall soldier in his blue coat with the long rows of shiny buttons with eagles on each one. Shoulders draped with gold panels, and the cuffs of each sleeve dripping with glimmering braid.

Oh, how he wanted that coat.

His palms itched with sweat. Jack rubbed them on the front of his pants, ruining the leaf on one of the cigars. He lit it anyway, with a twig from the fire, when the rest lit their cigars.

"Good, here come the others," Thomas announced.

The entire group turned to watch the final two commissioners enter the meadow on horseback, followed by the Riddles.

"Look at the clothes the old man wears," snarled Schonchin John in Modoc with great disappointment. "Old and worn—not like the Sunday Doctor's new suit."

"Even Winema's white man is wearing old clothes," Shacknasty Jim added. "They are not worth taking from his body."

Jack turned on Jim. "You remember the words of Scar-Faced Charley? He will kill you if you harm Winema or her husband."

Jim laughed. "Scar-Faced Charley? Ha! He is not here to hurt me."

"I would not be so sure," Jack said, enjoying the way his words made the smile drain from Jim's face.

Meacham did not like the smell of things as he rode down into that meadow, reining his horse up on the right side of the council tent.

Winema and Dyar dismounted on the left side of the tent. Frank Riddle strode to the front flaps, clearly anxious as he looked over the Modocs, then poked his head suspiciously into the tent itself.

Satisfied, he glanced at Meacham and shook his head slightly. Meacham was somewhat relieved. Still, seeing the two Charleys with rifles in plain view did nothing to make him more comfortable. He paused but a moment, looking over the warriors, wondering what weapons they carried beneath their coats.

"Weren't we told there would be only five Modocs here?" Dyar asked.

Meacham nodded. "Looks like there were six to begin with—then Bogus and Boston came on down from our camp."

"Eight," Dyar said, smiling at the Modocs who were jostling for position, indicating seating positions for the white men. He accepted a cigar from Canby.

"I don't like it any better than you do," Meacham replied, noticing that Thomas did not take a cigar.

Then a cold shot of realization hit him.

He looked at the fire-ring on the east side of the tent again to be sure. Then at the signal tower back up on the bluff.

"They've moved the council area," he whispered to Dyar.

The agent looked up the hill. "Yes. If we sit where the Modocs want us to sit, the tent will hide us from view of the lookout tower."

Meacham nodded, lips pursed as he removed his overcoat and draped it over the saddle of his horse. As he bent to tie the reins where Winema had secured her horse to a small bush growing beside the tent, Meacham noticed Shacknasty Jim eyeing his horse.

With a tug at his heart, Meacham decided he would not make it easy for any of the Modocs to get their hands on the animal. He let the reins fall to the ground.

You'll have your chance to run for it, girl, he thought as he straightened. I can help you no more than that.

Casually he ran his fingers across the derringer in his suit pocket as he stepped up to the council circle.

The Modocs set about jostling into position with such abandon that Meacham grew sure they were lining themselves up to shoot him and the rest. As if they had already chosen their targets and now needed to assure themselves of a clear shot at the white men. Meacham glanced at Dyar. They traded places, and watched four Modocs immediately switch places as well.

Riddle inched in front of Winema. She touched his hand, then moved away slightly. He moved back in front of her protectively, following Hooker Jim's gloating eyes as they followed his wife from the far side of the fire.

Through all the movement, Canby and Thomas remained aloof to the unvarnished hatred coming to a boil. Tobacco smoke joined the greasewood smoke in obscuring the scene from time to time as another strong breeze gusted across the meadow. Canby finally squatted on a stump near the fire, directly across from Captain Jack.

Meacham rose and circled the ring, followed by Shacknasty Jim. He got to the west side of the tent, where he stopped, hoping to somehow signal the soldiers in the lookout post.

But Jim stepped in front of him, pointing back to the council fire, making strong gestures and babbling in Modoc.

"He wants you back here so they can start talking," Frank Riddle said.

Meacham glanced across the meadow, hoping to catch the eye of one of the soldiers in the tower, or one of those soldiers and civilians squatting on the hillside far, far away to watch what they could of the proceedings. Jim suddenly tugged on Meacham's coat, the right side.

Afraid the Modoc would discover the derringer if he delayed any more, Meacham consented and returned to the fire. He settled just to the left of Canby. Schonchin John plopped down across from him as Winema came up and settled to the ground slightly in front of Meacham.

He turned, finding Dyar content to remain standing by his horse a little south of the tent.

He's ready to bolt at the first wrong move, Meacham thought, without blaming Dyar in the least for his lack of temerity.

A fussy man, Reverend Thomas carefully laid his overcoat over a thick clump of sagebrush to the left of Meacham. When he sat upon the seat he had prepared himself, Thomas was positioned slightly behind the head commissioner.

Riddle finally came up to stand behind his wife, just as the Modocs became suddenly agitated. They chattered, pointing up the hill sloping toward the soldier camp.

When Meacham turned, he saw a man walking along the high ground, silhouetted against the skyline. "Is he Modoc, Frank?"

Riddle shook his head. "They think it's a white man . . . maybe a soldier."

"Whoever it is—get rid of him, and now," Canby ordered.

"They're afraid he's a soldier and he's armed," Riddle said, translating some of the jabber from the warriors, his own voice edged with more nervous fear.

"Dyar . . ." Meacham turned, finding the agent quite anxious beside his horse. "Go up there and find out what's going on. Tell him this is a private meeting."

Dyar was in the saddle and up the hill before anything more was said. He spoke briefly to the stranger, and as the Klamath subagent turned away and headed back to the tent, the stranger disappeared over the hill in the direction of the soldier camp.

Dyar slid from his saddle and held onto the reins as he explained, "A teamster . . . civilian from camp. Looking for a lost horse."

"You explained what was going on here?" Canby asked, straightening his blue tunic.

"Yes. That's why he skeedaddled so damned fast," Dyar added without humor. "He wanted no part of anything to do with your talk with Captain Jack's cutthroats."

"Let's proceed," Canby instructed, turning back to Meacham.

He cleared his throat, unable to put things off any longer. Meacham began by making the sort of speech that was expected of a white man desiring to make peace with Indians. At the end of explaining their desire to forge a lasting peace with the Modocs, Meacham asked why Jack had requested this meeting with the commissioners.

"We want the soldiers to leave the Lava Beds," Jack replied.

Meacham waited a moment for more, impatient and growing more anxious with the foot-dragging. "You have said that before, Jack. For once, let us talk like men now —and not like children. Don't you have anything new to say to us that we might make peace between us here today?"

"The women and children are afraid of the soldiers."

He thought on it a moment. None of the other commissioners spoke up. Meacham felt alone as he answered. "The soldiers can protect your women and children—to keep other people away, to keep them from harming your families. If you wish, they can stay in safety at Fairchild's ranch while we decide on a reservation to your liking."

Meacham shifted on his perch. He did not like the way Hooker Jim paced back and forth behind the others—still studying the rocks and the rise of land that separated the meadow from the soldier camp. He caught Hooker's eyes for a moment. The Modoc lingered there a moment, then smiled as he went back to watching the distance.

"What will become of our men? My warriors?" Jack asked.

"If you wish, your men can stay in the Lava Beds until you have decided and we have agreed upon where you will live out your days." Meacham placed a hand on Schonchin John's shoulder to show some sincerity. The warrior shrugged the hand off and backed away slightly.

"Why don't you shut up, old man!" Schonchin snapped.

Hooker Jim stopped pacing at that moment, then turned and inched past Meacham, striding purposefully toward the head commissioner's horse.

"We won't live anywhere without our women and children," Jack said, shaking his head.

Turning on his stump as he listened to the Modoc chief,

Meacham watched Hooker Jim tie the horse to some brush, knotting the rein close to the ground. The warrior called the horse by name.

"You know this horse, Jim?" Meacham asked.

Hooker nodded, that crooked smile growing. "Fairchild's horse, no? Yes, I know this horse. A good mare. A fine mare."

Jim then stepped alongside the saddle, where he removed Meacham's overcoat. Making a grand show of it for his fellow warriors, Jim slipped on the coat as if he were selecting it from a mercantile over in Yreka. All talk stopped as Jim buttoned up the coat from bottom to neck, then strutted back to the council ring.

"Bogus Charley—you think me look like old man Mee-Cham now?"

The Modocs all had a good laugh as Jim strutted like a proud cock in a wide circle. "Me old man Mee-Cham now!"

Meacham glanced at Thomas and Canby. They grinned and clapped with the Modocs, as if this were some childish show. In his bowels, Meacham knew different. Perhaps they were trying to provoke something— only that. But, knowing that, perhaps he could keep the warriors off-balance by joking along with them.

He took his wide-brimmed pinch hat from his head and stood, handing the hat to a surprised Hooker Jim. "Here. Take my hat too. Then you can be Meacham."

A smile grew on Jim's face. The eyes lit with a sinister fire. "I will have hat . . . by and by. Don't hurry me, old man."

Dyar moved behind his horse, acting as if he were adjusting a stirrup. Realizing Dyar must think the time for shooting had arrived, Meacham watched Riddle inch back behind Winema's horse. Seated all this time on the ground in front of Thomas, Toby now stretched out on the ground as if relaxing, pantomiming a wide yawn. It appeared she was hopeful the bullets she expected at any moment might pass over her when the gunfire erupted.

Meacham attempted to catch Canby's eye, but the general appeared intent on pursuing the council. Unperturbed by others' fears, the soldier plunged ahead with his own speech to Captain Jack, while black and gray storm clouds scudded in off the lake.

"Since I don't have the authority to take the soldiers away, I want the Modocs to understand I do wish peace with them. These soldiers are here for the protection of whites and the Modocs. This commission makes no promises it cannot keep to your people. I have always been a friend to the Indian. You have no reason to distrust my word. My soldiers are not here to harm your women and children. When I was a young soldier myself—I helped move a band of Indians to a new home. Their hearts were bad for me at first—but they soon came to call me 'Friend-of-the-Indian.' I want to be a trusted friend of the Modoc too."

When he had completed his remarks, Canby gestured to Thomas. The reverend held up his Bible as he moved off his perch, so that he was now on his knees, as if praying. It was a fervent, heart-felt sermon he delivered: asking the Modocs to renounce their heathen ways and return to a belief in Christ Jesus, their only savior. He ended by saying how long he had known the other commissioners, that they were righteous, God-fearing men, with the welfare of the Modocs high in their hearts.

"None of these men wants to see any more blood shed on this ground. We are your friends. God asks us to be brothers and to care for one another. Help us help you, Jack. Let God's will be done in this land."

The chief snorted audibly as Toby translated the minister's words. Meacham watched the others, noticing now that they too watched Jack, as if distrustful of him.

"If the soldiers go away, we can talk about the Modocs leaving the Lava Beds," Jack repeated the old demand, wringing his hands anxiously as he turned to Canby.

"This is your last chance, soldier chief. Give us what we want—now." He stood, backing away a moment.

Meacham sensed that urgency in the chief's voice, somewhere inside him knowing what must surely come next. He leaned to the right, whispering to Canby.

"In the name of God, Canby—tell them you'll give them what they want!"

The general shook his head, irritated. "I cannot bear false trust with these men."

Into Jack's spot leaped Schonchin John, who suddenly announced, "We want the valley south of Cottonwood Creek."

Meacham was surprised by this unexpected news. "That's—no . . . that's John Fairchild's land."

"Give us the valley," Schonchin repeated, leaning forward with unmasked hostility and not slowing to allow Toby Riddle time to translate. "Move Fairchild out and we can live there in peace. Take your soldiers far away and we can be happy hunting and fishing again."

"We . . . why, we can't give you another man's land," Meacham said.

"It is not his land," Jack said, rubbing his palms across his thighs nervously. "It was Modoc land. He is only there because we let him stay there."

"No. I have no right to give you that land."

Jack turned to Canby. "Will soldier chief give us Fairchild's land? This is soldier chief's chance—last chance."

Canby waited for the translation from Winema. "Tell them I have no right to give them land. Only the commission can decide on a new reservation for the Modocs."

"You give us the land we want," Schonchin growled, holding a fist before Meacham's face. "Take away your soldiers—give us Fairchild's land—or we talk no more. We're tired. No more talk!"

Toby was not yet finished with translating the warrior's words into English when Jack bolted to his feet.

"I go now to wet the bushes."

"Wet the bushes?" Thomas asked.

"He's going to take a damn piss," Meacham growled, not sure what this turn of events meant. "Indians are damned direct, preacher. Best get used to that."

If we live to get used to anything, he thought to himself as Jack moved away from the council fire.

Chapter 22

April 11, 1873

*O*n the east side of the Modocs' Stronghold in the Lava Beds, Major E. C. Mason's men, who were camped near Hospital Rock, had established a series of outposts at the top of the broken ridges overlooking the Indian camp.

Private Charles Hardin was on picket duty that morning when young Lieutenant William Sherwood showed up with good news.

"Good morning, private," Sherwood said buoyantly. "This will be the last day of the bloody war, don't you know?"

"Those red devils in there really going to make peace today, sir?"

"Just received a heliograph from Gillem's camp. The peace commissioners headed down to their council tent a few minutes ago. We're to be on the lookout for any Modocs who might want to come in to surrender to our camp."

"Yes, sir. I'll keep my eyes open," Hardin replied, watching the lieutenant salute and walk off into the brush and rocks, heading back toward camp.

Spare minutes later, Private Hardin spotted a white flag being waved by a pair of Indians standing some four hun-

dred yards away. He turned and flung his voice back at
the soldier camp.

"Lieutenant! I've spotted some warriors want to talk!"

Sherwood trotted up in a matter of moments, stopping
to catch his breath, and staring squint-eyed at the distant
pair beneath their waving flag. He patted Hardin on the
shoulder.

"By God—peace is really happening, private!" he
gushed. "We've never seen them show the white flag before. I'm going down there and see what those two want."

Hardin dug a toe in the damp ground. "I wouldn't go if
I was you, Lieutenant."

"It'll be just fine. Keep me covered with that Sharps of
yours."

Hardin gulped, watching Sherwood head down the
rocky slope. The lieutenant came loping back after a few
minutes.

"They want to talk with the little tyee—the major. In
just a little bit—around noon. I'm going to fetch him."

Sherwood could not convince Mason to come for that
impromptu parley with the Modoc warriors, but Sherwood did convince a friend of his to join him in the conference: Lieutenant Boyle. A few curious soldiers climbed
atop Hospital Rock to watch the meeting with Hardin
while the two lieutenants strode into open ground.

They watched the officers stop when a single Indian
came out from the group of a half-dozen warriors now
gathered around the white flag. There was much gesturing, but no voices could be heard . . . when both officers turned suddenly and began walking away briskly.

The lone warrior signaled. Riflemen hidden in the
rocks appeared, their weapons raising smoky puffs on
the chill midday air before the loud reports echoed all the
way to Hospital Rock.

With the first shot, Sherwood was winged in the arm.
He was running when another shot clipped him through
the leg, causing him to stumble. Boyle was still on his feet,
turning back to help Sherwood. Together they hurried as

fast as they could toward the rocks, disappearing from view behind a low ridge of lava.

"They'll be butchered, we don't get down there!" Hardin shouted, already on foot and leading the rest down the slope.

"I'll lead this command, private!" hollered an officer Hardin did not know. "Follow me, men!"

Hardin stopped, shook his head and yelled at the officer's back. "Sir—you're going in the wrong direction!"

The rest of the soldiers followed the officer off into the maze of lava flow. Hardin followed for a few minutes, slowly dropping farther and farther behind. When he could no longer be seen by the officer hurrying ahead to his own destination, Hardin quickly ducked behind the hogback of lava where he figured he could find the lieutenants forted up.

By the time he made it over the sharp, slashing rocks, Hardin found Boyle already disappearing up the slope to Hospital Rock, making his own way back to camp. The wounded Sherwood lay hiding in a crevice, bleeding from his two wounds. He tried to rise when Hardin came close.

"Get down, Lieutenant!" he shouted, taking cover. "Are you hurt badly?"

Sherwood answered after a moment, "Afraid I am, Hardin."

When the private crawled to Sherwood's side, he looked over the wounds then tore a bandanna from his neck, tying it around the man's leg wound.

Hardin stood, scanning the far ground. Off to the right along the hogback he caught sight of the rest of the soldiers still tromping behind their confused commander.

"Here! Over here!" Hardin shouted, and waved. His voice echoed loudly off the black rocks.

Most of the soldiers stopped, trying to locate Hardin among the labyrinth. He waved his hat now, which caused them to abandon their commander and start down toward the crevice where he and Sherwood huddled.

"I'm still bleeding, private. Badly," the lieutenant said bravely, watching the bandanna grow dark and shiny.

"You rest, sir. We'll get you back to a surgeon right off."

Sherwood gripped Hardin's arm, whispering harshly. "You gotta let 'em know!"

"Who, sir?"

"The other camp!"

"Why, Lieutenant?"

Sherwood's head sank back, his eyes beginning to roll into sweet oblivion. "They'll murder them too."

At that very moment the commissioners and their interpreters were sitting in stunned silence while Jack moved off several yards and urinated, loudly spraying the hard, rocky ground.

When he turned back to the council ring, the Modoc chief shouted toward the nearby rocks.

With growing alarm, Meacham saw two warriors rise from hiding, weighed down with rifles cradled across their arms as they hurried into the meadow. A third, who Meacham recognized as Steamboat Frank, appeared from another direction.

The Modocs at the council ring stood, backing slightly.

Meacham realized the moment was at hand. He lunged for Captain Jack as the chief made a beeline for Canby.

"Jack, what is the meaning of this?" he hollered above the growing clamor.

His face suddenly pinched with horror, the Modoc chief shouted, *"Ot-we-kau-tux!"*

Riddle understood. So did Toby. Her uncle had announced, "All is ready!"

Flinging his coat flap aside, Jack yanked out a revolver he had stuffed in the waist of his britches. At point-blank range he aimed it at Canby's face.

Meacham stood transfixed for the next few seconds, unable to lunge to help the soldier. Watching Canby stare transfixed at the gaping muzzle of that pistol held only inches from his face.

Jack pulled the trigger, but the weapon misfired with a loud click—the cap useless.

Canby sat motionless, disbelieving perhaps, paralyzed in the sudden terror of those seconds while Jack muttered over the pistol, recocked the hammer and brought it back to the white soldier's face.

This time when he pulled the trigger, the bullet smashed into the general's head, just below the left eye, coursing downward and exiting from the back of the soldier's neck.

Canby's head was driven back violently, shattering his jaw as he landed on some rocks. His body plopped in the grass for but a moment as Canby groaned. Rolling onto his hands and knees out of some reservoir of inner strength, the soldier somehow clambered to his feet, weaving, and lurched into a lumbering run away from the tent. Perhaps by some primitive instinct heading back to Gillem's camp.

The bleeding, heaving general had covered just over forty yards when, blinded by his own blood, he tripped, sprawling in the grass and dust.

By this moment Ellen's Man had swept up one of the rifles brought into the meadow by Barncho and Sloluck and was dashing after his wounded prey. As Canby lay choking on his own blood, clawing fingers into the damp soil, attempting to rise, the warrior stood over his quarry and fired a bullet into the soldier's head.

Jack was on the quivering body in that next instant, stabbing Canby in the throat to bleed his victim. Grunting to one another, he and Ellen's Man rolled the still-warm carcass over and roughly yanked the blue army tunic from the body. Jack stood proudly with it as Ellen's Man spotted Canby's watch, tearing it from the dead man's vest pocket.

Both turned to gaze with satisfaction across the meadow at the other murderers.

At the moment Jack's pistol misfired its first shot, Reverend Thomas bolted to his feet in horror, still clutching his Bible, his knees still damp and dirty from his prayerful position in the grass.

Boston Charley brought up the rifle he had carried to and from the soldier camp, jerking back on the trigger as Thomas's eyes grew wide and he started to run. The bullet hit the minister squarely in the chest, knocking him backward over the stump where he had been sitting.

Clutching his wound, watching the blood seep between his white fingers, Thomas whimpered as he struggled onto his knees and one hand. With the bloodied hand outstretched and imploring at his attacker, Thomas moaned.

"Don't shoot me again, Boston—I'm going to die anyway . . ."

The Modoc stepped over his victim's legs, ramming home another cartridge into the breech of his rifle. He stood over Thomas, a sneer on his face. "Why you no turn bullets, Sunday Doctor? Your spirit medicine not strong as mine, eh?"

Whimpering more loudly now, at times calling upon his God to help him, Thomas struggled to his feet, still clawing feebly at his bleeding wound. He made two, then three steps before Boston tripped him, sending him facedown into the grass.

"Goddamn you, Sunday Doctor! Maybe you should believe what squaw tell you next time."

Boston brutally swung the butt of his rifle, crushing the side of the reverend's jaw. Thomas sprawled for a moment, gurgling in blood, yet somehow struggled to rise once more.

"Our Father . . . who art in heaven . . ."

Bogus Charley shoved Boston aside, raising his rifle. As Thomas watched, Bogus placed the muzzle against the side of the white man's head . . .

". . . Hallowed be Thy name—"

Bogus pulled the trigger. The grass below the preacher was of a sudden littered with blood and bone and gore.

As the body convulsed on the grass, its bowels voided, adding a sudden stench to the clean, spring air.

Holding their breath, the two Charleys quickly stripped their victim of the gray tweed suit, laughing that they had eaten from the Sunday Doctor's plate and drank from his coffee cup that same morning.

"Give me that!" ordered Steamboat Frank.

"Where you come from?" Bogus asked, yanking back on the minister's coat. He was not about to give it up so easily.

"I watch from the rock," Frank said, adding another yank to the coat. He stood a full head taller than either of the Charleys.

"You take the coat and go away," Boston Charley said, handing the dead man's garment to the newcomer to the meadow.

When Canby was shot and Thomas chased down for the fatal shot to the head, Alfred B. Meacham was already on his feet, trying to run backward up the slope toward the soldier camp. He took very few steps, fighting to get the derringer out of his pocket while Schonchin John brought out from under his coat both a knife and a pistol, steadily stalking his quarry with a wide smile slashed across his face, swinging the knife in a wide arc.

Yanking the derringer from his coat, Meacham brought it up at arm's length and pulled the trigger. Nothing happened—he had failed to cock the hammer. Yet the mere sight of the muzzles of the tiny gun stopped Schonchin dead in his tracks.

That heartbeat gave Meacham a chance to see why the pistol had not fired. He backed away again, faster this time, cocking the hammer. Stumbling in panic, Meacham passed by the body of the preacher, then the soldier's body, before Schonchin regained his courage and fired his own pistol at the fleeing white man.

The bullet whined past Meacham, barely nicking the whiskers beneath his chin. The blood seeping from the grazing scratch felt both hot and cold at the same time as a gust of spring wind wafted into the bloody meadow.

Meacham pounded his breast, and, in a loud voice, called out, "Shoot me here, you devils!"

Meacham had little time for thought—only action. Shacknasty Jim, Sloluck and Barncho all had rifles to their shoulders now, aiming them at the fleeing white man. Bullets whistled like angry hornets all around him. One found the top of an ear. He felt the warm blood seeping down his neck as he stumbled up the slope backward, the derringer still held out at the end of his arm in utter panic. Another shot grazed his shoulder, causing him to wince in pain.

He fell over a boulder suddenly, pitching backward, driving the breath from his aching lungs. Meacham heard them coming—perhaps sensed them running. Their shouts of bloodlust, their war-cries—that wild laughter that comes of sudden but long-awaited victory. His hand beat the grass beside him, desperate . . . then finding the derringer.

Meacham brought the weapon up as he peered around the boulder he had fallen over. The three warriors were loping toward him. On instinct the commissioner pulled the derringer trigger as the same moment Shacknasty Jim fired another shot from his rifle.

The Modoc's bullet struck the rock, a fragment of lead splintering off to strike Meacham across the forehead—knocking him back, dazed and semiconscious.

Shacknasty was on his victim like a mountain panther, tugging, pulling, tearing and yanking to remove the white man's boots and clothing.

The dull-witted Sloluck came up to watch with that smile of his. Then brought his rifle up and laid it against Meacham's temple.

With a growl, Jim shoved the rifle away. "You need not shoot no more. This one is dead already."

Cowed, Sloluck just bobbed his head eagerly in agreement. "Don't get the clothes bloody, Jim. No bloody clothes, right?"

Jim muttered something as he yanked on Meacham's

belt, tearing at the buttons on the fly. Boston Charley trotted up, finished with Thomas. He knelt at Meacham's head, slipping his skinning knife from his belt.

"I take old man Mee-Cham's scalp."

Jim looked at him a moment as he yanked down the britches. "What for you want it?"

"Old man's hide is tough. Make a good shot pouch for me, Jim."

Shacknasty grunted his approval. Charley pressed the blade down on the white man's brow, close to the hairline, and dragged the dull blade around the side of the skull\ toward and down behind the ear. Impatient and unfinished, he was nonetheless yanking on Meacham's hair when Hooker Jim strode up and laughed.

"If that old man Mee-Cham's bald head makes a good scalp for a warrior—you're welcome to it, Boston!"

There was a little bitter laughter among them when Winema ran up, screeching in horror as Boston tried ripping the ear and all from the balding man's head.

"Soldiers coming! Soldiers coming!"

As one, their eyes glanced up in fear, wide and glassy and blooded. Like scampering children caught in the act of mischief, the warriors abandoned the commissioner's body.

When the shooting had started, Toby had been stretched on the ground to protect herself from flying bullets. But when the screaming and firing began, she was climbing to her feet to run when Sloluck struck her on the side of the head with a rifle butt.

Perhaps the slow-witted warrior was only caught up in the excitement, but Black Jim and Captain Jack instantly turned on Sloluck, their pistols held ready—reminding him of Scar-Faced Charley's vow to kill any man who harmed Winema.

"If Scar-Faced does not kill you for hurting the woman —Jack will . . . here and now!"

Sloluck grinned wickedly, laughed his dull laugh and trotted away up the hill after other prey.

When his wife was knocked down, Frank Riddle was stopped from going to her side. He stared into the muzzles of weapons held by Shacknasty Jim, Ellen's Man and Barncho. Without thought, but only the screams of the victims and the oaths of the murderers in his ears, Riddle sprinted across the meadow, following the fleeing Dyar. None of the three warriors followed the white interpreter, who caught a glimpse of movement as Scar-Faced Charley stood among the brush and rocks on the east side of the meadow. As he ran for his life, Riddle remembered Charley was as good a shot with a rifle as he was at keeping his promises.

Like Riddle, L. S. Dyar had been on his feet when the shooting began. But unlike the interpreter, the subagent from the Klamath reservation had not delayed those precious seconds in starting toward Winema.

Hooker Jim was three steps behind Dyar as the white man pulled Applegate's derringer from his coat. Cocking it as it came out of the pocket, Dyar turned and stopped, pointing it at his pursuer.

Skidding to a stop, Jim ducked and threw up his hands, stumbling backward as Dyar's shot buzzed overhead. Jim turned and ran off. Dyar needed no more of an invitation to flee the scene himself. For several yards Black Jim followed the white man across the meadow, then gave up and came huffing back to join the others tearing the clothing from Meacham's body.

It was a few minutes past noon.

When Winema rushed toward the little pack hunkered over the old man's body, shouting her warning, Jack added his own voice to the panic, believing that his niece had truly seen soldiers on their way.

"Come! Come now! Run—all of you! Back to our fortress where we can fight them off!"

As a group they rose and darted past their chief, tearing by the canvas tent rattling in the cool breeze. Each of them carried something away from the scene. Clothing, watches and rings. Jack himself wore the soldier chief's hat on his head, the shiny sword slung from his own waist, rattling loudly as he turned round and round, anxiously scanning the meadow.

"How you like the old man Mee-Cham now?" Jack shouted back at Winema. "Keep your white heart—you no longer are a Modoc!"

Watching the murderers disappear across the slope, she came to a stop at the bloody body. In a rage, fear like acid at the back of her throat, Winema collapsed over Meacham's stripped and battered form, sheltering it with her own.

There she lay as all noise drained from the meadow. Overhead, the clouds roiled across the sun in ugly streaks, blotting out most of the light.

Slowly, painfully, she laid her head over Meacham's heart, listening for some clue. When Winema heard nothing, she held her own above the white man's face a moment, stroking the old man's cheeks, smearing his blood and her tears across the wrinkled flesh as she sobbed bitterly. Rivers of frustration and rage at the treachery of the people of her birth exacted against her adopted people.

Suddenly resolved, Toby drew back, snorting and swiping at her eyes. She gently turned the body flat on its back, straightened Meacham's legs and folded the arms over the torso in death's repose.

With one last glance in the direction taken by the Modocs, Toby darted past the other two bodies, to the council tent where she tore loose the rein to her horse, leaped to Frank's saddle and pounded her heels into the animal's flanks.

It was eleven minutes past noon.

There was nothing more she could do for the old man now.

Chapter 23

April 11, 1873

"*You* still see them, don't you?" Ian asked Seamus. "Your eyes younger, lad."

Donegan stood, straining his eyes on the far meadow as the light faded beneath the clouds whipped off Tule Lake. "I see 'em moving around some. Not sure what—"

"They're firing at the peace tent!"

In shock, Seamus looked up at the signal sergeant yelling atop the signal station erected on the bluff.

All around the Irishman soldiers snatched up their rifles and started away without command or orders. Donegan and O'Roarke found themselves among them, skidding, sliding, careening down the bluff toward the site as the sound of distant gunfire could now be plainly made out as they clattered along.

After covering no more than a half-mile, the soldiers in the lead spotted a man hurrying in their direction on foot.

"Hold your fire!" someone shouted.

"Is it a white man?" another asked.

Seamus sprinted along the side of the crude formation. "Bloody well won't be no damned Modoc running toward us, will it?"

"It's one of them peace fellas!"

Ian huffed to Donegan's side and stopped. "It is at that —Dyar."

"In God's name help me!" Dyar screeched, tearing up the footpath. "Help them! Murdering butchers—oh, the blood! The blood!"

O'Roarke grabbed Dyar as the agent collapsed against him. Dyar's eyes held the frightened, cornered look of a snowshoe hare chased beyond its limits by a winter-gaunt coyote.

A sergeant came up with several others. "Mr. Dyar— what happened?"

"We damned well know what happened, Sergeant," Donegan said. "Get this man back to camp and let's go see to the rest!"

The soldier was about to speak, his mouth hung open to protest—and instead he turned to order a squad to accompany the commissioner back to camp and a surgeon. Seamus tapped Ian on the shoulder and they were off, followed by a dozen soldiers who were leaving their sergeant behind.

The clatter of hoofbeats grew louder. Seamus turned, flinging his arms this way then that. Some of the soldiers took the left side of the road, the rest hid on the right.

Around the bend Toby Riddle galloped into view, laying low along the neck of her mount. Her hair streaming, her bloodstained hands gripping the reins close to the horse's bit, she began to rein up, terror filling her eyes as Donegan stepped into the road.

But instead of stopping, she flailed at the horse, laying on its withers again, tearing past the Irishman in a death race.

"She looks like she's seen the devil himself," a soldier said, coming back onto the road.

"Maybe she has, sojur. Maybe she has at that."

Ian was beside Donegan that next moment, gripping his nephew's arm. "I've got to find Frank. He was a friend of mine."

Seamus nodded as Ian started off again at a fast clip.

Just over the rise the small meadow opened up before them. Down to the right of center was the off-white canvas of the wall-tent. Gray smudges of smoke still climbed ghostly from the sagebrush fire ringed with deadfall and rocks used as seats.

Donegan had seen enough of war and death to know what the two dark forms were as he raced for the tent.

They stopped at Canby's body, stripped of all clothing, lying some twenty feet from the tent.

"He's dead," Seamus announced quietly to the first soldiers arriving as he stood over the general's corpse.

He trotted over to the second body, utterly naked as well. "Got in over your head, preacher."

Quickly making the sign of the cross as the breeze shifted and his nose wrinkled with the stench of voided bowels, he rose and moved to the final dark form as more soldiers appeared in formation at the edge of the meadow.

The head commissioner still had his red flannel underwear on, some of it soaked with blood turning brown. Seamus placed an ear against Meacham's chest.

"You got a surgeon with you?" Seamus asked the arriving soldiers.

"I'm a surgeon. Dr. Cabaniss," an older man in army blue announced. At the end of his arm hung a tiny bag he dropped as he knelt on the far side of the body.

"This one still alive—for now," Donegan said.

After a quick examination, Cabaniss clucked. "Damned lucky to be hanging on, I'd say."

"Maybe not. Sometimes it's better to get it over with quick."

"Perhaps," Cabaniss replied icily, pulling a flask from his kit. "Help me get him up to drink this."

"Brandy?"

Cabaniss shook his head. "That's all gone. Straight corn whiskey."

"If he don't lose it when you pour it down him, he might have a chance, surgeon."

"Help me hold him up," Cabaniss asked again. "He's a

bloody mess, this one." The surgeon began to pour a dribble past the commissioner's lips.

Meacham sputtered at the taste. "B-Brandy! No—"

"It's whiskey, Meacham," Cabaniss said.

"I . . . I can't," he replied weakly, trying to turn his bleeding head against the clamp the surgeon had on him. "I'm a t-temperance man, by God!"

"Stop this nonsense, Meacham. Down with it, I say. That's it—good. By God you just might live—you've got that much fight in you still!" the gruff surgeon growled, then pursed his lips into a sour smile aimed at the Irishman.

"I . . . hit Schonchin—bleeding . . ." Meacham muttered.

"Shut up, man—and drink," ordered the surgeon.

When Cabaniss called three soldiers over to help him, Seamus stood and trotted down to the tent. Reporter H. Wallace Atwell was removing his overcoat and draping it over the bloody, naked Canby.

"Get the general a goddamned shroud, sojur," Seamus hissed at a youngster nearby.

"Sir?" the young man asked, his eyes wide, face drained of color. He repeatedly licked his lips, refusing to look down at the bloodied corpses.

"Cut some canvas from that tent for General Canby."

"I . . . I don't have me a knife—"

"Use mine," Ian said, slapping the handle of his skinning knife into the young soldier's hand.

When the wide strip had been hacked from the tent, three soldiers helped wrap the general's body in the canvas.

"An army tent," Seamus said quietly. "No more fitting shroud for a fighting man."

The soldiers laid the two dead and the severely wounded Meacham on stretchers and prepared to carry them back to Gillem's camp after attending to the possibility they would be attacked by the Modocs they believed still lurking on the fringes of the meadow.

But Jack's murderers never looked back as they escaped into their Stronghold.

There was no one to fight, and no resistance offered by the Indians, yet the officers ordered their eager soldiers about-face and returned to the tent rather than have a repeat of the debacle of 17 January.

It was there that Seamus and Ian learned how the camp had been alerted to the trouble at the peace tent.

When some unexplained shooting erupted on the far side of the Modocs' stronghold, Mason's signalmen sent word to Gillem's camp that there was an attack made on two of his soldiers under a Modoc flag of truce. Gillem's signal officer wrote his hasty note and dispatched a soldier with the news for the colonel himself, still taken to his cot.

"Gillem was just completing his own note of warning to General Canby—telling the commissioners to be watchful, suggesting they should return to camp because of the attack on Mason's men—when another messenger come running down the hill," explained John Fairchild who had been at the colonel's tent during the outbreak of excitement. "You should have seen the look on Gillem's face when that soldier ran up shouting: 'The commissioners! The Modocs are firing on the commissioners!' "

"You get yourself a crack at any of Jack's warriors?" Pressley Dorris asked the two Irishmen, his face hopeful as he peered at the gravity etched on every face around him. He had been in camp with Fairchild during it all.

Ian O'Roarke shook his head. "We scoured the nearby rocks hoping to find any that might be skulking about—but all Seamus could find was the three places where four of 'em stayed in hiding until it came time for the bastards to do their terrible deed."

"The news roared through here like prairie fire," Dorris said as they all waited quietly outside the surgeon's tent where Meacham lay horribly wounded. "If it weren't for a few old sergeants taking control of things—and Captain Biddle pressing things with Gillem—they'd never got that doctor down there for Alfred as fast as they did."

Seamus turned to Dorris and gripped his arm. "What do you mean, Biddle pressed Gillem?"

Dorris glanced this way then that before he whispered, "The colonel was downright froze in indecision, he was. I don't known if it was because he was so sick . . . but the bugle was already blown, and the captains already had their men lined up and ready to march—still Gillem couldn't decide what to do. So in come Biddle, marching right into the colonel's tent. Don't know what he said to Gillem, but when the captain came back out, he ordered Captain Thomas to stay on duty with his battery of artillery to guard the camp. The rest of the troops Biddle was going to lead out to rescue the commissioners and do battle with the murderers if they caught up with any of 'em."

Seamus shook his head and spit into the grass between his boots. "Damn, if that don't sound like the truth: officers sitting on their thumbs—afraid to do something, anything! And all the while folks are butchered in cold blood."

"Gillem's officers and men are hopping mad to get a crack at the Modocs now, but the colonel won't let 'em," said Dorris.

"Why won't he turn 'em loose?"

Dorris shrugged. "Gillem said he's waiting for the Warm Springs Indians to get here to help before he moves in on Jack's Stronghold."

"You should have looked at Dyar's face when he came running in here," Fairchild said. "Never have I seen someone in such a state of shock."

"Still, he got off his telegram to Washington, John," said Dorris.

"Yes, direct to General Sherman himself," Fairchild added.

Seamus clucked his tongue inside his cheek. "Uncle

Billy? I'll bet that old war-horse will have a lot to say about this Indian carnival now!"

"Those reporters too," Fairchild added, with a thumb indicating a handful who stood about, asking questions of soldiers just back from the meadow, scratching on their pads with pencils. "Especially that Bill Dadd."

Newsman H. Wallace Atwell hunched over his notes, perched on a camp stool, his pad braced atop one knee as he scribbled furiously, hoping to be the first to have this story get out to the world.

"By the saints," Seamus said quietly, "this is the biggest story of the war yet."

"Atwell's hired Bill Ticknor—fella who surveyed the road around the lake," Fairchild said. "Ticknor will carry the reporter's story into Yreka to get it telegraphed to his paper in Sacramento."

Seamus wagged his head. "First time a general's been killed by Indians . . ."

As the sobbing wails drew closer, ever louder, the Irishman turned. Stretcher-bearers were bringing the canvas-wrapped body of General Edward R.S. Canby into camp. Half lying across the stretcher himself, stumbling along beside it at a clumsy gait, was Canby's young orderly, Scott. He screeched in rage and lamented in grief. Captain Biddle ordered three men to comfort Scott at a nearby fire while the body was carried on to the general's tent.

"Not a man could blame him for crying the way he is," Ian said quietly.

Seamus saw the mist growing in his uncle's eyes. "We all have tears inside us for someone."

Ian gently took his nephew's wrist in his big, callused, field-worn hand. "Were that I had been there with Liam when my brother took his last breath."

Donegan peered at the ground a few heartbeats, his chest growing heavier. "I—I wasn't with Liam when he died." He gazed into Ian's moist eyes. "Away down that bloody island when he was murdered."

Ian put a hand to his mouth in shock. "Murdered? No. I—I thought he died—a head wound—fighting the Cheyenne."*

"He did," Seamus started, lips quivering of a sudden. The muscles of his face pinched in their fight to maintain composure. "We all figured he was dying already, Ian. Maybe . . . Lord help me, I've never told anyone this— had I been there, he might'n made it until the surgeon showed up nine days later."

Ian gripped the back of his nephew's neck, pulling the big man into a rough embrace. "Don't go blaming yourself for the acts of other men, Seamus. Only God knows how I've beat myself with that same rod too many years already. It's not yours to carry any longer, son. Set that load down and go on. Go on."

At that moment Fairchild and Dorris turned away, perhaps a little embarrassed at Donegan's sobbing, although it was an age of strong and open sentiment. Seamus stood there among them all, inches taller than even his uncle, hunched over into the older man's shoulder like a child—shedding himself of that grief carried for too long, a burden much too heavy for any one man to bear alone for all those miles and all those sleepless nights spent alone.

Overhead the heavy, gray clouds had finally filled to their limit with cold. A light but icy snow began to lance out of the heavy sky, covering the countryside with a thin layer of white while the day drained out of the land.

Captain Biddle ordered three wooden rifle cases emptied of their Springfields by two regimental carpenters who would be kept busy beneath lamplight converting the boxes into tin-lined coffins.

"Three?" Ian asked in a whisper as they walked slowly by the canvas awning where the muffled hammering of nails and the screech of bending sheet tin carried through the sleety night.

---

* THE PLAINSMEN Series, vol. 3, *The Stalkers*

Donegan shook his head. "No one expects Meacham to make it to morning with those bullet wounds."

"They're taking the bodies to Yreka," Ian replied. "Thomas to San Francisco. Canby and Meacham to Portland."

"Then this army can get back to dealing with the Modocs."

"No one's saying a word about talking peace with Jack any longer, Seamus."

"I figure it's a blood debt now."

Ian dragged the back of his hand across his dry lips. "Jack and his bunch don't have an idea what they've started now."

He sighed anxiously. "I'm tired of this pacing, Ian. Going back to wait by the surgeon's tent."

"Maybe they have some news on Alfred," O'Roarke said as they started back.

As they were coming back up to the quartermaster's tent lit by firelight and kerosene lamps, crowded with newsmen and the curious, one of the surgeon's hospital stewards poked his head out the tent flaps.

"Captain? Captain Biddle?"

Biddle came forward, taking his slouch hat from his head. "Is Mr. Meacham dead, private?"

"No—no, sir," the young soldier replied in wonder. "He . . . he just asked to have an officer send to Linkville for his brother-in-law."

"I'll be goddamned," Biddle replied. "Who's this brother-in-law?"

"Captain Ferree—Fort Klamath."

"Ferree—I'll send someone for him now," Biddle said, turning back into the crowd that parted for his passing.

"Liam had that when he died, Seamus," Ian whispered beneath the murky lamplight as the snow scudded icily along the ground. Sparks from nearby fires kicked up fireflies into the black sky.

"Had what, Ian?"

"Family."

"Family."

"Always lonely work—this thing of dying," Ian said. "Made a little easier having family near."

Chapter 24

Shining Leaf Moon

*A*lthough Captain Jack might still be leader of the Modocs, he was nonetheless doing just as he was told to do.

Curly Headed Doctor and his Lost River murderers had full control of the band now.

Hours ago they had scurried back into their rocky Stronghold to learn that Curly Jack and his bunch had killed one soldier and chased another away on the east side of the Lava Beds. But Curly Jack's warriors had nothing to show for their efforts.

The peace tent murderers argued and shoved and argued some more over the scanty spoils carried from the bloody meadow: a few items of clothing, a derringer and a horse, along with the soldier chief's sword and uniform.

As much as some of the murderers tried, they did not succeed in getting Captain Jack to back down from his claim to everything that belonged to Canby.

"I killed him," Jack told the crowd, pantomiming with his outstretched finger like a pistol he held right in Ellen's Man's face.

"I killed him," Ellen's Man said, knocking the chief's hand aside. "He was running away after you shot him. I made him dead."

Ellen's Man did not win the contest.

Once Canby's belongings were securely in Jack's possession, Ellen's Man kept the soldier tyee's pocket watch and chain. The Sunday Doctor's clothing was divided between Bogus and Boston Charley. Old man Mee-Cham's possessions were split between Shacknasty Jim, Schonchin John and the ridiculed Hooker Jim.

He sat to the side of things now, this Hooker Jim—ignored even by his father-in-law, the shaman.

Hooker had bungled his job: killing Commissioner Dyar. He had run when faced with the white man's gun. Captain Jack led the chorus of those who believed Hooker did not deserve anything taken from the murder scene. So rather than celebrate with the others, Jim had instead to suffer the ridicule heaped on him by the band as they prepared to celebrate their victory with the falling of the sun from the cold, snowy sky.

"We must be ready when the soldiers come," Jack reminded them as the greasewood bonfire was built, flames radiating off the black rocks surrounding their Stronghold.

"Kientpoos is mad with fear! Ha! The soldiers will all run away now," said the Doctor with scorn.

"We have killed their chief right before their eyes!" added Schonchin John.

"That will make the soldiers angry!" said Scar-Faced Charley.

"He speaks the truth," Jack said. "And the Teninos from Warm Springs are coming to lead the white men in this fight!"

"Let them come," boasted the Doctor. "We will be ready for them. The full power of my medicine is not yet tested. Tonight we dance!"

The women and young warriors screeched their approval as the Doctor turned away to complete his preparations at the pole where he hung more feathers and animal skins, along with two more fresh scalps. When the drums began their soul-stirring beat, the young warriors

and squaws alike removed some of their clothing despite
the dropping temperatures and falling snow. The huge
fire coupled with the furious dancing kept them warm
until the moon sank far in the west.

As a murky sun rose in the east, shedding gray light
over the white land, Jack's scouts reported no movement
of troops from the soldier camp west of the Stronghold.
And instead of marching toward the Lava Beds, the
soldiers camped by Hospital Rock were seen marching
south.

The night-long dancing and medicine making seemed
to consolidate the Doctor's power. No soldiers were coming to avenge the murders the Modocs had hoped would
cause the white men to resume the war.

So they danced through that next day and into the
night, knowing the white man's army and the white man's
government were powerless to act against the magic of
their shaman.

They danced.

By dawn on Saturday the carpenters had three coffins
prepared.

Canby and Thomas were gently laid to rest and the lids
nailed shut for their trip north to Yreka for embalming.

Meacham clung tenaciously to life, arousing himself
from time to time to curse surgeon Cabaniss for forcing
the whiskey past his lips, and to clutch the hand of Captain Ferree as he once more slipped into blessed sleep.

Word spread through camp that twelfth day of April
that at dawn some Modocs had fired on a young sentry
posted near the signal tower on the bluff.

Later in the day word was flashed from Mason's camp
that a scouting party sent south under Lieutenant E. R.
Theller had been shot at by a small war-party stalking
them. Although a lot of bullets were fired between the
groups, apparently no damage was done to either party.

As the clocks inched toward noon on Easter Sunday,
the thirteenth, the soldiers in Gillem's camp learned that

Lieutenant Sherwood had finally succumbed to his wounds, suffered just minutes before the slaughter began at the peace tent.

Solemnly, the two commissioners' coffins were laid side by side in the back of an army ambulance for the trip to Yreka. From there Thomas was to be transferred to his family in San Francisco, Canby transported on for burial in Indianapolis.

While the general had not been all that popular among the officers and troops during the months of posturing and waiting, Canby's brutal death now stirred talk of rage and recrimination for the Modocs. The soldiers were ready to storm the Stronghold—but Gillem held his hand from smiting the warriors.

The colonel's signal sergeant brought word down from the signal tower not long after the bodies were on their way west to Yreka: chief of scouts Donald McKay had arrived at Mason's camp with his Tenino mercenaries from the Warm Springs reservation in northern Oregon.

As far back as 22 March the War Department had authorized signing on the Warm Springs Indians to fight the Modocs in the Lava Beds. Canby had believed he had a powerful negotiating tool in telling Captain Jack that his enemies were on their way to fight the renegades.

But while Canby and the army might have faith in Donald McKay, the Tenino mercenaries did not.

McKay himself represented both bloods involved in this fight. While his father had been a famous fur trader with the Northwest Fur Company working out of Astoria on the Columbia River, his mother was a Cayuse Chinook woman. McKay's whole life had been spent traversing the wilds of the northwest, either as a trapper himself, a guide for the army, or as an interpreter for hire. It was while serving as scout for the army during the Snake War that McKay first crossed swords with the Warm Springs fighters, who claimed the underhanded half-breed swindled them of much of their army pay.

But with the army that spring of 1873, it was a matter

of moving out under the command of Donald McKay or not going at all. And if they did not go, the Warm Springs scouts would not be paid anything.

Seventy-two of them headed south for Tule Lake on 4 April.

Their arrival on Easter Sunday caused a stir in both camps as the troops realized they would be marching into the Stronghold at last. Only one small problem: these converted Christian soldiers refused to fight on Sunday.

Monday would be soon enough for the Teninos.

Quartermasters prepared weapons and rations as officers laid out a plan of attack. While most of the troops were buoyant in expectation of a quick and decisive fight of it, the few soldiers who had been in on the debacle of 17 January were decidedly more solemn.

Amid the revelry that night before the planned assault, some of the men in both camps sat talking with comrades of other wars and faraway battles, of places called Antietam and Cold Harbor, Manassas and the Wilderness, Kennesaw Mountain and the James River. Toasting one another's health come dawn and the orders to advance on that impregnable fortress of black rock where the Modocs danced and sang and celebrated over the scalps of good soldiers.

A few made oral wills or scribbled down their final requests and stuffed them into the hands of friends. To see that a wedding ring made it back home to a wife; a cabinet photo back to children waiting in the east; a little extra pay forwarded to some aging parents somewhere in southern Ohio.

A few of the many faceless enlisted who could not write asked friends who could to put down their name on a piece of paper they would pin to their uniform come morning. So that when they died, the men burying them would know them, at least by name.

And there were always the songs to be sung: "The Girl I Left Behind Me" given voice repeatedly over those campfires where gathered the men in blue, young and old

alike; along with the "Doxology" and "Annie Laurie,"
sung as a bittersweet lament for love's anguish.

Likewise the many raised their tin cups to toast to
success with the coming light of day. Seamus Donegan
stood among them, soldiers all at that moment, adding
his roughened, off-key brogue of a voice to theirs.

> "Then stand by your glasses steady,
> This world's a round of lies;
> Three cheers for the dead already,
> And hurrah for the next who dies!"

Not only in Yreka that day, but elsewhere across the
land, a terrible grief was sweeping through every heart.
As ink was smeared across long sheets of newsprint, the
shocking headlines reached a stunned nation that Easter
Sunday. On every street corner from big city to small
hamlet, newsboys hawked their wares to angry custom-
ers, eager for any scrap of news from the bloody Lava
Beds.

Slowly, but steadily, the cries for a war of extermination were heard echoing across the land.

In the far west, two long lines of silent, bare-headed
mourners lined the streets of that California mining town
beneath flags dropped to half-mast. The army's black-
draped ambulance pulled up before the only mortician in
Yreka, and the two rifle-case coffins unloaded while the
loud cries of vengeance against Captain Jack rose to the
leaden skies once more.

Outside in the streets they hung a life-size effigy of
Interior Secretary Columbus Delano, who had urged his
peace policy on the Grant administration's War Department.

"Give them bullets and grapeshot!" was the shout
raised that day.

"No talk of peace with murderers—let 'em choke on
their own blood!"

Canby lay in state for most of the day and into that

black evening while thousands for many miles around, even schoolchildren dismissed from classes, came in to pay their respects and glimpse the mortal remains of the man who had given his life, sacrificed on the altar of the hope of making peace with Jack's Modoc renegades.

Late that Sunday night a recovering A. B. Meacham's own brief telegram outlining the murders at the peace tent in horrid details was speeding to officials in Washington. His painful conclusion: "We believe that complete subjugation by the military is the only method by which to deal with these Indians."

Receiving word of Canby's murder at a late supper, General William Tecumseh Sherman immediately hurried to a midnight counsel with President Grant before wiring General Schofield, Commanding Officer of the Military Division of the Pacific, recently returned from Hawaii.

> The President now sanctions the most severe punishment of the Modocs and I hope to hear that they have met the doom they so richly have earned by their insolence and perfidy.

More to the gritty business of waging war on the Modocs, Sherman selected Colonel Jefferson C. Davis to fill Canby's role as Commander of the Department of the Columbia. But Davis would be some time in arriving on the scene. For the present, it would fall to Colonel Alvan C. Gillem to prosecute Sherman's war of annihilation on sixty Modoc warriors.

At his command, Gillem had fully five troops of cavalry and five companies of infantry, in addition to four artillery batteries and the newly-arrived mercenaries under Donald McKay. His firepower had recently been augmented by the addition of four Coehorn mortars capable of effective bombardment of the Stronghold. For every soldier to carry into battle was a supply of five hundred hand grenades from the armory at Benicia Barracks near San Francisco.

Yet Gillem's officers continued to shrink from the idea of a direct frontal assault on an impregnable position backed by a determined enemy. Their idea was to soften up the Modoc positions by judicious use of the mountain howitzers and mortars before the foot soldiers moved in: Major Mason from the east with some three hundred men, Major Green marching from the west with 375 soldiers.

Gillem's final orders, "Tell your men to remember General Canby, Lieutenant Sherwood and the flag."

They didn't get moving until Monday. By that night of the fourteenth, Mason moved his troops and the Warm Springs Indians into position on the east. There was a slight delay while the seventy-two Indians held a Christian service of song, thanksgiving and prayer before going into battle.

So different from the attack of last January—no blinding, confusing fog awaited them now. Only a balmy, moonless sky, undisturbed by a single breeze.

After bugles blew reveille at midnight, Green ordered his soldiers forward at two A.M. across the sharp rocks in the dim starshine to the nearby peninsula to await the coming of dawn less than a mile from the hostiles. Mortars and mountain howitzers had been broken down and packed on foot-sure mules for the trip into the Lava Beds. Each man carried sixty rounds for his Springfield. On his back was a haversack containing fifteen hardtack and a skimpy supply of salt-pork.

Unlike the disaster of January, this time the troops were no longer dependent upon doing the job in one day. This time they were prepared to stay until the job was done.

A handful of the infantrymen left behind to guard Gillem's camp decided they had the best idea for starting the war to annihilate the Modocs. As pickets who hid among the rocks a few yards east of the soldier tents, they watched with surprise as a lone warrior strode up out of the darkness.

Slow-witted Long Jim had decided he would like to visit the soldier camp again, as he had done so many times in the past weeks of negotiation and wrangling. Yet he walked right into a far different reception than the one he had enjoyed before the murder of the peace commissioners.

Seizing Long Jim, the soldiers argued as to the best way to kill the Modoc, something no soldier could boast of having yet done in the war of the Lava Beds. They decided to convince Jim to escape—then shoot him as an escaping prisoner of war. While they were arguing over their options, Jim took it upon himself to flee toward the Stronghold.

The hapless infantrymen fired, and fired again at their escaping prisoner, until the starlit darkness swallowed Long Jim from pursuit.

"Now I know why we were left here and the rest of 'em got orders to do the fighting," grumbled one of the infantrymen. "Ain't none of us can shoot to hit a Modoc, even a old slow-witted one like that'un."

As the minutes crawled into hours and the stars whirled overhead, Green's troops inched closer and closer to the peninsula where they would await first light. Off to Donegan's right a soldier stumbled and fell clambering over the black rocks. His Springfield clattered to the ground, discharging.

Every man dropped to his belly, most believing they had been spotted by Modoc snipers—a repeat of the horror encountered in last January's defeat.

But as that solitary shot echoed away over the silent stronghold, only harsh whispers from confused and harried soldiers were heard beneath the black of night.

No Modoc warriors were waiting to swallow the soldiers this time.

* * *

Jack issued orders to William Faithful and Scar-Faced Charley to roust everyone from their sleep. After that single gunshot had echoed over their Stronghold, wasn't many of the Modocs still sleeping anyway.

Everyone knew the attack was coming.

Old women and men took charge of the children and moved them farther back into the deepest of the caves, fortified with their skimpy supplies of water and what food they had.

The young women went out with the warriors to help reload the captured Springfield rifles, keep powder and ball supplies near at hand for the older muzzle-loaders, along with carrying water skins and canteens to their men who would stand the brunt of the coming assault.

In the dim light of coal-bright fires, the women wrapped rawhide around the hands, elbows, knees and feet of the warriors for protection from the sharp rocks they would be called upon to scale during the battle.

All Captain Jack could do now was to wait for dawn, anxious to see if the shaman's magic still possessed enough power to hold the white soldiers at bay.

Chapter 25

April 15–16, 1873

*A*s ready as everything was, the order for the attack did not come until after eight o'clock.

By midmorning the soldiers were still advancing slowly, only inching toward the outer defenses of the Stronghold. No man had yet seen a Modoc defender.

The ground was broken and serrated, strewn with sharp rock and rough going for men on foot. Even more than that, the company commanders themselves kept the advance slowed to a crawl to prevent a repeat of the disastrous attack of 17 January.

Those soldiers on the far right flank of Green's advance were "hanging in the air" and without much support should the Modocs throw themselves against that end of things. Which is just how and where the Second Battle for the Stronghold began.

Eight warriors had left the rest and crawled toward the lava flow to the south of their Stronghold. Their intention was to prevent the soldiers from sweeping to the south and thereby joining Mason's forces coming in from the east. Riflefire from those eight Modocs stopped Green's entire advance where they stood.

Officers dashed up, shouting orders to renew the advance and return the enemy fire.

Either the soldiers could not, or they simply would not, advance into the sound of the random Modoc gunfire. Angrily, the officers surged up and down their lines, bullying and cajoling—until the Irishman rose up and trotted over to present himself to Captain Evan Thomas.

"You find me a dozen men, Cap'n—we'll get this flank in sight of the red divils' main Stronghold."

"You can see it?"

"Ain't much more than a thousand yards from the far end of our flank now."

"How you know that?" asked a grizzled sergeant coming up.

"I can see Cap'n Jack's medicine flag fluttering out there meself, and a few specks moving around it that I take to be some of his warriors."

The captain turned to his old sergeant. "By glory—get me a dozen men, Holcomb. We'll put them behind this bull-headed Irishman and see if we can't get this line moving again."

"Aye, Captain!"

Inside of a handful of minutes Seamus had his squad, led by the grizzled sergeant himself, as they moved out in silence.

"I didn't believe you at first, mister," whispered the older man as they came to a halt at a rocky ledge. Peering over it, looking north, they could make out the outline of the central Stronghold held by the Modocs, encircled with caves where the Indians had retreated and several pockets fortified with rocks.

"We're not going to get any closer than this without a hard fight of it, I'm thinking," Seamus replied.

"I do believe you're right on that count too," replied the sergeant.

"Go back and tell the cap'n what you've seen here," Seamus suggested. "If he and the others can get their lines moving when we start our charge—we might do some good."

The sergeant nodded and backed down the rocky ledge,

wincing as he went, his knees and hands shredded on the sharp soil.

He was back in a matter of minutes. "Cap'n sends his compliments to the civilian, mister," the sergeant said as he crawled back up. "Says we can advance with the rest of the force in our reserve."

Seamus's eyes narrowed. "I'm a horseman myself, Sergeant. Don't know much about playing infantry. How does your captain figure us to advance on our own?"

"You ever play leapfrog as a boy, Irishman?"

"Aye—tell me how we'll play it here."

"We'll leave half of our men back to cover the other half what's advancing."

Seamus nodded then. "Then the bunch left to cover will come up while the others cover them."

" 'At's right, son. You Irish will make good soldiers yet."

It took the better part of the afternoon, clawing their way across the rough terrain and sharp rocks, exposing themselves to Modoc snipers as they gained yard by yard of ground, inching ever closer to the enemy's Stronghold.

Four hundred pitted against but eight warriors, yet those eight riflemen made it tough and gritty work for the soldiers across six long hours.

Along about mid-afternoon Seamus got his first clear view of the Modoc position. It was plain to him that when the natural rock formations did not meet the warriors' needs, they had built up fortifications of stone to a minimum of four feet, leaving loopholes in those improvised bastions for their rifles. One by one the soldiers attacked these small bastions of defense, only to find them abandoned by the enemy moments before the walls were breached.

At one rock formation four soldiers crabbed forward, expecting it to be as abandoned as the rest had been. A Modoc warrior had bravely remained behind, drawing the soldiers in by refusing to fire until the white men were dangerously close. He fired at the closest soldier, then retreated and disappeared among the rocks.

Private Charles Johnson reeled backward, a bullet between the eyes, blood slowly seeping from the purplish hole in his forehead as he collapsed against his companions.

Near the same time on that long afternoon, a California sutler hired by the army saddled his mule in Gillem's camp, curious to see what he could of the protracted fighting. Patrick McManus was not cut of heroic cloth.

The sutler hadn't gotten very close to the action when Steamboat Frank shot the mule out from under the white man, forcing McManus to huddle behind some rocks for the remainder of the afternoon while the Modocs fired an occasional shot to keep the frightened sutler cowering and hollering for assistance.

As soon as the light drained from the sky behind the Cascades, sutler McManus dared scurry back to camp on foot, leaving his saddle on the mule's stiffening carcass. As he neared the outer videttes, a picket's voice called out in warning ahead of him and a single shot whined over the civilian's head.

"Goddamn you, soldier! Don't shoot a friend!"

"Friend?" came the reply. "How I know you ain't one of them sneaking Modocs talking white man talk—"

"Dry up there, you idiot!" he snarled, more angry now than afraid. "It's me—McManus, the sutler. Don't you know a white man on his knees from an Indian on his belly?"

For the time being the white men had no way of knowing how many Modocs they had killed or wounded, if any, throughout their day-long assault. But as the count stood with the falling of the sun, five soldiers had been killed and nine wounded.

At about the same time, just after dusk, Captain Perry's cavalry advanced from the peninsula through the stationary line of attack where the infantry had halted at the end of the day's fighting. Within minutes Perry had his horse soldiers in control of the ridge at the far north-western border of the Stronghold. It was from that very ridge on 17 January that the Modocs had delivered such devastating fire on the soldiers blinded by the cold fog.

Matters were looking up as orders were passed down through the line to dig in for the night. With each previous assault, the soldiers were ordered out of the battle arena come dark. But this time was different. The men were now to find themselves a tiny piece of the rugged, sharp ground where they could fortify themselves and try for some sleep until the morning brought a renewed assault on the Modocs.

As the light drained from the sky, Colonel Gillem proudly stomped up to the edge of the bluff to once more overlook the progress his troops had made through that long day. Dorris, O'Roarke and Fairchild stood among a few others, trying one last time to catch a glimpse of Donegan out there among the blue-clad men hunkered behind dark shadows of black rock.

Gillem sighed, a bit too satisfied with himself to Fairchild's way of thinking. Ever since Gillem had taken to being sick the morning the commissioners were attacked, then stood about frozen with indecision once the murders were committed, then compounded everything by refusing to attack the Modocs until the Warm Springs mercenaries arrived—John Fairchild had grown to despise the soldier.

"Well, gentlemen," Gillem said, moving right in among the civilians. "I'm satisfied. Don't you agree, Mr. Fairchild—this is a splendid day's work? How long did it take Wheaton to get this far?"

Fairchild's chance had arrived. He looked squarely at the colonel to say, "General, I don't remember exactly, but as near as I can judge, it was about twenty minutes."

Gillem hemmed and hawed and huffed at the insult, finally turning away with the members of his staff.

As he disappeared into the growing darkness, Ian said quietly, "You bloody well know that wasn't true, John."

Then he had to grin and slap Fairchild on the back. "But it served that pompous windbag right, didn't it?"

The three laughed among themselves, if only to relieve some of the tension that had every man wound like a watch mainspring.

"I pray your nephew will fare the night, Ian."

"Aye—Seamus is one to always need your prayers."

Not that a man could get any sleep, even someone as bone-weary as Seamus Donegan, once the artillery opened up with their nighttime pounding of the Stronghold.

In the dark, the first mortar round landed less than twenty feet from Perry's cavalry troop. As the shell whirled, spewing and hissing on the ground near them, the soldiers clambered to their feet and began to panic. Pandemonium: horses rearing and whinnying, men screaming in total abandon and anger. But the captain regained control of his soldiers, ordering them to flatten themselves on the ground. No man was hurt when the shell exploded.

Four times an hour either the mortars or the mountain howitzers were touched off. While little actual damage was done to the Modocs burrowed like badgers back in their caves, the noise did serve to keep the Indians awake, anxious and off-balance throughout the night.

After each new bombardment, the warriors would shout back at the soldiers who lay not that far away from the Modoc positions.

"Charley, say—you think soldier big-guns do good that time?"

Answered by another Modoc, "No, Frank. These boys don't even shoot straight when they shooting between a woman's legs!"

Whereupon the warriors would laugh until one or more of the soldiers would fire into the dark, aiming only at the sound of the sneering voices or the cackling laughter. Back and forth they would vent their spleens, hurling their profane oaths at one another—promising what they would do to one another once daylight came to permit a resumption of the fighting.

Seamus was certain the Modocs learned a few new words that long night—new expressions regarding a man's sexual abilities or his lack of legal ancestry.

Nothing more to do than occasionally fire your rifle and try to doze between the artillery fire coming every fifteen minutes. Perhaps chew on the hard-bread and salt-pork stuffed down in your haversack. And wait for first light.

Few white men slept that night.

Captain Jack moved most of his strength to the west side of the Lava Beds during the blackest part of that night, feeling as he did that the great massing of soldiers on Green's side of things meant he should meet the coming assault there. On the east, Mason had already disobeyed Gillem's orders and stalled, allowing his men to dig in far from their objective. From where they sat in safety, Mason's forces were little threat to the Modocs.

When dawn came, Gillem sent Mason his terse dispatch:

> We will endeavor to end the Modoc War today. Try to join Col. Green's right. Let us exterminate the tribe. Push when Green attacks. I will be over this A.M.

Minutes later Gillem received Mason's reply:

> The Indians are on our left and rear. We have to fight them, but will do all we can to help Green.

It was nothing more than pure fabrication, invented to excuse Mason with his superior for failing to punch his troops through to the south of the Stronghold and effect a junction with Green as Gillem's battle plan outlined. Had Mason done his duty, the Lava Beds would have been entirely ringed, from one shore of Tule Lake to the other, with no means of escape from the Stronghold.

Further communication between Green and Mason themselves brought about another deviation from the original battle plan. The majors agreed to effect a junction between their forces on the north side of the Stronghold, along the shore of the lake. Both officers disobeyed Gillem when he ordered them to stick with his plan of attack and united their flanks, effectively shutting the Modocs off from their water supply.

Still, few men on Green's right flank, or on Mason's far left flank, gave much thought to the fact that there were several hundred yards of very rugged, jagged, yet very open terrain left between them.

"They've been firing all day up there," the old sergeant muttered, turning to Donegan as he pointed north to the far side of the Stronghold.

They lay together with three soldiers in a shallow depression, within sight of Mason's troops, who had advanced less than three hundred yards ever since the first moment of attack twenty-four hours before.

"Maybe that's why things have been so quiet down here," Seamus replied. "Maybe they're making some ground, for all the lead flying up there."

"I should hope, Irishman," growled the sergeant. "I sure as hell didn't get any sleep last night—what with all the noise meant to soften those red bastards up."

"I figure those guns kept the Modocs up too, Sergeant."

He grunted. "Gimme a chance to get my hands on a Modoc—or one of those artillery sergeants, either one. I'll knock the cork out of his bunghole for him, I will."

They laughed easily, the camaraderie growing by the hour among those black rocks occasionally smeared with blood.

"Those boys up north there push in much farther, they're gonna have some up-close fighting to do," Seamus said. "And that's what them Injins will like—getting up close enough to see the fear in them sojurs' eyes."

His people were in the middle of the Shining Leaf Moon —five days since he had put the pistol to the soldier tyee's face and pulled the trigger, twice.

Captain Jack had enjoyed little sleep since that day, and last night he had been moving, constantly, from one position to another to make sure his warriors were where he wanted them before the soldiers renewed their attack at dawn. The rattle and hiss and boom of the big guns every few minutes made the women and children scream at each report. But they were brave under the fire and quickly quieted down. By the gray of predawn, in fact, few of them screamed in surprise or fear any longer at the bombardment.

Yet, with the coming of the second night, one foolish warrior had attempted to pull a burning fuse from a shell fired from one of the big guns into the Stronghold. Jack had been crawling close enough to watch the explosion make the warrior's head disappear in a blinding flash of flame and smoke and gore. What was left of the body lay thrashing on the ground for only a moment.

As soon as it had grown dark, Jack ordered some warriors north to attempt to sneak through the soldier lines to secure some water from the lakeshore. Their first attempt failed. As did a second and a third. The soldiers were completely in control of the shoreline. After a final attempt by some warriors failed, Jack pulled his men back to the council area just as a mortar landed in the council fire, scattering coals and burning limbs with a spectacular show.

"Listen to me!" he shouted as the men gathered around and the women poked their heads from their black burrows. "We can no longer count on the power of Curly Headed Doctor."

The shaman leaped forward, his face pinched in rage. "Do not listen to Kientpoos—he would give some of us over to the white man's hanging rope just to save his own neck!"

Jack pointed a long finger at the shaman. "This crazed man will get you all killed. Look for yourselves!" he said as William Faithful dragged the beheaded warrior into the center of the council ring. "Didn't the Doctor promise you no warrior would be killed?"

The shaman stood over the remains of the dismembered warrior. "He did not do as my medicine told him," he snarled.

"No—you speak without any truth to your words," Jack replied. "Your power is gone. The soldiers have even crossed your magic red rope!"

"Yes—the white men are coming!" Scar-Faced Charley added, jumping to the center.

"We can still kill them all," Hooker Jim said, coming to stand by his father-in-law. "Let them come so we can finish the blood work our medicine demands of us."

"You stay and die on these rocks, Hooker," Boston Charley said. "I am willing now to listen to what Jack tells us to do."

"He will lead us to the gallows!" Hooker cried.

Jack wagged his head, grabbing the front of Jim's shirt in a fist, waving his pistol with the other hand. "Tell me how I can give you over to the soldiers now? Not without giving myself over to their hanging rope! I murdered the soldier tyee for you, Hooker. We are all going to flee so we can again fight together—or we are going to hang together. What will it be?"

"Escape!" came the cry from the weary women and children.

"Escape!" echoed the resounding voices of the warriors.

"When the moon reaches mid-sky, all warriors must fire their guns into the soldier positions," Jack instructed. "Make them think we are preparing to attack them. While we are doing that, our women and children and the old ones can escape. You must keep the little ones very quiet. And only after they are on their way through the soldier lines to the south will I let the warriors go . . . one by one by one."

"What will we do once we have fled our Stronghold?" asked Ellen's Man George.

Jack turned to him. "You are still eager to fight these white men?"

"Yes, always—to my last breath."

"Good. Then you will take Hooker and the rest who want to fight. Once you are out of the Stronghold, move west toward the big soldier camp. If you attack the soldiers there—they will have to bring some white men back to help them. And that will keep them from pursuing our families for some time."

"Where are we going, Jack?" asked a woman from the crowd.

"Far from here," he answered. "All I know is that we must go far, far from here."

Chapter 26

April 16–20, 1873

"So what's kicking 'round in your craw, Eugene?" Ian O'Roarke asked early that third morning of fighting at the Stronghold as he walked up to the young man who had recently celebrated his nineteenth birthday.

Eugene Hovey ground the back of a dirty hand under his nose. "I asked that officer over there to back off on me."

"He working you too hard?" Ian asked, knowing full well that Hovey was among several of the braver civilians who had volunteered to take their mule teams into the Lava Beds for the purpose of transporting supplies into and hauling the dead and wounded soldiers away from the battle lines.

"Not that, Mr. O'Roarke," the young man answered. "I just got me a hunch this morning—a feeling something's bound to happen to me in that infernal place if I keep pushing it the way I've been."

"You ask the quartermaster if you can back down for 'while?"

Hovey nodded. "He said he knew how I felt, going in there with them Modoc sharpshooters and all—but he had his job to do, and that was getting the wounded and dead soldiers out."

"Suppose you just sit things out here awhile and let them come find you."

This time the youngster shook his head violently. "Oh, no, Mr. O'Roarke! I can't do that—that'd be like being a coward. Not doing what I was called on to do for the soldiers."

O'Roarke's heart felt tugged for this young son of a Yreka friend of his. One day Ian's own sons would be this age. "Ain't no law says you gotta go back in there, Eugene."

"I'll go. My daddy wouldn't want to know I backed down from doing what I could for the soldiers."

"Your daddy's a fair man. He wouldn't hold it against you if you got a bad feeling about it. Besides, you've done a hell of a lot already. No man can call you coward."

Eugene sighed and shrugged, reaching down deep into his worn britches. He pulled out his old pocket watch. "My pa give me that a few years back—sixteenth birthday. I figure it ought'n go back to him now."

Ian felt strange, standing there with that watch plopped in his palm, unable to find words for the sudden, cold feeling that spilled down his spine at that very minute.

Hovey stuffed a handful of crumpled scrip into O'Roarke's hand on top of the watch. "This here money's for my ma and pa. Got good wages working for the army while I could."

"I—I can't—"

"You gotta take it, Mr. O'Roarke. 'Cepting John Fairchild and Press Dorris—I don't know nobody else here. And I'm gonna find some paper now—write my ma a letter telling her what's in my heart before I go on out there again. You wait—"

Ian gripped the young man's shoulder. "Get hold of yourself, Eugene. You aren't acting like you're in your right mind."

The boy tried a thin smile out, so thin that it quickly drained from his freckled face. "I've never been more sure of anything in my life, Mr. O'Roarke. So, I'm asking you again if you'll wait while I write my ma a letter."

Ian felt a burn in his throat as he answered, "I'll wait, Eugene. You go ahead and take your time writing that letter."

Since the official word had it that the Modocs were surrounded and only a mopping-up action was required, the quartermaster in charge of removing army casualties from the battlefield could not assign Eugene Hovey an escort for his first trip into the Lava Beds that morning. Eugene was only able to talk another young teamster from Yreka into accompanying him as soon as the sun made its appearance for the day at the eastern edge of the Modoc's Stronghold.

Alone, the two men were crossing the meadow below the bluff where the peace tent had stood less than a week before.

"You hear something?" Hovey asked, stopping.

His companion came up with his pair of mules. "Not a thing, Eugene."

Hovey's eyes strained into the surrounding rocks and brush. He glanced at the mules a moment, trying to pick out if they were acting at all strangely. "Sure you didn't hear nothing?"

"Not a thing. C'mon. This is the place they murdered that general and the preacher. Gives me the willies. C'mon, Eugene."

The crack of a rifle from the nearby rocks alerted the men that they were under attack. But as the young teamster turned to yell at Hovey, he found Eugene holding a blood-soaked hand over his eye and forehead, collapsing back against his frantic mules.

Another shot whined overhead, close enough that the youngster heard it hiss past with his name on it.

The teamster bolted off, abandoning the mules and his friend, Eugene Hovey.

Hooker Jim and four young warriors who were among

those who had escaped the Stronghold under cover of darkness and were circling around to the southwest that early morning to create some diversionary ruckus at the soldier camp had spotted the two white men coming into the meadow leading their mules.

The five fired a few more shots at the fleeing teamster, then turned back to the body of the white man they had wounded.

They found Hovey barely alive, moaning and calling for someone to be sure to give a letter to his mother. To tell her good-bye for him.

With a savage laugh, Hooker Jim himself put his boot on the young man's neck and began slashing off the white man's scalp. Hovey cried out in pain and rage, not able to struggle much as he was already nearing death from the head wound. Venting all their own pent-up rage at the white men and soldiers, the other warriors stripped the young man naked and cut off his manhood parts, stuffing them into the teamster's mouth. Then, while the others slashed at arms and legs, feet and hands, to dismember the white man, Hooker Jim found a rock he could hold in his hand.

And with it he smashed the young teamster's head until it was no more than the thickness of two fingers.

The Modoc warriors then followed Hooker Jim, whose idea it was to go through with their original plan of attacking the soldier camp to cause confusion among the white men. They were joined by a dozen more men at the base of the bluff. The warriors hurled themselves against the outlying pickets.

"Sergeant!" hollered Grier, the lieutenant left behind by Gillem to guard his headquarters. "We've got Indians in camp!"

Fairchild, Dorris and O'Roarke came running with their weapons, joining other civilians and the soldiers hurrying to meet the attack. Grier quickly scribbled a note for the signal sergeant to send a message to Major Green somewhere near the shoreline of Tule Lake.

Modocs out of stronghold and attacking camp.

A brisk, hot fight held the white men down as the eighteen Modocs spread out, giving the impression of far more warriors firing into camp. O'Roarke and the others had no way of knowing how many Modocs they were facing.

Ian was one certain that Captain Jack would come out of the Stronghold fighting to avenge the damage done him by the soldiers—and what smarter way was there than to totally abandon their Stronghold and immediately attack the soldier camp with his entire force?

Minutes dragged by as bullets whistled overhead and the crack of enemy rifles drew nearer and nearer to Grier's small band of defenders—until the Modocs crossed into the camp itself.

But just as everything appeared darkest for that small band of defenders, they watched as the Modocs turned, their fire being drawn behind them.

A cheer went up among the civilians and the few soldiers in camp.

Another cheer erupted from a band of reinforcements sent by Major Green from the Lava Beds to rescue Gillem's headquarters.

"They won't be back any time soon," the young lieutenant said confidently.

Ian turned to him. "Wouldn't be so sure. Captain Jack is out and on the loose now. And there's no telling what a wounded animal will do."

The best thing that could be said about the fighting on the sixteenth was that the soldiers had forced the Modocs out of the Stronghold.

Trouble was, they paid a terrible price for that black rubble and honeycomb of caves.

On through that long night of the sixteenth, the mortars and howitzers hammered away at the center of the Lava Beds. In the pauses between bombardments, Donegan listened to volleys of rifle shots coming from the soldier camp.

"The Modocs attacking camp again?" Seamus wondered out loud, digging into his haversack for something to eat. It was as empty as every other haversack in the Lava Beds.

He sighed, laying his head back against the sharp rocks, scratching at his many open lacerations from those rocks, angry at the mosquitoes that came in vapors each night to torment every man.

"No," replied the old sergeant. "Sounds to me like they're burying some boys."

Donegan nodded, eyes squinting in the darkness, knowing no man would see those gray eyes moisten. Too many times Seamus had dug midnight graves for brothers-in-arms, fellow soldiers who would be left behind in unmarked holes. Nameless dead all too often unknown by their own officers.

"Always hated funerals meself," Donegan said eventually as the riflefire faded away across the darkened rocks. "Suppose I'll even hate my own."

"The only one a man's allowed to hate," replied the sergeant.

By the next morning, the army discovered its quarry had flown.

Only a handful of Modoc sharpshooters remained anywhere near their old fortifications to slow both Green's and Mason's troops as they ordered every able-bodied man to push south from the shore of Tule Lake into the Stronghold. As quiet as it was among those rocks, most men feared they were again walking into some sort of trap as they advanced farther, and farther still.

But the three-day battle was over.

The fissures and crevices and fractures all converged at the edge of the central ravine of the Stronghold itself.

"God only knows where that bastard Captain Jack is now," a soldier grumbled.

"I thought those Warm Springs Injuns were supposed to tighten a noose around them sonsabitches," cried another.

"Injun blood is Injun blood," complained a third. "Them Tenino mercenaries was just watching out for their own, is what they was doing."

While Colonel Gillem had been failed by his officers in their attempts to either capture or kill the renegade Modocs, the arrival of soldiers in the Stronghold did nonetheless mark the turning point of the Modoc War. From 29 November, when Captain James Jackson had unknowingly bungled himself into beginning the conflict, until the predawn darkness of 17 April, this had been a war of siege and assault on impregnable fortifications that had caused union veterans to recall the vivid horrors of action suffered at Atlanta or even Vicksburg itself.

Unfortunately for the army, the Modocs were now no longer tied down where the soldiers could find them and hammer them at will. Shutting them off from food and water.

Now the Indians were on the run, free to hit when and where they wanted.

When the first soldiers advanced into the heart of the Stronghold, they found the Modocs had abandoned the bodies of three men of fighting age, along with the bodies of eight women evidently killed during the incessant artillery bombardment.

Officers ordered squads to cautiously search every cave and depression, every single structure, to eliminate the chance of ambush by hidden warriors.

At the resounding rifle shot, Seamus yanked his head into his shoulders and dropped to a knee. His eyes scanned the far rocks.

"Sounds like it come from up ahead where that other outfit is searching," said the old infantry sergeant.

It had been too many hours without sleep and with too little food for Donegan to have too much a sense of humor. He joined the sergeant's patrol as they continued into the labyrinth of caves and fissures. At the entrance to a small cave, they found a handful of soldiers busy over the corpse of an old man.

"You boys just kill that ol' Injun?" asked the sergeant.

One of the soldiers rolled his head around to smile a gap-toothed grin that reminded Seamus of a coyote loping on the fringes of the slaughter yard at Fort Phil Kearny, Dakota Territory, seven years gone now.*

"Ol' Injun—young Injun . . . what's it matter to you, Sergeant? We're just doing what the cap'n ordered."

"You was ordered to kill that unarmed old man?"

"We was ordered to kill Modocs, Sergeant," he replied. "Besides, he wasn't helpless. He was holding a knife at us when we come up on him."

Seamus stepped forward. "A brave one, ain't you? Killing an old man with a knife . . . and the five of you with loaded Springfields."

The gap-toothed one waved his knife at the Irishman as he asked the sergeant, "Who's this big-talking Mick now? Where's your uniform?"

"Here you go," interrupted one of the soldiers working over the old Modoc. "You can have a piece of his scalp, Avery—since't one of your bullets hit him too."

Seamus wagged his head as the gap-toothed Avery held up his little chunk of the old man's scalp, still dripping with blood. Another private was cutting off the Indian's eyebrows for souvenirs as well.

Donegan stepped away, walking on among the black rocks as the knot of soldiers laughed at his back.

He heard another shot and a third that morning of the seventeenth, in what had been the Modocs' Stronghold. Later he learned the soldiers had killed two old women, too feeble to escape with the others when Captain Jack led his band south into the maze of lava flow, deep into the heart of darkness.

---

* THE PLAINSMEN Series, vol. 1, *Sioux Dawn*

The total casualties for the three days of battle were six killed and seventeen wounded from Green's command. Mason suffered no casualties.

Gillem took but brief satisfaction in securing the Stronghold. He now had to find the Modocs, and as quickly as was humanly possible. Captain Jack's people needed water, which would send them scattering across the surrounding countryside. But for the time being the colonel ordered Captain Perry's cavalry to make a wide circuit of the southern fringe of the Lava Beds. Perry was to ascertain if the hostiles had escaped into more open country, or if they were still hidden somewhere, anywhere in the great expanse of the lava flows.

"Might not be all that bad, though," Gillem confided to his officers late that afternoon while they awaited the results of Perry's reconnaissance. "If we do flush Captain Jack's henchmen into the open to fight for the first time in this bloody little war—we can damn well finish them in a matter of minutes."

For three days things were quiet.

No one heard or saw sign of the Modocs.

Gillem expected news to arrive at almost any time from either Captain Perry's reconnaissance or from Donald McKay's scout with his Warm Springs mercenaries.

Then Lieutenant Howe rode in with his twenty-man escort for a wagon train of supplies coming in from Scorpion Point to the new soldier camp at the Stronghold. A clearly agitated Howe saluted and reported to Colonel Gillem himself.

"What happened?" snapped the colonel as he watched a limp body being eased down from one of the wagons, another soldier wounded and helped to the ground by two of his own outfit.

"A band of Modocs hit us, Colonel," Howe explained. "We were caught between the lakeshore and a high ridge of rock."

"Damn," Gillem muttered. "They're not staying in one

spot, for fear we'll find 'em and wipe 'em out." He turned back to the lieutenant. "Get your man seen to . . . and your man buried with proper rights."

Howe saluted and was leaving when Donald McKay made a grand entrance into camp, causing quite a stir. He had been gone for the better part of two days, sniffing around with his scouts.

McKay accepted the offer of coffee and drank an entire cup with lots of sugar poured in before he appeared ready to report. Gillem realized the man was, after all, half Indian and would talk when he got damned ready to talk.

"We counted forty warriors left in there—give or take a couple."

"You're sure about that?" Gillem asked.

"They weren't moving around much. Forty is what we counted."

Gillem turned to Green and Mason with a smile. "If we add another ten for those who attacked Lieutenant Howe —looks like we're dealing with something on the order of fifty fighting men, gentlemen." He looked back at McKay. "Where'd you find them?"

McKay pointed south. "About four miles from here . . . in a long ravine formed from the lava rock."

"Good," Gillem allowed. "It looks like they haven't busted out of the Lava Beds yet and scattered all over hell's acre, boys. We can still get a crack at them, and soon."

"The sooner the better," Green said. "I don't trust 'em to stay in one place too much longer, Colonel."

Later that afternoon of the twentieth, when Perry rode in with his exhausted and hungry troops mounted on trail-weary horses, the captain confirmed Gillem's hunch. It had taken his outfit three days fighting the brutal terrain and the unfit mounts, but the news was good.

"We did not run across any sign that showed the Modocs have fled the Lava Beds. It's my considered opinion they're still holed up somewhere . . . just to the south of us."

Chapter 27

April 24–26, 1873

"They've got Canby's replacement coming," Seamus announced to A. B. Meacham.

Each day, the Irishman had made it a point to visit the peace commissioner in the hospital. For almost a week now there had been little going on in any other army camps.

But today word had it that Gillem was sending out his artillery officers on a reconnaissance south of the Stronghold into the Lava Beds, where all reports had the Modocs holed up. The officers could then tell the colonel what his chances were of driving the hostiles out of their position without investing the lives of more infantry over that rugged and unforgiving ground.

"I've heard as well," Meacham replied. "A dyed-in-the-wool soldier, I'm told. Jefferson C. Davis: colonel of the Twenty-third Infantry up at Fort Townsend, Washington Territory."

"Breveted a major general during the rebellion down south."

Meacham coughed a bit of a chuckle, wincing with the pain of his head wounds. "How you put on, Irishman. Don't you think I know that was more than a damned rebellion? For the likes of you it was nothing less than the pure hell of war, was it not?"

Donegan peered at the ground between his cracked boots and for a moment brooded of how he could talk the quartermaster out of a new pair. But like a troublesome prairie buffalo gnat, Meacham's question still invaded his thoughts as much as he might try to evade the brutal memories.

"Davis ought to show up here any day now." It had been ten days since the War Department appointed the hard-bitten colonel to fill Canby's shoes.

Meacham lay back against the pillow made of a rolled army blanket. "This war's hell by itself, Seamus. Can you believe those young soldiers cut off the head of an old man they killed in the Modocs' Stronghold and presented it to Dr. Cabaniss?"

"What for?"

"I suppose for a souvenir—an oddity of sorts. Cabaniss says he will keep it preserved in a glass morning jar. Perhaps for display someday as the head of Schonchin John."

"Was it his head?"

Meacham's eyes told it with a glint of fire. "I ought to know, shouldn't I? He was one who tried to kill me." He sighed. "No. Whoever that poor old man was—it wasn't Schonchin John, brother of the Yainax chief. Riddle agrees with me . . . but it's no use telling any of these soldiers—even that butcher of a surgeon Cabaniss."

"Now, the man's good on bones and bleeding, Alfred."

"Lot you know, Seamus. It's not been your wounds he's been jabbing with his probe three times daily. And a lot he lacks in civility as well—I've had to take another vow of temperance because of that man!"

"That whiskey was just what you needed right then."

"That's where you're wrong, lad. I needed to get my hands on Schonchin John at that moment."

Seamus wiped his palms across the tops of his thighs. It was warm in the tent today, the sun beating down on the canvas, making things much warmer in here than they were outside in the gentle spring breezes.

"I hear Gillem's sent those Tenino Indians down to hold the Stronghold," Meacham said.

He nodded. "They've got themselves a nice camp there now, so the Modocs can't come running back in to reoccupy the area. But there's not much going on over there except that Muybridge fella from San Francisco."

"The photographer I've heard about?"

"Yes, that's the one. Been taking stereoscopic views of the Stronghold caves and fortifications, officers and the Warm Springs scouts—even this camp."

"Perhaps I should pretty myself up and let him take a photograph of me—warts, scars and all."

Donegan smiled. "Don't you joke now—Muybridge would jump at the chance to immortalize one of the survivors of the peace tent massacre."

"Him and every other hack newsman west of the Missouri River."

"They've been hounding you again."

"Every day it seems someone new arrives here from Linkville or Yreka—representing one newspaper back east or the other. And all wanting my story of the murders. I bloody well keep those young guards at the tent flaps busy turning reporters away."

"Don't be so hard on them, Meacham. Their kind will bite at any little morsel any one of us feed them—blowing it up into a story of their heroic exploits for their readers back home."

He sighed deeply. "I'm growing weary again, Irishman. I apologize."

"No need. I'll find me something else to do, and leave you sleep in peace. At least in here you don't have to worry about looking yourself over at least once a day to check for wood ticks." Seamus scratched at his collar absently. "Just came down to see you after Gillem sent his artillery officers off to study the terrain where he figures the Modocs are hiding. When they get back, the

colonel will know better how to drive Captain Jack's warriors out into the open—"

The not too distant crack of rifles interrupted Donegan
and aroused the dozing Meacham.

"That sounded damned close, Irishman."

"Too close," Donegan replied, already on his feet and
halfway to the tent flaps. "I'll see what's doing."

Outside, the camp was a mass of confusion, soldiers
going this way, teamsters in another, most dragging
teams of horses or mules to the far side of the tent village.
Seamus grabbed the arm of a young soldier as he was
trotting by.

"What's the commotion?"

"Modocs attacking the camp." He pointed, pulled his
arm free and trotted on toward the sound of the firing.

The first shot to actually reach camp whistled through
the leafy branches of a tree overhead.

"Donegan!"

He was back in the tent before Meacham could holler
out again.

"Are we in danger?"

He shrugged. "Can't tell—but I wouldn't put it past
those red bastards to boldly stomp on in here to try to
finish the job they started on you two weeks ago."

Seamus watched Meacham shift uneasily on his bed,
eyes squinted as he adjusted the bandages wrapped about
his skull.

"I'll stay with you, friend." Donegan took a pistol from
his belt and laid it on the side of the cot in easy reach of
Meacham's hand. Then took his revolver from its holster
at his hip. Meacham laid his hand on the pistol and closed
his eyes a minute.

"No man is ever going to try for my scalp again—I've
sworn to that, Donegan."

Seamus winked as a flurry of shots landed close by,
snapping canvas and banging pots and pans in a nearby
mess-kitchen.

"Why would anyone want your poor scalp? There's too

damned much fallow ground there between the fertile grasslands for one of Captain Jack's boys to make much of a fuss over."

Meacham reached up to rub a few fingers over the very top of his bald head not covered with bandages. "I suppose you're right. But just the same—I'll keep your pistol here till the ruckus is over. With that fine head of curly hair, you might need my help saving your scalp, Irishman."

The sudden roar of one of the mountain howitzers shook the sides of the tent. A second cannon erupted. In the distance they could hear the impact of the shells. Ian O'Roarke poked his head through the flaps, then strode on in with a look of relief on his face.

"By glory—I feared I'd lost you to the Modocs, Seamus. Pardon me, Alfred."

"Come in and pull your pistol free, Ian. We're preparing for the bastirds to breech the walls."

Ian dragged up an empty hardtack case and settled atop it. "Everytime the cannon fires, the Modocs scuttle for the rocks. After the shell explodes, they come prancing back out to show us their brown bottoms and call the soldiers by every name the miners in Yreka taught them!"

"A lively show of it, eh?" Meacham asked, stroking the blued metal on the pistol.

"They come out laughing at the soldiers, line up and point their rifles at an angle—just like Gillem's mortars—then one of 'em gives the command to fire and the bullets rattle into camp."

"You're sure they're not storming the camp?"

Ian shook his head. "Not a chance of it, my friend. Rest easy now until it's over. Captain Biddle is mustering a force of infantry to go chase the warriors back to wherever they came from."

"Hell, most likely," Meacham muttered, his head sinking into the blanket pillow.

"Aye, hell is where they ought to return as well."

* * *

Late the next afternoon, 25 April, word came from the signal station located high on the bluff that they had spotted a thin column of smoke rising some five or more miles south of the army's camp, away in the heart of the Lava Beds. The tallest landmark in that inhospitable area was what the soldiers had come to nickname Sugar Loaf, called Big Sand Butte by the local settlers.

And to the west of that ugly, bald cinder cone was hell on earth—a place called Black Ledge.

Despite the austere conditions to be found in that country, John Fairchild along with other civilians advised Colonel Gillem that the Modocs could survive in there for some time.

"There's enough water back in some of those lava caves cut through the Black Ledge," Pressley Dorris explained.

"And enough seeps in the ledge that's been catching water one rainy season after another," added Ian O'Roarke. "Likely that smoke your men spotted was the Modocs burning their dead."

The colonel looked up in amused wonder. "They cremate their dead?"

O'Roarke nodded. "No other reason I can think of for Indians on the run to be making such a big fire."

Gillem drummed the fingers of one hand on the map he had spread beneath his elbows, his eyes focused on something more than the rugged terrain of the Black Ledge country.

"All right," he sighed. "Thank you very much, fellas. Now I need you to excuse the rest of us so we can discuss our plans for a reconnaissance in force down to that Big Sand Butte."

Seamus recalled how John Fairchild had stopped at the flaps of the colonel's tent and turned to speak to Gillem.

"That purgatory of the devil is where you'll find the Modocs—I'll lay my ranch on it."

Gillem grinned without humor. "We'll see if there's anything substantial about your hunch on the Black

Ledge, Mr. Fairchild. Now, if you and the others would step aside and let the army do its job."

By the time the stars came out that night, Seamus had talked his way into accompanying the patrol that would be leaving in the morning, as one of three civilian packers assigned to go along. Lieutenant Thomas F. Wright of the Twelfth Infantry readily agreed, but said he would have to clear it with his company commander for the reconnaissance, Captain Evan Thomas of the Fourth Artillery.

"Artillery?" Seamus asked.

"Gillem wants Thomas heading things up so he and his boys can determine if cannon can be used to blast the red devils out of the rocks once the Teninos find them for us."

"We're taking scouts?"

"They're meeting us somewhere down the line," Wright explained. His father, George Wright, had been a brigadier general of volunteers and had commanded the Military Division of the Pacific until he drowned at sea in 1865. Young Wright had attended West Point in the forties, then served with distinction during the Civil War. "Gillem's going to send them heliograph orders come sunrise. McKay's to take fourteen with him from their camp in the Stronghold and meet us near that Big Sand Butte and Black Ledge everyone's talking about."

With the gray of dawn creeping over the land, Seamus stood with the others that Saturday morning, 26 April, drinking steaming coffee and eating hardtack soaked in pork grease at the fires that drove a chill from the spring morning. Fifty-nine enlisted soldiers would be led by Captain Thomas and Lieutenant Wright, in addition to three more officers: Lt. Albion Howe, son of General A. P. Howe, and a Civil War veteran of Cold Harbor and Petersburg in his own right; along with lieutenants George M. Harris and Arthur Cranston.

In command of the mule-train was head packer Louis Webber, who welcomed the offer of help from Donegan and another assistant packer. Assistant Surgeon Dr. Bernard A. Semig was assigned to accompany the scouting detail to be guided by H. C. "Bill" Ticknor, a civilian familiar with the area and surveyor of the Ticknor Road south of the Lava Beds.

As the infantry and artillery troops lined up in double columns preparing to march out, many handed their comrades letters they had written to family back home. Those young men and those not so young were cheerful as they pulled out at sunrise, marching south into some of the most rugged country to be found in the Lava Beds. Guide Ticknor suggested they march down a wide depression that existed between two up-vaulted lava flows that had long ago heaped themselves ominously on either side of the eroded valley.

Not long after leaving Gillem's camp, the land began to slowly rise toward the south. Thomas ordered twelve soldiers from Company E out as skirmishers to march in front of the column, as they were forced to slow their pace in making the climb, along with the difficulty encountered upon entering the rugged terrain characterized by the passing of the two great lava flows: rocks of all sizes, from knife-sharp pebbles to house-sized boulders; cinder cones left behind by ancient geologic activity; buttes composed of crumbling black pumice.

It was as if Seamus could almost smell the stench of the devil's own sulfur and brimstone exuding all along their path through the wavelike layers of frozen lava.

For better than a mile they had marched without any flankers to cover the higher ground on either side of their column. Growing more anxious as they moved farther into the unknown, bleak and forbidding country, Seamus sensed the scar on his back burn like someone had poured coal-oil down his spine and set that strip of pain afire with a match.

On the outside of the columns, he edged up to Sergeant Robert Romer, attached to the Fourth Artillery. "Say, Sergeant. You remember those Modocs we saw far to the east when we marched out of camp this morning?"

Romer nodded, his eyes scanning the higher elevations on the right side of their march.

"I sure don't feel good with Cap'n Thomas not putting out flankers."

"We usually push cannon around, so you see why we're not used to this marching like foot-sloggers," Romer replied. "I'll go talk with the captain myself."

He strode up to Thomas with Donegan along.

"It's a good idea, Romer," responded the artillery captain. "Mr. Wright, let's order out some flankers."

A half-dozen men were ordered out on the right, another six for the left flank. Yet the farther Thomas's men left Gillem's camp behind, the more the flankers tended to ease back toward the column of twos.

Growing angrier by the mile, infantry sergeant Malachi Clinton sped up to growl at Lieutenant Wright.

"I don't figure it's any use forcing these fellas out any farther than they're willing to go for now, Sergeant," Wright said.

"The hell, you say?" Sergeant Romer growled, disgusted. "We need flankers out, Malachi. If those privates won't do it—and the lieutenants won't make 'em—then it's up to the sergeants to do it."

Romer strode off alone, walking the far right flank by himself, intently watching the countryside.

Seamus grew more and more anxious as with every yard the soldiers in the columns bunched closer and closer together, purposely slowing their march as they began the tedious climb to higher country.

"You going to cover the left flank?" Donegan asked Clinton.

The sergeant wagged his head. "No need, mister. We haven't seen a sign of those Injuns since we pulled away from camp."

Wright glanced at the Irishman, clearly disgusted with the performance of the soldiers so far on the patrol. "I haven't been out here in the west all that long, but, Sergeant—I do know that when you don't see Indians, that's when you better be on the lookout for them."

"Where the devil you going this morning, Patrick?" Ian O'Roarke asked of the civilian sutler who was whistling as he saddled his mule at the corral when the settler walked up with Frank and Winema Riddle. "Heading into Linkville for more supplies today?"

"No," McManus answered. At the outbreak of war the government had awarded him the sutlering contract for the campaign. "Been thinking some about riding out to catch up with that bunch headed down to Big Sand Butte."

"What the hell for?"

McManus smiled. "See for myself some of that country, since there's soldiers enough going that way for Gillem." From the corner of his eye he suddenly caught some movement off to his side. "Hey, what'd you do that for?"

He lunged for Winema as she slapped the rump of his mule, sending it galloping off through the tents into the soldier camp.

"Goddamn you!" he whirled, glaring at the woman, then Frank Riddle. "What's got in your wife, Frank?" He ripped the bridle Winema had taken off the mule from her hand. "Gimme that—goddamn!"

McManus stood there frustrated, swearing, shaking a fist at the frightened woman as Frank pushed her behind him, pointing his own finger at the sutler.

"Stay back, McManus—Toby's trying to tell you something."

He stopped in his tracks. "What the hell's she trying to say? That your squaw don't like me?"

"I like you, McManus. You good white man," Winema started to explain. "I like your wife."

He shook with anger. "Then why go and run off my mule like that?"

"Don't go with soldiers."

Ian craned closer. "She . . . you mean you don't want him to go with that bunch marched out this morning?"

Winema nodded.

"Why?"

"I have bad feeling."

Ian rocked back on his heels, his eyes moving to Frank. "Same kind of bad feeling she had when Canby and the others went down to meet Jack in the meadow?"

Frank nodded.

But McManus still refused to believe. "Why there's over sixty armed soldiers in that bunch—against only forty some Modocs—if there was to be a fight. And I can't see it likely that—"

"I run mule off for the sake of your wife." Winema came around Frank at last, her hands supplicating McManus. "Please," she begged. "Please! Stay in camp—for sake of your wife."

Chapter 28

April 26, 1873

The last two miles reaching the Black Ledge had proved a hard march for the soldiers. New topsoil lay atop the older lava flow broken down by millions of years of weathering. In that soil among the sharp-edged stones the size of a man's fist emerged the new green bunch-grass, scrub oak and sage. As they climbed, the soldiers entered a land of stunted mahogany trees that would at least provide some shade for the coming noon hour.

For the past two hours the soldiers had been observed by Captain Jack, who had brought along twenty-two warriors.

At first Scar-Faced Charley and his men had been worried the approaching white men intended on attacking their camp of women and children. But when the soldiers kept on moving directly south instead of angling east into the rougher lava-flow country where Jack's band had their camp, the Modocs began to skulk along the soldiers' path to the Big Sand Butte. At times the warriors were no farther than a half-mile from the white men, remaining hidden behind the higher ridges bordering the valley. And as the soldiers bunched tighter and tighter together, it became easier and easier to watch them. Especially when the soldiers marched slower and slower.

Even though Captain Jack's warriors had to cross much more difficult terrain, they were able to keep up with the soldiers' plodding progress.

As the sun climbed to mid-sky, Jack and Charley conferred, figuring the objective of the white men was the tall singular butte near at hand. Jack ordered his warriors to hurry on ahead to set up an ambush in a good place on the far side of the Black Ledge where the soldiers would pass.

As ordered, the warriors climbed the eastern slopes of the butte and concealed themselves behind outcroppings of black rock and settled in to wait for the soldiers who would soon be marching beneath them to their deaths. There was plenty of cover to hide them, what with the grass and sage and stunted mahogany trees.

The soldiers came on, marching tightly together at their plodding pace, even the few skirmishers in the vanguard slowing now as they climbed the gradual slope up Black Ledge.

"Once they are over the top, and past that large depression," Charley explained to Jack, "we can fire on them at once and kill them all."

Jack nodded, approving the plan, just as one of the soldiers leading the group two hundred feet below them held up his arm and shouted to the rest.

"They've seen us?" asked the chief anxiously.

Charley's eyes grew big with fear that they had been discovered. But below them the soldiers did a very strange thing.

They stopped their march far short of the planned ambush site—then milled about a moment while they stacked their rifles. This done, they gathered in knots to plop in the shade of the mahogany trees.

Seamus joined the rest as the soldiers broke ranks and settled on the sparse, new grasses in the patches of welcome shade, while guide Ticknor assured Captain Thomas.

"Ain't a Modoc in fifteen miles, Captain. I know this country—and those damned Modocs too."

They pulled their haversacks from their arms and drank greedily at the canteens before digging out their lunch. Some men yanked off their dusty broughams, rubbing their sweaty, aching feet with a primitive, carnal pleasure as they joked and jabbered like a bunch of boys playing hooky, slipping away from school to cavort at the local swimming hole.

"Say, Malachi," hollered a soldier. "Sing us that song you was trying to teach us last night."

Sergeant Clinton beamed. "You mean the one Perry's cavalry boys taught me about Cap'n Jack?"

"Yeah," answered another soldier. "The one about Cap'n Jack!"

Clinton swiped crumbs of hardtack from his bushy mustache and downed a swallow of lukewarm water from his canteen before he attempted his off-key rendition of the current popular song.

> "I'm Captain Jack of the Lava Beds,
> I'm cock o' the walk and chief of the reds.
> I can lift the hair and scalp the heads
> Of the whole United States Army!"

Most of the men, officers included, roared with glee at that first verse and begged Clinton to sing more.

"Let me have my lunch, boys—then I'll teach all the words to you."

Seamus nudged Romer and asked quietly, "Where are those Warm Springs scouts supposed to meet up with us all morning?"

"That's a good question," replied Captain Thomas, overhearing the civilian. He stood, dusting off his blue britches, ramming the cork back in the neck of his canteen. "They damned well should have joined up by now."

"We've seen 'em from time to time all morning, sir,"

Lieutenant Harris said as he too stood. "It's almost like they didn't want to march with us, sir."

"C'mon, Mr. Harris," Thomas replied. "Bring a couple signalmen and their heliograph with you." He pointed up the slope of the tall butte. "We'll go up there, give the country a look for McKay's scouts—then signal back to camp that we've seen nothing and will be turning back soon."

Minutes later Lieutenant Wright approached a pair of soldiers finishing their meal and pulling on their boots. "You men—go up that little ridge to the east there. Keep an eye out for us. I don't want any of Captain Jack's butchers sneaking up on us from the place yonder where we spotted that smoke yesterday."

As an afterthought, the two infantrymen picked up their rifles and plodded toward the slope. They were halfway up when the first bullets from long range cut the air around them. Diving and dodging, the pair scurried downhill.

Up the slope, Captain Thomas turned at the first shot, his face gone chalky. Grabbing the shoulder of the signalman kneeling over his heliographic equipment on the slope, the captain demanded, "Are you set up to send to camp?"

"I—I am, sir!"

"Then by damn tell them we've found the Indians—behind the bluff!"

It was the only message received by Lieutenant John Quincy Adams in the signal tower at Gillem's camp.

Almost immediately firing broke out above the soldiers on a wide front. In panic some of the men dove alone or in pairs for cover among the fissures in the black rocks, without weapons or their shoes. Others jostled and fought among themselves for their clothing and weapons, knocking over the stacks of rifles.

It was precious minutes before any fire was returned at the Modocs. But in that time Jack's warriors moved one by one down the butte until they ringed that wide depression where the soldiers huddled. For the most part the warriors were behind the rocky ridges bordering that hollow the white men had chosen for the noon stop.

Seamus slid up beside Sergeant Romer. "We're trapped."

"Like fish in a barrel here, mister. Only way out is to make a dash through their flanking fire—or charge face-on up that slope into the jaws of it."

"This bunch listen to you?" Donegan asked.

"Look at 'em," Romer growled, indicating some who were breaking and running. "They're peeing their pants right now. This bunch won't make a charge like that!"

"Mr. Wright!" barked Thomas as he made it back to the depression, bullets spouting earth around his heels.

"Sir?"

"Rally some of these men and take that ledge."

Wright swallowed hard. "That's more than five hundred yards of open ground, Captain."

Thomas's eyes implored him. "We're taking the hardest fire from that quarter, Lieutenant. And this patrol's done for if something isn't done about that bunch of snipers."

"We'll open up a path, sir," Wright replied with a swallow, turning to call upon his company to follow him in the assault.

"Pray these boys can make it through what you open up, Lieutenant," Thomas whispered as he turned to dash off to the southwest.

In a matter of seconds after Wright disappeared from the depression with his men, Seamus heard a volley of shots, then the rattle of withering gunshots. A handful of Wright's soldiers came scurrying back in the face of devastating fire. The rest were scattering off Black Ledge, running north for their lives.

Up top of the rocky ledges, Donegan watched one of the older Modocs pointing with his rifle, sending some of his warriors to follow the fleeing soldiers.

They'll follow those sojurs down like dogs—picking them off one by one, Seamus thought as he brought the

Henry to his shoulder again and squeezed off a shot at the warrior directing the attack. The bullet smashed against the top of the ledge, splattering and kicking up a spray of black dust.

"Wright needs help," Thomas was thinking out loud as he listened, watched, and grew more despondent.

"I'll go, sir," the young lieutenant volunteered.

Thomas turned to Arthur Cranston. "See if you can drive them back and give Wright a chance to break out."

Cranston could find only five soldiers who would accompany him into the open. Three were from Artillery Battery A, the other two from Wright's own infantry outfit. Seamus watched the lieutenant go, then decided to join the six. He reached the edge of the depression in time to watch Cranston turn his men to the west—right into the face of some Modoc flanking fire.

The six troopers lasted as many seconds, driven back and shot down to the man, their bodies shattered on the black rocks.

His heart in his throat, Seamus dropped to his belly behind some gray sage. *You've not been in it like this for a long time, Seamus. Hopeless, it is. Perhaps this is it—one by one . . . by one—*

"Mister!"

He turned to find Ticknor hollering at him, waving at him. Behind the guide, Thomas was leading what he had left of men. Something over thirty.

Donegan's mind burned, realizing in the space of a handful of minutes half of the captain's command had been slaughtered.

Slowing behind Ticknor, surgeon Semig waved the Irishman on as he passed.

"We're busting through! Going north!" Ticknor yelled, pointing, then hurrying to join Thomas's soldiers.

Thomas stopped, stood a moment, hollering. "Wright! Where the devil are you, Lieutenant? *Wright!*"

Semig halted suddenly as Donegan crabbed up through

the mahogany trees and grass, bullets spewing dirt clods around him.

"There's two here still alive," Semig muttered in a low voice, as if he were talking only to himself.

Seamus turned, watching a half-dozen, then more of the Modocs, leap off the ledges, working their way down into the depression to follow the retreating soldiers, shrieking their horrific war-cries. Some of them stopped momentarily, pointed their rifles at the ground and with a victorious screech fired their weapons.

"They're killing the wounded Thomas left behind!" Seamus started to rise, his instinct to defend those who had taken shelter in the confining fissures of rock, only to find that there was no escape once the Modocs came down from the ledge.

Semig yanked him back down. "I need you here, dammit! Help me stop this bleeding. Look at this," he implored, showing the Irishman his two hands glistening with crimson beneath the noonday sun.

"That's Wright," Seamus said, finally realizing.

"Four bullets—abdomen, thorax and head. Lord, how the man holds on—"

Donegan jerked Semig around. "Look around you. The Injins flanked us now."

Semig gazed up for a moment, seeing that the warriors were hotly pursuing the soldiers, mixing in among the fleeing troopers now, picking them off one by one in their wild flight. The Modocs were letting Ticknor escape.

Looming out of the shadow of the ledge, Thomas reappeared, waving his pistol, his other arm hanging limp and useless, blood dripping from it in huge glops to the sandy, rocky soil beneath him.

Semig looked up. "I found Wright for you, Captain."

Thomas did not glance down. "Good, Surgeon. Perhaps together we'll get out of here."

"Wright's not traveling anywhere, Cap'n," Donegan snapped. "He's too far gone."

Thomas fired his pistol up at the ledge above them,

then wagged his head dolefully. Only then did he stare down at his lieutenant. At last his eyes turned to the Irishman, glazed.

"Then, I'll not retreat a step farther. This is as good a place as any to die."

"There's no retreat for any of us now," Donegan said as he watched the troopers hurrying away to the north, followed by a few Modocs who continued to cut the soldiers down one at a time and fall on them with glee.

"The rest of you!" Thomas shouted at what he had left of his command. "Gather in here with us—now! We'll make a stand right here."

A few, then a dozen, and finally sixteen, crawled, crabbed and slid into the depression to join Thomas, Semig and the tall, gray-eyed civilian with the Henry at work and the big, brass .44 caliber shells dangling between the fingers of both hands like glossy sausages.

There was nowhere to go now. The Modocs were up on the high ledges two hundred feet above them. And many were circling on the slopes, dropping into the depression where the last survivors had gathered around the captain.

"Pile up what rocks you can around you, men. We can hold—"

Thomas spun around, the side of his face gone in a red explosion. He sprawled atop a soldier who shrieked in terror as the captain trembled. Then lay still. Seamus pulled Thomas off the frightened youngster.

"Turn around, you bloody idiot—and shoot that gun of yours!"

Semig cried out in pain and anger.

He was clutching his lower calf when Donegan slid down beside him. Blood oozed between the surgeon's fingers.

"At least they didn't kill me," he gritted his words out between his clenched teeth.

"Can you help yourself?" Seamus asked.

He nodded as the Irishman rolled away, plopping on his belly to fire the Henry. Up the slope he heard another unearthly scream that raised the hair on the back of his neck. He figured the Modocs had run across another wounded soldier and were making sport of their victim. He vowed they would not take him alive.

Seamus rolled on his side to pull free the pistol at his hip, not wanting to have it pinned under him when the final moments came.

That's when the bullet burrowed through him.

Cracking the collarbone, splintering it into sharp shards of icy pain that drove on through the Irishman's shoulder and upper arm.

Never since that day when the surgeons had poured fumaric acid into the wide saber slash along the great muscles of his back had he experienced such pain. So icy-hot and intense it took his breath away. He blinked with the creeping darkness threatening to swallow him, sure it was night and him staring into the black canopy overhead filled with a meteoric splendor.

Forcing his eyes open, he clambered for the pistol, hearing more and more of the shots whine and rattle into the depression Thomas had chosen for their last stand. A few men cried out. And he knew he could hear Semig muttering in pain. Others just breathing, raspy and fluid-filled with every terror-filled suck at life into their shattered lungs.

Somewhere close a man was cursing up a storm, his voice low and filled with rage. Cursing God and Jesus and the Virgin Mary and a litany of saints all in the same breath for his bad luck.

Then Seamus realized it was his voice—finding that he was doing the cursing. Consciously he bit down on his tongue until it hurt—but refused to cry out.

Instead he grabbed for the pistol, feeling how sticky it was in his hand. He could not see the hand for the shooting stars, but he knew where the hammer was beneath his thumb and pulled it back, listening to the cylinder roll amid the war-cries.

He hoped the chamber was loaded. A funny thing to

pray for now. If not to shoot the first Modoc who he heard inching close, then to shoot himself—

"All you fellows that ain't dead!" echoed a loud Indian voice from high on the ledge, speaking his best pidgin English, "you better go home now. We don't wanna kill you all in one day!"

Laughter resounded off the black ledges above him, all around him, as more and more of the Modocs took up the wild cackle that first erupted from their war-leader.

Donegan listened carefully, blinking his eyes again and again to clear them. He couldn't. One of the Modoc bullets had splattered against a nearby rock and blinded him. But the tears came for the pain. Tears come of the relief swelling in his breast now as he heard nearby footsteps moving off, slowly—no longer concerned with creeping in silence.

Now the many footsteps rattled rocks and rustled through the underbrush and grass along the slope of the depression.

Seamus brought the pistol up as his vision cleared for a moment in blinding sunlight. He looked down at his hand, within it the blood-covered revolver. The arm of his shirt and the entire front of his body covered with glistening crimson.

He felt faint again and fought the first eruption of his stomach with the fresh hardtack and warm water he had forced down for lunch minutes ago as the Modocs circled in for their attack.

Slowly, as his eyes cleared, Seamus rolled his head to see if anyone else was alive. The only one moving was Dr. Semig.

If you called his shallow breathing *moving*. Seamus watched the rise and fall of the surgeon's chest until a blessed blackness dripped over him once more. Purging the pain from his soul.

This time Seamus did not fight its long-awaited relief.

Chapter 29

April 26, 1873

*A*fter Winema had done all she could to give sutler Patrick McManus the willies, Ian O'Roarke strolled over to the bluff and found himself a spot in the grass near the signal tower.

Through that morning the soldiers atop the tower reported that they had the Thomas patrol in sight for the first three miles or so after the troops entered the heart of the Lava Beds. But the Warm Springs scouts who had marched out of their camp at the Stronghold that morning were still holding back and had not joined up with the soldiers by eleven o'clock.

That's when the patrol disappeared behind a high ledge better than halfway to Big Sand Butte.

Despite the confidence of Lieutenant John Adams's signal crew, Ian sensed the first flutters of fear trouble his belly.

"Thomas got sixty goddamned men, Mr. O'Roarke," one of the signalmen said. "And with another platoon of those scouts going to join up with 'em—the Modocs would be crazy to try anything."

"That's right," joined in another soldier. "There ain't but forty warriors left to that bastard Jack now. We can lick 'em, they choose to come out and fight."

"If they'll fight," echoed the first soldier.

"Squash 'em like bugs in those rocks!"

It was shortly after noon when Ian sensed real hunger rumbling in his belly. He rose, dusting off his canvas britches as Lieutenant Adams hollered down to the pickets at the foot of the signal tower.

"Tell the colonel I'm observing some activity from the bluff, private. Receiving a signal from them . . . wait."

Ian waited too, his hands gripping one of the tower support poles, knuckles gone white.

"We—have—found—the—Indians . . . They—are—behind—the—bluff." Adams tore the field glasses from his eyes. "Take that message to Colonel Gillem."

In a matter of minutes Gillem came trotting up with his staff, still buttoning his tunic.

"Is Thomas in danger?"

Adams looked down at the colonel, shaking his head. "Not from what I can see, sir. I've heard some distant firing—but it looks like they're hammering the Modocs pretty hard. From the looks of it, they've got the Injuns running, and hard—even driving 'em this way. About fifteen of our own behind them, and heading north through a narrow gap in the rock, coming this way quick as well."

This report would prove the beginning of another very dark day for the frontier army.

"Very well, Lieutenant," Gillem replied with a sigh that showed his irritation at being disturbed. "Send a messenger to let me know how things develop."

Nearly two hours of uncertainty passed. The hunger in Ian's belly grew every bit as much as the not knowing.

"Someone's coming in!" shouted a signalman atop the tower.

Many of the soldiers and a group of civilians hurried to the edge of the bluff to watch the first of the survivors reach Gillem's camp. They had covered more than four miles across formidable country in something less than an hour. These first were escorted into camp to find Dr. Cabaniss.

More showed up, straggling in alone or in pairs, exhausted but all telling the same story of terror.

When all these stragglers could tell was that Thomas had been in a fight with the Modocs and that they had been cut off from the captain, Gillem decided the enlisted men were simply overcome with shock and incapacitated with fear.

"Thomas outnumbers them, pure and simple," Gillem announced, replying to calls to send out a relief party. "I'm not alarmed in the least."

Nearly a half hour later a bugler stumbled into camp, telling for the first time a hair-raising story that was believed. In running from the scene of the attack, the soldier had dashed right into the arms of McKay's Tenino scouts. They had heard the firing and were finally hurrying to the scene when they were pinned down by the twenty-some men of Wright's company who had escaped the massacre and were fleeing pell-mell from the scene.

On their way those soldiers bumped into McKay's scouts—and in their terrified state, any dark face appeared to be an enemy. The soldiers fired on the Warm Springs Indians, cutting the scouts off and preventing them from marching to rescue the troops still pinned down at Black Ledge.

McKay had ordered the bugler to blow every call he knew. The half-breed declared that if the soldiers back in Gillem's camp didn't respond to the frantic call of the bugle, perhaps the Modocs killing the soldiers at Black Ledge would become fearful, believing that soldiers were on the way to rescue the encircled patrol.

More than an hour after his own capture by the Teninos, the bugler watched McKay's men bring in a captured artillery sergeant. The half-breed asked the two soldiers to go to their frightened comrades and tell them to stop firing so his Teninos could go on to help those who were still up near the Big Sand Butte.

But when the sergeant and bugler got clear of the Indian scouts, the pair doubled back and around, heading directly for Gillem's camp in great haste.

Only then did Gillem wake up and realize Thomas was in serious trouble.

Ordering Major Green to take all available men with him, Green found sixty-five soldiers ready to move out immediately. At the same time, Lieutenant Adams signaled the news to Major Mason's camp near the Stronghold. Mason dispatched Captain James Jackson along with lieutenants Kyle and Miller to lead a detachment of cavalrymen to the scene.

As Green was marching his troops out of Gillem's camp, O'Roarke watched assistant surgeon McElderry present himself to the colonel and volunteer to go along with the major.

"There's no need of that, Doctor," Gillem replied. "Mason will be sending out one of his three physicians with his rescue party."

After an hour and a half of rapid march to the south, Captain Jackson joined up with Major Green's men. A few minutes later McKay hailed the column and brought his scouts in.

The half-breed told the soldier leaders that his Teninos had gone on in to the battlesite and found only a handful of wounded men left alive. While they were certain they had not found all those who might have survived the attack, the scouts gave water and wrapped some wounds before they turned back toward Gillem's camp.

The rest were dead.

It was only then, as darkness was beginning to swallow the land and McKay told them of the few wounded they had found, that the soldiers realized there was not a surgeon among them. After conferring, Jackson and Green agreed that the peril faced by any survivors far outweighed any difficulty in negotiating the difficult terrain in the dark. They chose to plunge ahead through the Lava

Beds, heading for the faraway Big Sand Butte slowly as it slowly disappeared in the deepening twilight.

For more than three hours they fought their way through the unforgiving landforms until it became clear they might be in danger of injuring their own men as darkness seeped down upon the jagged countryside.

"We're lost—there's nothing else to do until morning." Lieutenant Kyle moved among the men to explain as they were ordered to find themselves a patch of ground and pile up rocks around them in the event the Modocs returned to fight.

"We going on in the morning?" asked a soldier near Ian.

"As soon as it's light enough for us to pass over this godforsaken ground," Kyle replied before disappearing into the dark, only the whisper of his voice to tell a man where the lieutenant was going.

The moon hung just past mid-sky when a commotion was caused by the arrival of five soldiers—survivors of the Thomas-Wright patrol. Three were injured, limping, groaning, hauled along by the other two soldiers who had escaped with them after darkness eased their fears of being discovered by wandering Modocs.

While the three wounded troopers were sent on to Gillem's camp with a pair of McKay's scouts to guide them, Green asked the other two survivors if they could lead his men to the scene of the battle.

After more than an hour of wandering over the broken country, searching for some clue as to where they were or how they could reach the Thomas command, the two young soldiers admitted they too were hopelessly lost in the dark. Even though they had drawn close to the butte that loomed like a dark monolith nearby, Green decided his men had had enough of the dangerous gamble. Again the order was passed to settle in and fortify for the shank of the night.

Far behind them, to the north, the men watched the glow of a huge bonfire built at the edge of the bluff near

Gillem's camp. It made a cold, lonely light against the far sky.

"They'll keep that lit all night—to shine as a beacon to any survivors still wandering out there in the Lava Beds," said a soldier quietly as he settled down near O'Roarke.

Ian dragged a hand beneath his nose, hoping it was only the cold that made it and his eyes run here in the darkness. "I pray there's survivors left to see that light, son."

From where he lay, Seamus Donegan could not see that beacon when he came to sometime after sundown.

The depression cradled him down in its rocky bosom. As he slowly moved his eyes, he could make out the blacker outline of the rocky ledges high above him against the night sky. There were only stars out in the sky, but he was sure the moon must be up by now, as dark as the canopy was overhead. Hidden, perhaps, behind that tall butte to the east of him.

He called out once, quietly. No one answered. Then he tried to move, his right arm gone to sleep and aching. The pain was so intense he swallowed air then suddenly puked on the ground beside him. Seamus gasped as the waves of nausea subsided and blessed sleep overtook him again.

The thin rind of a linen moon hung against the starry sky when next he opened his eyes. That taste in his mouth was something awful, reminding him of younger days when he would pass out drunk after puking up a bellyful of good whiskey.

But that was before he had learned how to drink and hold it down like a man.

A lot of good that done you, Seamus, he growled at himself.

Gritting his teeth as pain swamped over him, Donegan dragged the sticky arm up and across his belly, which relieved some of the agony in the shattered shoulder. He wondered if gangrene would set in soon.

They should have been here by now.

Perhaps he would lose the arm. And that made him cry more than the fear of dying here alone.

Snorting back the tears of loneliness, Seamus decided to call out quietly again, still fearful the Modocs may have left some guards behind to watch over the white men.

He whispered, and listened to some rocks tumble nearby, sure that a Modoc was creeping, crawling, skulking in on him out of the darkness. His finger was stuck to the trigger of his pistol—dried in blood. With his left hand he found the hammer still cocked, and prepared to sell his life when a weak voice answered his.

"That you, Irishman?"

"Doc?"

"It's me, lad."

"You hit bad, Doc?"

"No," and Semig coughed up some phlegm. "Just the leg. Lost a lotta blood and both bones broke clean through."

"Anyone else around you alive?"

There was a long silence that made Seamus grow fearful Semig had passed out again. It made him feel even more alone than before.

"Doc? You hear me, Doc?"

"No—no one else around me appears alive, Irishman. How—How about you. Can you crawl over here in the dark to help me?"

"I ain't moving good at all, Doc," he tried to explain, feeling guilty that he should try. "My shoulder—whole front of me covered in blood—can't feel my arm no more."

He listened to some far-off sound of some rocks clattering. There were more and more over the next few moments. Then Semig whispered harshly.

"You got a weapon, Irishman?"

"Yeah—my revolver. You?"

"Can't find it—not now anyway. But just listen. Those rocks . . ."

"I heard 'em."

"If that's the red devils coming back to take us alive—
you take that pistol of yours and shoot in the direction of
my voice."

Seamus realized he too did not want to be fodder for
the Modocs. "Don't worry, Doc. I'll take you with me.
We won't let the bastirds get us alive."

"Bless you, Irishman. I don't know if I'll come out of
this alive —so I'll pray now for a while that the Lord our
God will bless you for your kindness to a dying man."

"You're not dying, Doc. Not—Not just yet."

"But I'm very, very tired. I think I want to sleep now."

"You get that leg of yours bandaged up yet?" Seamus
asked, of a sudden frantic that the physician had not
ministered to himself since the battle.

He finally answered after several minutes. "No. But
I'm a doctor. I should know if I'm going to be all right.
I'm just . . . tired now."

"Doc?" A few seconds later as more of the distant
rattle of rocks floated to his ears again, he called out once
more, "Doc?"

And for the first time that night the chill breeze that
brushed over his shirt drenched in blood made Seamus
Donegan feel cold inside.

And more alone than he had been since coming to
Amerikay.

They sounded far off at first, those falling rocks. Tum-
bling from the high places in his mind. Clattering, skitter-
ing as they fell.

Then he realized it was not a dream but part of his very
real ordeal as he blinked his eyes open to find the sky
going gray along the east behind the tall butte above him.
The sun would be coming up soon enough.

It only made him thirst all the more for something to
drink.

The blood on his shirt had grown stiff and cold. He
shuddered, his lips quivering with the chill made more

painful with each new gust of breeze that swept down into the depression.

He stiffened instinctually with the new rattle of rocks falling. Closer and closer still. Much nearer than they had been last night. Coming out of the northeast—where the Modocs had come yesterday at noon.

Yesterday seemed so long ago. The right arm tingled with cold. As painful as it was, that tingle brought him hope that he would not lose it. He could hold out until they came today. Surely someone had heard the shooting yesterday. Surely Gillem would send out a rescue party today at dawn.

It was dawn now. He had only to wait until about noon.

The rocks rattled again, a stone's throw away now. Closer still.

He brought up his weary left arm, unsure of his aim, and saw the hammer was cocked back. Drawing up his left leg, he balanced the barrel on his knee and prepared to take the head off the first Modoc who poked his head over the lip of the ledge. Four.

Maybe he could take four of them with him before he shot the doctor, then himself.

"Glory!" came a voice to his far right.

Seamus jerked, frightened.

There were dusty kepis and dirty faces popping up all around him now, looking down into the shallow depression where Thomas's men had waged their last fight.

He started to cry when he recognized his uncle's drawn and haggard face, the tracks of Ian's first tears starting to smear the black dust on his cheeks.

For the longest time Ian sat hunched over him, letting his tears drop one by one on Seamus's devastated shirt, mixing with the dried, browned blood—not knowing whether to pick his nephew up and cradle him in his arms or not.

"Hold me, Ian. Just hold me and tell me it's really you."

Seamus swallowed the pain come of that rough embrace, listening as the soldiers continued to call out to one another as they found Semig alive. Then another. And another. And finally another who had somehow lasted the attack and the mutilation suffered by those back along the ledge.

And beyond that they had lasted the long, black night of fear and despair, and aloneness.

As much as it hurt to cling here to his uncle, Seamus did not want to let go.

But a soldier came to help O'Roarke, and together they bound up the right arm, lashing it against Donegan's body, and then gave him another drink from a warm canteen. Water had never tasted that good on his tongue.

"It's almost enough to make a man swear off whiskey, that water is," Seamus whispered to Ian as they watched the soldiers doing what they could for the rest of the wounded, those few survivors of the Black Ledge Massacre.

"Whiskey? You're a damned Irishman, Seamus Donegan," Ian said, his eyes going moist. "Your blood's half whiskey as it is!"

"I was scared last night, Ian," he said later when he came to again as the sun climbed high in the sky and Green's men had fanned out, bringing in the bodies of the dead they had found scattered over a wide area.

O'Roarke nodded. "I was fearful too, Seamus. I'd lost my own brother by something foolish. I did not want to lose you too."

"All night I heard the rocks clattering."

Ian smiled. "Weren't no Modocs, son. Us: Green's outfit—where we spent the night, piling up rocks to protect ourselves from the wind and Injuns."

"The wind made it so cold . . ."

"I know, Seamus. You hear it blowing softly at first. Then finally it seems like it's blowing right through you, making the pure marrow of you cold with it." He watched some soldiers tearing up sagebrush they threw on the fires to heat water to wash the wounds of the survivors. "To think you laid here all night—and we weren't no more than a few hundred yards off from this ground while you lay here, alone."

"Never want to be that cold, or alone again, Ian."

"Perhaps you'll think about staying on with me and Dimity now. Help me—help make this a place that belongs to you too. That's all I ask of you, lad."

He nearly choked on the thick ball of sentiment, his eyes welling. "I'll think about it . . . this staying with you."

Chapter 30

April 27–May 7, 1873

*T*hat morning of the twenty-seventh was spent gathering the wounded who could be found and caring for them with what warm water and torn rags could do. An occasional Modoc was spied on the skyline of some distant ridge, curiously watching the knots of soldiers clambering over the bloody ground.

In the afternoon, as cold, gray clouds scudded out of the mountains looming to the south laden with frozen moisture, Green ordered patrols out to locate the dead. First came the cold rain, which quickly turned to icy sleet mixed with wet snow as the soldiers clattered over the slickened black rocks, dragging out the naked, bloodied, mutilated dead.

The Modocs had killed most with shots to the head, then taken guns and ammunition, canteens and boots, uniforms and hats. Leaving the silent dead among the bunch-grass and mahogany trees dotting Black Ledge.

With the weather closing in and the falling of the sun, Green made a decision to leave the dead enlisted men in one group there in the depression, hidden as well as possible beneath sagebrush gathered by his soldiers. He would remove the five dead officers strapped to mules and the nine wounded tied down on stretchers, forging their way across the forbidding expanse of the Lava Beds as night was calling close at hand.

Lieutenant Boutelle mustered the rescuers into three squads: the first group would carry the stretchers for a distance, while a second group carried the rifles of those handling the stretchers and a third group rested, ready to relieve those bearing the wounded.

McKay and his scouts took the lead, guiding the solemn procession into the bleak purgatory that lay between them and Gillem's camp.

Up and down, climbing and descending, the stretcher-bearers fought the cruel terrain while other soldiers followed behind, weighed down, their arms loaded with rifles. The men grumbled, their arms aching from the load of stretchers or weapons, wishing they could use lanterns to light the uneven ground where they often stumbled and fell, crying out. Yet not one man among them failed to realize that any light might bring the feared Modocs down upon them as they clattered on into the night later described by one soldier "as black as a wolf's mouth."

They stopped to rest beneath the battering of freezing snow and driving wind, more and more frequently as the night wore on. And each time the stretcher-bearers found themselves more alone: each succeeding stop meaning more and more of the others had abandoned them, hurrying on ahead to the safety of the soldier camp. As much as Boutelle tried, he could not rally enough men to return to the stretchers to relieve those who wearily carried the nine wounded.

The lieutenant finally determined that his muscle was worth more through that long march than were the bars sewn on those weary shoulders.

During that dark night's ordeal, pulling the dead and wounded over the rough ground, the soldiers watched distant watch-fires lit on the high ground to the east. If a man were to look long enough, he could discern the flickering movement of Modoc warriors circling their fires. Such a sight did nothing but make each hour seem longer, each mile more excruciating than the last, waiting for the Modocs to come sweeping down out of the night.

So dark was their loneliness on that march, that many of the men at the front of each stretcher had to keep a hand out to tap on the last man of the stretcher before them. That, or intently listen to the sound of broughams and boots stumbling over rocks up ahead, guided only by those noises on into the icy darkness.

After midnight the signal fires were blotted out by the full fury of the raging storm, blowing before it sheets of driving, lancing snow. As difficult as it was for a man to keep his bearings in that swirling buckshot of white, the strong-hearted pushed ahead relentlessly.

But by sunrise the last of the stretcher-bearers came within sight of the signal tower high on the bluff, like a homing beacon on a rocky coast in that first light of day. Miraculously, only one of those nine wounded brought in about six A.M. would die in the days to come: Lieutenant George Harris, shot in the lower back.

It was only then that Gillem realized the full extent of the destruction. Twelve men were unaccounted for, not found during the day-long search of the rocks.

But what was even more telling was that in one brief flurry of riflefire, Captain Thomas had lost almost as many men as the army had lost in all battles since 29 November. Two thirds of his patrol had been killed or wounded by enemy fire. Those who weren't injured had run, abandoning the field and their comrades.

"Wright was dropped when a bullet pierced his groin. He was unable to walk," explained the young corporal named Noble from Battery A, talking to all those who quietly listened throughout that day to the many individual tales of horror. "That's when most of his men jumped and run. As Wright gritted his teeth, the rest of us watched, while the lieutenant buried his watch. He wasn't 'bout to let them savages get the watch his wife give him three Christmases ago."

"How many of you were left at that time?" asked Major Green.

"I wasn't counting, sir. I was shooting best I could."

"Try to figure for me, Corporal."

"Seven . . . maybe eight is all—'cluding me. No more'n that—because the rest had gone down in blood . . . or run off, deserting us like a pack of sheep."

Gillem drew himself up, the stress of the defeat clearly etched on his pudgy face as he tried to make some sense of the senseless. "I'm going to officially commend every last enlisted man who died with Captain Thomas. Yet, it seems to me that two men seem to require special mention. Their conduct was the subject of commendation by those—there is no easier way to say this—by those who fled the fight . . . as well as those who remained behind and survived."

There was a nervous shuffling of boots and a patter of clearing throats in the hospital tent as Gillem glanced over the beds bearing those who had been wounded at the Black Ledge.

"These gallant men were First Sergeant Robert Romer, Fourth Artillery, and First Sergeant Malachi Clinton, Twelfth Infantry. Both were soldiers to the last, who not only stayed their ground to the end, but attempted to enlist others to do so as well. Sergeant Romer was killed at his commander's side, and was found with Captain Thomas. Sergeant Clinton was killed holding ground with Lieutenant Wright."

Seamus waited until the officers and their staff had left the tent before he sat up and spoke to his uncle and Commissioner Meacham, still confined to the cot beside his. "Those soldiers died without taking one damned Modoc with 'em," he whispered harshly. "A lot that makes me bleed inside."

Ian watched his nephew wince as he settled himself. "That collarbone of yours won't heal, along with that hole the bullet made clear down through your shoulder, if you don't keep the arm still, lad."

"It don't hurt that much, Ian." He smiled weakly.

Meacham said, "I'd like to know if Captain Jack and the rest are dancing in the Lava Beds over the scalps of those poor soldiers."

Seamus grinned even more, his teeth bright in lamplight. "They'd be doing less dancing and more running— if they knew what was good for 'em."

"Why would you say that?" Ian asked. "What with the way they've soundly whipped the army time and again."

Seamus gazed at his uncle. "Why, Cap'n Jack and his renegades ain't yet had the pleasure of meeting the iron-ass General Jefferson C. Davis."

On the twenty-eighth Gillem sent a detail to Black Ledge, assigned to retrieve the bodies of the dead enlisted men who had been left the day before beneath a scant pile of sagebrush as the sky had unloaded with sleet and icy snow.

"They found nothing of the bodies except ashes and bones," Ian whispered in Donegan's ear, fearful of alarming the other wounded men in the hospital tent.

Seamus grit his teeth. "They burned those sojurs?"

Ian nodded. "That patrol came back in pretty riled up against the Modocs."

"It's about time somebody got riled up, don't you think?"

"Colonel Davis coming soon."

"He is, eh?"

"Sounds like he's the sort to kick the Modocs' asses."

"I'll be up in a few days to help Davis spread his special cheer across Modoc land," Seamus said, starting to rise in adjusting his position.

Ian gently pushed him back into his blanket pillows. "You're staying here until Cabaniss says your fit enough to go home to stay with Dimity and the children."

He squinted at his uncle severely. "If there's fighting to be done—I'll not be going home to be with the women and children. By the saints, Uncle—half me own blood is O'Roarke blood—"

"And the other half is fool, dunderheaded Donegan blood."

"Damn you, Ian O'Roarke," he spat angrily. "I can't have no fool blood in me, because you yourself told me the other half is pure Irish whiskey!"

Colonel Jefferson C. Davis himself reached Gillem's camp four days later, on Friday, 2 May, having suffered a long trip in coming by train, coach and horseback to the Modoc theater.

Colonel Alvan C. Gillem handed Davis a telegram received before his arrival.

The Western Union Telegraph Company
San Fran Cal Apr 30 1873

TO COL J C DAVIS
   LAVA BEDS VIA YREKA
I WISH YOU TO STUDY THE SITUATION CAREFULLY AND
LET ME KNOW IF POSSIBLE WHAT IS NECESSARY TO BE
DONE LET THERE BE NO MORE FRUITLESS SACRIFICES OF
OUR TROOPS THERE CAN BE NO NECESSITY FOR EXPOS-
ING DETACHMENTS TO SUCH SLAUGHTER AS OCCURRED
ON TWENTY SIXTH ASCERTAIN WHO IS RESPONSIBLE
FOR THAT AFFAIR IF THE TROOPS OR THE NUMBER OF
WHITE OR INDIAN SCOUTS & GUIDES AT THE LAVA BEDS
ARE NOT SUFFICIENT TRY TO INFORM ME HOW MANY
MORE ARE NEEDED WE SEEM TO BE ACTING SOMEWHAT
IN THE DARK

J M SCHOFIELD
MAJ GEN'L

From Washington itself as well, William Tecumseh Sherman sent a wire to Davis, telling the colonel that all he had to do was ask and he, Sherman, would immediately dispatch the entire Fourth Regiment then stationed in Arkansas. More raw recruits were on their way to San Francisco from New York City.

But green soldiers were the last thing Davis needed.

The colonel had to determine a way of locating troops
with the sand and tallow enough to fight a dirty war
where there was no front line as there had been in the
Civil War. Almost eight years to the day after the armi-
stice was signed at McLean's farmhouse in Appomattox,
the army was finally figuring out that Indians fought
without rules of engagement.

Worse still, among what he had for an army in the Lava
Beds, Davis found enlisted morale dangerously low, while
their contempt for the courage and effectiveness of their
officers was exceedingly high. The first order of business
for the colonel appeared to be that he take the reins into
hand—ordering rest and restructuring of the entire command while he worked on this critical matter of morale
and gained the trust of his enlisted.

A West Point graduate and a veteran of the Mexican
War, Davis had served at Fort Sumter prior to its bombardment by the Confederates. In fact, nothing got in the
man's craw more than anyone mentioning that he had the
same name as the president of the former Confederate
States of America. But he was, most of all, a soldier.

In 1862 during the war, Davis had killed his commanding general in a heated personal argument, but was nonetheless spared punishment by the testimony of an
eyewitness to the deadly confrontation: Indiana Governor
Oliver P. Morton. Davis was certain the killing prevented
his subsequent rise to wearing a general's stars.

Later in the war, down in Georgia, as a trusted member
of Sherman's command, Davis's troops were soon over-
whelmed with slaves fleeing their plantation and demanding the Union soldiers protect them from their former
masters and confederate Johnnies alike. Their numbers
swelled so greatly that Davis was soon unable to move his
troops when informed of the approach of Confederate
regiments under General Wheeler.

When the former slaves would not abandon the Union
soldiers, Davis gave the order for his troops to march
across a bridge at Ebenezer Creek, then ordered the

bridge put to the torch. Many of the slaves were killed when Wheeler's troops arrived, or were drowned, driven into the swollen creek by Wheeler's cavalry.

For the longest time there was no end to the criticism suffered by Jefferson C. Davis. Some went so far as to claim that the man bearing such a name had proven his true colors by ordering the deaths of so many coloreds.

At the end of the war Davis was made colonel of the Twenty-third Infantry and sent to Sitka to receive the nation's new purchase of Alaska from the Czar's troops, staying on for a time to act as temporary governor of the country's newest territory. With that duty at a close, Davis had been sent in obscurity to northwest Washington Territory, where many expected the soldier who had amassed a brilliant war record would run out his days.

But with Canby's murder, General Sherman once more notified his trusted friend. With twenty-seven years in the army, Davis was again given a chance at field duty.

On the third of May, McKay's Tenino scouts returned from five fruitless days of scouring the Lava Beds for Captain Jack.

"By damn," Davis exploded, pounding a fist on the camp table, scattering maps and surprising McKay, Gillem and the gathered officers, "why can't anybody find this miserable band of Indians?"

No one answered, nervously shuffling their feet and watching to see who would dare speak up. Davis was rough as a cob against new skin, but he did have one facet of his personality that endeared him to his rank and file soldiers: the colonel could remember what it meant to be an enlisted man. Unlike every other officer who would serve under him until the end of the Modoc War, Jefferson C. Davis had risen from the ranks, the hard way.

"That chunk of country is like nothing I've seen before," Davis continued, pointing south. "I'll grant you that. But by all that's holy—the Lava Beds are not insuperable! We must, and gentlemen—we will—operate on the terrain our enemy has given us to operate on. Do I make myself clear?"

A few of the braver souls muttered their agreement.

"If you ask for what I saw when I arrived here, gentlemen—well, I'll not mince words. As for the soldiers as fighters, a great many . . . are utterly unfit for Indian fighting of this kind, being only cowardly beef-eaters!"

He paused and let that sink in while he rolled the cheroot around on his tongue. "When your men are fit enough to fight—I will be expecting them to fight the Modocs on the Modocs' ground. But, unlike previous tactics, I now plan to bring an end to the Modoc War with one, crushing blow." He pounded a fist into the palm of his left hand.

"Tomorrow, in fact, I'm ordering a patrol out to the scene of the Thomas-Wright massacre. I want to find the bodies of the missing enlisted and Lieutenant Cranston. I won't stand by and abandon the remains of our dead to the enemy. We won't stand for it!"

That Sunday, the fourth of May, the patrol found no bodies, but they did manage to surprise a small, miserable camp of Modoc women and children. As the Indians scattered, the soldiers captured two of the older women unable to escape quickly enough into the rocks surrounding Big Sand Butte and Black Ledge.

The soldiers kept one of the squaws hostage while they sent One-Eyed Dixie out to discover where the rest of Jack's warriors could be found. The soldiers returned to headquarters to await the outcome of the squaw's travels.

Not until Wednesday did Dixie come in to Colonel Davis's camp to report not only that the Modocs with Captain Jack had abandoned the Lava Beds and were moving into the higher country to the south, but also that she had discovered the bodies of six soldiers. Davis assigned McKay and a patrol of soldiers to recover the remains. Five enlisted men were buried where they were found, and the body of Lieutenant Cranston was returned to camp for full military honors.

The very same day the burial detail was out recovering the dead, some of McKay's Teninos came in to report that they believed the Modocs were still operating within the Lava Beds and had not left their old stomping grounds, as One-Eyed Dixie had led the army to believe.

Davis and the others were beginning to distrust the reports of the Warm Springs scouts when word came in from Mason's camp near the Stronghold of some trouble suffered days before.

"They waited this long to tell us about a fight?" Davis demanded of the nervous signalman standing at the tent flaps.

"Yes," replied Lieutenant Adams, pressing by his corporal. He saluted Davis. "I figured I'd come tell you this one myself, Colonel."

"Tell it."

"Three supply wagons on their way under escort to our outpost at Scorpion Point."

"They were jumped?"

Adams nodded.

"Casualties?"

The lieutenant swallowed. "Only two wounded. The rest abandoned the wagons and were not pursued by the Modocs."

Davis's eyes narrowed. "What did the warriors capture?"

"A little bit of everything, it seems," answered Major Green, looking up from his papers. "Appears from these manifests that they got everything from biscuits to bullets to bacon, General."

Davis absorbed it all for the next few minutes as he chewed on the stub of a cheroot. Then his piercing eyes touched everyone in that tent as he rolled the cheroot off his lips with his tongue.

"An affair no man can be proud of—I'm sure we'll all agree. Once again I am sorely impressed that the men of this command are in no condition, either mentally or physically, to stand their ground against these thieving raiders."

"Thieving is right, Colonel," muttered Green.

"What was that, Major?" asked Davis. "I failed to hear you."

"Thieving is right, Colonel," Green repeated, much louder this time, but still grumbling.

"Explain yourself."

He rattled the manifests for that three-wagon shipment of supplies. "Something I just found out the Modocs got their hands on in that shipment."

"Some weapons perhaps?" Davis growled, his lips pursed beneath the bushy mustache.

"No, sir. Not exactly. Captain Jack and his henchmen are now the proud possessors of two kegs of army whiskey."

Chapter 31

Tule Reed Moon

*A*nother week and they would be in the middle of the Tule Reed Moon. Time for the women to gather the stalks when they were greenest, strongest, and most resilient for weaving, with all the spring moisture.

But for now there could be no thought of the women going in their canoes to ply the lakeshore, gathering the green stalks. For now Jack had to keep his people moving, constantly moving, always on the lookout for army patrols and those cross-blooded Teninos from up north who searched for the Modocs like the white man's paid hunting dogs.

Jack was growing so tired after all these weeks of fighting and running and moving to fight again. He closed his eyes from time to time, but it was never anything he could call sleep. Above all the others, he alone had to be constantly on the alert. Not only from the white men and their Warm Springs hunters—but also keenly aware of any subtle changes in the mood of the Lost River murderers.

He was as worried about being stabbed and left to bleed to death by Curly Headed Doctor, Hooker Jim or Schonchin John—his own people—as he was worried about being captured and hung at the end of the white man's cruel rope.

Captain Jack did not sleep well these days.

This running forced his mind to always work, and that was hard on any man. Especially a Modoc. For generations they had been a people of leisure, with much time to consider things of substance, carefully. Now he no longer had time to deliberate—always having to think about where to find food for his people; where they could find their next drink of fresh water.

The pockets of melted snow and sleet that had collected in the rocks and down at the bottom of the ice caves in the Lava Beds had kept his 165 people alive for many days. But without a source of food his warriors could count on, Jack had watched the faces change. Mostly the faces of the women and children, and the old ones—all growing thinner, more pale and gaunt, their eyes grown sunken like the swallowed eyes of a skull picked clean by thieving ravens.

For several days he had camped his band near Juniper Butte, where they chopped ice from the cave walls with their metal axes and hauled the chunks back to their fires to melt. It was a small cave, however, and when the ice was depleted, Jack was forced to move his people on to the Frozen River Cave less than a mile away. It was like that every few days. Moving on a little more —the women keeping at the ice while the men were out trying to bring in a little game to feed the many hungry bellies.

From Frozen River he had pointed them south into the rising country where they were forced to look at the mountains looming over them. At the Caldwell Ice Cave, Jack tried to tell them for the first time that to live in freedom, they might have to live far from Lost River— perhaps even among the summer pines and winter snows of that high country above them now.

When the ice and seepage at Caldwell ran out, Jack led his people east past three low buttes left behind by the volcanic activity millions of years before. His people called them the Three Sisters. Jack's band had never been this far east, camping now as they were almost directly south of a thumb of land that jutted into Tule Lake, a place the white man called Scorpion Point. They made their camp on the shores of a long-ago dried lakebed. The women scraped and dug at the sandy soil until a murky, gritty water began to slowly seep into the holes.

The water was cold though, and some of the men brought in a few small animals to cook over their tiny fires. But if the band was to make it to freedom farther south into the high country, they would need supplies of food, perhaps even ammunition. The warriors wanted to capture some of the army's supply wagons.

Jack agreed. Even though it meant letting the soldiers and their Teninos know where they were, he agreed with the young warriors who Scar-Faced Charley would lead in the raid.

On the road running in from Land's ranch they spotted a small escort riding along with three freight wagons nearing Scorpion Point. It proved far easier than Jack had expected to run off the soldiers after the warriors wounded two of the white men.

Like children, two dozen warriors swarmed over their new-gotten booty. Tossing bales of clothing and boxes of hardtack down onto the road, the warriors bypassed barrels of beans but sniffed closely at the barrels of salt-pork the white man was so fond of. To crack open every crate and keg just to be sure what to take and what to leave behind, Scar-Faced Charley ordered some of the warriors to search for some hammers among the soldiers' toolboxes.

In the long wooden toolboxes, Boston Charley and the others found two smaller kegs carefully concealed under army blankets.

"Perhaps it's better food than this pig meat," Hooker Jim said, causing the others to laugh as Charley dropped one of the kegs to the ground.

They gathered around it as Scar-Faced Charley hammered away at the end of the keg and found it to be filled with liquid—a fragrant, potent liquid most of the warriors knew well enough already.

But Ellen's Man George shouldered his way into the tight circle and dipped a finger into the keg. He smacked his lips with the taste.

"Whiskey!"

Rifling through other bundles, the warriors found a supply of tin cups and proceeded to bust the head off the second keg as they grew uproariously drunk. Weaving and bobbing, some of them clambered into the backs of the wagons and hefted out every case, keg and bale into the middle of the road.

Then others slapped and whipped the mule teams, firing their pistols overhead as the frightened animals bolted off into the labyrinth of the Lava Beds. Wagon boxes rolled from running gears, running gears splintered from singletrees, as the warriors had themselves their first good laugh in many, many days. As the splintered wood came to a rest among the rain-soaked rocks, and the horses clattered on into the distance, Captain Jack and his men finished their revelry, not in the least fearing an attack by the soldiers.

When they had their fill, the warriors stumbled and weaved and careened back into the confusing maze of the Lava Beds, carrying what they could after destroying the last of the whiskey kegs.

"Whiskey's no good for white men," Ellen's Man slurred. "He don't know how to have him a good time like Modoc."

Nearly a full month had passed since the murder of Canby and Thomas.

Seamus lay beneath the first streaks of gray cracking the sky this morning of 10 May, in a temporary camp comprised of two troops of cavalry and one company of artillerymen Colonel Davis had ordered out yesterday with five days rations behind a select group of McKay's

Tenino scouts. Davis had instructed the patrol commander, Captain H. C. Hasbrouck, to determine why in two weeks no one had been able to find a trace of the Modocs—while the warriors seemed to come and go through the Lava Beds with impunity.

The patrol had covered a little better than twenty-five miles almost southwest of the main headquarters camp before stopping for the night at the shore of Sorass Lake, a small, dry depression of cracked alkali mud lying in the midst of rugged buttes and scarred foothills. What water stood in parched pockets was laden with salts, unfit for man or animal to drink.

For better than two hours that afternoon, Hasbrouck had details of his men digging at wells in the hope they could find water. When this plan failed to produce any seepage, the captain stated he had no other choice but to send some men back to Scorpion Point after breakfast the following morning to bring out water for the patrol. That evening Hasbrouck fondly named the place Dry Lake in his daily report.

While the cavalry had hobbled their mounts and put them out to graze on what skimpy grass could be found, the artillery company moved on, something less than a mile to the south, encamping among the stands of mahogany and juniper. McKay's scouts spread their bedrolls near the horse soldiers, certain of safety there. Just two hundred yards north of them extended three humps of low rock outcroppings, while another two hundred yards beyond these humps stood a rocky, volcanic ridge rising a minimum of thirty feet above the lakeshore.

Not a single Modoc had been seen along the skyline throughout the long march of the ninth, but Hasbrouck had nonetheless warily placed his pickets atop this higher bluff for the night.

Rolling over within the warm cocoon of his two wool blankets, surrounded by the darkness of the early morning, Seamus set too much pressure on the healing wounds suffered only two weeks before. Wincing in pain, he cursed himself for his sleepy stupidity and ground his hip into the sandy, grassy soil, taking respite that no one was stirring that early—forcing the command to move out before sunrise.

The fingers of his right hand tingled with pinpricks. Gently he urged his left hand under the thick bandage Dr. McElderry had looped tightly over the injured shoulder, across the broken collarbone, firmly imprisoning the upper arm against the right side of his chest.

It felt good to move the arm, even though the collarbone nagged at him when he adjusted the wrap.

"Shut-up!" said Charley Larengel in a harsh whisper to his blue tick hound stretched out beside its master's bedroll. The dog growled back in its throat, his muzzle snarling, teeth bared.

"He smells something," said Larengel, rustling at last and turning to Donegan as if in apology for waking him.

"Injins," Seamus said. "By the saints—I'll put my money on your dog's nose before I'll bet on those worthless Teninos any day! Go find one of the guards and get him to alert the camp."

Larengel took his growling dog at the end of a chunk of rope and set off into the predawn darkness to find a guard. The first picket he happened across laughed at the civilian's claim that there were Indians near by. But he took Larengel to awaken the sergeant of the guard.

The sergeant grumbled something fitting about civilians knowing their place in the army's war and told Larengel to go back to his blankets until reveille was blown.

"You get out of your blankets and take me to see Captain Hasbrouck right now, laddie—or you're going to find my boot heel under your goddamned chin!"

Evidently the sergeant clearly read the look in Larengel's eye, because he pushed himself out of his own blankets, squared his clothing and set off with the civilian in tow to find Hasbrouck.

Seamus was chuckling to himself, cradling the right

arm as he eased back against his blankets, knowing
Larengel would convince Hasbrouck to believe him as
well and send out some of the scouts to make a circuit of
the camp.

He closed his eyes. Perhaps a few more minutes of sleep
before dawn came calling . . . would be a blessing—

He bolted upright, blankets falling away and the
wounds crying out in sudden, sharp anguish. Hair stood
on the back of his neck, as he vividly remembered those
war-cries that echoed through the cavalry camp.

Horses tied at the picket-lines reared and kicked and
whinnied in fear and pain as bullets rattled among them.
Those rope picket-lines strung between trees were but
momentary obstacles. Half of the horses bolted through
the camp, leaping over the crouching mounds of soldiers
fleeing the hammering hooves.

Through the night, the Modocs had slipped past the
pickets and crept into position on the high ridge. Some of
the warriors had quietly made their way down to the
lower humps before dawn, that much closer to the sleeping soldier camp.

Here and there on this northern fringe of camp, a soldier cried out to his fellows, saying he was hit. There were
the screams of others as bullets found their marks among
the cavalry and Teninos alike as they rolled behind saddles and blankets, pulling on boots or simply running for
cover barefooted. Others fell without a sound at all. They
were trapped between the lakeshore and the rocks where
the Modocs hid, firing with impunity.

His searching left hand found the Henry, but for a
moment.

Seamus threw the blankets back over the rifle and
swept up the two pistol belts. The enemy was already
pressing past the outer pickets they had killed, pushing
into the camp itself. No need for the long-range Henry—
even if he could have forced the butt against the healing
shoulder. Pistols would have to do in the dirty little fight-

ing when you got close enough to see the eyes of your enemy.

With gritty pleasure, Seamus knew he had a personal score to settle after the horror of the Black Ledge. He wanted to get close enough to see the look on the face of every warrior he cut down with a .44.

Captain Hasbrouck came out of the gloom, hollering his orders, scrambling to regain control of the panicked soldiers diving for cover, others scrambling to retrieve their Springfields. He sent veteran lieutenant Boutelle with a squad of proven men to attempt circling behind the enemy so they could get word to the artillerymen camped nearby.

Captain Jackson, second in command, cried out his orders as well among his own B Troop. His men huddled on the lakeshore in terror—believing they were now to be massacred like Thomas's men before them.

Lieutenant Kyle attempted to reassume control of his Troop G and went after the horses before the Modocs could escape with the company's mounts.

Skirmish lines were established as bullets whizzed past the soldiers fighting first of all to see their enemy in the gray light. This time the white men did not flee and run like some headless creatures. Instead, Jackson and Kyle held a firm grip on their soldiers, pushing them ahead almost two hundred yards as McKay brought up his Teninos on the left flank.

"Remember Thomas and Wright!" shouted some soldier down the line.

"Avenge Canby!" cried another.

The hail of Modoc lead was coming from a series of three low ridges directly to the north of camp.

"The bastards followed us yesterday," Kyle growled at Donegan as they forged ahead, foot by foot. "I'd lay money on it."

"Then laid in wait for first light," Donegan replied. The pistol bucked reassuringly in his left hand.

"You any good with that hand?"

Donegan smiled. "Good enough as a man needs to be at this range."

"Lookit that!" cried a soldier nearby as some of the firing quieted.

"Glory—who's that?"

"Who can it be?"

For the space of a half-dozen heartbeats, the riflefire coming from the cavalry and scouts tapered off and withered to nothing as they all noticed the form standing alone on the ridgetop, outlined by the new light in the east.

"He's wearing a army uniform!"

"Lookit that hat—the medals—a officer to boot!"

"Did those devils capture a officer?"

"Sure—that's it! The red bastards got one of our men up there, holding him hostage."

"Going to kill their prisoner—cease fire, men! Cease fire!" became the yell up and down the skirmish lines.

As the soldiers halted their fire, the figure paced to the left grandly, then back to the right. With a smart about-face, he marched to the left once more as the soldiers grumbled and the Teninos chaffed at this suspension of the fight.

"The scouts say that ain't a white man!" hollered a soldier down on the left flank near the Teninos.

"By God—that's Cap'n Jack hisself!" screamed another.

"Wearing Canby's bloody uniform!"

"Shoot him—pray do it! Shoot the murderer!"

The soldiers opened up once more with a wild barrage of fire. Those bullets were as quickly answered with a hideous war cry as the Modoc chief beat his chest provocatively.

"Bastard thinks he can't be killed, eh?" Kyle hissed, slamming a cartridge into his Springfield carbine.

As the soldiers plunged to the base of the ridge, a Modoc dropped. Then a second. And suddenly the warriors were falling back, sagebrush tied to their bodies, providing the perfect concealment in the gray light of this new day. Soldiers shrieked out their own throat-searing war-cry now, following their quarry at a sprint, stopping only to fire at each new puff of smoke spotted among the retreating Modocs.

But a sudden, wild shriek ignited the warriors, causing them to wheel and stand their ground, more accurately returning the soldier bullets.

Within seconds the soldiers halted in the face of the renewed and devastating fire. Then the retreat began as the camouflaged Modocs surged back toward the white men. Yard by yard the white men gave up, a soldier falling here. Another there. Then a second of the Tenino scouts cried out, dead before he crumpled to the ground.

Before they knew it, six soldiers were dead, another seven lay bleeding in the grass.

Then behind the cavalry arose a rattle of riflefire, and another volley. Shouts climbed above the clamor as Captain Hasbrouck's artillerymen arrived to reinforce the battered, confused and angry cavalry under Jackson and Kyle.

Slowly at first, the Modocs gave ground again, this time carrying the body of a mortally wounded warrior. Then of a sudden they found bullets falling among them from a new direction. McKay's scouts were flanking the surprised warriors on two sides, preparing to surround them in minutes.

Now the warriors buckled in—foot by foot then yard by yard, until they were fully sprinting, leaping over the rocks, having abandoned their ponies in a mad flight due west into the heart of the lava flows just north of Big Sand Butte. But in that escape, with the Modocs having to break through the encircling flanks, the fighting became something more ferocious and primal.

Then the warriors broke through the tightening noose.

For three tortuous miles the soldiers followed the escaping warriors, harassing them, firing into the Modocs disappearing among the boulders and fissures. Hasbrouck ordered McKay's scouts to mount what horses Kyle had succeeded in rounding up. Still the Teninos were unsuccessful in capturing their prey in that rugged, cruel terrain. Not another warrior was killed.

"We've gone far enough!" yelled Captain Jackson.

The Teninos howled in disappointment. McKay tried to explain to the soldier that his scouts wanted more scalps. The soldier told his guide to clamp it for good and follow orders.

"We're not stringing this patrol out across the whole extent of these goddamned Lava Beds—and us on foot to boot!" Jackson shouted down the complainers.

"By gor—look at you fellas!" Lieutenant Kyle hollered at his dismounted company as they milled. "This is the first victory we've had—driving the bastards off the way we did—and still you whimper and cry for more!"

"Damn right, Lieutenant! If this is what turning the tables on the Modocs feels like—we want more!"

"Give us more Modoc blood!"

"And scalps!"

As they turned about and made their way back to their Sorass Lake camp, the soldiers found for all their own casualties, they had killed but one warrior. Two dozen captured Modoc ponies would in no way salve the wounds caused in losing so many good soldiers. Those animals, along with some powder and blankets discovered on the field following the battle, were awarded the Teninos for their part in the victory.

Still, the complexion of the Modoc War was changing at last. No more would the army turn its back on Jack's ragtag band of renegades living hand-to-mouth, striking from the hills and running to fight another day.

Victory was at hand. One more fight, the soldiers cheered one another lustily—and they would have this dirty little war won.

Chapter 32

May 10–18, 1873

*T*he sun had not yet fully risen when Captain Hasbrouck dispatched a mounted messenger bearing a quickly written report of the Modoc attack on the patrol camp.

When Davis received word of the encounter, the colonel ordered another 170 men moved out as reinforcements, with his command to follow the Modocs into hell once and for all.

At the same time, Hasbrouck had McKay's scouts follow the foot-trail of the fleeing warriors into the black labyrinth of the Lava Beds. The Teninos returned shortly after noon to report they had located the Modoc camp near the base of Big Sand Butte, less than seven miles from where the soldiers stood at Sorass Lake.

The captain determined he had less than twenty gallons of water and would now have to temporarily delay his trip back to Scorpion Point for more. He forbade all ablebodied personnel from what water they had left. It was to be used for the wounded.

"You must take the blame for the death of Ellen's Man George!" snapped Hooker Jim.

While never an endearing friend of Ellen's Man, Jim

seized upon the warrior's death by the soldiers at Dry
Lake as an occasion to chop away at Captain Jack's
power.

It was Ellen's Man whom soldier bullets had struck in
the dawn attack that morning. He was unconscious and
mortally wounded when they dragged him from the fight.
Lingering in a fitful delirium for a few hours, Ellen's Man
finally died.

The whole world had tipped on its side for the Modocs.
Until this day, in every battle fought with the soldiers,
there had been booty abandoned on the field with the
dead white men: rifles and ammunition, clothing and
boots and even food. But this morning the warriors themselves had been forced to flee—leaving behind two dozen
horses. Back in the Ice Moon they had lost some horses to
the soldiers, then more were captured by the white man
several weeks later. Besides being a serious blow to their
pride as a people, Jack's band had lost nearly all its mobil-
ity.

But at that moment the death of a warrior like Ellen's
Man hit them the hardest.

The band carried the body to a clearing a few miles
from their camp and scratched an oblong hole out of the
ground. Sagebrush, juniper and mahogany were heaped
into the pit before Ellen's Man was laid atop. The pyre
was lit as the men and women and children stepped back,
flames clawing higher and higher into the spring sky.

Jack stood watching, surrounded by his tribal enemies,
who hurt most at this loss of one of their own. As they
witnessed this cremation which marked the Modoc manner of freeing the spirit into the afterlife, a gold pocket
watch slipped from the clothing being quickly consumed.

General Edward R.S. Canby's watch—twisting now,
its painted face crackling under the extreme heat of the
flames totally engulfing the body of one of the two
Modocs who had killed the soldier chief. The watch too,
freed now of its temporary imprisonment.

Others like Shacknasty Jim and Steamboat Frank, both

Boston and Bogus Charleys, all stood ready to side with Curly Headed Doctor in blaming their chief for the warrior's death when they returned in silence from the funeral. The time for respectful quiet was done. Emotions exploded like a sudden, volcanic eruption.

"You only think about protecting your own hide," Shacknasty cursed. "You never worry about others."

Rarely had Jack felt this alone.

"I'm done fighting for you," vowed Steamboat Frank.

"Good!" Jack shouted. "Go, run away from here and let men do the fighting now."

"Men—ha!" Boston Charley lunged forward, his breath hot in Jack's face. "No more will we fight for a coward, Kientpoos!"

Knowing the soldiers and their Tenino trackers would soon be coming along their backtrail, Jack was nonetheless forced to listen to this tirade from the lips of the feckless murderers the moment they had arrived back at their camp.

"These warriors are ready to fight for me again. Your magic is only as strong as a dog raising its leg to piss against these soldiers. No coward should lead fighting men!" declared the Doctor.

That singular insult was the straw. The words had barely crossed the shaman's lips when Jack crumpled the Doctor's shirt in both fists, pulling him off his feet.

"Coward? You call me coward?"

With a mighty shove, Jack hurled the shaman backward into the arms of his supporters.

"You—each of *you* are the cowards. Spineless dogs, the lot of you. Come to me after your bloody murders of innocent, unarmed men, didn't you? Whined and cried for help hiding you from the white man you knew would come, didn't you? Everything was good when you had the protection of my people, my warriors—while you were killing soldiers. You even called me a squaw, dressed me as a woman—shamed me before my family!

"But when one of your faithless ones is killed—you

come crying to me," Jack hissed. "Me a coward? You are the cowards—killing good men in cold blood when they come to talk peace."

"You waited a long time to pull your gun on the soldier tyee," Shacknasty dared speak.

Jack whirled on him, raising his hand and watching the warrior cower beneath its shadow. "That soldier chief was a better man than any of you! He was brave, facing death when it stared him in the face . . . while all of you run and cry out to the sky when one man gets killed."

"How many more of us will fall dead if we follow Kientpoos?" asked Hooker Jim, his voice an impassioned shriek. "We must go before this man gets us all killed."

Jack turned on him. "Go! Yes, go! I do not want you here anymore. Run far, far away now while you can—all of you who want to go. I will stop the soldiers as long as my body stands to receive their bullets. Yes—I will stay and fight. For I am the only true Modoc of you."

"Maybe we kill you instead before we go!" Hooker shouted back, angry at the rebuke and reaching for the pistol stuffed in his waistband.

Scar-Faced Charley stopped the gun hand. "You want to kill—go kill white men. Lots of soldiers left. We can't kill each other now. Not enough Modocs left."

Jim yanked his hand away from Charley's grip and stomped away a few steps, then turned, burning with indignation.

"Yes, go, Hooker!" Jack taunted his enemy before Jim could speak. "You can never kill me!"

Hooker suddenly lunged back through the knot of warriors for Jack, hands like hawk's talons aimed at the chief's neck. Charley and the others kept the two men separated as they hurled their threats at one another.

"I kill you—with my bare hands I kill you!"

"Ha! I will not die by Modoc hands, Hooker. I will die fighting! No cowardly Modoc like you will ever kill Captain Jack!"

"Let me go!" demanded Hooker Jim. "I show you how you die by Modoc hands! Mine!"

His father-in-law, the shaman, pulled Jim back from the chief. "We go."

Jack watched them load up a few horses with what few possessions they had been able to carry all these weeks since leaving their Lava Bed Stronghold. Hooker Jim and the shaman led twelve warriors and their families, sixty-two women and children, away, heading west.

When the Tule Lake murderers were gone, Jack turned once more to those who were left. "Now we must flee ourselves."

"There is time," said Schonchin John.

"Yes, let us rest," William Faithful added. "Every time we have fought the white man, he is many days coming after us."

"Yes, your words are true," Jack replied. "But today is the first time we have been driven off, fully beaten—"

"Soldiers coming!"

They all turned together to find a young warrior they had stationed on their backtrail running into their camp near the base of Big Sand Butte.

"Soldiers?"

"Many, many soldiers." The young one huffed to a halt, catching his breath, hunched over and hands on his knees as the warriors crowded around him.

"How many?"

"Many, many—"

"The soldiers from the dried lake?"

"More—twice that number."

"The Teninos with them?"

"Yes—and they bring their big guns that shoot twice too!"

The army was moving, but not against the Modocs that tenth day of May.

Instead, Captain Hasbrouck finally ordered his men north with their dead and wounded for Scorpion Point to reoutfit and obtain more water. The next morning, Davis signaled Hasbrouck to take his three companies back south to Big Sand Butte. The colonel was also ordering Major E. C. Mason out of the camp in the Stronghold, with plans to link up with Hasbrouck's patrol and make a concerted, overwhelming attack on the Modocs' mobile camp.

By the night of the twelfth, as the soldiers made their bivouac, Mason and Hasbrouck were less than three miles apart, with not only Big Sand Butte, but what they believed would be the Modoc camp between them. On the thirteenth, when the two patrol leaders met to plan their attack, they determined to delay the offensive until more water could be transported in for both wings.

By the next afternoon a Tenino scout informed Hasbrouck that he believed the Modocs had fled their camp and were now in parts unknown. Lieutenant J. B. Hazelton volunteered to take a patrol in to find out conclusively if the Modocs were gone. Twenty-six men immediately lined up to join Hazelton's reconnaissance. It would not be the first indication that Colonel Jefferson C. Davis had indeed infused these tired, frightened, battle-whipped soldiers with a new sense of courage and hope.

A few hours later Hazelton returned, reporting that the Modocs had disappeared. The war was no longer one of searching for Captain Jack's band, hoping to surprise the Modocs in their camps. From Davis on down, the officers now realized how liquid the situation had become. Needed now were the cavalry.

The chase was on.

On 15 May the Teninos guided Hasbrouck's men west on the trail of the fleeing Modocs. For some miles Captain Jack had led his people down the Ticknor Road. Soon, however, the soldiers found the Indian trail leading away toward Antelope Springs. It was there Hasbrouck gave up the chase and returned to Big Sand Butte while Mason transferred his command back to Juniper Butte to await more water and horses.

His plans for following the Modocs renewed on the sixteenth, when he received fresh horses, Hasbrouck led his men west from Big Sand Butte toward Van Bremmer's ranch. After several miles the captain met Captain Perry's troop of First Cavalry out on a reconnaissance south from Davis's camp. They camped together, and on the morning of 18 May continued in their search: Perry would ride south toward Antelope Springs, while Hasbrouck plodded north toward Van Bremmer's Mountain, hoping to either find the Modocs trapped between them or, at the outside, to at least run across a fresh trail.

On that same Sunday, the Modocs fleeing with Hooker Jim had already skirted south of Van Bremmer's Mountain then crossed over Ticknor Road, heading west toward a long, J-shaped ridge of higher ground that joined Sheep Mountain in the south with Mahogany Mountain farther north, directly across the road from John Fairchild's ranch.

Moving on horseback still bothered Donegan's tender wounds. Not as much as it had days ago. But this morning, the eighteenth, his shoulder was again stiff with the cold and damp after a night spent on the ground at Van Bremmer's ranch with Captain Hasbrouck's troops. Ian O'Roarke had come out from Davis's camp with Captain Perry's cavalry, and when they camped together on the seventeenth, Ian decided to stay on with his nephew.

After a breakfast of strong coffee and hardtack, along with strips of fried pork, Hasbrouck moved his command south along the Ticknor Road.

Approximately three miles down the wide trace, the captain came upon McKay's scouts waiting in the middle of the road. They had something to show him.

"Tracks?"

McKay answered. "Hurrying west."

"How many?"

"Seventy. Maybe eighty."

"Damn. That's only half of what we were expecting to

find." Hasbrouck sounded disappointed in spite of the good news.

"They split up on us," McKay said with a shrug.

"And maybe they haven't. Maybe this isn't the main trail. Perhaps it's only something to throw us off."

The half-breed shook his head. "These Modocs. Warriors—with some women and children and some poor ponies. If they are not the big bunch you want, they lead you to Jack one day."

"All right. Tell me how old these tracks are. How many days ago were they here?"

McKay gave the captain a quizzical look. "They crossed the road this morning. Maybe before dawn."

Hasbrouck tingled with anticipation as he looked to the west at the shadowy bulk of the ridge, encapsulated at either end by mountain peaks. "All right. Put your boys on the trail, McKay. We'll be serving Modoc soup for dinner tonight."

A half-mile later the captain signaled Captain James Jackson forward. "I want you to take a squad of a dozen good horsemen ahead with two of McKay's best. Press the trail hard."

"You really believe they're just ahead of us?"

"I do—and you're going to find out for us, Jackson."

"Very well." Jackson saluted Hasbrouck and loped back along the column to pick his dozen.

"You mind if I ride along?" Donegan asked as Jackson was moving by.

The captain reined up, glancing first at O'Roarke. "I appreciate the offer, Irishman. I do. But with that bad wing of yours, you might just hamper us if we get ourselves in trouble."

"Nothing I'm not accustomed to."

"But in this case, having you out of commission might mean an added danger to my men."

Ian had watched the disappointed look cross his nephew's face. "What if I go along, Captain? I'd cover the lad's ass. You'd not be responsible."

Jackson considered it, then grinned slightly. "I suppose we cut our teeth together in the Modoc War, didn't we, Irishman?"

Seamus sagged a little with relief. "We did, that, Captain."

"All right, you both come along. And by the way Mr. O'Roarke—if you ride with James Jackson—we all cover each other's asses in this outfit."

Jackson reined away to ride on down the column of his B Troop, choosing the best horsemen and shots he could from among his soldiers.

O'Roarke nodded approvingly. "Maybe I'd done all right riding cavalry in the war like you, nephew. Sometimes I've wondered. So, why you want to try to get your head blown off again?"

"Better than eating the dust of a long column of horse."

"Still I don't like the idea of us riding up there in that timber—just daring those Modocs to jump us again."

He loosened the flap on his holster and eased the extra pistol from his belt. "Chances are good—a man goes riding with the likes of that Captain Jackson will come out of any tangle with the enemy."

Chapter 33

May 18–22, 1873

*G*unfire greeted them before they had gone three miles up the Modoc trail, headed for Mahogany Mountain, across Ticknor Road from John Fairchild's place.

In among the trees flitted light and shadow, then rapid, bright muzzle flashes.

The Modoc men had doubled back on their trail once rear scouts learned the soldiers were drawing close. The warriors waited until Jackson's fifteen horsemen were into the thick timber, then cut loose.

Riding down at the tail end of the long column, Seamus could only hear the rattle of riflefire mixing with war-cries and the screams of horses up ahead on the trail. Gray smoke puffed from the stands of juniper and mahogany. Soldier mounts reared, crying out in surprise and agony —painfully reminding him of that summer sunrise on the high plains when a band of fifty frightened men raced their own horses to a sandy island in the middle of a nameless river, then one by one shot those animals for barricades from the screaming Cheyenne of Roman Nose.*

A solitary soldier tore past Donegan and O'Roarke,

---

headed down the mountain, clinging to the neck of his mount.

Spurring his snorting horse into action, Seamus freed the pistol from his belt. Only yards ahead around the hard twist in the trail, Jackson's squad was a confused jumble of men and animals.

More shadow and light flitted through the trees to his right this time. A puff of smoke followed the cruel whine of a bullet creasing the air near him. The horse jumped.

Soldiers were on the ground, two of them hollering out and pinned under horses that lay thrashing, crying out in pain. Others were still in the saddle fighting wounded animals. A few already crouched behind their slain horses.

"They're shooting the horses!" Jackson called out as Seamus leaped forward, his animal clearing first one then another writhing horse sprawled on the narrow mountain trail. Nostrils flaring, its eyes wide as saucers, the horse fought the bit.

With one good arm and the other in nagging pain, he yanked on the reins, nearly bringing the horse down as he brought it around on its haunches, ending its panicked race.

"You've got them running, Captain!" O'Roarke shouted, pointing up the trail.

It appeared the warriors were only covering the retreat of their women and children, delaying the soldiers long enough so they themselves could escape.

"Damn those bastards!"

Seamus quickly glanced over the carnage, wagging his head. "They didn't hit a single one of your men, did they?"

Jackson as quickly appraised the littered trail as men were pulled out from under horse carcasses. "Not a man. I—I don't understand it."

"That bunch is telling you something, Captain," O'Roarke declared. "I figure those warriors could have whittled your outfit down to nothing in a heartbeat."

"But instead they only shot the horses out from under us. What does that tell you, Mr. O'Roarke?"

Ian looked at Seamus for help.

"Seems they don't want any more killing," Donegan replied quietly. "I think they realize that the army will track them to the end—but if they can slow you down by killing the horses, maybe they'll buy themselves a little more time to run."

"Trying hard not to kill us, eh?"

Seamus had no time to answer Jackson's question. The clatter of bit and the squeak of leather joined the clatter of hoofbeats on the backtrail as that solitary soldier sent for help led the rest of Company B and a full contingent of McKay's Tenino scouts.

The new arrivals had but a few seconds for disappointment in not finding a hot fight of it on the trail, for Captain Jackson formed up what he had for mounted men and ordered them forward on the heels of the fleeing Modocs. Those troopers who had lost horses were ordered down the backtrail.

For the rest of that long afternoon, the soldiers pursued the unseen warriors covering the retreat of their women and children in a sporadic yet bitter running fight across some eight miles of rugged terrain marked by boulders and precipitous ridges covered with pine, juniper and mahogany.

As the ground grew rougher, steeper still, the Modocs splintered. Lieutenants split their commands. Sergeants further divided their squads. Lathered army mounts lagged farther and farther behind their fleeing quarry as the day grew old, the warriors using every tree and boulder and tree again to fight and hide behind.

Up and down the ridge the echo rang as the various units relayed Captain Jackson's order to halt and turn about.

"Pushing on now might jeopardize my men and mounts even more than they already are," the captain explained after he had rejoined the main command down the slope of Mahogany Mountain.

"I quite agree," said Captain Hasbrouck. "Did we capture any?"

"About ten—women and children only. Along with two dozen of their ponies."

"Enemy casualties?"

"My men counted five dead."

"Warriors?"

Jackson wagged his head wearily. "Two males. Three females."

Hasbrouck pushed his cap back on his head and scratched his brow. "Not to be ashamed of, Captain Jackson. The way those warriors were mixing in with their women and children in that mad flight—no wonder some of the innocents were sacrificed."

"That bunch was doing just what any man would do," Seamus Donegan grumbled as he began to rein away, grown disgusted with the artillery officer.

Hasbrouck jerked. "What was that you said, mister?"

Seamus halted, reined about and glared at the captain. "I said those warriors were doing what any of us would do to protect their families."

Hasbrouck glanced quickly over his men, finding many of them nodding in grudging agreement as Jackson called out to his sergeant.

"Reform the men into column of twos. Halt at the base of the ridge to await me." The captain turned to Hasbrouck. "Damn, but I hate making war like this."

The cavalry officer nudged his exhausted horse onto the narrow foot-trail that descended the ridge.

As soon as word of the running fight was relayed to Davis that afternoon, the colonel gave the command for his cavalry and infantry to hurry to John Fairchild's ranch.

"We know where they are," Davis explained to his officers just before they moved out to Mahogany Mountain. "The Modocs are now within our grasp."

On the nineteenth Hasbrouck moved his combined command of artillery and cavalry up the Ticknor Road to Fairchild's ranch from Van Bremmer's place. The following day the remaining infantry was led from Davis's camp by Major Mason. Likewise, the rest of the artillery units moved up the Pit River Road in the opposite direction toward the Peninsula.

Davis had stripped the Lava Beds.

That same Tuesday morning, while the breakfast fires still smoked, reeking of fried salt-pork and harsh coffee, and while the cavalry was saddling up for a renewed pursuit, John Fairchild strode up to Davis's headquarters tent. He had with him a reluctant Modoc woman.

"You're trying to tell me that bunch of renegades claims they were coming to your place to surrender when Jackson caught them up the mountainside?" Davis asked, disbelief etched in every one of the wrinkles that gave such distinction to his face.

Fairchild nodded as other civilian ranchers and settlers from the region drew close, curious all. "That's what this woman came down yesterday to tell me. She didn't make it all the way in when darkness came—but at first light she continued on down to my place. My wife fed her before I brought her over to you this morning. Look at her—how they must all be slowly starving to death."

Davis eyed the stocky, middle-aged Modoc squaw. "Don't you figure they're just buying time with this maneuver, Fairchild?"

"No, I don't," answered Ian O'Roarke.

Davis turned, as if pulled by a string.

"I think they've had enough. Being in the Lava Beds, where they could come out and raid at will—and had good protection from army attack—that was one thing," O'Roarke explained. "Having to run now . . . harried by your soldiers. Just look at her—look at her, Colonel. These people are done in. They haven't eaten fit food. They grab water on the run when they can find it. They sleep curled under trees. Take a goddamned look there,

Colonel—and any fair-minded man would know these people are done in."

A glare of anger flashed in Davis's eyes, then as if something had doused the flames, that ire disappeared. He sighed, his great shoulders heaving.

"Perhaps you're right, Mr. O'Roarke. Maybe—Maybe we've had all we can take too." Davis turned back to Fairchild. "All right. Let's see if these people really want to come in. Among our prisoners, I want you to find those two squaws who went out to find the bodies of Lieutenant Cranston's men in the Lava Beds. They're trustworthy."

"What you have in mind?" Fairchild asked.

"Tell them to go with this woman. Find the Modocs up there in the hills. Tell them the specific terms of surrender."

"Colonel, if I may?" Hasbrouck asked, waiting for Davis to nod. "Do you want to put a time limit on it? We've waited before and they've scattered to the four winds on us, sir."

Davis sighed again behind lips pursed in resignation. "The captain's right, Fairchild. Tell the Modocs they have two days to come in. After that, we'll hunt them down. If it means taking them one at a time as prisoner, or shooting them down where we find them on this mountain—we'll do what we have to in bringing a conclusion to this war."

"I want O'Roarke along," Fairchild said.

Davis eyed the other civilian. "All right. Whatever it takes. Looks like we're back to trying to make peace with this bunch, gentlemen. But I won't be responsible if you go up there without any weapons."

Fairchild flicked his eyes at O'Roarke. "Neither one of us is going up that mountain without a gun, Colonel."

By midmorning Fairchild and O'Roarke were saddled and pulling away from the rancher's corral set to the side of the log home and outbuildings. Behind them rode Fairchild's wife and the three squaws. Seamus watched them disappear across Ticknor Road, up the pine-studded ridge that climbed toward Mahogany Mountain. In silence he prayed beneath those scattered, fluffy clouds dotting the blue canopy that the Modocs truly wanted to come in.

But try as he might, Donegan couldn't squeeze from his mind the horrible vision of Canby's scalped and butchered body, or Meacham's brutal wounds which nearly took his life.

On the following day, the twenty-first, Colonel Davis completed the inevitable. He relieved Colonel Gillem of his command of the Modoc War.

In his Special Orders 59a, Davis declared that since Gillem's infantry "must be made to conform to the new order of things," present and future operations would now "more conveniently be carried on under the immediate orders of the Department Commander, while on the spot, than under those of a special commander of the expedition . . . Colonel A. C. Gillem is therefore relieved from duty with this command and will proceed to Benicia Barracks."

The time of that change could not have been more unfortunate, perhaps even ruinous for Gillem's career. In fact, it was perhaps a senseless deed that the last words of Davis's order returned Lieutenant Colonel Frank Wheaton to command of the Modoc campaign, although there was no mistake to be made in the fact that he would be serving under Davis. Perhaps this was Davis's manner of saying, if not the army's way of apologizing, in publicly declaring that it had not been Wheaton's responsibility for those catastrophes at Lost River and in that first attack on the Stronghold.

"Here they come!"

Seamus turned at the shout of the young picket stationed up high along a rocky outcrop above the Ticknor Road, across from the yard in front of the Fairchild house. The soldier was pointing up the hillside, into the trees at something those in the valley could not yet see.

"The civilians bringing 'em in!" hollered the picket, waving his hat at the end of his arm to the soldiers stand-

ing in curious attention at their noon fires that Thursday,
22 May.

With a flick of his wrist, Donegan slopped the rest of
his coffee in his cup onto the ground. The entire camp was
on its feet in breathless wonder by the time the leader of
the procession appeared from the distant trees. Seamus
found a sudden, hot and scratchy lump in his throat as he
recognized Fairchild. Slowly the rancher came on, as Colonel Davis and his staff officers pushed across the road to
the base of the trail. Many more troops surged forward
silently, jostling for a good view of the narrow trail that
slashed down the hillside like a brown scar amidst the
green kissed by spring rains.

Riding some fifty yards behind the rancher, Mrs.
Fairchild appeared from the trees into the brilliant sunshine of that midday. Riding right behind her on the trail
came the two squaws Davis had twice trusted to help his
soldiers. As yet, no one in the valley could tell if they had
been successful in bringing in the renegades.

More important still, Seamus had not seen a glimpse of
his uncle.

Then, from the shadows emerged the first pair of warriors. Their ponies halted, then moved, halting again before inching forward at an agonizing pace, heads slung
low, weary of the weeks and miles of chase.

Another pair, then a third—until twelve warriors had
emerged from the trees, following the Fairchilds down the
green slope. Behind the men came the women, some with
little children clutched in their blankets. Others riding
double and triple on ribby ponies clearly done in and in
need of proper grazing. A dozen men and fifty-one others,
including a handful of old ones who hooded their faces
from the soldiers beneath tattered, dirty blankets. Nearly
all wore some scuffed and greasy part of a soldier uniform, taken from the army's dead.

"Dear Lord," whispered Captain Jackson. "Half-naked
children, aged squaws who can scarcely hobble. Blind,

lame and halt. The scum of the tribe—how this war has made beggars of them!"

"By the Virgin Mary," Seamus whispered in a sudden gasp.

"What was that?" Jackson asked, then turned to find what had caused the Irishman to utter his quiet, prayerful exclamation.

Ian O'Roarke brought up the rear, the last down the trail on his own weary animal. And in front of him, on the old saddle the settler had ridden all those years since mining the creeks of Colorado, sat a young girl not more than five or six summers. Her hair in hung greasy sprigs, her face smudged with dirt and the smoke of many desperate fires, and clutching Ian's coat about her trembling shoulders, beneath it her own dress in wind-whipped tatters.

Try as he might, Seamus could not swallow down the hot lump of glorious pride caught in his throat at the sight. Seeing even now that his uncle was more of a family man than any others might suspect. In his heart swelled a fierce love for that man bringing up the rear of the sad procession. His eyes grew moist as a rustle crossed the crowd.

Davis started forward with his officers, stepping onto the road. Soldiers surged forward and the colonel whirled on them, flinging his arm and ordering them back. He went on with a handful of his staff. Fifty yards from Fairchild's cabin, they stopped. Waiting for the rancher.

Fairchild, then his wife, came to a stop without a word spoken. When the first pair of warriors came to a halt with Fairchild, the rancher finally said, "Colonel Davis—this here is Bogus Charley."

"One of the murderers?"

"Yes." Fairchild turned, nodding to Charley. "This is the soldier tyee, Charley. It's time—like we talked about . . . now."

The dirty Modoc drew himself up as he slipped from the back of his skinny pony. He strode over to the officer who towered over him in the bright sunlight, rubbed his Springfield rifle affectionately one last time, then laid the weapon at the colonel's feet.

Without another word being spoken, the rest of the warriors dismounted as they rode into the ranch yard and laid their weapons, rifles and pistols, at the soldier's feet.

"Tell them I want their knives too, Fairchild."

When the rancher told the warriors, there were some flinty glares from the black eyes. But one by one the Modocs came up to lay their skinning and scalping knives with the firearms.

"Now tell them I am much pleased," Davis instructed. "Show them a place where they can camp across Cottonwood Creek, Fairchild. And remind them that any attempt to escape will be dealt with in a swift and harsh manner."

By the time O'Roarke was into the yard and handing the young girl down to a squaw, Seamus was at his side, taking off his own coat to wrap about the shoulders of an old woman who hobbled along near the end of the procession, dragging an injured foot.

"Didn't know how long I could wait . . . to know . . . to see you," Seamus admitted when he had his uncle locked in an embrace.

"You would have waited as long as it took, lad. Same you done already . . . getting here to find me."

As the sixty-three Modocs turned to cross the creek with their infantry escort, Davis caught up with Fairchild once more. "Call Captain Jack from the group. I wish to see the man for myself."

Fairchild slowly lidded his eyes. "Jack's not with them." He turned to the warriors and called out. "Charley—come here!"

Bogus Charley returned, shading his eyes as he looked up at the tall soldier chief.

Fairchild said, "Tell the tyee about splitting from Jack."

"We go another way . . . many days ago. Jack go there. We come west."

It was clear to read the disappointment in Davis's face. He scratched at his beard. "Correct me if I'm wrong, Fairchild. But this means that the staunchest of the warriors are still at large—still on the run."

"That's right, Colonel."

Davis turned back to Bogus Charley. "You lead this bunch?"

The Modoc nodded. "Now I do. Hooker Jim not want to surrender. Me? Tired of fighting. Running. Look at the people. Hungry. Their clothes no more keep out the cold. The little ones cry too much. Mothers no have the food, or milk to feed them no more. Charley so tired . . . tired of running."

Before supper late that afternoon, Hooker Jim—leader of the Lost River murderers—came down the ridge on foot to surrender to the troops at Fairchild's Ranch.

He too was tired of running.

Chapter 34

May 23–29, 1873

Six weeks had passed since the murders of Canby and Thomas on that Good Friday. Yet, this next to the last Friday in May had wrought its own surprise.

"For two hours this morning, Davis interrogated Bogus and Hooker and the rest," explained Ian O'Roarke around a last mouthful of Dimity's tender white beans. He sopped the last of the pork gravy from his cracked plate with a slab of her special cornbread, then popped it in his mouth, carefully licking each finger before he went on.

"But it was this afternoon that we watched the best show of all, Dimity."

She set two refilled cups of coffee before the men and quickly gathered dishes licked clean by children and adults alike. If Ian and Dimity O'Roarke had done anything right—it had been to teach their children not to take food for granted. Bones were always picked clean before they went to the hounds, and the last drop of milk from the cow was always argued over before the pitcher was drained.

Seamus himself was full and well-satisfied as he pulled the battered corncob from his pouch. Well-used it was, for back in the fall of '69 he had bought it from trader Mc-

Donald, sutler at Fort McPherson, Nebraska, shortly before pulling out for Denver City, Colorado Territory.*

Dimity finally perched herself on one of the long
benches that ran along both sides of the table. She
smoothed the long, patched apron. "Those dishes can
wait, Ian. I figure your story can't."

Ian smiled, nodding his head in approval. "See, Seamus
—how a good woman knows what it takes to make a man
happy. She fixes him the best meal we've wrapped ourselves around in many weeks . . . and then she politely
listens to his stories without complaint—like they was the
most important bits of news around."

She slapped at his shoulder, then swiped the corner of
the table with her apron as she said, "I'd listen to you talk
about the price of dirt, were you to do that, Ian O'Roarke.
Just to hear your voice . . . after so, so long."

Ian realized she was going to cry were he not careful.
Quickly clutching her hand in both of his, he stroked the
roughened, callused skin battered from so many dunkings
in soapy water, washing dishes and home and children
alike. "After suffering in the company of so many male
voices for so long now myself, Dimity—the Lord knows
how best to bless me with what's most important: the
heavenly music of your voice."

For a moment Seamus felt like a sham outsider, watching the couple embrace once more every bit as fiercely as
they had when the men had come riding into the yard
from Fairchild's place not far down the road as the sun
eased out of the day.

"This war ain't long in lasting now, Dimity," Ian reminded her as she drew back and swiped at the corners of
her eyes with the apron.

She blinked the pretty, reddened eyes clear and forced a
smile for Donegan's benefit. With a swallow she said, "So,
Ian O'Roarke—tell me what business you've got in this
war any longer."

---

* THE PLAINSMEN Series, vol. 3, *The Stalkers*

Ian still held her rough hand in both of his. "I figure I can only speak for myself—but I was there when this whole thing started last November, woman. And I've vowed I'll see it through."

"As well for me," Seamus replied.

"How long will it take for the army to round the rest of them up?" she asked.

Her husband wagged his head. "I can only pray it won't be long."

"You can't give me anything—nothing to hold onto while you're gone off to fight Modocs again, Ian O'Roarke?"

He smiled, stroking the back of her hand. "Two weeks."

"At the most," Seamus added, seeing something akin to gratitude come across his uncle's face.

"How are you so sure this time—either one of you?"

Ian glanced at his nephew. "I suppose because this time Davis is sending Modocs out to track down Captain Jack."

She sat up a little straighter, looking at him sternly from the corners of her eyes. "Is that what Hooker and Bogus had to do with the colonel?"

"I suppose they talked about it among themselves before they volunteered—but they told Davis they would help him track down their old chief. Captain Jack himself."

"Those cutthroats turning on Jack now, is it?" she said, making a clucking sound with her tongue. "Can you trust 'em, Ian?"

"I suppose we can. I rode up the mountain with John and Millie Fairchild—"

"And I'll never forgive you for taking such a stupid chance with your hide for all my days, Ian O'Roarke!" she replied, yanking her hand from his clutch.

"I'm here now, Dimity!" he cried, patting his chest and belly. "Look at me—not a hole anywhere. Seamus . . .

well, just look at him. The lad's a bullet magnet if I ever saw him."

She pouted a moment more, then said, "I suppose if you've got to go see this thing through, Ian—then take your nephew here along. With his luck, maybe he'll attract the bullet meant for you."

Seamus straightened in mock alarm. "I thank you both for your loving concern! If this shoulder would allow— I'd get up and throttle you both!"

"Dimity would not need my help in the least, whipping you soundly, Seamus!"

"Best keep your seat, young man," she warned. "Ian knows whereof he speaks!"

Donegan collapsed back on his bench, laughing. "All right—you've won this one, you have. But I'll have you know I've caught my own share of bullets and I'm not about to step in front of any more."

Colonel Jefferson C. Davis had been dubious at first, believing that Captain Jack was somewhere south of Fairchild's ranch, in the vicinity of Sheep Mountain. But the Hot Creek warriors continued to shake their heads. The rest of the Modocs, they asserted, could be found in one of three places a person could find drinking water: at the Boiling Springs on Pit River, or at the Coyote Springs southeast of Clear Lake, or somewhere along Willow Creek just east of Clear Lake.

After some discussion among themselves, the warriors had told Fairchild and O'Roarke they had decided the best bet would be to scout over the Willow Creek country. Besides good water, it was there Jack's people could find plenty of roots to dig, fish to catch and game to hunt.

After ordering Major Mason to remain with his infantry to guard the Modoc prisoners at Fairchild's ranch, followed by placing Major Green in charge of all cavalry, Davis dispatched Jackson's B Troop to Scorpion Point on the outside chance Jack would be found in that area. By Wednesday, 28 May, Hasbrouck and Perry had themselves come into the Scorpion Point camp, making it

Davis's new headquarters for the capture of the last of the renegades.

By now the colonel had convinced himself the four volunteers were to be trusted in tracking down their chief.

"I'll let Indians fight Indians any day if it will save one soldier's life," Davis told his officers in that Scorpion Point camp he had established for the final hunt.

On the twenty-seventh he issued orders to have rations, used uniforms, Springfield rifles and army mounts given to the four who were now being called the Modoc "bloodhounds" : Bogus Charley, Hooker Jim, Steamboat Frank and Shacknasty Jim.

Instead of staying out for a full four days as rationed by Davis, the Modocs had decided to come in just before dark that Tuesday. After they had scouted the area south of Tule Lake, they explained to Davis, and were searching the Horse Mountain area toward Clear Lake, the four knew they had to give the soldier chief their sobering alarm.

Sure that Jack's band had recently used the road going past Applegate's ranch, Bogus and the other bloodhounds were just as certain that Jack might now be in the hills above the ranch, planning a raid in retaliation for the parts played by Oliver and Ivan Applegate in the early days of what had become the long and bloody Modoc War.

On Wednesday, 28 May, the four Modoc bloodhounds once more rode away from the soldier camp and headed for Willow Creek, which drained the tall and timbered high country, eventually flowing west into Lost River, which drains into Clear Lake. Early that afternoon, after riding some fifteen miles into the hills, clouds gathered with ominous warning over the shrouded peaks above them as the four Modocs were climbing the pine-covered slopes.

"Stop!"

The echo of that warning bounced from ridge to ridge

as the four horsemen reined to a halt. Captain Jack stared
down the slope as a half dozen of his sentries surrounded
the four Modocs who had bitterly abandoned him weeks
before.

"We come to see Jack," announced Bogus Charley.

Without a word the sentries led the way off the trail, up
the slope through the timber. Then the guards stopped,
pointed to the narrow meadow a quarter of a mile off, and
disappeared to watch the backtrail for soldiers.

As the four watched, they found the Modocs in camp
emerging from the trees, forming a cordon across the
footpath.

"Let them pass," Jack said, stepping from the shadows
behind the line, his fiery eyes taking in every detail of the
quartet's army garb and equipment.

"You did not bring anyone with you?" asked the chief
before the four could dismount.

"No one," Bogus replied. He started to ease out of the
saddle.

"Do not get down," Jack ordered. There was a quiet
rustling of weapons behind the chief. "You are welcome
to stay in our camp—if you give up your weapons and
will be my prisoners while you are here."

"I will be no man's prisoner!" Shacknasty Jim railed.

"Why do you expect us to give you our guns?" asked
Bogus.

"You deserted the rest of us three weeks ago. You are
not welcome as guests. But you can come to talk as my
prisoners."

"Prisoners?" Bogus squeaked.

"Yes!" Jack said. "You sold your honor as Modoc warriors to the white man—just to hunt me down. Your freedom . . . for my neck, right?"

"I am no man's prisoner. I will keep my gun," Hooker
Jim said, his finger clearly on the trigger of his rifle. "I
won't be the first to kill a Modoc here today."

Jack glanced up at Hooker. "Strange, isn't it—how you
sing such a new song now. Only days ago you were ready

to kill me with your bare hands. Like the coward that you are: ready to kill a brother Modoc." He turned from Hooker, stepping over to Bogus Charley's horse.

The chief gazed up at the warrior. "These are John Fairchild's horses, aren't they?"

"I don't deny that they are."

Jack stroked the neck of the animal. "Good horses, Fairchild's. Where did you get them?"

"From Fairchild's ranch," Shacknasty answered.

"Then my suspicions are right," Jack replied, looking over the four. "The white men sent you here to track us down."

Bogus glanced at Hooker, then replied, "A few days ago we surrendered to the soldiers. Everyone who went west with us. The white man has been good to us—gave us blankets and food to eat. It is good to stop running."

He felt the bile rising high in his throat. "You are saying that Kientpoos should stop running too?"

"Yes," Bogus replied. "Come, give yourself up to the soldiers."

Jack snatched the bridle, yanking it in his anger so hard the horse reared back, nearly unseating Bogus Charley.

"You! All of you—spineless cowards who called me a squaw! It was you who tied the woman's dress around my waist. The hat on my head and the shawl over my shoulders. Saying I had the heart of a squaw! But look at you —now you are hunting dogs for the white man. Brave hearts are you? Ha!"

"The white man guaranteed we would not be harmed," Hooker explained.

"You believe them?" He wagged his head. "There is no truth waiting for me on the white man's tongue. Only a rope—because I did what the four of you wanted me to do! To kill an honorable man in cold blood—simply to show that I was not a coward."

"We too have killed, Jack," Shacknasty tried to explain. "Come in and surrender too."

The chief wheeled on him. "I will die with a gun in my

hand, hot from firing and killing many before me. I will never—never—die at the end of a white man's hanging rope!"

"Your people are hungry and cold, Jack," Bogus said. "Let them come surrender now."

"You have talked too much already!" Jack snapped, flinging his arms up and cutting off further discussion. "Go now while I still let you live. Go live with the white man if you want. But remember this: if I ever see your faces again . . . if you come within range of my gun—I will shoot each one of you down like dogs."

For a long time no one spoke. The four sat nervously atop their horses. Jack stood glaring at them, his arms crossed haughtily.

"Will you leave, Jack?" asked Bogus. "I want to talk with my friends without you making problems for us."

"You ask me to leave?" Jack shrieked in rage. "It is you who must leave—and now! Go before there is great trouble."

But Scar-Faced Charley suddenly pushed past his old friend the chief, striding up to Bogus Charley. "I will talk with my friends, Jack. I am a Modoc warrior, and no one will tell me I can't talk to my friends."

So, it had come to this. Jack brooded, his eyes darkening as his best friend whispered among the four Hot Creek Modocs.

In those last few weeks since the great split, things had not gone well between Jack and Scar-Faced Charley. More fissures were splintering Jack's band. More grumbling all the time. He had done everything he could to keep his people together—even killing a good white man to do it—and now the people were slowly deserting him. These unfaithful, ungrateful people who had followed the shaman's bloody magic and now wanted to abandon the fight.

How much pain, he wondered—how much pain must one man have to endure?

"Are you here to guide the soldiers to us?" demanded

William Faithful as he stepped up to where Bogus Charley was talking to a few of Jack's band.

"The soldiers are coming whether we guide them here or not," Bogus answered.

"This talk is no good," Jack grumbled again. "I cannot allow you."

"We will talk," Scar-Faced Charley said. He turned back to the four and continued to tell them how bad things had become within Jack's dwindling band. "There are many who would leave him—if they could sneak away. He stays up the nights now—watching everyone so they cannot flee. Like a madman . . . possessed he's become."

"As bad as my father-in-law?" Hooker asked, half a crooked smile on his face.

Scar-Faced Charley wagged his head. "This is something else again, Hooker. It is like he holds us prisoner now with the chains of his own great pride."

Now knowing for certain that Captain Jack was on Willow Creek, Colonel Davis dispatched Jackson's B Troop, a squad of Perry's cavalry and some of Hasbrouck's mounted artillery to Applegate's ranch in the event the hostiles did make a vengeful attack on the settlement. It was there Davis would establish his final headquarters for the campaign.

Lieutenant Colonel Wheaton had arrived on the scene, vowing he would now see the end to the whole sad affair he had begun the previous November. When he told fellow officers that the next few days would see Jack captured or killed—Davis told Wheaton it would be far more prudent to keep his mouth shut and his ears open.

Jefferson C. Davis was clearly in command of the Modoc campaign.

That Friday, 30 May, when Major Green led mounted squads under Captains Jackson and Hasbrouck away from Applegate's ranch, a wet, deepening snow began to fall that would make it easier to track the fleeing Modocs.

It slowed most travel into the Willow Creek area as well, but the soldiers knew that reports from the Hot Creek Modocs who had visited Jack's camp had told Colonel Davis there was growing discontent in the band. In all likelihood, more of Jack's warriors would defect as the noose tightened around the chief.

Three miles out from where the four bloodhounds said the soldiers would find the camp, Major Green divided his troops into three wings, each with a contingent of McKay's Tenino scouts: Hasbrouck's men, guided by Hooker Jim, rode to the north side of the Willow Creek canyon, in the event Jack attempted to flee by crossing the creek itself; Green and most of the rest moved along the south side of the creek with Steamboat Frank as their guide; and meanwhile, Fairchild, O'Roarke and Donegan, along with the other two bloodhounds and some Warm Springs scouts, inched their way up the snowy floor of the valley.

Perhaps the snow had made Jack's pickets less watchful. Perhaps they were more mindful of their own cold, wet feet and chattering teeth. Green's soldiers drew to within a mile of the Modoc camp before they were spotted by Jack's warriors.

"You go around that hill," Steamboat Frank advised Major Green, "your soldiers get so close to camp Jack won't see you come."

Green obediently dispatched Lieutenant Bacon and a dozen infantry to the backside of the enemy position. In the meantime, McKay and his Teninos got to within three hundred yards of the soggy, blanket shelters when four warriors appeared, about the time the civilians and more scouts showed up from the creek bottom.

"Why you Indians come to our camp?" one of them hollered to the Warm Springs mercenaries.

"Yes—why you bring so many men with you?" demanded another, waving his rifle at the three civilians.

To Seamus Donegan it was as clear as rinsed crystal

that Jack's warriors were now more interested in negotiating than in firing the first shot.

"Bogus, get one of them to come over here and surrender," John Fairchild suggested in a loud whisper.

"Yes," O'Roarke echoed. "If they see one do it without harm—the rest will come up and lay down their arms."

Bogus Charley hollered out his offer. "These men will not harm you. You know Fairchild and O'Roarke. They have always been good to us."

"Bogus? Is that you with O'Roarke?"

Bogus turned to flash a big grin at the civilians as the snow gently fell, soaking into their wool coats. "That Boston Charley. Know his talk anywhere." He turned back to his friend back in the timber. "Boston—come talk with us."

The warrior looked at his companions, then alone he crossed the open ground between the camp and the white men. With the look of a harried, frightened animal, Boston stopped before Fairchild, still clutching his rifle nervously as he eyed the Teninos.

"McKay, tell your scouts to lay down their weapons," Fairchild suggested. "To let the Modocs know they will not be killed by us."

As the Teninos laid their weapons on the ground, Boston Charley laid his rifle at Fairchild's feet, then stood with a smile of a man suddenly relieved of an awful burden.

"I thought you were dead, Boston," O'Roarke said as they performed the normal handshaking ritual so popular with the Modocs.

Across the open ground more and more of Jack's band appeared, watching warily in the mid-distance, from behind boulders and trees, making certain by watching Boston that they would not be killed if they showed themselves.

"Me? Boston no dead. Bogus tell you that?"

"Yes," answered Fairchild.

Boston laughed, easily now. "Bogus. Him all time tell

lies about Boston. Good jokes, this Bogus tell!" They
pounded each other on the back like reunited brothers
who enjoyed the most primitive of practical jokes.

"You hungry, Boston?" asked Steamboat Frank.

"Me? Always hungry. You got some soldier food?"

Frank nodded and strode back to his horse, forgetting
that he had cocked the hammer of his rifle. When the
animal shied while he was busy at his saddlebags, Steamboat lunged for the horse, catching the heavy hammer on
a stirrup fender.

The rifle fired.

As one, the group of scouts and civilians jumped and
whirled. Steamboat Frank stood there with a sheepish
look on his face, and with a shrug of his shoulders continued to dig in his saddlebag for something to eat.

But the damage had been done.

Those Modocs who had been watching Boston's surrender had disappeared before the last echo of that gun's
blast had rolled down the canyon. As far as they were
concerned, Boston had been lured into a trap and slaughtered by the white men and Teninos.

"You better go get them, Boston," O'Roarke suggested.
"Likely they think you're dead."

"Boston Charley no dead. He hungry." The Modoc
ravenously gnawed off a chunk of dried salt-beef. "I go.
Bring them back. Tonight. Maybe in morning."

Seamus watched the Modoc cross the open ground and
disappear into the timber toward the camp. "Does he
have a chance of talking the others in?"

Fairchild shrugged. "It's the only chance we've got that
doesn't mean more blood spilled."

Chapter 35

May 29–31, 1873

"*I* think we've been played the fool, Fairchild," growled Major John Green.

O'Roarke glanced at the pocket watch Fairchild held in his palm. Seamus looked into the sky at the falling sun. Boston Charley had been gone for better than two hours.

"You think he could have done us wrong?" Fairchild asked of O'Roarke.

"Didn't really figure him to, John."

Green stood suddenly, his own frame taut with tension. "We'll get something salvaged out of the day. Davis sent me here to end this war—and end it I will. McKay!"

The half-breed loped over. "Major."

"Take a few of your men and see if you can advance into the village. Find out what happened to Boston Charley—if he's played a hoax on us. I'm not waiting any longer to attack if he has."

In a half an hour McKay was back—but coming in from the south, in the opposite direction of the camp.

"Didn't you go looking for Boston as I ordered you?" Green snapped.

McKay's dark face flushed with anger. "Charley not in the camp. He got to camp about the time your god-damned soldiers with Captain Hasbrouck showed up in the village on other side—coming from another direction. They captured Boston more than two hours ago after he left us here. They sent him down the valley with guards."

"The fools!" Green yelped as if bit.

"Hasbrouck said he didn't know any better—thought Charley was lying to him about going to get the others to come in and surrender to you."

"Damn!" Green wheeled on Fairchild and O'Roarke. "Do you see what I'm saddled with at times? Hasbrouck captures what he thinks is an enemy warrior—and doesn't even think to tell me. Had I known two hours ago . . . god*damn!* I'd love to swear like a gut-cut sea swabby!"

The major whirled back on McKay suddenly. "All right—go back to Hasbrouck and tell him Boston Charley is to be released—to you. Bring that Modoc here so we can get the rest of these people with Jack induced to surrender."

By the time Boston Charley reached Major Green and was again sent into Jack's camp with the army's message, most of the Modocs had flown.

"They don't ever come back here," Charley explained when he showed up at dusk, shadows grown long and the air more cold than it had been in many days.

"No one?" Green cried. "You can't find a one of them?"

Boston shook his head. "Find some: squaws, children. Queen Mary too—she come to soldiers."

"Queen Mary? Who's this?" Green asked, turning to O'Roarke.

"The chief's sister. Jack's own family," Ian answered. "It means something if she's surrendering."

"Likely they're hungry, Major," said Fairchild. "Cold too. Army blankets and hard crackers sound mighty good to them right about now."

The major turned back to the Modoc bloodhound. "Go bring this Queen Mary in, Charley. With the rest. Tell them they can eat their fill tonight and sleep warm by our fires."

Those who did not surrender that evening bolted north into the Langell Valley, intending to make it all the way to the Yainax Agency where Old Schonchin and his small band were still living in some safety. Although the various groups of them were all heading in the same general direction, with Steamboat Frank's careless accident with the rifle, Captain Jack's holdouts had gone the way of feathers tossed on the wind, scattering over the hills and ridges along Willow Creek in pairs and small groups—every one of them certain the soldiers had come to butcher them all.

If only they could make it back to Yainax alive . . .

Just past midday that thirtieth of May, Fairchild and O'Roarke crossed some fresh tracks cut through the soggy new snow. Six grueling miles later, after following a trail only a mountain goat could have made, they spotted three warriors who kept running and dodging, despite what assurances the civilians could holler across the distance. The warriors disappeared into another steep canyon cluttered with boulders and deadfall—impossible for a horse to follow.

An hour later Green's footbound troops discovered still another small group of Modocs and drove them over the hills toward the civilians. Thirteen more warriors now disappeared into the narrow canyon.

The uncertain terrain took its toll on the soldiers, who repeatedly slipped and fell on the soggy ground and slick snow. While they all grumped for their horses, not one man among them failed to understand that there wasn't a horse yet born could have followed the Modocs' trail into the Langell Valley.

Green halted his command for a breather, calling up McKay.

"Take your best trackers and find out where those warriors have forted up," the major ordered. "I want no bloodshed if we can help it. Don't fight—just find them for me."

Time dragged by for soldiers forced to sit, unable to move about much at all. First one hour, then a second passed. And finally McKay showed up at the bottom of the valley, waving in greeting to the soldiers.

Green was pacing, slapping a glove against the side of his leg by the time the half-breed climbed the slope.

"You found them?"

"Fifteen of 'em. Not many more than that left, Major."

"Lead me down there to them."

"Your surgeon already talking to them."

That brought the major up as if someone had yanked hard on the back of his hair. "My surgeon? Cabaniss?"

"He came down, alone," McKay explained. "While we were talking to the Modocs."

"You two actually talked to them?" asked Captain Hasbrouck.

"Yes. We talk some after they fire four shots over our heads."

"You said over your heads," Fairchild repeated. "You think they were avoiding hitting you and your men."

McKay nodded. "They didn't mean to hit us—just scare us off."

"What were they telling Dr. Cabaniss?" Green asked.

"Scar-Faced Charley came down close to talk with the surgeon," McKay declared. "He said they are hungry and tired of running now. They have nothing no more. Without food for many days. Charley and four others surrendered to doctor."

"By God, that's good news. We're slowly whittling them down now!" The major was clearly exuberant.

"Scar-Faced Charley tell surgeon that Jack probably come in morning to see you."

"See me in the morning?"

"Charley says so. But that wasn't good enough for your surgeon."

Green began pulling his glove on. "Where's Cabaniss now?"

"He go with Scar-Faced Charley to talk with Jack himself."

"He's gone in to talk with Jack? I hope to hell he doesn't botch this."

Fairchild wagged his head. "Cabaniss can't possibly do any worse than what your soldiers have done to botch things up the last few days, Major."

"I've never seen them more anxious, uneasy—downright scared," Dr. Cabaniss explained to those who had gathered at Major Green's fire after the surgeon came into camp that mid-afternoon of the thirtieth, accompanied by one of Jack's warriors, One-Eyed Mose.

"They damn well have reason to be afraid," Green said. "We're rounding them up at last. You did talk to Jack personally—see him yourself?"

"Yes, of course. His head was in his hands when I came up. He's terribly despondent. More lonely than I've seen anyone in my life, Major. But we sat and had a good talk. Still, he doesn't look like the man I knew before all this started. The toll this has taken on him."

"He's not the only one, Surgeon," snapped Green. "Tell me when he's going to surrender."

Cabaniss sighed at the affront. "Jack wants to know what you're going to do with him if he surrenders to you."

Green hunched forward. "You didn't tell him he was going to be hanged, did you?"

The doctor leaned back, staring at the fire. "I told him nothing, Major."

"Good. Did the two of you discuss anything else?"

"That his people had been without food and warm clothing for many days. I promised him I would return with some."

One of Green's eyes flickered slightly. "You were sticking your neck out there, Doctor."

"If you didn't order the requisition—I was sure I could ride down and secure permission from Colonel Davis."

Green rubbed his gloves atop his thighs, his turn to suffer an affront. "I'm sure you would have, Dr. Cabaniss. All right—you have my permission to draw foodstuffs, clothing and blankets from the quartermaster's stores." He stood. "And, in fact—you'll return with something more. Tell Jack I'm going to pull my soldiers back a few miles before we bivouac for the night."

"That will go a long way to easing some of the Modocs' fears, Major. Thank you," Cabaniss replied.

"Not at all, Doctor. It seems you've made some headway with Jack's bunch—so I want you to continue to win their confidence. I won't do a thing to spoil your hard work. You see, I've got this war almost in my palm. We don't want anything to go wrong, do we?"

Green was good at his word. As Cabaniss and One-Eyed Mose took the food and supplies into the canyon, the major ordered his troops to move due west some five miles down the Langell Valley to the Wilson ranch, where they would establish a short-term outpost as the sun again fell from the sky.

As clear as it was after the recent storm, tonight would be even colder than expected.

It made a man shiver to watch the light bleed from that sky, wondering on the morrow.

"He what?"

"Jack slipped away on me, Major," Cabaniss tried to explain with a shrug of his shoulders.

"I trusted him. Hell, I trusted you!"

"He was there in camp when I went to sleep. It was late. This morning at sunrise he was gone. Up before me."

"You know where?"

Cabaniss shook his head. It was more from sympathizing with the hunted chief than from his own grave error in trusting Jack. "He told the other warriors he was leaving early to find a new campsite where they would be safer from the soldiers. But the others knew."

"Knew what?" Green demanded, seething.

"They knew that was just an excuse."

"An excuse?"

"Jack could not bear to surrender himself—knowing you're going to hang him."

"How does he know that? Did you tell him, Doctor?"

Cabaniss shook his head. "No one had to tell him. Jack knows the white man needs to hang someone for all the civilian and soldier deaths. So, he still doesn't think surrender is the end for him."

"No—a bullet will be, by God!"

O'Roarke and Fairchild inched up on Cabaniss. Ian spoke first. "He couldn't bear to watch the others surrender either, could he?"

The surgeon nodded. "That's right. He left his people so they would not have to go on fighting and running. Mostly running."

"There's something to admire in the man even yet," Seamus said quietly.

"So, what about these others who want to surrender?" Green asked, tossing a twig into the fire at his feet. It sent sparks into the air as it plopped among the red, writhing coals.

"They'll be along shortly."

"You're positive about this, Cabaniss?"

"As sure as I am that you'll hunt Jack down until he no longer has any strength left in his legs to run."

"By damned—you might be starting to understand me, Doctor."

They didn't have to wait long that Saturday, the thirty-first day of May, for the first weary warrior to make his appearance on the hillside overlooking the Wilson ranch.

"That's Scar-Faced Charley," O'Roarke told his nephew.

"I've seen him before," Seamus replied quietly, his mind digging at it the way a child would dig at a muddy creek bottom with his bare toes. He was sure he had seen the warrior someplace before.

"Charley does all his fighting out in the open—like a man, Seamus," said John Fairchild. "He's not one of them murderers like the others."

It came clear for Donegan of a sudden, like a gust of wind blowing fog from the creek bottom. "He directed the attack on Captain Thomas's patrol up at the Black Ledge. I saw him, standing up on the ridge. It was a bloody fight, but no way was it murder. And—Charley— he called it off before the rest of us were all killed."

Ian turned, amazement written on his face. "You never told me that, Seamus."

"I know. Seeing him now, I'll never forget that long scar down the whole side of his face . . . making me remember some pieces of it now—how he hollered down at those of us who were still alive. Laying in that brush, afraid of dying. He could see us down in that hollow— every man bleeding and unable to defend himself if they truly wanted to wipe us out."

"But he called off the attack?" Fairchild asked.

"That's right," Seamus said as the warrior drew closer, holding his rifle up in one hand, the other open, palm out and empty. "I suppose . . . this man might be a little grateful to that Injin for sparing my life."

Ten more warriors came in, each one walking the same path out of the hills that Scar-Faced Charley had taken. Each one came alone. One by one they laid their weapons down at the feet of Major Green, then went with an escort to the Wilson barn, where they were kept under guard.

The twelfth warrior to give up came in knowing for certain what he was to face at the hands of the white man.

"Schonchin John." Fairchild said it like a curse. "The old Yainax chief's younger brother."

"Meacham said he was one of the murderers at the peace tent," Seamus reflected.

"It will go hard on Schonchin," O'Roarke replied. "In

a way, you've got to admire him too. Coming in—giving up—knowing what faces him now."

Dr. Cabaniss walked up to their group a few minutes later. "Scar-Faced Charley said it was hard to leave his friend Jack."

"He knows where Jack is?"

The surgeon nodded. "Up there, doing what's hardest: watching his warriors surrender."

"Will he?" O'Roarke asked. "Or will he force the army to shoot him in the end?"

"Charley told me Jack wants to see me," Cabaniss said quietly. "Jack wants to surrender in the morning."

"You still believe him—after what he pulled on you?" Fairchild asked.

The surgeon finally said, "Yes. I still believe Jack. None of us can imagine—we have no idea what agony it must be for him—knowing what faces him now. Not one of us can truly understand what it means to stand in his place at this moment: knowing that to give up means certain death."

Chapter 36

June 1, 1873

With the coming of the sun that morning, burning the last wisps of fog from the low places, Colonel Jefferson C. Davis learned that his regulars were being rejoined in the chase by three companies of Oregon volunteer militia.

"Sounds to me like General Ross, who's leading all those volunteers, wants to get into the field to make a show of protecting his Oregon settlers," said Captain David Perry as the sun rose, spraying his men with warmth as they saddled their mounts at Applegate's ranch, preparing to move out for the final chase.

"I don't think so," Seamus replied as he stroked the neck of his own mount. He and John Fairchild were again riding along with Perry's F Troop, First Cavalry.

"I figure the Irishman's right. Seems more like Ross and his volunteers are coming in now as the war ends for their grand show," added Fairchild on the far side of the captain's mount.

Perry considered it, finally dropping the stirrup over the cinch, watching McKay's Tenino scouts mounting up. "Could be, Irishman. His kind figures that the war's all but done—so he comes in to grab some of the glory."

"That," Seamus replied, "and so his volunteers can come pick Jack's bones clean."

Captains Jackson and Hasbrouck had flushed the last of the Modoc holdouts from the Willow Creek country. Both had reveled in capturing half of those who had stayed with Jack when the band splintered at Big Sand Butte. Now Colonel Davis was ordering Perry's cavalry to finish the job.

From Applegate's place Perry ordered his guides to take them back across Lost River toward the trail the other Modocs had taken two days before. From there the captain planned to backtrack in their march to the south toward Willow Creek. Everything seemed to point to Jack remaining in the high-walled valley that tumbled down to Clear Lake.

The sun hadn't climbed all that high in the sky by the time Perry's advance squad found the Tenino scouts stopped and waiting for the soldiers to come up.

"Jack's men splitting up," McKay said as Perry walked up on foot. He showed the captain some moccasin and boot tracks leading off in more than a half-dozen directions at the edge of the clearing still several miles north of Willow Creek.

Perry chewed on it like it was a piece of gristle while Donegan stepped up, leading his mount. The Irishman looked over the tracks, then peered into the far distance. "Cap'n, these tracks are breaking up, for sure. But I've gotta tell you, I've seen a lot of this same thing out on the high plains."

"Not the same kind of country," McKay said, seeming to sneer a little at the Irishman's news. "Not the same kind of Indians neither."

Seamus let it slide from his back like water off greased rawhide. "Believe what you will, Cap'n. But I'll put this in for what it's worth: this bunch is splitting up—but I'll lay good wages on these trails joining back up today."

"You're sure of that, Donegan?"

He nodded, scratching at his chin whiskers. "You look

close, then imagine this trail going out there into the distance—see how every one of these paths is heading in the same general direction."

"All due south, aren't they?" Perry asked himself. "Right for Willow Creek?"

"Any of them. Or all."

Perry turned to McKay. "Divide your men, McKay. Lead a squad of them yourself and take one of these trails. We'll divide the rest of your scouts between my squad, Captain Trimble and Sergeant McCarthy. That way we'll have four of these trails covered."

After progressing five more miles, Perry found the other three squads awaiting him near the north bank of Willow Creek. The various trails had converged at the ford.

"Some of them crossed over," McKay explained.

"You've been over there?"

"Yes. And the rest—most of the tracks—move upstream on this north bank."

Perry drank slowly from his canteen, then replaced it in a saddlebag. "All right. Captain Trimble," he called to his junior captain. "Take your squad and cross the creek. Move upstream the way Hasbrouck did two days back."

"You'll be on this bank, Captain?" asked William Trimble.

"Yes. One of us is bound to find something before dark."

"Won't be long now," McKay said before Trimble moved off. "Jack not far ahead of you now."

Nudging his mount up beside Fairchild's, Seamus said, "John, I'll cross over with Trimble if you're staying close to Perry."

"All right." The rancher held his hand out and they shook. "Your uncle told me to watch out for you—but I figure from what happened at Black Ledge, you don't need me watching out for you, what with the Lord doing it for you."

Donegan smiled briefly as Fairchild reined away. Sens-

ing once again that there was no other reason for him and
the others to be alive now but for Scar-Faced Charley
calling off the attack. It would be something more he
would carry with him for the rest of his days—this wondering what it was that had made the Modoc leader recall
his warriors when they could have slaughtered all the
white men.

Why had he been left to live, when so many other good
soldiers who had stayed behind to fight—had died?

Was it, as Ian's friend John Fairchild had just claimed:
the Lord Himself was watching over him?

It brought the hairs up on the back of his neck as the
horse nimbly stepped across the high-running stream behind Captain Trimble now, looking back as he did at each
of those times since the Civil War when he had been
hurled so close to the stinking maw of death itself.

Beneath a broiling day-long July sun at the Crazy
Woman Crossing of the Bozeman Road . . .

. . . had he not been a prisoner in Fort Phil Kearny's
guardhouse, he likely would have marched out that cold
morning of 21 December 1866, with fellow civilians and
friends, Wheatley and Fisher, who chose to join Captain
William Judd Fetterman and eighty men in crossing
Lodge Trail Ridge . . .

. . . had he quit the hayfield corral that morning of 1
August 1867, instead of waiting for the paymaster to
come down and muster him out, chances were good he
would have been cut off, alone and helpless, by the hundreds of Cheyenne and Sioux warriors gathering in the
surrounding hills, coming to attack Fort C. F. Smith . . .

. . . had things been different, the shots fired by renegade Confederate Bob North would have hit him as he
made that frantic crossing to the sandy island in the middle of the Arickaree Fork . . .

. . . or perhaps the Cheyenne bullet fired by one of
those fighting for Roman Nose would have hit him in the
head instead of Uncle Liam . . .

. . . and had it not been for the thirst of a good friend

wanting to have one last drink with a fellow plainsman, Bill Cody would not have ventured out one October sunset to that stinking latrine behind trader McDonald's to find the hulking, wild-eyed mulatto about to slit an Irishman's throat like a hog at slaughter.

Was it that a man lives so much by luck? he wondered as the two Tenino scouts led them into the trees on the south bank of Willow Creek. Are most affairs really left in the hands of man? And when man himself botches those affairs badly, does an angel step forward to right the wrongs of man?

He dared not tempt the fates by thinking on them, trying now to squeeze the fears and uncertainties from his mind as the foot-trail took them higher into the rugged, precipitous rocks and timber overlooking the creek gurgling farther and farther below.

All that training at his mother's knee had taught him not to question, but to accept the will of God. It was enough for her to do what she was told was God's will by the priests. That was all that was expected of a man, she in turn taught him.

"Do ye God's will—and the saints will always protect thee," she had oft repeated to her son as he grew to young manhood.

In less than a mile of narrow, twisting trail, Willow Creek bent sharply to the left. From time to time through the thick stands of timber, Seamus could see Perry's men moving along the high rocks across the creek. The valley seemed so tranquil, he doubted Jack and his last holdouts could be anywhere close. Not a sound but the occasional muted squeak and rattle of horse-trappings, the snort of an animal blowing on the steady climb, forever climbing up the high valley wall, perhaps a muffled cough of one of those fourteen troopers following their corporal and Sergeant McCarthy and Captain Trimble and two Teninos ever higher. From time to time the Indian scouts dismounted, getting down on their knees to look over the foot-trail.

They would stand after each inspection, smiling at the soldier chief, and say something.

"Squaw trail. Squaws' moccasins." And point up the slope.

The next inspection, farther up the canyon, would cause the guides to smile even wider, placing their hands in the dim footprints, then rise, saying, "Hot trail, soldiers. This is hot trail."

Donegan was struck with how much had changed in this fighting the Modocs. No more was it anything that the pundits could describe as a war. In the past few days it had become nothing more than a ragged pursuit of wild beasts through the wilderness.

Something close to an hour had passed since Trimble led them across the creek now far below. Up ahead the scouts were signaling to the captain to take a shortcut to avoid a rocky promontory off to their left where some clumps of juniper obscured the sharp drop into the creek bottom far below.

Instead of immediately following his guides, Trimble trusted his intuition and raised his arm, signaling a halt. He signaled one of his older soldiers to come up from the column.

"Shay, stick your nose up there on those rocks and see what you can. If nothing else, take a look across the creek and see if you can spot Captain Perry's men on the far side."

The old private slid from his mount, handing his reins to Sergeant McCarthy. He moved quietly into the shadows.

In less than five minutes he was back, constantly craning his neck behind him.

"By jiminy, Cap'n—we've caught us one for sure!" he said in an excited whisper.

"You found a warrior?"

"One, sir," he said, turning to point. "On the edge of them rocks—cutting on a root, something. He's got a dog, and they're sitting there—staring off at Perry's men moving along the far side of the creek."

"The warrior doesn't know we're here?"

Shay shook his head. "No, Cap'n. Not yet."

Trimble turned to the two Teninos. "See that the Modoc is alone—then take him prisoner. There must be no shooting. Do you understand? No guns. I don't want to scare the rest away."

They all watched the Teninos move into the shadows, following Private Shay.

"You figure there's more warriors close by?" asked McCarthy.

"Where you'll find one, we'll find the rest, Sergeant," answered Donegan.

In minutes the Teninos reappeared with their prisoner, a hunch-backed warrior.

"Humpy Joe," said one of the Warm Springs scouts. "Half brother to Captain Jack."

The fourteen troopers all dismounted noisily, excited, bunching forward to make the last charge of the Modoc War.

"Quiet!" Trimble ordered as the Teninos grew alarmed at the sudden noise.

"Keep soldiers quiet," ordered one of the scouts, his mind clawing for the English words. "We wait for Jack. He won't run when we wait."

Trimble turned on his squad. "Sit, men. We'll play this hand out like the scouts say."

"I talk to Fairchild now," Humpy Joe said as he strode up to Trimble, sure now who was the leader of the soldiers.

"He's on the far side of the creek," Seamus explained. "You know Fairchild?"

Humpy Joe nodded, his eyes moving down, then back up the Irishman's frame. The Modoc stood less than five and a half feet tall, bent over as he was with the severely deformed spine, making him appear all the more small beside the tall civilian.

"I know Fairchild. Friend . . . Fairchild."

"Yes, Fairchild will be glad to see Humpy Joe again," Seamus said quietly, putting his hand out.

Humpy Joe stared at it a moment, then put out his dirty hand covered in dried blood. They shook as the Modoc smiled.

"Where is Captain Jack?" asked Seamus.

With a bigger smile, the Modoc shrugged and turned to point down into the canyon. "Jack not far. There."

"You saw soldiers across the creek?"

Humpy Joe nodded.

"We have Jack surrounded now," Seamus explained. "Go now—tell Jack to come give himself up to us. We want no more of your people to be hurt."

"You come with Humpy Joe?" asked the Modoc.

Donegan turned to Trimble.

The captain nodded. "We'll both go with him."

"Take us to see Jack," Seamus said.

Humpy Joe turned, shuffling into the junipers. The long trail led through less than fifty yards of shadow and sunlight until they reached another jutting promontory of rock. The warrior stepped to the edge and called out in Modoc.

"Kientpoos!" echoed from side to side in the narrow canyon.

There was no answer from below as the sound died away, and with it some of Donegan's hope.

Humpy Joe turned back to the two white men and shrugged.

"Call him again," Trimble directed. "Tell him we won't shoot if he comes out now."

Before Humpy Joe could turn back and utter a word, Captain Jack himself appeared on a rocky shelf above them, a Springfield rifle hung carelessly at the end of his arm. It struck Donegan by surprise that things should end so quietly—so bloody and so long a war should wind down like a clock's mainspring running out of tension and just slowing, slowing, slowing until it stopped.

"Fairchild?" Jack called out.

"He's not here," Trimble shouted back, shading his eyes with a hand.

The chief took a single step forward. "Fairchild—that you?"

Trimble glanced back at Donegan, waving the civilian forward.

"He's across the creek, Captain Jack," explained the Irishman as he stepped more into the light.

"Fairchild not here?"

"Soon. He'll come soon."

Jack appeared very tired as he took a few more steps forward, the rifle still slung carelessly beside him, then he appeared to think better of it and collapsed slowly to the nearby shelf of rocks.

Tremble and Donegan moved forward warily, both watching the rest of the trees for anything that could spell an ambush. But in less than a minute they both stood feet from the chief of the Modocs.

Dressed in tattered soldier britches and a dirty, bloodied army tunic, Captain Jack looked up at them, his eyes red and puffy from the smoke of many fires and too many nights without sleep. He shielded his eyes with a hand as he looked them both over. There was no flinching, no indication of fear as he gave himself over to his captors.

Then his eyes dropped to the ground, where he laid the rifle at Trimble's feet.

Jack dragged a hand beneath his runny nose, quietly snorting. He wagged his head wearily and sighed, as if a great burden had been lifted from him.

Two more warriors now appeared, off to the right, as if they had been waiting—watching the scene. They slowly moved down to stand near their chief and surrendered their rifles. Seconds later the first of the squaws and children came into the tiny clearing. Five women and seven youngsters stood with the men, every one of them looking emaciated and exhausted, having hung on during the chase of the last few days by nothing more than sheer will alone.

Kientpoos, chief of his people to the end, looked over those of his band who had come into the tiny clearing to stand around him. Then Jack squinted up at the white men and spoke quietly.

"Jack's legs give out."

Chapter 37

June 1–14, 1873

"*Y*ou are Captain Jack?" Trimble asked his prisoner.

The Modoc nodded, scratching at the back of his neck for a louse. "I am Jack."

"Chief of the Modocs."

He squinted up at the officer for a moment. Then gazed back at the ground. "Yes, I am Kientpoos. Chief of the Lost River Modocs."

Captain Trimble turned, signaling. "Sergeant McCarthy! Bring the men up! We have captured Captain Jack!"

As the sixteen soldiers and pair of scouts came into the clearing, William Trimble himself ripped his hat from his head and tossed it into the air with a throaty cheer. The rest of the men did the same, each one of them rushing forward to get a look at the ragged, forlorn figure of the man they had been making war on for more than six months.

"He don't look so mean to me," muttered one young soldier.

"It ain't how he looks," commented another. "It's what a black-hearted bastard like that does that'll give you bad dreams, boy."

Seamus Donegan listened to the not so quiet mutterings of the soldiers as they encircled their few captives, all the while never taking his eyes from the man who had stood off the might of the United States Army with less than seventy warriors, with no supply lines and no logistical support, for more than half a year.

The longest Indian war in history.

"I'll bet he ain't no older'n you," commented Private Shay as he came to stand beside the Irishman.

"Lot younger than any of us would've thought."

After the captured Modocs performed the social rite of shaking hands all around with the Tenino scouts, and Sergeant McCarthy had signaled Captain Perry on the far side of the narrow canyon, Trimble gave the order to move out. Each of the four warriors was placed behind a soldier on horseback. Then each of the five squaws and children were ordered to climb behind a soldier as well. The scouts turned the party down the trail toward the Willow Creek crossing, where they met the expectant Captain Perry, Donald McKay and John Fairchild.

As the entire band of Warm Springs scouts drew closer to Colonel Davis's camp sprawled on the grounds of Applegate's ranch, they began to sing victory songs one after another, each one louder than the one sung before.

Ian O'Roarke stood with the others, soldiers and civilians, newspapermen as well, who had heard the distant singing that early Sunday afternoon, sensing those songs meant something momentous. In moments hundreds of people lined the main path winding through camp, bodies parting like a wave, cheering and crying out, waving at their prisoners and throwing their hats in the air as the procession of Perry's cavalry plodded into camp.

Ian shouldered his way out of the crowd and was at Seamus's side, trotting along beside the horse. "The Modoc War is over, lad. Welcome . . . welcome home."

Remembering for a moment the far-off life they had shared in Ireland—thinking now of a young boy carried bouncing down muddy, rocky roads on his tall uncle's shoulder—Seamus reached down, gripping his uncle's hand for but a moment. Then he lifted the young Modoc boy who had ridden down the mountain on Donegan's horse, handing the youngster to Ian.

The words came hard then. "This one needs something to eat in a bad way, Uncle."

Ian stopped, rubbing the youth's wounded shoulder as Seamus pulled his horse out of the long procession. "Let's find us all something to eat."

"And, maybe we can talk Cabaniss out of some of his brandy," Seamus added quietly, eyes smarting.

Ian smiled, his own eyes glistening. "It has been a long, long and dirty war for us all, Seamus. I don't think the surgeon will see a damned thing wrong with the two of us having a toast—for medicinal purposes."

The Warm Springs scouts made a grand show of presenting their prisoners to Colonel Davis in the sunlight of that Sunday afternoon. Davis received Jack without ceremony, then ordered that the chief immediately be taken to a regimental blacksmith and fitted with leg shackles.

"Lock him to Schonchin John," the colonel ordered. "I want this one to run no more."

As the two warriors were separated from the rest of the entire band, rejoined just moments before in the soldier camp, the Modocs' fears grew palatable. Six soldiers appeared, nudging the two leaders away. Other soldiers held the rest of the Modocs at bay. Children began to scream when squaws set to wailing, keening in grief.

"They think those two are being taken for execution," explained John Fairchild as the guard marched their prisoners by.

"Fairchild!" Jack called out, his eyes wild, filled with fright. "Where they take me? Time now to kill Jack?"

The civilian pushed aside a young guard to walk alongside the Modoc chief. "No. Not time now, Jack. They're taking you to put irons on your legs."

"Irons?"

"Heavy chains. So you will run no more."

Jack wagged his head again. "Jack no can run no more, Fairchild. Legs very tired. Jack ready to die now."

Fairchild turned from the guards, looking for an officer. When he found one, he suggested that Jack would need an interpreter: Scar-Faced Charley.

The chief and Schonchin John both protested vehemently when they arrived at the blacksmith's forge to find they were to be chained together. When Charley explained that protest was useless, both men submitted to the long, hot process of wrapping sheet iron around the ragged cuffs of the army trousers they both wore. John and Jack were in this way wedded by the army for the rest of their lives.

Bogus Charley stood on the side, watching, himself wailing to the late afternoon sky. "Now all Modocs will hang. We all die now, Jack!"

That evening, as twilight sank over Tule Lake and the victorious Teninos began their night-long celebration of dancing and feasting, Davis sent orders to Major Mason to bring the rest of the prisoners from Fairchild's ranch and meet him at the Peninsula camp. Most of the soldiers watched that entire, barbaric performance by the Warm Springs scouts into the long evening, as the Teninos acted out each incident of the war, accompanied by drums, war-cries and firing their guns in the air.

Over the next few days Davis learned that some of the Oregon militia had run across a few of the remaining Modocs in the northern part of the Langell Valley, looking for someone who would accept their surrender. General Ross was preparing to turn his prisoners over to the Jackson County sheriff for execution.

At hearing that news, Jefferson C. Davis grew livid with anger. He immediately dispatched an escort of soldiers to return all Modocs held by the Oregon militia to his camp as prisoners of war. In a tersely-worded message, the colonel informed Ross of the consequences he faced if any of the Modocs were tried in civil courts, for he believed Oregon held no jurisdiction over the prisoners.

Ross at first intended to ignore the federal government

and the U.S. Army as well, until his men began showing the captured Modocs to the widows of the slain settlers. Neither of the women were able to conclusively identify any of the murderers.

"You can now take possession of them all," Ross informed Davis indignantly. "Prisoners of war, murderers of Oregon civilians—all."

By Friday, 6 June, when all the troops and the Modocs were gathered in the Peninsula camp, the colonel assured Ross that executions would be held, for he had ordered his regimental carpenters to construct a gallows he would use to hang the Modoc leaders.

"I firmly believe the best way to bring an end to all Indian trouble across the breadth of the frontier is to summarily execute every leader of this ignominious Modoc War as quickly as possible, with the end in mind of showing by example what awaits other red men who would take up arms against us."

He was prepared to hang at least seven of the ringleaders at sunset that Friday night.

Yet in an eleventh-hour telegram from General William Tecumseh Sherman, Davis's superiors could not authorize the hangings unless the murderers could be positively identified and convicted in a court of law. In addition, Davis was told to spare the lives of the four warriors who had helped track down their chief.

"Damn!" Davis blurted out as he read the last part of the telegram. "They wish to reward murder—as long as these butchers have seen the light and hunted Jack down!"

"They actually want you to spare those fiends who killed the civilians?" asked Major Green.

"Damn them—sitting back there—making decisions for me a whole country away!" Davis fumed. "If I had any way of making a living for my family outside of the army, I would resign today!"

"I suggest you write General Sherman, sir," said Major Mason.

"Yes, I'll damn well tell them that I believe delay will destroy the moral effect that the prompt execution of these red devils would have upon other tribes, as well as dampening the inspiring effect their execution would have upon the troops."

Then he suddenly turned, as if struck with a thought, and pushed through his tent flaps. In a flurry of motion, Davis led his staff and officers fluttering behind him as he hurried to the compound where the Modocs were held. As the sun sank behind the mountains, the colonel let fly with his anger. He stepped up before the sullen Captain Jack, shaking his fist in the chief's face.

"From the first contact my people had with the Modocs, yours has been a history of murder and rapine, plunder and thievery. Even among your own Indian neighbors you are known as a domineering and tyrannical tribe. Old settlers in the country report as many as three hundred murders committed by your people . . .

"For these many crimes, no adequate punishment upon the guilty, even as a tribe or individually, has been made . . .

"A few years ago, regardless of these acts of treachery, the government gave you a reservation of land for a home, where, if you chose, you could have remained and enjoyed the annual bounties of the government unmolested . . .

"You all went upon the reservation, and part of your tribe has remained, but you and your band seemed to have preferred the warpath. You left the reservation, you spurned the kindness of the government, and even resisted the soldiers in the execution of their duty in forcing you to the reservation . . .

"Now that I have recounted your history and that of your tribe, the recent acts of yourself and your band, I will close this interview by informing you that I have this day directed that you and your confederates, members of your band, be executed . . .

"But while I was preparing a list of those I intended to

execute, a courier arrived from Washington, saying, 'Hold the prisoners till further orders.' "

Davis was on his way back to his tent when the reporter from the New York *Herald* dashed up to inform the colonel that the two widows were trying to kill some of the prisoners.

The colonel and his party found Mrs. Schira jabbing at a cowering Hooker Jim with a large, double-edged knife. Nearby, Mrs. Boddy was trying to get a pistol cocked.

Davis was himself nicked by Mrs. Schira's knife in disarming her.

Two days later Seamus found himself sitting in afternoon shade with his uncle and a handful of civilians near the newly constructed gallows. A soldier dashed into camp shouting in panic that some Modocs who had come in to surrender at Fairchild's ranch had been attacked on the road to the Peninsula camp.

"They've been murdered! Modoc prisoners coming in from Fairchild's ranch—up at Adams Point!"

John Fairchild, Pressley Dorris and Ian O'Roarke were on their feet, bolting toward their horses.

"My brother—James!" cried Fairchild, the words seizing in his throat as he galloped away from the soldier camp.

Spurring their mounts to a lather down the Pit River Road, they found the horrid, bloody scene. Already at the site they found a squad of ten soldiers who had hurried to the Fairchild wagon when they heard the repeated gunfire.

"James!"

"John!" young Fairchild called out, recognizing his brother's voice amid the crying and wailing of the Modoc women as they rubbed their hands over their dead husbands.

The brothers embraced, tears in each man's eyes as they stared into one another's face.

"How close . . . so many times how close we have come to death, James."

"They spared me," the younger man said.

As the other civilians came up, glancing over the bloody scene, John asked his brother, "Tell us what happened, James."

He drank another short swallow from Dorris's canteen, then started. "Four warriors came in yesterday. With their wives and children. About a dozen altogether. Gave themselves up to Millie and me. We started out for here yesterday afternoon."

"Who knew you were coming over?" Seamus asked.

James shook his head. "It was no secret, I suppose. But, far as I knew—no one had any idea I was heading here."

"Go on," John asked of his brother.

"As we crossed the Lost River Ford, north of here, we were met by some Oregon volunteers—under a fella named Hyzer."

"They cause you trouble?"

"No. Not really. Just looking the bunch over in the wagon real hard. I know a couple of those men on sight. Raised like we was here in Klamath country."

"They went on down the road?" Dorris asked.

Fairchild nodded. "West. And I kept on east another seven miles or so—right here—when two strangers come up from the trees with their guns out."

"You ever seen 'em before?" O'Roarke said, bristling.

"Never."

"Were they wearing uniforms of any kind?"

"No."

"Had to be them volunteers," Dorris hissed. "Tell us the rest."

James Fairchild nodded. "They ordered me down from the wagon, waving their guns at me. I thought they were joking at first, but they wasn't. While one of 'em kept me covered, the other one cut the mules free and drove them off. That's when I knew the fat was in the fire. I started to tell them two just to go and nothing would come of it, when they up and turned their guns into the wagon and started shooting it up."

"They killed the four warriors and wounded one of the squaws before they lit out," O'Roarke said, turning at the sound of hoofbeats.

Lieutenant John Kyle arrived on the scene with a squad of another fifteen troopers.

"Mr. Fairchild," Kyle said as he slid from his horse, quickly surveying the scene. He stepped back after looking at the bodies. "You have any clues who did this?"

John Fairchild shook his head. "My brother was driving the wagon. He didn't know either one of 'em."

"You here to catch the murderers, Lieutenant?" asked Pressley Dorris.

"No, sir. General Davis sent us along to bury the dead and escort the rest into camp."

"You'll bury 'em here?"

Kyle looked over his shoulder and nodded. "Alongside the road there, I suppose." He turned away and began giving orders to his squad to busy themselves with shovels.

"That's four more won't get cremated," John Fairchild muttered.

"Meaning their Modoc souls can't be freed if they aren't," explained Ian O'Roarke.

On 11 June, Colonel Davis dispatched Captain Jackson to take Troops B and K of the First Cavalry back to Fort Klamath, where they were instructed to build a stockade and adequate shelter for the Modoc prisoners: forty-four men, forty-nine women and sixty-two children.

Three days later, on the fourteenth, Davis marched his prisoners north, escorted by Mason's Twelfth and Twenty-first Infantry. That first night out, a pair of prisoners shackled together thought they saw their chance to escape. Black Jim and Curly Headed Doctor did not get far into the darkness before the chain between them snagged on a clump of sagebrush and brought them both crashing down.

Soldiers dragged their cursing prisoners back to the night's camp.

The next night another prisoner determined to escape or die trying. He had sworn he would not hang at the end of the white man's rope.

Curly Headed Jack, one of the trio who had boasted of shooting Lieutenant Sherwood east of the Stronghold just moments before the murders at the peace tent began, had somehow gotten his hands on a pistol in the past few days and kept it hidden under his clothes.

When he arose to go relieve himself in the dark, a guard followed behind. Curly Headed Jack tried to run, and when he saw his flight was hopeless, brought the pistol up and shot himself in the head.

He was buried in another unmarked grave beside that long road to Fort Klamath.

By the end of the third week of the month, Captain Jack's people were prisoners in Captain Jackson's stockade. At sunset on 20 June the soldiers divided the band: prisoners destined for trial kept apart from those who were nothing more than luckless participants in Jack's bloody war.

Epilogue

Mid-June 1873

"*I* still can't talk you into staying here with us?" Ian asked one last time as he came around behind his nephew's packhorse.

Donegan snagged O'Roarke by the scruff of the neck and brought his uncle close, into a fierce embrace, then tore himself away after but a moment, afraid of weakening.

He went back to lashing the gum poncho that enclosed his blankets behind his saddle.

"At least give it more time before you decide."

Seamus turned to look into the man's moist eyes as they caught the first light of predawn just now creeping over the hills into the yard outside the house. "I've had plenty of time to think, Uncle. It's time I go back."

"Still set on home?"

"Aye, Ian," he sighed. "It sounds so far . . . far away right now—doesn't it?"

"Why won't you even head southwest to San Francisco, catch a packet from there, around the horn and back to New York or Boston?"

He wagged his head, the big smile cutting a wide swath in the chill air. "I must do this my way, Ian. Back over the mountains."

"What's out there for you, Seamus? Out there for any half-civilized white man anymore?"

Seamus thought on it a moment before answering. "To see it one last time before going home to Eire. To be sure I have gleaned all that I can carry of it home in my heart before I go. That's why."

Ian dragged a battered pipe from his pocket and with a finger retamped the old tobacco in the bowl. "That godforsaken wilderness claimed one of your uncles. And it nearly claimed another—had I not come here when I did."

"But look at you," Seamus said, his big arm sweeping in a wide arc, "this very country nearly swallowed you as much as the plains swallowed Liam. That ground is no more a hell than this has been for some."

O'Roarke dragged the lucifer along the sole of his boot, sucking the flame into the bowl and its charge of dark leaf. When he had inspected the red cherry and tossed the lucifer aside, he said, "When it comes down to it, Seamus —I suppose I have chosen my place to stand . . . as much as Liam chose his on that nameless river you've not talked about much."

"In the end," Donegan replied, slapping the big mare on the rump as he finished his preparations for the trail, "that's all any of us can ask of ourselves, isn't it? That we find our own place."

"So—you've decided this isn't yours."

"A fine place it is, Ian. A land so steeped in moisture that the roots don't have to grow so deep here as they do on the far plains. A rich land where a man can grow his crops and raise his stock without worry of having enough water, or worrying about the next Sioux or Cheyenne war-party to come riding over the hill."

Ian looked up at his nephew's face, studying it closely. "That's it—at least part of it, ain't it? You like not knowing—perhaps the uncertainty of that life on those far plains and in those mountains still. Aye?"

Seamus pursed his lips in concentration. "Perhaps

that's part of it. All I know is that this is a good place to
raise children as well as those crops and cattle you tend to
so well, Uncle. So here is where Ian O'Roarke should
stay," he said, looking over the older man's shoulder as
Dimity dragged the front door back into shadow and
stepped into the light. "To stay here . . . with a good
woman who will stand beside him. With that—no man is
ever in the wrong place."

Seamus crossed the muddy yard to meet her halfway.
She put out both her hands for him. He held them but a
moment then pushed them aside, sweeping her up into his
big arms.

"He so wants you to stay, Seamus," Dimity whispered
against his chest, so that only Donegan could hear.

He squeezed her tight, one last time. "There will be a
time when I can return," he whispered against the fragrant top of her head. "Keep telling him that. Remind
him of that for me whenever he grows too wistful—and
yearns for my return."

The children poured into the muddy yard to stand behind their mother as Seamus pulled back to hold the
woman at arm's length. She reached up and with finger-
tips swiped some tears from the tall man's ruddy cheek.

"As long as Ian had talked and talked about his
nephew, I always wondered what you would be like—you
and me so close in age." Then Dimity smiled, bravely,
swiping Donegan's other cheek. "And now it fills my
heart with warmth to know you are so much like Ian. Not
just reminding him of your mother—but he loves you so
just for being what you are. And finding you so much like
him."

"That must hurt most of all then," Seamus said quietly
as he let her go and took a step back, "to know that even
though I am so much like Ian . . . I can still tear myself
away from places and people and move on, like Liam."

"But like Ian—I am certain it hurts you more than you
would ever let us know."

Seamus sensed the salty sting blurring his eyes once

more and turned to the children who had clustered at the doorjamb. With both arms he waved them into his embrace. All five at once: tall Patience and young Seamus, his namesake, little Liam and Charity and, last to scurry up atop his short legs, young Thomas.

Each grabbing and clutching for a piece of this giant of a cousin who had ridden into their lives more than half a year ago, and now was heartbeats away from riding back out again.

He touched each cheek, kissed each forehead, gave the three boys a tousle of their hair and both the girls a gentlemanly bow as he called out their names one last time, as if to let his own heart vow to return to this home and warmth when needed most.

Then all six of them met again in that embrace no man is ever ashamed to share with loved ones . . . before Seamus tore himself away and strode through the softening mud to his uncle's side.

"You'll send us word—something—each place you stop on your way?"

Seamus nodded, swallowing down the hot ball that threatened to choke him still. "I plan on riding to St. Louis, from there catching a boat down the Mississippi to New Orleans. Surely there I can find something heading home—perhaps some captain who could use my muscle in payment for my steerage."

"Aye," Ian said, his voice growing low and raspy as he swallowed down his own pain. "Amerikay will not easily claim Mother Donegan's firstborn son, will she?"

"Home," he said wistfully. "Where that woman has too long waited for me to return. If that homecoming cannot be with her brothers, then best it be that I return before she breathes her last prayer."

"Tell her of my love, Seamus. And how I love this family of mine—and this new land . . . in so many ways like Eire."

"Yes, the land. You really do feel that in your heart—don't you?"

Ian watched his nephew climb into the saddle. Then reached up and grabbed Donegan's hand as it adjusted the rein. "My prayers go with you, nephew. Knowing now how for the rest of your life you will have that struggle waging within your heart. At last I know you carry within you the best and the worst of your uncles. And for the rest of your days, you will suffer that struggle between what Liam loved most, and what Ian held most dear."

Seamus bent far over, with one arm dragging his uncle to his toes in one last embrace. Then he suddenly jabbed the heels of his muddy, new army boots into the mare's flanks, demanding she take him from this place. And quickly.

It was not until he was far down the rutted lane, when he thought he would not be discovered, that Seamus turned to look at what he was leaving behind. Wondering if such happiness of hearth and home and family would ever be his to have . . . fearing that it would not.

The O'Roarkes still stood, long after he had passed from sight through the trees—the seven of them. The children huddled close, arms entwined with their parents: two people so fiercely in love that nothing—not this brutal land, not enemies pale-skinned nor red, and certainly not time and distance—could keep apart.

Seamus prayed he would one day find a home for his heart.

Author's Afterword

This time around, I'd like to do things differently and give you something to read *after* you're done with *Devil's Backbone.*

Students of the era of the Indian Wars have largely neglected the long and bloody conflict in the Lava Beds of northern California. Fewer would even be able to locate on a map where the many battles and ambushes took place. But there are yet a few reminders here in the Lava Beds that more than 127 years ago a great and exhausting struggle took place not far from where I sit.

One can gaze across the remnant of what was once the pristine Tule Lake, and find along what was once its southern shoreline the crude cairn, that tower of rocks the soldiers of 1873 themselves erected to commemorate the murder of their revered leader. Atop the rocks stands a wooden cross, dutifully inscribed by a soldier these words on the cross-arm:

> Major General E.R.S. Canby,
> U.S.A., was killed here by Modoc Indians
> April 11, 1873

You can still walk below the bluff the soldiers first descended at dawn on 17 January 1873, to attack the Modocs in their Stronghold, at the bottom of which Colonel Alvan C. Gillem would later erect his great encampment, and to this day find the places where the real actors in this great drama stood and breathed. At the base of that same bluff is Toby's Cave, where interpreters Winema and Frank Riddle lived during their tenure with Meacham's peace commission and where (incidentally) many of the Modocs visiting from the Stronghold would stay the night.

About fifty feet above the flat ground at the base of the bluff, you can still recognize Signal Rock, used to communicate with the eastern camps, either by semaphore flags or by heliograph on sunnier days. It was from this rock that the soldiers witnessed the murders of Canby and Reverend Thomas.

Now that you have finished the story, keep in mind that Captain Jack fought the U.S. Army, and eventually surrendered to soldiers of that frontier army only three short years to the month before troops under the command of General George Armstrong Custer were massacred in faraway Montana Territory.

There were factors that made the struggles on the plains and the continuing conflicts in Apache country different from this final eruption of war on the Pacific Coast. But for every difference—there were as many, and greater, similarities. It cannot be emphasized enough that the Indian of America, no matter his geographic location, was fighting against extermination. If not extermination of his species, then most certainly extermination of his culture, his way of life, his spirit.

And for a brief, glorious moment experienced by these Modoc red men some three years before another brief and glorious moment for the plains Indian, a few ragtag, ill-equipped Modocs fought off the pride of the U.S. Army. Captain Jack's warriors totally befuddled the soldiers ordered into battle against them. In the end, Jack's young lieutenants also confounded proven, able army officers who had served and fought with distinction in the Army of the Potomac or the Army of the Shenandoah or in Sherman's army that left Georgia in ruins.

Jack was grinding the army down—if not by bullets and blood, then most surely grinding down his enemy through despair and confusion.

It is clear now, if not then, that the white man, both soldier on the scene and the civilians back at the War Department in Washington, had completely underestimated their enemy in the Modocs. Not only that, but prior to the outbreak of hostilities on 29 November 1872, the Indian Bureau had totally underestimated Captain Jack's resolve not to be moved from his traditional homeland.

Yet in the end the Modocs brought about their own destruction with the mindless murders of General Edward R.S. Canby and Reverend Eleazar Thomas. Deaths that stunned the nation and enraged the army to finish the task at hand.

This was the only war in which a general of the U.S. Army was killed by Indians.

And it was most certainly a perfect study of the cultural conflicts already raging in the Apache southwest and on the great plains, for in this study of the Indian Wars, one is continually struck with the fact that both sides failed to grasp an essential ingredient to the conflict:

. . . While the Indian could not understand just how great a value the white man placed on the material ownership of the land, the white man in kind failed to understand to what extremes the Indian would go to maintain the universal freedom of the land.

In addition, the differences between the two opposing cultures were already racing toward inevitable conflict in 1872 when Jack executed a Klamath shaman who had failed to cure a Modoc girl after accepting payment for his services prior to conducting his mystical rites. Under

Indian law, Jack was by all rights allowed to kill the medicine man.

Yet, Jack and the other prisoners months later would find the intricate machinations of military and American jurisprudence more baffling still than the straightforward meting out of Indian justice.

What occurred through more than six long months of fighting, negotiating, sniping, ambushes and full-scale battles was in fact the most costly Indian war in U.S. history. When a few angry warriors broke away from their Lost River camp and swept around the shore of Tule Lake, killing white settlers, they set in motion a military machine that would eventually require more than a thousand soldiers, scouts and civilian teamsters to surround, subdue, chase, and do battle with no more than seventy poorly-armed red warriors.

Beyond the human terms, the long, protracted months meant that the total cost of the war in dollars multiplied every day. An army in the field requires fodder. Civilians were hired to haul in those supplies—which opened the door to what became the general practice throughout the era of the Indian Wars: civilian profiteering.

Read here how author Keith Murray lists the prices charged the army during its stay near the Lava Beds:

soap	50 cents a cake
iodine	50 cents per ounce
rubbing alcohol	$1.25 per quart
calomel	$4.00 per pound
horseshoeing	$1.25 per shoe.

In a time when, as Murray shows, a man might be extremely happy to earn two dollars per day, most teamsters working out of Yreka, California, and Linkville, Oregon, were charging the army a minimum of twenty dollars per day for their services—if they were hauling supplies or not.

And that's where the grand total for Captain Jack's

war swelled every day—with this matter of transportation from the rail depot at Redding, California, to the various camps in the Lava Beds. One teamster alone received $118,132.86 for hauling men and matériel to the scene of the fighting!

The final tally of direct costs to the federal government exceeded $420,000. They paid Oregon and California more than $76,000 for the use of their militias. Other costs such as pensions and medical expenses billed to the government by veterans of the conflict are, in Murray's opinion, sure to total more than an additional $100,000.

A half-million dollars—and, mind you, nineteenth century dollars at that!

In the end, whether the Modoc warriors were killed with army bullets or at the end of an army rope, for each of those seventeen warriors, the government sacrificed the lives of a dozen soldiers, volunteer militia or civilian employees of the army. Eight officers, thirty-nine enlisted men, sixteen citizens and two Tenino scouts, in addition to another sixty-seven wounded. Almost as many white men killed by Captain Jack's people as we had servicemen killed twenty-five years later in the whole of the Spanish-American War.

To allow you firm footing once more, let me bring you up to date on what transpired in this story once the Modocs arrived at Fort Klamath, Oregon—when the wheels of military justice began to grind.

It must surely have caused Captain Jack great pain those last few weeks of his life to feel each waking minute the weight of those iron shackles binding him to Schonchin John, while outside the guardhouse on the parade stood four separate tents, one each for the four men who had murdered innocent white settlers, then surrendered to the army and volunteered to hunt down their former chief.

On 9 June 1873, the U. S. Attorney General made a determination that all the actions of the Modocs following the skirmish in their village on 29 November 1872, did most certainly "constitute war in a technical sense that crimes afterwards committed against the laws of war are triable and punishable by military courts preferably Military Commissions."

This put to rest all but one last-minute attempt by Oregon officials to put the Tule Lake murderers on trial in their own state courts. General Schofield ordered Colonel Davis to immediately form a military commission to try six prisoners. In addition, Schofield left it up to Davis as to whether or not to punish those Modoc "bloodhounds" who had helped hunt down and capture the notorious Captain Jack.

In the next few days the War Department itself would direct its military commission to try only those warriors who had killed General Canby, Reverend Thomas or Lieutenant Sherwood. The rest were to be treated as prisoners of war.

And ultimately, only those who had taken part in the killings at the peace tent would face that military tribunal seated at Fort Klamath.

Six only: Captain Jack, Schonchin John, Black Jim, Boston Charley, Barncho and Sloluck.

On a day marked elsewhere for a celebration of independence, the trial of the Modocs opened on the Fourth of July, 1873. The large assembly hall at Fort Klamath had been prepared with tables for the military commission, chairs for the prisoners and witnesses—including the four "bloodhounds" still free to roam the fort grounds at will—and the American flag. No spectators were allowed during the few days of testimony.

To a reading of the charges, and a request for a plea, all prisoners answered: "Not guilty."

On the second day of the trial, while William Faithful sat in the witness chair, a hush fell over the courtroom as peace commissioner Alfred B. Meacham quietly entered by a side door. This was the first time since the 11 April murders that the prisoners and the "bloodhounds" had seen Meacham, who they had all along believed to be every bit as dead as Canby and Thomas.

One can imagine the looks on those dark faces as the old man moved among them, their eyes inspecting the wounds where Boston Charley had attempted to remove his ear and scalp.

It is an interesting sidelight to history to note that Meacham later made a modest living on the lecture circuit, talking of the great Modoc War and the murder at the peace tent, showing his scars and exhibiting his lecture assistant, and former interpreter, Winema Riddle. During that same time period, Meacham made Winema the heroine of his story of the Modoc War, *Wi-Ne-Ma.* The Riddles' son, Jefferson Davis Riddle, himself wrote a story of the conflict, *The Indian History of the Modoc War.*

But in that hot July of 1873, Meacham was himself called forward as a witness. Following his firsthand testimony that sealed the fate of the murderers, he nonetheless asked the stunned military commission if the prisoners had been assigned counsel. When he was informed they had not, Meacham fumed, angry that counsel had not been appointed for them. No one at the fort would accept the post of defending the prisoners.

With great credit to the character of the man, a still-weakened Meacham volunteered, but never served, as defense counsel—on the advice of his physicians, who believed so great an emotional strain would most certainly kill their aging patient.

By the fourth day the prosecution had completed its testimony. With no defense counsel to offer rebuttal or its own witnesses, the prisoners were then granted only the formality of an opportunity to speak for themselves. While it is a common belief that when great chiefs rise to give their death statements, great oratory pours forth, such was not the case with Captain Jack. Instead, his speech was more an enraged indictment than silver-tongued epitaph.

"You palefaces did not conquer me . . . my own braves conquered me . . . You say I killed Canby. Yes, I did kill him, but I see no crime in my heart. My heart is not bad. The ones most guilty are the ones now free. If the white man's law were not crooked like a snake, they would be here in chains along with these others . . .

I am ashamed to die with a rope around my neck. I wanted to die on the battlefield with a gun in my hand. But I am not afraid. I only think of my people and hope you don't treat them bad on account of what wrongs I did . . .

But do we Indians stand a chance to be treated fair by white people? I say no! . . . [White man] can shoot Indian any time he wants . . . Can you tell me where one white man has been punished for killing a Modoc? . . .

"Now here I am . . . killed one man, after I had been fooled by him many times and forced to do the act by my own warriors. The law says, hang him. He is nothing but an Indian, anyhow . . . Let me hang, then! I am not afraid to die. I will show you how a Modoc can die. I am done."*

Following the stunned silence that marked Jack's suddenly resuming his seat on the floor, the other five prisoners made their brief statements, each one similar in their condemnation that the "bloodhounds" who had murdered the innocent white settlers were free while as warriors they would be hanged.

It should come as no surprise to you that in that short matter of days, after taking testimony from all concerned, all six Modocs were found guilty of two charges:

---

* Compiled from the following: Doris Palmer Payne, *Captain Jack, Modoc Renegade;* Dee Brown, *Bury My Heart at Wounded Knee;* and, U. S. 43rd Congress, 1st Session, Executive Document 122

Charge 1: murder, in violation of the articles of war (General Canby and Reverend Thomas);

Charge 2: assault, with intent to kill, in violation of the articles of war (A. B. Meacham and L. S. Dyar).

The sentence handed down: "To be hanged by the neck until they be dead."

Throughout the rest of that July and into August, the six were held in the steamy guardhouse, allowed only infrequent visits with their families, while outside at the corner of the parade post carpenter Hiram Fields put his saw and hammer to work, building a scaffold thirty feet long, large enough to accommodate six men at once. Every log cut, every nail pounded, every rope knotted from the huge cross-beam, was witnessed in detail from the windows of that guardhouse. But that was not the only torture.

Not far from the scaffold soldiers were seen pounding stakes into the ground and looping string around the six rectangles. As sweating soldiers dug those six holes deeper and deeper, no white man had to tell the Modocs that one day soon their lifeless bodies would lie at the bottom of those dark graves.

As you have read in the Prologue, while there were six graves dug outside the prisoners' guardhouse window and six ropes hung ready from the gallows' cross-beam, only four coffins were in that wagon carrying the six to the scaffold. President Grant himself had determined at the end to commute the death sentences for Barncho and Sloluck, who, many back east were convinced, were mentally retarded. (Sloluck had in fact slept on the floor throughout most of the trial, unable to understand not only the white man's English, but the import of the entire process.) Grant's orders specified that the two not be informed until moments before the execution of the other four.

An unnecessary cruelty for men who would spend the

rest of their days imprisoned on the little island called Alcatraz.

When the execution was finally scheduled for ten A.M. on 3 October 1873, a lone newspaperman was allowed to witness the last visit the condemned would have with their families. That night before the hanging, the prisoners were "seated on the floor, each with space enough that his family might gather around him where they engaged in their death chant. The condemned men sat stolidly without uttering a word."

As the six were led from the guardhouse on the following, fateful morning to the strains of the army band's rendition of the "Dead March," Captain Jack found nearly the whole of the Klamath tribe come to witness the execution. In addition, many of old Chief Schonchin's Modocs from the Yainax Reservation had journeyed to see this hanging of the renegades.

Jack mounted the scaffold last, and atop the platform saw that the army had given preferential treatment to the four "bloodhounds." They had front-row seats to watch the execution.

Five minutes after the nooses were fitted tight and the black hoods draped over the prisoners' heads, a captain dropped his handkerchief, signaling a young lieutenant to use his axe to cut the rope holding the heavy drop.

The platform fell away, and with it the four prisoners.

A reporter recorded that a quiet gasp of horror went through the crowd. Eerie keening burst from the gaps between the pine logs of the stockade where the women and children were held. "The bodies swing round and round, Jack and Jim apparently dying easily, but Boston and Schonchin suffering terrible convulsions."

Eight minutes later the surgeon pronounced all four dead.

Later that afternoon another reporter found himself passing by a wall tent erected nearby on the Fort Klamath parade, its flaps open enough to show a long table in its center, "similar to those used in the dissecting-room of a medical college." An Indian gum-rubber sheet was spread over the table, while in a corner the reporter saw a barrel of water, nearby a small table on which were laid surgical instruments.

The reporter later informed San Francisco *Chronicle* readers that the heads of all four executed prisoners were cut off and shipped east to the Surgeon General's Army Medical Museum in Washington for display.

A ghoulish end to a dirty little war.

Only days later the rest of the Modocs were loaded aboard wagons and transported under Captain Hasbrouck's escort to Yreka, from there to the railhead at Redding, California. Barncho and Sloluck were carried south to Alcatraz.

Two weeks after the executions, the remnants of Jack's band were themselves herded onto a Central Pacific train bound for Fort McPherson, Nebraska. By the order of Lieutenant Colonel Frank Wheaton, no one was to know of the final destination of these prisoners until the Modocs had reached their first stop in Wyoming.

Twelve days later Captain Hasbrouck turned over his 153 prisoners to Colonel John J. Reynolds (who we will meet in future episodes of the war on the plains). Reynolds gave Hasbrouck a receipt for his prisoners, then escorted the Modocs south into Indian Territory, where they were given a grant of land only two and a half miles square at Seneca Springs, near the Quapaw Agency, just south of Baxter Springs, Kansas.

With scrap lumber given them by the government and the help of three local white squaw-men, in one day the Modocs erected a "barracks" where they would live only two hundred yards from the agent's watchful eye and under the leadership of their new chief, Bogus Charley.

In 1879, Steamboat Frank was ordained as a pastor for the Modoc church on the reservation.

Yet in the end, for all their attempts to walk down the white man's road, it was typhus, tuberculosis, despair and starvation that would eventually accomplish what the U.S. Army could not in six bloody months of war.

By 1909 the fifty-one surviving Modocs were allowed to return to the Klamath's reservation in Oregon, where they would once again be unwelcome intruders on another tribe's land. No more would they have anything but dreams of what they once possessed—a land rich and free and belonging only to the Modoc people.

I find it important to note here before closing, two important features of the story I chose not to deal with in the narrative of this novel.

First of all, I want to emphasize the character of the man, Alvan C. Gillem, who for many weeks was the commander of the Modoc War and would eventually be sent home in disgrace by Colonel Davis. Yet, as I have noted in our story, Gillem recommended many of his enlisted men for special commendation for heroism in the face of enemy fire.

I want the reader to fully understand just how unheard of was such an act in that era of the Indian Wars—an era when documentation shows us that no other officers recommended their enlisted men, the front-line troops, for meritorious conduct. A star for Gillem's crown perhaps.

And secondly, the reader might wonder just who were the two killers of those four Modocs in James Fairchild's wagon?

While the Oregon volunteers would to their deaths continue to deny they had anything to do with the killings, peace commissioner Meacham would likewise continue to assert that nothing was ever done to find the killers.

Although Colonel Jefferson C. Davis refused to launch an investigation of his own into the matter, one can find among the official military documents of the era evidence that the U.S. Army never doubted the fact that the guilty parties belonged to Ross's militia: ". . . the Indian captives . . . were fired into by Volunteers."

* * *

Should you find that you now want to know more about
this little-known but very costly and dramatic chapter of
the Indian Wars, you can refer to the few reliable books
available on the subject. And, I do want to emphasize
how little is available on Captain Jack's war of the Lava
Beds. But what you will find for the effort is richly re-
warding.

For a contemporary account, written from interviews
of participants and witnesses, you can always trust Cyrus
Townsend Brady's *Northwestern Fights and Fighters*. In
this case, the spectacularly readable reminiscences of
Captain Trimble.

An overview of the entire war and its place in the larger
conflict of "winning the west" will be found in Robert M.
Utley's brilliant work, *Frontier Regulars*.

Time and again I was drawn from the purely military
and dryly historic accounts of the entire conflict to read
again the pages of Doris Palmer Payne's stunning book,
Captain Jack, Modoc Renegade. She, more than any other
account, has been able to breathe life into the central
character of the war: his early years, his coming of age,
and his tragic few years of manhood attempting to lead
his people.

What is in my opinion the classic work on the subject
should remain so for all time. *The Modocs and Their War*
by Keith A. Murray, who was the first writer to approach
the entire history of this little-known conflict between
white and Modoc from its earliest days, which dated back
to the time of explorer John Charles Fremont.

Yet Murray himself, in a foreword written for Erwin N.
Thompson's *Modoc War—Its Military History & Topogra-
phy*, candidly stated that he wished he had had Thompson's book available when he was writing his own many
years before. Not only does Thompson draw heavily on
the formal military record for every shred of the engross-
ing narrative, but he has combed the press of the day as
well, to glean a feel of what the newspapermen assigned to

the war had to report to their readers, both in California and back east. Thompson's book is worth a trip to the library if only to study the stunning and engagingly understandable maps on the history of the whole conflict. With these maps, a student thirsting for knowledge of Jack's tragic fight with the army would not have to himself visit this beautifully-austere scar of landscape. One can take a most satisfying tour of the entire area by thumbing through those masterfully executed maps.

But in the end I wish to leave the reader with one of the author's primary impressions of this little piece of our history, this little piece of what we are as a people.

This is a story all too representative of other battles during the Indian Wars, a story of an Indian chief representative as well of other chiefs gone before, and after. But while there might be others who died tragically and at most dramatic times— (Crazy Horse or Sitting Bull, among others)—there is no other chief *more* symbolic of his own people's struggle to find a way to deal with the coming of the white man.

In the beginning the small but hearty band of Modocs attempted to keep the white man away from their Lost River country. Then, over time, these people came to see the white man was there to stay. The Modocs attempted some adaptation, some accommodation with the new intruders. In fact, it is plain to see that the young Kientpoos himself attempted to amalgamate both cultures within his own band. That was not an easy task, and (some might argue) a task ultimately doomed to failure.

In the end, when Captain Jack decided that he was going to live outside the bounds of white society and wanted that culture to leave his people alone—his personal death warrant was sealed.

From that point on, in the press of the day, this tragic figure was known as "the red Judas."

Let me close by saying that Jack's one-time hope to amalgamate both cultures is what should live on in our history, not only a recitation of the bullets fired and the blood shed in the Lava Beds.

This sharing of the best we all have to offer one another's spirits is to be remembered and cherished. I would argue that this sharing was, and still is, possible—and most assuredly something that would enrich both societies.

The wind blows here still, across this dark and rumpled ground rarely visited. Fire came here first to cleanse, millions of years ago. Now the wind blows with a ghostly whisper across these ravines and ridges and bluffs and caves. And you can hear the whispers on that wind.

It's always here, this wind that comes at last to cleanse the terror, the horror, the sheer tragedy of man's passing from this place. The wind always blows.

—Terry C. Johnston
Lava Beds National Monument
June 1, 1990

Prologue

July 1873

With a nerve-rattling screech of iron upon iron, the great hissing weight of the eastbound freight was eased into the station at Hays City, Kansas beside the Smoky Hill River.

It was almost as if the great black monster sighed as it settled itself there this early evening beside the battered platform that had seen countless thousands of boots and moccasin soles over all those years it had stood here beside the Kansas-Pacific. To most who found themselves meeting this train at twilight, this appeared to be just another eastbound chain of freight cars and passenger wagons shuddering to a stop behind the wheezing engine as it hissed its first of many spouts of steam among the legs of those gathered in the fading summer sunlight on that scuffed platform of cottonwood planks.

Seamus Donegan rose slowly from his horsehair, leather-covered seat beside the window on the far side of the train, away from the station platform. He was in no real hurry, he figured; time enough to let the other passengers scurry down the aisle in their rush, down the iron steps and into another life than the smoky, dusty, confined life they had all shared for what time they gave themselves over to this black snorting monster that had pulled the Irishman here all the way from Redding, California and the land his uncle Ian O'Roarke had come to call his own.

Seamus was moving east, heading back to the only place he could ever admit to feeling was home. Ireland.

With a sense of some completeness now fully a part of him, the tall Irishman set the battered brown slouch hat atop his shoulder-length curls, then tugged the heavy canvas mackinaw onto his arms. The sun had just settled at the edge of the far prairie, giving a pink tint to the underbellies of the summer flecks of clouds overhead. The air would be growing cool soon enough.

Seamus had been a long time returning to these plains, gone to the edge of the western world, tracking down uncle Ian and fighting Modocs in the devil's playground called the Lava Beds. And he had spent more nights than he cared to now remember wrapped in his bedroll at the edge of this endless prairie wilderness.

The plaintive howls of wolf and coyote, the whisper of wind and the hammering hoofbeats of summer thunderstorm on his gum poncho, the minute cry of insects at work in the dark, a sound almost lost against the aching immensity of the whirring of the faraway stars a man could almost make out coming from that great black velvet canopy overhead. A great, arching skyscape just out of reach above the bed he made in that lonely land of the high plains that only a true, wandering soul could learn to love.

"This land will bake your brains in the summer . . . freeze your balls in the winter. Nothing like the high plains, Seamus."

He snagged the worn leather of his holster belt, slung it over his shoulder as he recalled those words of Abner Grover, the prairie scout who had for a time shared a rifle pit on a stinking island in the middle of a nameless river bottom somewhere up high on the Colorado plains.

Pulling up the scarred remains of his trail-weary saddlebags, he hefted the saddle that had cradled his ass for so many miles, and half that many years. With his free hand, Seamus retrieved that last item of his belongings wedged into the narrow seat: the brass-mounted, blue-barrelled .44-caliber Henry repeater. Much as if the rifle were coming home, he swept his huge paw around the action, his hand cupped in a made-to-order groove ready to receive the weapon.

He was alone in the car. The noise was all outside now: the calls of friends and family to those who had stepped off the wheezing monster. Stevedores hustled, shouldered back the huge doors and disappeared into baggage cars to retrieve luggage and trunks and freight bound for off-loading at this stop on the central plains. A clanging of bells, a rush of pouring water from the rail-side tank and another loud exhaust of steam greeted the Irishman's ears as he turned his bulk sideways and eased down the aisle for the narrow door at the end of the passenger car.

Three steps and his tall, mule-eared boots clattered to a halt on the platform. He glanced up, then down, and found a uniformed station man hurrying past with papers rolled beneath his arm. Seamus held out the Henry rifle like a man who required a toll to be paid before passing.

"Where might I get my animals?"

"What sort of animals, Mister?" he asked, irritated.

"Horses."

"You bring with you in from Denver City?"

"Aye. Farther still. California."

The harried man pointed back down the track. "Likely they were loaded in the last few cars. There ain't another platform, but they run a ramp up to the cars and put 'em down in the corrals."

Seamus looked downtrack, then turned around to utter his thanks but found the small man hurrying on to other duties at the far end of the passenger platform.

In the fading light of this early summer's eve, every form took on a unique texture here in the clear air of the central plains. Ever since the iron rails had catapulted him over the California mountains and on to the plains, his nose had reveled in that special quality to the air that bespoke this high land yearning against and for the endless sky. Not that the land hugging the boundary of California and Oregon wasn't pretty. It just wasn't country for him.

But, saints almighty, if that hadn't been land that reminded every fiber within him of his native soil so far from his bootsoles now. The air of that Oregon-California borderland smelled of the same high, chilling dampness of County Kilkenny. That same rugged blending of rock and turf and those brittle plants that clung tenaciously resisting a brutal environment. And in passing up the western slope of those California mountains, looking down one last time into the land his uncle had adopted, Seamus finally and fully understood why Ian O'Roarke had chosen that rainy land as the spot where he would send down his roots and raise up a family with his sweet Dimity.

That far land had reminded Ian of all that he had once had back in Ireland, before so many started slowly dying off from hunger and disease, or from nothing more complicated than simple despair.

Seamus started for the far end of the platform, hoping the green land of his birth had come on better times in all the years he had been gone from Town Callan. Were that those better times would not be too much to hope. . . .

He was nearing the edge of the platform, having just found the steps that would take him down into the dust and the dung that lay stretched clear to the corrals hugging the tracks run endlessly back across the flats of western Kansas and into Colorado Territory—where twice already he had fought the Cheyenne: once beside Sharp Grover at Beecher Island, and a year later helping Major Eugene Asa Carr's Fifth Cavalry scatter the mighty Dog Soldiers plundering the high plains under chief Tall Bull.*

So deep in thought was he of those places and the

---

* THE PLAINSMEN Series, Vol. 4, *Black Sun*

weeping scars they had left upon his soul that the Irishman really did not hear the voice call out his name the first time. It came more like an unsettling part of the damning recollections he carried with him in his waking hours. Yet, too, ringing with every bit as much stark terror and physical pain as the dreams he suffered when he closed his eyes each night. Alone.

"Seamus? Is that you?"

But this was a real voice, not one of those who haunted the unplumbed depths of his solitude. Donegan turned.

A figure moved toward him from the shadows cast beneath the rail station awning. Then the dark shadow halted.

"Lord, Seamus—it *is* you!"

He strained his eyes, inching the finger into the guard, encircling the trigger of his Henry, a cold prickling at the back of his neck as the stranger swept out of the shadows, wearing the flaring drape of a long coat that nearly reached the platform etched with the inky clomp of the thin man's bootheels.

But the stranger stopped as Seamus brought up the Henry.

"Seamus—it's me—don't mean you no harm."

The thin man raised his arms out in a way that reminded the Irishman of the crucifix hung over the head of his bed, where he slept as a boy in Town Callan, listening to the lonely sobbing of his mother on the far side of the thin wall, crying herself to sleep each night for want of the return of her husband—now dead and buried beneath the loamy soil of Eire so stingy and refusing to give back life to its own.

"It's Jack. Jack Stillwell, Seamus."

"Jack . . . young Stillwell, is it?"

The stranger stepped fully into the last pink light of the sun as it eased off into the far side of the prairie behind the Rocky Mountains, days away in Colorado Territory.

"Damn—but I don't believe it's you, young Jack!" He

dropped pistol belt and saddle and bags in a mad rush at the tall, thin man, sweeping Stillwell against him in a crushing embrace.

They pounded one another on the back until weary in a close-cropped dance of glee that hammered the cotton-wood platform until Seamus stepped back, moistness at his eyes and a lump come again to his throat.

"Good to see you, young Jack."

"It's been five years, Seamus," Stillwell said, gone serious. "None of us so young now as we was then. On that bloody island where Lieutenant Beecher fell."

"Aye," he answered softly, the sting come again to his eyes. "But were it not for the grit of a likely lad by the name of Stillwell who went to fetch us relief from Fort Wallace, likely that island would have proved a grave for Major Forsyth and the rest of us what rode after Roman Nose."

"Then you know . . . it was Roman Nose you killed in that first charge?"

"If it weren't me—likely it was Ian."

"Everyone here on the plains talks of you being the one who brought that red bastard down."

"They do?"

"It's a story makes the round of every barrack and barroom that I know of."

"And what would Jack Stillwell be knowing of barracks and barrooms? You ain't gone and become wolf on me, have you?"

"No—ain't likely. But I enjoy army food—and two squares of it a day, as a matter of fact. Gotten used to it."

"You still scouting for them out here?"

"I am, Seamus. In fact," he said, craning his neck, "I'm here to pick up two gentlemen I'm to guide down into the southern part of Indian Territory with an army escort from Fort Dodge."

"Sounds like it might be a dangerous ride."

"Naw. Ever since Custer and his Seventh settled things

back to 'sixty-nine—been mostly quiet down there. Look, I think I see them two off the train and looking for someone who's supposed to be waiting for them. So, here," Stillwell said as he stuffed a hand into the inside pocket of his long trail coat. He brought out a small, folded bundle, none too thick and about six inches square, tied up in brown bailing twine. He dusted off the flat package, much rumpled, wrinkled and trail-worn.

"Damn my soul if I walk off from you and didn't give you this."

"What is this?" he asked, staring down at the bundle.

"Letters," Stillwell answered, as if it were the most normal thing in the world to hand such a thing over to a friend one has not seen in the span of five years.

"How long you—"

"Been carrying 'em for Sharp Grover. He toted 'em around for you for two year. Listen—I gotta be getting, Seamus. Those two fancy fellas getting nervous. Meet me later in town. Where you gonna stay?"

"You tell me."

"Henshaw's place. I'll find you there tonight, Irishman." Stillwell held out his hand. They shook. "Damn but I'm glad to bump into you. And finally get shet of those letters Sharp's had me lugging around for you the last three years—hoping I'd run onto word of you somewhere after you quit scouting for Bill Cody and the Fifth."

"That's a story we'll share over some whiskey tonight."

"Damn right we will, Irishman. I figure we got a lot of tales to share."

"Five years' worth, Jack."

"I'll see you to Henshaw's after I get these two gentlemen with their paper collars tucked in for the night."

"Watch your backside, Stillwell."

"I'll watch yours as well, Seamus!"

As the young scout disappeared into the twilight of that station platform, oily, yellow light beginning to spill

from the multi-paned windows, Donegan stared down
into the package suddenly going heavy in his hand. With
nervous fingers he tore apart the twine knot and un-
wrapped the coarse, browned paper that enclosed two
envelopes.

After dragging his trail gear into the splash of saffron
lamplight pouring from a window, Seamus spread the
wrinkled brown paper with his fingers and began reading
what appeared to be the unfamiliar handwriting of a
woman.

Dear Irishman,

If you are reading this, then you are alive. I've carried
these two letters with me for close to two years now, but
am fixing to move on south and do something new with
my life. My woman's had enough of Kansas and hears
good things from her family gone to Texas. That's where
I'm going, south across the Red River. So I'm giving
these two letters over to Jack Stillwell.

Lord, has that fella growed. But as I give them over to
him for safekeeping for you to show back up, I'm having
the wife of a storekeeper in Sheridan write this letter for
me since I can't make no word on paper but my name.

Want you to think about coming south with me,
Seamus. Plenty of ranching land for a man down there.
Good timber and water. We can make a go of it and live
out our days as peaceful country gents. Something me
and Liam always talked about. It does still give me pain
to think on Liam now—how he talked so on one day
settling down with me and we could run some cattle and
raise some fine-strutting horses.

Won't you come look me up? Jack will always know
where I end up roosting. I'll let him know how you can
track me down. ·

Don't blame this on the woman, Seamus. I gave the
army my best years, and owe that woman the rest of what
I got left in me. Come on down to Texas, put your boots

up on the rail with mine for a change. Neither one of us meant to be an Injun fighter the rest of our natural days.

Abner Grover

There was a trembling of emotion that threatened to spill over as he stared down at that name illuminated by the lamplight on that Hays City station platform. "You always hated that name, Sharp. Thank you, Abner—but I don't figure I got any business coming south to Texas, when I've got something stronger still tugging me back to Ireland."

Stuffing the brown paper in the pocket of his mackinaw, Seamus stared at the top letter, much wrinkled as well, addresses crossed out and new ones squeezed into what blank space was left on the folded envelope. A litany of posts and forts and towns up and down the Platte River Road and on up the Bozeman Road. It had been better than seven years now since he had started up that bloody trail into Red Cloud's country, looking for yellow gold but finding instead an unrelenting red wall.*

Unfolding the envelope, Seamus found it hard to believe his eyes.

Dear son,

I am writing this at the old table where we all used to sit for what meals I could place before my family. It brings back so many memories of you now. Gone so long from this place. How I would love to see your face come past the window one more time.

Ian has written me. From someplace on the far side of America. Calls the place Linkville Town. Oregon must be the county he's settled in from the sounds of it. Happy he is too. God bless him now that Liam's gone. Your letter telling me how Liam died reached me here several months ago. How scared I am for you still.

Come on home now. Liam has gone on to stay with

God and Ian is putting down deep roots with his family in that new land. He writes like I remember him as a boy, not like the hard man he became before leaving Eire. But now full of hopes and dreams once more, like our papa, like your papa too, had dreams for you living close to the earth. Ian has that now, and a good woman to love him and stand by him.

Come home now so you too can be far, far away from those savages who have claimed your uncle and nearly took your life too. I wait every day watching for your face at the window, to hear your steps on the stones at the stoop before you open the door.

Your mother loves you, Seamus.

For a moment he held the letter against his breast, almost as if the warmth of her hand were still there upon the page despite the years and the miles and the aching loneliness that had separated them for so long.

"I'm coming home, Mother."

Carefully folding her letter, Seamus put it in the pocket with Grover's, then glanced at the last letter, nothing more really than a twice-folded page, addressed much as the first had been. And from Town Callan in Ireland as well.

Dear Seamus Donegan,

You will not remember me, nor know me. I came to the parish several months after you were bound over to America, as your mother told me of you on so many occasions. I was her priest all these years. She became a friend to me, one of the few I could count on in this land and a time of little to count on.

It is not easy when anyone dies, but especially a friend. So it is that I hope you can feel my remorse and pain in losing your mother. We share that loss together.

He blinked his eyes, smarting with the sudden tears, straining at the words swimming now in that smear of lamplight splashing from the window where he stood. Then slowly, ever slowly he sank to his knees, sobbing silently, falling back against the clapboards beneath the station window.

Seamus ground a fist into both eyes angrily and read on.

> She died peacefully, after a hard illness, Seamus. And she died with the love of God in her heart and a smile on her face. But, I am writing you since she asked me to, just before she breathed her last, and to tell you that in those final moments, your mother prayed for your welfare in a far and savage land, at the hands of strangers, and not among the bosom of your family.
>
> She is laid in a small spot beside your father, as she wanted. Your brothers and sisters come to the grave often these past two weeks, for I always find fresh sprigs of this or that on her resting place. You would be settled to see it for yourself someday.
>
> My prayers are for you, as your mother asked me to ask God to watch over you now that she can't pray for you. But I feel she is watching still, Seamus. Now much closer to you than she was in her last days here in Eire. Her spirit is with you, and her love as well.
>
> Father Colin Mulvaney

The moon rose full on the horizon and climbed toward mid-sky before Seamus felt capable of arising without shaking. He folded the last letter neatly and found a place for all three in the inside pocket of his mackinaw.

Dragging a hand beneath his nose while the summer night cooled the Kansas tableland, the Irishman hoisted his saddle and gear to his shoulder, then stepped off the platform.

He was moving into Hays City now, to Henshaw's place. To find Jack Stillwell.

Ireland lay behind him now.

He would ride south through Indian Territory with

Stillwell's government men and army escort to find Sharp Grover. Seamus Donegan was heading south for the Red River country of Texas.

SHADOW RIDERS—VOLUME 6 IN TERRY C. JOHNSTON'S *PLAINSMEN* SERIES—COMING IN DECEMBER 1991. DON'T MISS IT!

IN THE SHADOW OF THE BIG HORNS, TWO
PROUD NATIONS CLASHED—AND IGNITED THE
LONGEST, MOST DRAMATIC WAR IN AMERICAN
HISTORY.

THE PLAINSMEN

The rugged new Western series by the award-winning
author of *Carry the Wind*

TERRY C. JOHNSTON

Terry C. Johnston was nominated twice for the Golden
Spur Award and won the Medicine Pipe Bearer's Award
for *Carry the Wind*.

SIOUX DAWN (Book 1)
92732-0 _____ $4.99 U.S. _____ $5.99 CAN.

RED CLOUD'S REVENGE (Book 2)
92733-9 _____ $4.99 U.S. _____ $5.99 CAN.

THE STALKERS (Book 3)
92336-8 _____ $4.50 U.S. _____ $5.50 CAN.